Joy of the Widow's Tears

Other Books Available from Geoff and Coy:

Saul Imbierowicz Series
Unremarkable
Untouchable

Constable Inspector Lunaria Adventures
Wrath of the Fury Blade
Joy of the Widow's Tears

ISBN: 978-1-951122-01-0 (paperback)
ISBN: 978-1-951122-02-7 (ebook)
LCCN: 2020931615
Copyright © 2020 by Geoff Habiger & Coy Kissee
Cover Art: © Mike Wagner
Cover Design: Geoff Habiger

Printed in the United States of America.

Shadow Dragon Press
9 Mockingbird Hill Rd
Tijeras, New Mexico 87059
www.shadowdragonpress.com
info@shadowdragonpress.com

Joy

of the

Widow's Tears

A Constable Inspector Lunaria Adventure

Geoff Habiger

&

Coy Kissee

Albuquerque

Chapter 1

Constable Inspector Reva Lunaria carefully set down the cup of tea, avoiding the parchmentwork before her, and stifled a smile as she saw Senior Constable Ghrellstone walking up to the table. Seeker Ansee Carya's nose twitched, and he glanced up from his own work, his quill pausing on the parchment. Before he could say anything, Willem thrust an open cloth, piled high with gingerbread cookies, under Ansee's nose. "Cookie?"

Ansee's reaction was as sudden as it was hilarious, as he recoiled away from the proffered dessert, and his skin took on a sickly, moss-green color. One hand flew to his mouth, and he puffed out his cheeks in an apparent attempt to keep his breakfast in check. Reva thought that he might succeed, but Willem grabbed one of the cookies and took a slow, deliberate bite, causing Ansee to jump up from his seat and rush toward the water closet. Willem let out a deep-throated laugh.

"I don't think that will ever get old," he said, between laughs.

Reva couldn't help laughing either, though she did say, "If you do that, and he doesn't reach the bucket in time, you're the one who has to clean it up."

Willem gave it a thought, and said, "It might be worth it if I can start my day like this all the time." He offered the cookies to Reva, and she took one. They were still warm, and the aroma of the ginger emanated from them, which was probably the reason that Ansee had reacted so strongly. Willem took another one and, as he bit into it, Reva saw Ansee step up behind the Senior Constable, a flash of blue sparking between the fingers of his outstretched hand. She managed to hide her smile again.

Willem gave a bark of pain as Ansee's hand grabbed his neck, and his mouth spasmed shut. His body shook violently for a second, the cookies spilling onto the table, and then returned to normal as Ansee released his grip.

"Son of a succubus!" Willem bellowed, putting a hand to his mouth. His fingers came back bloody. "I bit my tongue!"

"It serves you right," Ansee said, pulling out his chair. He knocked several cookies to the floor with a contemptuous swipe of his arm. "I told you yesterday to stop doing that, but you apparently just won't listen. You should know better than to get a spell caster angry."

"It was all just a bit of fun," Willem countered.

"Losing my breakfast for the past week has not been what I would call 'fun.'"

"Aw, you just can't take a joke."

Reva finally let out the laugh she'd been holding in, and the outburst was enough to calm both Ansee and Willem. "Enough, both of you," she finally said. "We're about to close this case, so that means that the pranks have to stop," she pointed a finger at Willem, "and no more retaliation," she turned the finger toward Ansee. Both of them cast their eyes down and mumbled an acknowledgment.

"Hells, you two are worse than children. I'm tempted to make Constable Gania sit between you."

"I'd really prefer to be left out of this, ma'am," Gania's voice came from the table next to her. Everybody smiled, and the tension eased.

Ansee gingerly picked up one of the fallen cookies and tossed it to Willem. "I may have been faking earlier, but I don't think I will ever be able to eat a gingerbread cookie again in my life."

Willem picked up the rest of the cookies and took them to his table. He purposefully took a large bite from one of them and then cringed in pain as he'd forgotten about his wounded tongue.

"You'll get over it at some point," Reva said.

Ansee looked at her dubiously. "A baker was killed by having three stone of raw gingerbread mysteriously appear in his stomach. The crime scene at the bakery was bad enough, but having to go through Thea's dissection was the worst experience of my life."

Reva picked up her cup of tea. "It was a new one for me, that's for sure."

"Death by gingerbread suffocation," said Willem. "I think that's a new one for anybody."

"Too bad we don't know how it happened," added Gania.

"Life is full of mysteries," Willem elucidated.

"Yeah, well, that might work for the Sucra and the mages at Auros," Reva said, "but I'd rather know the truth."

"We know it was a spell," Ansee said.

"But you haven't found out how it works, or who cast it." Reva countered—a bit too harshly, she realized, seeing Ansee flinch ever so slightly. "And my main suspect has a wizard-locked alibi. I was so sure that the wife was involved." She sighed, drained her tea, and set the cup down. "Well, for now, we're stuck, so this case is going nowhere for the time being."

She turned to Willem and Gania. "Make sure you document what evidence we collected, then go ahead and get rid of it. Constable Whitlocke has been complaining about the lack of space in there."

"Come on, Kai," Willem stood up. "Let's go clean house."

"There are still possible leads with the spell," Ansee offered. "I'm sure somebody at Auros can help us."

3

"If you want to do it in your spare time, you can, but I told Aescel that we'd be winding this one up today. We still have that suspicious fire over in West Gate to investigate, along with that rash of burglaries in Old Grove. Our branch is heavy right now."

Ansee nodded, "I know. I just don't like leaving things unfinished."

Reva could understand that sentiment since she shared it. She didn't bother to respond, and went back to recording her notes into her personal notebook. If they did get a chance to come back to this case, or if their mysterious cookie dough murderer made a repeat performance, she'd have something to remind her.

She'd not gotten very far when the sharp bark of First Constable Aescel's voice flew across the Stable. "Reva, get in here!"

Reva set her quill down, not even bothering to sigh. She exchanged a look with Ansee that said, *What did I do this time?* He shrugged, but looked relieved that he was not being called out onto the stump with her. She took her time to walk to Aescel's office. The door was open, so she walked in. Reva was surprised to see that the First Constable was not alone; a Green Cloak was standing at the window, keenly taking in the Stable.

The Sucra officer was about Reva's height, with long, light-brown hair tied in a simple braid. As Reva closed the door, he turned around and gave her the kind of glare that the Sucra was infamous for across the entire kingdom. Other than the glare from his acorn-brown eyes, he kept his face impassive. Reva hadn't seen him come up the main stairs, and she wondered why this Green Cloak had bothered to sneak up the back stairs. If he was trying to be mysterious, it wasn't working on her. She returned his glare with her own, adding a slight curl of disdain to her lips.

"What did you want, sir?" she asked, finally taking her

eyes off the Green Cloak. "We'll have the baker case set aside by lunch."

"Good, good," Aescel acknowledged. "This is Inquisitor Rhus Amalaki. He's the new liaison between the Sucra and the RTC." Aescel let the sarcasm coat his words. "But you knew that already, right?"

"Oh, it's so nice of the Sucra to inform us. I thought we'd been given a reprieve after they shipped Malvaceä off somewhere."

"I sent you three letters informing you of the change in liaison and requesting a meeting." Amalaki let his voice rise in indignation.

Reva smiled inwardly. *Point for me.*

"They must have been misplaced or lost," Reva said. She did remember getting the letters, stamped with the Sucra coat of arms, and promptly tossing them into a waste bin to be burned. She didn't need any more interference from the Sucra.

The Inquisitor gave her a hard look that told Reva that he didn't believe her.

Like I care.

"It's important that we maintain a positive relationship between our two organizations," he said, managing to keep the edge off the comment.

"Malvaceä never cared about building a positive relationship."

"Yes, well, the Senior Inquisitor and I have different opinions about how we should interact with the Constabulary."

Reva gave a shrug. "Where is our favorite Senior Inquisitor these days?"

"Not here." Amalaki gave her a smug smile so it was clear that he knew, he just wasn't going to say.

Typical Sucra attitude.

"What did you want, sir?" she turned her attention back to Aescel.

"To get you to play nice with the Sucra." Reva sighed and rolled her eyes. "I'm serious, Reva. The Sucra have a critical role to play, and it's important that we keep them informed of what we are doing."

"I thought they already knew everything," she said, giving Amalaki another sneering smile.

"We don't spy on the Constabulary."

Reva turned to him, her eyes narrowed. "That's hawk-shit, and you know it. The Green Cloaks spy on everybody. It's your *raison d'etre*, to use the Arisportian term." The way the color rose in his cheeks, and his frustrated silence, told Reva that her words had struck true. Spying was the whole reason that they existed.

Another point for me.

"It is your duty to your King to inform us of any threats that you may come across." Amalaki stood taller as he stated, "That is why it is important for us to share information."

Reva again rolled her eyes. "The next time that the Green Cloaks share anything with us will be the very first time."

"It seems that I have a lot of damage to undo," Amalaki said with a sigh of his own. "I told you that I am not like my predecessor. Malvaceä had his own methods and his own motivations. The fact that he's been sent," Amalaki paused briefly.

Reva raised one eyebrow in anticipation of receiving some actual information.

"—away," he continued.

Reva let her eyebrow fall and briefly shook her head in disappointment.

"—is proof that the way he did things is out of favor with the Grand Inquisitor," Amalaki concluded.

Wow, are you really that clueless? Reva knew the real reason why Malvaceä had been sent away: he'd failed to recover the Fury Blade for Grand Inquisitor Agera. Whatever plot Agera's little cabal had been planning had been trimmed to the roots by the loss of the Fury Blade, but that didn't mean that the threat wasn't still there. Either Amalaki was really good at playing dumb, or he didn't know who Agera really was. She supposed the latter was possible—the Sucra was a large organization and not everybody would be plotting to overthrow the Kingdom—but she had never trusted a Sucra inquisitor before, and she wasn't about to start now.

"Reva," FC Aescel drew her attention. "I'm asking you to play nice and meet with Amalaki. If you don't, he's liable to take his request to the Lord Constable Inspector."

Reva nodded and looked at the Green Cloak. His expression remained impassive, so she didn't know what he might or might not know about the internal politics of the RTC. Aescel's "asking" was tantamount to an order and, while saving the lives of LCI Betulla and Grand Inquisitor Agera from Roya Locera's attack had earned Reva a nice commendation, she knew that the LCI was still holding a grudge for the embarrassment that Reva had caused her. Betulla was, without a doubt, looking for any way to cut the branches out from under Reva. Allowing Amalaki to take his grievance to her might be the justification that she needed to take Reva out of play.

She turned to Amalaki. "I am busy today, but I suppose we can meet tomorrow or the day after. Is that acceptable?"

Amalaki gave her a coy smile, "Your place or mine?"

"Mine. You can come here." Reva didn't smile back at him, but thought, *Humor from a Green Cloak. Who knew?*

Chapter 2

Four elves stepped out of a dank shop into the bustle of Cantull's paths and waterways. "Son of a succubus!" exclaimed Erroll as he looked at his right forearm. It was the only admission he'd allow himself for the pain that he felt. The skin was raw and red around the image of a bird—a graceful tern—its wings outstretched and its scissored tail spread wide.

"Does skin painting always hurt like this?" Liam asked, gingerly touching his own arm and wincing in obvious pain. The reaction drew the attention of the ship's *Isean*—the first mate—the tallest member of the quartet.

"Of course! Don't be such a *muschi*, Liam! You should be more like Erroll here." Loren slapped the fresh skin art on Erroll's arm, causing him to bite his tongue in order to keep from yelling out. Loren and the fourth member of the group, Aavril, erupted in laughter, causing the Cantullians around them to give the four elves odd looks and to steer a wide path around them. Ignoring the pain in his arm, which was somewhat eased by the rum in his belly, Erroll joined the other three elves in laughter. Loren set off into the crowd, leading the others through the throng and back to the docks.

"Did it hurt when you got yours?" Liam asked. Erroll thought it was a naïve question, clearly showing Liam's youth and inexperience. He smiled inwardly at the stupid comment. Erroll knew it was Liam's first time away from home, and the young elf never failed to show that he was a moss-behind-the-ears tree dweller.

"Hells, I don't remember!" Loren exclaimed. "We were very drunk at the time. Do you remember, Aavril?"

Aavril shook his head in laughter, his straw-brown hair shaking with the motion. He held out his right arm, which was bronzed from spending so much time under the ocean sun. He pointed at an identical tern that had been inked there. "Hells yes, it hurt, Loren! Especially after you poured that cheap rum on it!"

Loren threw his head back and laughed, his own straw-brown hair falling around his shoulders. Not for the first time, Erroll reflected that the two sailors actually looked so much alike that they could have been mistaken for brothers. "Oh, right. You squealed like a stuck kobold." He lifted the bottle of rum that he'd been holding and made a motion as though he was going to pour it on Erroll's arm. Erroll quickly pulled his arm away with a scowl, creating more laughter from the two senior sailors.

"Give me that," Erroll demanded, grabbing the bottle. "Don't waste it." He took a pull of the sweet, cheap liquor, and then handed the bottle to Liam, who took it tentatively. They headed across one of the hundreds of bridges that crossed the twisting waterways of Cantull.

"Now both of you are officially part of the crew," Loren proclaimed, taking the bottle back.

"So, what about the past three months, then?" Erroll asked, not bothering to hide his annoyance. He and Liam had hired onto the *Majestic Tern* the last time the ship had been in Tenyl. Liam was a year older than him, but Erroll had more experience sailing on merchant and fishing ships. True, all of his experience had been confined to the sheltered waters of Black Elf Bay, but he was the better sailor. He considered himself to be the senior of the two new crew-elves and had made Liam do all of the worst jobs on the ship whenever he could.

Since leaving Tenyl, they'd visited half a dozen ports in the Melapar Sea, up and down the west coast of the Sneveves Peninsula, before stopping here in Cantull on the east coast. On any normal ship, that would have been enough to make them both veteran crewmembers.

"Well, it's not really official until you get inked," Aavril said, with mock seriousness.

"What?" Liam asked, sounding confused. "You mean like us not being 'real' sailors 'til we crossed the line and did all them tasks for King Demar?"

"Exactly," Loren laughed. "If you are going to be a sailor, Liam, you have to understand how important tradition is."

Erroll reddened at the memory. *Tradition?* It was just like the *Isean* to joke about the hazing that the crew had given to him and Liam. The whole experience had been humiliating. Loren had dressed as King Demar, wearing a broken bucket for a crown and holding a mop handle as his spear. The *Isean* had made Erroll climb the mast, completely naked, in order to sing a prayer to Demar, and then had made them both kiss his feet before they could get their dinner. After a full day of hell, the Captain had declared them Ammonites—true disciples of Demar. The whole affair had been idiotic and childish, especially since Erroll had proven his worth ten times over by that point in the voyage. Crossing the equator and performing the stupid ceremony hadn't changed anything. The crew still treated him like a green-eared sailor, giving him all of the shittiest jobs on the ship. He resented the whole experience. *I've been sailing since I was a boy. I shouldn't have to prove myself to anybody on that pissant ship.*

"How many more of these rituals do we have to go through?" Liam asked, with a silly grin mortared to his face. Erroll wanted to slap it off of the idiot. "I never knew that being a sailor was so complicated."

Aavril and Loren laughed again, handing the rum back to Liam. The narrow paths and bridges opened onto a large square filled with dozens of stalls and merchants hawking their wares. The air was filled with the sounds of the odd Cantullian language and the exotic smells of food cooked in strange spices.

Erroll was wiping his mouth after his latest sip of the rum when a flicker of light caught his eye. There was a glint of gold coming from a stall, and something about it tugged at him, like a branch snagging on his clothes. He veered away from the others and headed toward the stall.

"Hey!" called Aavril. "You'd better stick with us or a thief will clean you out!"

Erroll ignored the Quartermaster, his eyes fixed on a necklace that was hanging in the vendor's stall. It hung from a peg in the top crossbeam, twisting slightly in the breeze. The chain was made of small, silver links and was four or five hands long. At the bottom was a twisted piece of gold with a single, small, tear-shaped grey-green gemstone. It seemed ugly at first, with the twist of gold looking like the squiggles that a child might draw, and due to the unappealing color of the gemstone. But as the necklace twisted in the air, the gold formed the seductive profile of a woman. The delicate metal twisted in such a way to expose a graceful neck, chin, nose, and forehead, then curved back to form sweeping, long, flowing hair. The gemstone wasn't set as the eye, as Erroll had expected, but instead, it was positioned slightly below the eye, as if it could be a tear, making it appear as though the woman was crying. He'd never had any interest in jewelry before, but the subtle, abstract beauty of the necklace struck a chord in him.

Erroll reached up to touch the necklace, but a thick, rough hand grabbed his wrist, and somebody shouted at him in the coarse Cantullian language. He turned his head to see the vendor; a pudgy human with a short, black beard, who was wearing a green and blue scarf wrapped around his head that was held in place by a black cord.

"What?" Errol exclaimed, and the human shook his hand at him.

"*Tikai pircēji var pieskarties precēm,*" the human said, and Erroll stared blankly at him, clearly not understanding the language.

"I. Want. To. See. The. Necklace." Erroll pointed, speaking the words loudly and slowly in Tenylese.

"*Tikai pircēji var pieskarties precēm,*" the human repeated, increasing his own volume in response.

"He said that only buyers can touch the goods," Aavril said. Loren and Liam stood behind the Quartermaster.

"Well, I want to buy it." Erroll didn't know why he said this. The words had just tumbled out of his mouth, but as he said them, he knew them to be true.

"It's probably expensive," Aavril cautioned.

Erroll's eyes narrowed. *I am not a child.* He reached for his coin purse. "Tell him I'll give him eight crowns for it."

"*Eight crowns?* Where'd you get *eight* crowns?" Liam asked. The tone of his voice made it clear that he'd never held a gold crown in his life.

Aavril sighed, his expression clearly indicating that he thought that this was a bad idea, but he told the vendor, "*Viņš tev došu astoņus zelta monētas.*"

The vendor shook his head and waved his arms. "*Nē,*" he said, followed by a considerable array of sounds that Errol thought were probably words, but sounded more like a cat coughing up a hairball.

Aavril listened, and then asked, "*Laime?*"

The vendor shook his head again, "*Nē. Prieks.*"

"What's he saying?" Erroll demanded. He was frustrated at not being able to follow the discussion.

"He said that he wants sixteen crowns for the 'Joy of the

Widow's Tears.'"

"Sixteen! Hells, he's trying to rip me off!" Erroll gestured to the necklace dangling from the peg. He spoke at the vendor in Tenylese slowly, in order to drive his point across. "There's not even sixteen crowns worth of gold in this if it was melted down and minted. And it's clear that you've had it for a while, so I'll offer you ten crowns to take it off your hands." Erroll knew that this ugly human was just trying to cheat him because he was not from around here. He'd haggled enough with merchants back home to know that.

Aavril smiled as he translated what Erroll had said. The vendor kept his face stern, his expression not giving anything away, but he slowly began to nod and reach for the necklace.

"*Divpadsmit!*" Loren suddenly spouted.

Erroll turned to stare at Loren. *What in the hells is he doing?*

The vendor smiled broadly and pointed at Loren. "*Jā, divpadsmit. Tas ir jūsu.*"

Aavril looked at the *Isean*, his own shock clearly displayed on his face.

Erroll didn't know what was happening until Loren handed several gold coins to the vendor. Then Erroll went off like a fireball. "Gods damn you, Loren, that's *my* necklace!" As the vendor was handing the necklace to Loren, Erroll made to grab for it with one hand while he threw a punch at the *Isean* with the other.

Loren managed to sidestep the punch and landed one of his own in Erroll's gut. Air exploded from his lungs, and he doubled over. Loren took the necklace from the vendor, who looked bemused by these two elves that were fighting each other at his stall. Liam grabbed Erroll by the shoulders, keeping him from both falling down and trying to strike back at the *Isean*.

"Watch your tongue, sailor, or you'll find yourself swimming home," Loren chided.

"Loren, what in the hells was that about?" Aavril said.

"It was a fair offer," Loren said.

"The hells it was. You're acting like a halpbloeden."

Loren's ears reddened at the insult, and he turned to face Erroll. "I gave a fair price for it, and it's mine now. Buy yourself some other trinket. This necklace is *mine*." He turned and walked away.

Erroll gritted his teeth as he stood up, then he spat on the ground. Liam continued to hold him back until Erroll shook him off. He and Liam followed the first mate, with Aavril following a pace behind them. Erroll's eyes bored two small holes in the *Isean's* back as they walked back to the ship. *I will get what is mine.*

Chapter 3

"Why are you being such a halpbloed?" Rhus groused. He saw Constable Inspector Lunaria bristle at the insult.

"Protecting my fellow constables is not the same thing as being stubborn," she countered. "I'm here to give you details about cases we are working on, not to help you on some sort of a sorcerer hunt for constables who may not think the way that you want them to."

Rhus shook his head. He was starting to see why Senior Inquisitor Malvaceä had always complained about working with Lunaria. She was worse than any halpbloed. It was like trying to work with a dwarf.

They sat in a tiny room—more of a closet, really—that was tucked into some corner of New Port. The room was located near the roofline, and the ceiling sloped down with the pitch of the roof. Lunaria, naturally, had forced Rhus to take the chair nearest the sloping ceiling so that he'd had to bend over in order to get to his seat. It made the room feel even smaller.

"Why are you not worried about threats against the King? It is our duty to root out these instigators. I don't know why you are so against this."

He watched as she gave him a cold glare with her turquoise eyes. He wondered what she was really thinking, because it was clear that she wanted to say exactly what was on her mind. Instead, she said, "Even if I believe you about these rumors, I won't rat out any constables. Not without evidence."

"I have statements from two witnesses who overheard Constable Sulwynd."

"*Real* evidence," Lunaria countered. "I'm not a Green Cloak. I don't make any arrests on just the word of an informant I don't know."

That's not what I've heard, Rhus told himself. Lunaria was a wild warhawk within the Constabulary, often doing her own thing, and usually suffering the consequences. She had been suspended or put on probation more than any other constable in the history of Acer Division. But she also had one of the highest rates of arrests, and had received commendations from the King on at least two occasions. She was tenacious, something that Malvaceä had complained about many times, but that made her a good constable. He figured that would make her a good inquisitor as well.

"And what if the evidence I bring you is a dead noble?"

"Then we'll take action," she said, matter-of-factly. "If you think that there's a threat, there's nothing stopping you from doing what the Sucra is good at." The disdain in her voice was crystal clear.

"We don't act without overwhelming evidence either."

Her laugh was filled with spite and anger, and Rhus felt the tips of his ears redden. The Sucra's work was, by necessity, done in secret, with much of the means and methods withheld from the army, from the constabulary, and sometimes, even from the King himself. There were too many ways that the wrong thing said in the wrong company, or a casual observer learning how the Sucra operated, could allow a traitor to escape justice. It was important for the Sucra to operate independently in order to keep the Kingdom safe. He knew that Lunaria wouldn't understand even if he could explain. The protection of the King was too important to let the rule of law get in the way.

He picked up the parchment from the table and made a mark next to Constable Sulwynd's name. He'd see what he could do about getting Lunaria the evidence that she wanted. He looked at the next item but, before he could say anything, Lunaria interrupted.

"How many more of these things are you going to go over? I have real work to do, you know."

"Oh, stopping petty thieves is more important than the safety of the Kingdom?" He was trying to make a joke, but he realized that his tone came across as more flippant than jovial. His training allowed him to keep his face neutral as Reva again furrowed her brow.

"Be careful, Inquisitor. Haven't you heard? The LCI says that crime is rampant in the city. It would be a shame if you were burglarized and no constables were around to help you."

It was a clear threat, and totally in keeping with what he knew of Lunaria's character. He was sure that Malvaceä would have risen to the bait and made his own snappy comeback or threat. Rhus decided to ignore the remark. The important work that he needed to do would only get done with Lunaria's help. If he ticked her off, she'd just leave.

"There are only a few more items left to discuss."

She rolled her eyes and drummed her fingers on the table, clearly bored, but she kept quiet. They covered the next two items on his list in less than ten minutes. Rhus smiled as he rolled up the parchment to put back into his satchel. "See, that wasn't so bad."

"I'd rather clean out a stable using a spoon, but that was certainly less painful than working with Ailan. Until next time, Inquisitor." She stood up to leave.

"Next time, I will host at the Red Keep. We certainly

have better accommodations." He stood up, careful to keep his back bent, and walked around the table.

"Maybe," she allowed. "Whenever I have to go there, I break out in hives."

"I assure you, Inspector, we've cleaned the place very thoroughly since the Senior Inquisitor left. You'll be fine." He walked out of the room with Lunaria escorting him. *You still don't trust me? Or is this just institutional paranoia against the Sucra?* As they reached the stairs, he figured it was probably a little of both.

Chapter 4

Aavril watched the sun touch the western horizon, the rays catching the few clouds and setting the whole sky ablaze with red and violet light. "There is nothing better than a sunset at sea," he said.

"Aye, that's tha truth," agreed Kelsey from the ship's wheel. Kelsey Pfallstaph had deep-set eyes and leathery, tough skin that made him look older than his 124 years. He'd spent nearly all of that time at sea, and it had tanned and aged him to the point that he looked more like a wizened monk than a sailor. As the *Majestic Tern's* Sailing Master, he was responsible for giving orders to the crew, maintaining the rigging, and generally keeping the ship repaired and fit for sea.

"It reminds me of tha *Voyage of the Blueswater Brothers*: 'And tha Lord Demar set tha sky aflame, tha Blueswater brothers chasing tha sun. Pursued by tha navies of two nations, tha three pirates on their mission from God, and saving their precious cargo from harm.'" He had a deep bass voice that was not only useful for bellowing orders, but it also gave a majestic character to the epics and other stories that he told at night to entertain the crew.

"Does everything remind you of an epic?" Aavril asked.

"Oh, aye. Don't it ya?"

Aavril laughed. "Sorry, no. I'd rather look to the future than live in the past."

"Oh, sure," agreed the Sailing Master. "But if ya don' keep an eye on where ya've been, ya may end up makin' tha same mistakes where ya are goin'. Tha past has much ta teach us, if'n we is willin' ta listen."

"Were you a philosopher in a former life?"

"Who's ta say I'm not one now?" Kelsey smiled and winked as he turned the wheel slightly.

Aavril gave a hearty laugh, watching as the sun finally dipped below the horizon. He noted the moment in the ship's navigation log, along with the current weather conditions. He looked up to the pennants flying from the central mast, gauging the wind speed and direction with a practiced eye. The large lateen sail was full, the wind moving the *Majestic Tern* at three leagues of speed. Aavril opened the sea chest that was bolted to the deck along the aft rail. He pulled out the astrolabe and walked to the starboard rail.

The polished oak and brass instrument was cool and smooth in his hands. He glanced skyward looking for Qurna, the north star, and Illoth, the brightest star that could be seen during High Summer. In less than a minute, he'd sighted both stars and made his measurements, mentally noting the numbers from the astrolabe. Returning to the navigation table, he recorded the numbers in the log and performed the calculation in his head, then recorded their latitude.

"Are we lost?" Kelsey asked as he lit the oil lamp now that the Quartermaster was finished.

"Nope. We're right where we are supposed to be."

"Damn," the Sailing Master muttered. "How'm I supposed ta meet a beautiful mermaid if'n ya always keeps us on course?"

Aavril laughed as he put away the instrument. "If it's all the same to you, I'd prefer to not meet any merfolk. They have a mean temper when it comes to surface people. I'd sooner stay away, no matter how beautiful they may be."

"Aye, ya gots a point," Kelsey agreed with a smile.

The two sailors fell silent, content to watch the stars come out and listen to the ship as she cut through the water. The *Majestic Tern* was a fine merchant ship, despite her age. Her hull was made from thick oak timbers with a clinker construction of overlapping planks. The *Tern* was not a big vessel, being only twenty-one paces long from the aft rail to the front of the foredeck, and she was only seven paces wide at her widest point, but her small size meant that she could be sailed with a crew of just eight elves plus the Captain. She could carry twenty *drasastone*—nearly 20,000 stone—in cargo, so Captain Sterna could make a decent profit on each voyage. Of course, finding a place for all of that cargo was hard on a small ship, but they managed.

Aavril stepped to the front rail of the quarterdeck and looked to the front of the ship. The Blueleaph brothers— Janish and Olwynn—were recounting their encounters in the Cantull brothels, each in vivid and complete detail, as they checked the ropes on the many crates that were lashed to the foredeck. Aavril smiled. He'd spent plenty of Skips in those brothels himself. A small part of his mind expressed some guilt about that, but he rationalized that he wasn't really cheating on Reva. He had his needs, and these trips kept him away for months at a time. Besides, what she didn't know wouldn't hurt her.

Though maybe opening a shop in Tenyl isn't such a bad idea, he thought. Reva had waved that branch the last time he'd been home. He'd told her that he would think about it, and she'd let it go. *It would be nice to be able to spend more time with Reva,* he admitted. He had plenty of contacts among the merchant captains, enough that he could open a good import shop, catering exotic goods to all the nobility who had more money than they knew what to do with. They could then see about settling down together. Maybe he'd be able to convince Reva to move out of her mother's house and they could get a nice place of their own. Maybe she'd even consider marriage. He'd waved that branch more than a few times, and Reva had always said yes...someday...just not now. He wasn't sure why she was so reluctant about it, but he'd not yet pressed the issue.

A splash pulled his attention to the port rail, and he saw a pod of dolphins swimming alongside the *Tern*, an iridescent green glow surrounding them as they leaped and played. It was a beautiful sight like the sunset had been; one of many he'd had the pleasure of witnessing at sea. Of course, being a merchant sailor was a hard life and it was full of risks, but times like this made it all worth it.

The dolphins raced ahead of the ship, green light flickering around them as they cavorted in the bow wave. Aavril smiled to himself. *Why would I ever give this up?* He didn't have an answer.

"Oy, Aavril!"

Aavril turned to see Donnel Whellsind standing on the main deck. He jerked a thumb toward the Captain's cabin. "Cap'n and the *Isean* wanna see ya."

"Alright." Aavril turned from the rail and grabbed the navigation log. He patted Kelsey on the shoulder as he passed. "Keep us out of any storms or coral dragon lairs."

"Aye, sure. 'And lo, did tha great beast rise from tha sea, tha serpent full of furious power...,'" his bass voice sang out across the deck as he related another epic.

Aavril took the four steps down to the main deck and entered the Captain's cabin. It was located directly under the quarterdeck and it was the only private space on the ship. Though private, it was small, only five paces wide at the front, five paces deep, and the cabin narrowed to just four paces along the aft wall. Still, Captain Sterna had neatly furnished the space with mostly functional items. A bunk, which also served as a bench, was positioned along the port wall, a chart table next to it. The table could fold open to allow for as many as ten people to sit around it for meals, though rather tightly if all the seats were occupied. A wardrobe was along the starboard wall, and a large sea chest sat under the aft windows. Aavril knew that there was a hidden compartment under the bunk where the Captain kept the money that he used to purchase trade goods and to pay the crew.

There were few personal decorations in the cabin: a large rug that was woven in the complex style from the Tave region of the Kingdom that the Captain called home, a family portrait, and a wooden plaque with a carved tern in flight. The portrait of the Captain, his wife, his son Loren, and his four daughters, hung over the bunk. The plaque hung over the aft windows.

A hooded lantern hung from the central beam, casting a soft yellow light across the cabin as it swayed slightly with the roll of the ship. The Captain sat on the bunk, one leg propped on the bed as he leaned back on several pillows. He held a clay goblet in one hand.

"All's well, Aavril?"

"Aye, Cap'n." Captain Sterna was 133 years old and had spent nearly all of that time at sea. His face was weathered, his blue eyes looking out from deeply set sockets. His brown hair was streaked through with grey. "We are on course and it looks like the winds will hold steady all night."

"Good." The Captain's voice was strong and gravelly. He picked up a curved pipe that was carved with a dragon's mouth gaping open as the bowl. Aavril knew that it was carved from a coral dragon's tooth and it was one of the Captain's favorite possessions. He packed in a sweet-smelling tabak. "The crew can spare you for a bit. Have a seat." He gestured with the pipe to a folding campstool sitting next to the table. Loren sat at the aft end of the table. As Aavril sat down, tossing the log onto the table, Loren poured a large helping of rum into the clay goblet sitting there.

"*Satee,*" Aavril said, picking up the goblet and taking a drink. Loren had already poured his own drink and held up his goblet, echoing the salutation.

The Captain finished lighting his pipe using a small fire-stone (another favorite possession) and puffed out a thick cloud of smoke. Instead of picking up the log, which was what he normally did during their evening ritual, he said, "So, Aavril, my son. How are you doing?"

Aavril was a bit put off by the unexpected question. Captain Sterna was a good elf and a great captain. Aavril considered him a second father and had learned much from him. But the Captain was usually more formal than this, not bothering with the feelings or well-being of his crew beyond what it took to get the job done.

"Umm...I'm doing fine, Captain."

Loren was not bothering to hide his mirth, chuckling softly to himself. But he didn't elaborate or give Aavril any clue as to what was going on.

"What about at home? You have a girlfriend, Loren tells me. Renna?"

"Reva."

"Right. Reva. And she's a constable."

"A Constable Inspector," Aavril couldn't help correcting him. *Reva always insisted on the use of her full title.*

Captain Sterna nodded. "A noble profession, keeping folks safe. Any chance she can help us with those greedy thieves who're always demanding a share of our hard earnings?"

Was this what the Captain wanted? Aavril knew that the many guilds and gangs were a pain in the ass, extorting money from ship captains. It was never as blatant as a thief in an alley robbing someone at dagger point, but the duties, fees, tariffs, and other hawkshit really just amounted to simple theft. Those who couldn't—or wouldn't—pay would find their cargo damaged or stolen, their crew attacked, or worse. It had gone on for so long that most captains considered it one of the expenses of doing business. "I'll see what she can do—"

The Captain waved him off. "No, son. Sorry. Idle curiosity. Though having a Constable Inspector for a friend is never a bad thing." He took another pull on his pipe. "Is she good with you being away for so long?"

Aavril was shocked by how close the Captain's question was to his earlier thoughts. "Well, she gripes about it like women do."

"Tell me about it," chimed in Loren. Aavril knew that Loren had his own issues with his girlfriend.

"But she supports me in what I do," Aavril continued. "Of course, it helps that I bring home gifts for her from each trip." All three smiled at that.

"Do you think she'd mind if you were gone longer?"

Aavril considered that as he took a pull from his goblet. "I don't know," he finally said. "She'd probably be mad—she thinks that we don't spend enough time together as it is. But if I could give her a good enough reason, I think that she'd understand. Why?"

Captain Sterna smiled around his pipe. "Do you know how long I've been at sea?"

"Ninety-six years, isn't it?"

"Yup. I began as a lowly seaelf, climbin' masts, and the riggin'. Muckin' out the bilge." He grimaced. "But I loved being at sea, especially at sunset and sunrise." Aavril again noted how close the Captain's own experiences were to his own. "I worked hard, becoming a Sailing Master, then Quartermaster, and then *Isean*. With a bit of help, I was able to buy the *Tern*." He ran a hand lovingly along the wall. "I've been her master for sixty-one years, and I've loved every minute of it."

"But being at sea is a hard life, and it's not for the old. I may still have a few decades left in me, and I want to spend them onshore in a simple home along the coast where I can spoil my grandchildren." Here he gave a pointed look toward Loren who merely grinned and drank his rum.

"So, I've decided to give the *Tern* to Loren. I'm retiring when we get back to port and he can take over as Captain. He and I have talked it over and we both agree. We want you to be his *Isean*."

Aavril was stunned. He'd been at sea for nearly two decades, starting out at the bottom. *As all sailors should.* He was certainly ambitious—no elf wanted to stay a deckhand—and he'd considered rising in rank, but he'd never looked beyond being a Quartermaster. Maybe in his early days he'd had thoughts of becoming a captain, but that had changed after meeting Reva. Before this moment, the best he could've hoped for was to be a merchant with his own shop onshore. *Isean?*

"I don't know what to say."

"Say yes, you fool," laughed Loren. "That's the other part of this. I have plans. Big plans." He held up his hands wide. "I want to break into the market in the Spice Islands. What cargo we get now is secondhand—stuff traded with the Torollans or Oromans. But if we can trade directly with the Nephrinians, we will rake in the crowns."

"There's already some ships doing that," Aavril said cautiously, but a small glimmer of excitement was building in his mind.

"This is why we need to act now, to be able to get in on the bottom branch. If we do, we can make the right contacts and connections. If we don't, we'll be left with the scraps. That's why father wanted to know how Reva would take it with you being gone longer."

Aavril nodded, a map of the coast and the Spice Islands forming in his head. "Heading to the Spice Islands, or to the mainland, will add several weeks to any voyage."

"Think of the challenge in navigating a route that could shorten the trip. Think of what profits we will make for the cacao, pepper, and other spices; not to mention the mahogany and teak if we cut out the middlemen—the merchants we buy from now."

The idea continued to germinate in Aavril, and he liked where this was heading. The possibilities of going to the suppliers directly were almost endless. *But*—"With only one ship, though, we'll spend so much time at sea. How would we ever make anything?"

Loren beamed with excitement. "I knew you'd see it. With one ship it would be impossible."

"Then how do you get this plan to work?"

"First, we get started right away. As soon as we've unloaded our cargo and get provisions we'll sail again."

"What? That fast?" Normally the *Tern* was docked for several weeks to replenish and prepare for the next trip. There were usually repairs to make and money had to be collected from buyers in advance to pay for cargo.

"Yes. Any sort of delay will mean that we run into the early winter storms, and that will not only be dangerous but would slow us down." Loren smiled and held up a finger. "But if we leave right away, we'll not only beat the weather but get in a shipment this season. We'll make enough crowns with that cargo to be able to buy a second ship and outfit it over the winter. Naturally, you'd be the captain of her."

Aavril had lifted his rum and taken a drink, and ended up spewing it out, "Captain!"

"Of course! Who else would I have? You and me, working together, as a merchant fleet. We'd rival the big, slow merchant ships, delivering the same cargo, but faster."

Aavril leaned back on his stool, rubbing a hand through his hair. *Captain?* He'd never earn enough money to be able to afford his own ship, but the commitment would mean spending even less time with Reva. *Captain Paroth.* He said the name to himself, and he liked how it sounded. To earn the title this way, so easily, made it all the more sweet-sounding. *Captain Paroth sounds so much better than Merchant Paroth.*

"Well? What do you say?" prodded Loren excitedly.

"I say yes!" Aavril reached his hand out, and Loren clasped the forearm and then slapped Aavril on the back.

"This calls for a celebration, then," Captain Sterna said. He reached down to open a secret panel, pulling out a bottle and setting it on the table. "North Highlands whiskey," he said proudly as he checked the date on the label. "Forty years old."

As they prepared to open the whiskey, a loud commotion outside the door drew their attention.

"I wasn't doin' nothin'!" proclaimed one voice.

"Tell it ta tha Cap'n!" countered another.

The cabin door shook with a loud pounding, followed by Kelsey's deep voice. "Beggin' yur pardon, Cap'n, but we gots us a...situation."

All three stood up and walked out on deck. A broad river of stars overhead and a half-moon gave a silvery illumination to the ship. Kelsey stood before them, holding Erroll by the collar of his shirt. The rest of the crew stood around in a semi-circle, except for Donnell. Aavril looked up to the quarterdeck and saw him standing at the wheel, one hand resting on the wood, but both eyes on what was going on below him.

"What's the matter here, Sailing Master?" The Captain's voice was grave, expecting a good reason for the disturbance.

"It's nothing, I say," yelled Erroll. "No one can prove I did anything!"

Kelsey cuffed Erroll on the back of the head. "Shuddup!" Turning to Liam, he said, "Tell 'em, lad."

Erroll turned to Liam, eyes wide. "You didn't see anything. Rat me out and I'll make you pay!"

Liam's own eyes were wide with fear. The Captain turned his gaze on the young elf. "Well, lad? Out with it!"

"Cap'n, sir—"

"Shut your trap!" Erroll yelled, earning him another cuffing from Kelsey.

"I saw him do it, Cap'n," Liam stammered.

"Do what?"

"He took it. Straight from the *Isean's* seabag."

"Took what?" Even before the question was asked, Loren stepped forward and grabbed Erroll, shaking him violently.

"Filthy thief! Where is it? Where did you hide it? Give it back to me!"

"It's mine!" Erroll shoved Loren back. "You stole it from me! You're the thief!"

Loren smacked Erroll hard, causing him to hit the deck. "Give me back my necklace!" He reached down and began searching Erroll, violently pulling at his clothes. Erroll tried to fight back, but Aavril and Kelsey grabbed him, holding him down. Finally, Loren stood up, holding the 'Joy of the Widow's Tears' in his hand. Aavril thought the gemstone had a soft glow to it in the moonlight.

"It's mine! Give it to me!" Erroll continued to struggle.

Loren cupped the necklace in his hand and then slid it into a pouch on his belt. Grabbing Erroll, he hauled him up off the deck. "You'll have a hard time claiming anything from the bottom of the sea!" He started dragging Erroll to the deck rail, while everyone else made a commotion.

"*Isean*, stop!" bellowed Captain Sterna, his voice breaking through the noise. Loren stopped, turning to look at his father.

"Justice will be meted out for this crime, but it will not be death." He looked hard at Erroll. "The accused, having been found with the stolen goods upon his person, is found guilty of theft. His sentence is twenty lashes, to be carried out immediately. Quartermaster, execute the sentence."

Aavril was stunned. Everything had happened so fast that he was still trying to comprehend what was going on. He managed to say, "Aye, Captain." Turning to Kelsey, he said, "Sailing Master. Bind the prisoner to the mast."

Kelsey nodded solemnly and carried out the task without a word. Loren entered the Captain's cabin and returned with a whip, handing it to Aavril. Aavril walked over to Erroll, pulling his shirt up to expose his back. He then stepped back a pace, letting the whip fall to the deck. Raising his hand, he struck, the whip cracking across Erroll's back. Everybody stood silent as Aavril began counting, "One."

Chapter 5

The double-doors to New Port burst open with a clatter. Constable Karen Whitlocke's mouth formed a sharp, thin line, and she folded her arms as she looked up from her parchmentwork. Raised voices and the clanking of weapons and armor preceded the gaggle of people entering the Royal Tenyl Constabulary headquarters. Whitlocke glared at the procession as the calm and order of her realm were disturbed.

"You have no right to do this!" bellowed a large, muscular human with thick red hair and wearing plate armor that was painted in red and black, several spikes sticking up from the shoulders. Whitlocke wondered to herself, *How does that idiot not stab his own head against those?*

"Shut yer knothole!" Senior Constable Ghrellstone yelled, shoving the human to Whitlocke's left. The Senior Constable carried a sheathed dagger, a weird-looking axe, and a large sword that he wore draped over one shoulder.

"Why are we being punished? We didn't do anything wrong!" hollered a stocky halfling with a magical gemstone hovering over his head. He was wearing a blue and gold silk cape, and had a large, golden holy symbol of Xuran hanging from a thick gold chain around his neck.

"Just keep moving," Constable Brillow said, as she used her foot to nudge the cleric to Whitlocke's right.

"But don't you see? It was their fault! We're the heroes

here. We were doing your job for you, doing Tenyl a favor. The mayor should give us all medals." This tripe came from a lithe, male elf wearing fine silversteel chain armor and a wood and silver inlaid brooch, which was made in the shape of Basvu's holy symbol and clasped a dark green cloak.

"Whatever," Constable Kai Gania said, pushing the elf to stand next to the human. Gania carried a heavy flanged mace that glowed with a soft, blue light, and several leather scroll cases.

"Our fault?" exclaimed a thin, busty, human female with raven black hair. "You attacked us! We only fought back in order to defend ourselves from your treachery!" She wore very ineffectual scale armor that barely covered her bosom and left her stomach entirely unprotected.

I could gut her like a fish without breaking a sweat, Whitlocke mused with a sneering smile.

"Tell it to the Magistrate," Constable Bluepflame said, pushing the underdressed human to Whitlocke's right.

A handful of Birches from Betula Division ushered in four more people, sending two each to Whitlocke's left and right. The eight armored, though currently unarmed, adventurers continued to argue, yelling insults and pointing accusing fingers at each other. It sounded like a waterfront pub in Port Grove after somebody was accused of cheating, and it had driven Whitlocke past her tipping point. This was her domain and she wasn't going to let these hooligans forget that.

"Everybody shut the hells up!" Whitlocke bellowed at the top of her lungs. She was petite of stature, but her voice was high and piercing, a shrill noise that easily cut through the din. Everybody stopped talking and turned to look at her. Constables from the two Stables upstairs came and leaned over the railings to see what the commotion was all about.

"I couldn't have said it any better myself, Constable

Whitlocke." Constable Inspector Reva Lunaria stated, as she and her partner, Seeker Ansee Carya, walked into New Port. Inspector Lunaria's silver-red hair was disheveled, having come loose from her headband. There was a long cut in her leather armor and the start of a bruise under her left eye. Seeker Carya held a wooden staff bedecked with bird feathers, bronze bangles, and small bones. His uniform was similarly damaged, and Whitlocke noticed that blood had smeared the red and black Acer Division bracer on his left arm. There were also the odors of burned hair and burnt cloth, and she saw that both of their cloaks were badly singed.

Between the pair walked a halpbloed who was well-known among the constabulary for causing mischief. Coleus Pfastbinder was slightly shorter than CI Lunaria and had long, loose to the point of being almost wild, chestnut-brown hair, though it looked to be graying some since Whitlocke had last seen the halpbloed. He had a round face with a broad nose and a prominent chin. His emerald green eyes were sparkling at all the commotion that was going on, and a gleeful smile was plastered to his face. His clothes were...eclectic. He wore a bright yellow vest over a green silk shirt and red-and-white diamond-patterned leggings. Over this colorful combination, he wore a patchwork cloak that was sewn from several different materials and colors.

Reva marched the halpbloed up to Whitlocke's table. "What's all this, then, Inspector?" Whitlocke asked, attempting to return some much-needed order to the proceedings.

"I'm charging all of these idiots," the Inspector waved a hand to take in everybody, "with being adventurers."

"Err...ma'am?" She raised one eyebrow quizzically at the Inspector and sighed to herself. *Why can't anybody follow the rules?* "I don't think being an adventurer is a crime."

"Well, it damn well should be," Lunaria groused, clearly upset by this legal setback. "Fine. If I can't charge them with

33

that, how about we start with assault on a Constable." She pointed to the bruise under her eye.

"Resisting arrest," Senior Constable Ghrellstone said. He gave the human a shove.

"Disturbing the public peace," Constable Gania added.

"Arson," Seeker Carya chimed in.

"Arson?" exclaimed a female elven wizard to Whitlocke's left.

The Seeker turned to her angrily. "You cast a fireball right in the middle of a crowded street, engulfing a bakery and a grocer's in flames! Not to mention the fact that it also caught me and the Constable Inspector in the blast!"

It was clear that Seeker Carya was quite upset by the event, and the elf shut up. Whitlocke was silently pleased that the wizard looked embarrassed. She wrote the final item into her booking ledger, and then looked up. "Anything else? What about him?" She pointed the quill at the halpbloed.

"Possession of an artifact of mass destruction with intent to sell," The Constable Inspector said.

Pfastbinder burst out with a laugh that echoed around the entry area. "Oh, Inspector, this is so much fun. I really do enjoy it when you play along with my games."

"Play along?" Lunaria asked, her voice rising in anger.

"Games?" asked several of the adventurers at once.

Pfastbinder's grin widened, and he laughed some more. "Of course. This isn't an artifact." He tapped the staff that Seeker Carya held.

"Wait," said the elven cleric to Whitlocke's left. "You told us that is The Staff of Kanob, and that we'd need it in order to gain access to Kanob's Tomb so that we could defeat the demi-lich there."

"No," interrupted the wizard to Whitlocke's right. He pointed to the other group. "Pfastbinder told us that you were stealing Knoab's Bane so that you could raise an undead army and take over the city."

"Why would we want to raise an undead army?" the cleric of Basvu asked indignantly.

"Who in the hells knows?" the halfling cleric retorted. "But we would have stopped your evil plot."

"There was no plot!" the red-haired human yelled. "You attacked us so that you could take the staff and command the lich, not to destroy it like we would have done."

More shouting broke out between the two groups and the constables had to get between them in order to keep them from restarting the fight. All the while, Pfastbinder stood next to the table laughing.

Inspector Lunaria glared at him, and then yelled, "Enough!"

Everyone quieted down again and looked at her. She shook her head slowly. "You are all idiots. And so am I."

More blustering started but the Inspector raised a hand for silence. "Don't you get it? Kanob? Knoab?" She looked at all eight adventurers who stared at her dumbly. "Hells, doesn't anyone here have any religious knowledge?" She looked meaningfully at the two clerics who tried to appear like this wasn't their responsibility. "Kanob and Knoab are anagrams—really bad anagrams—for Banok, the God of Mischief. And Pfastbinder here happens to be Banok's biggest follower here in Tenyl. He's been playing both of your groups against each other. There is no Kanob's Tomb, and nobody wants to raise any undead or control a lich. It was all a game for his amusement."

"Xuran's pox upon you!" the halfling exclaimed.

"By Basvu, I'll have you banished from the city," said the other cleric.

Pfastbinder continued to laugh, apparently unconcerned by the threats. "Very good, Inspector. Although it took you a while to figure it out. You're slipping," he chided playfully.

The Inspector ignored the remark. "So, this isn't an artifact?"

"Nope," he grinned. "The good Seeker here will be able to confirm that there's a simple illusion spell on it, but it has no magical properties of its own. And there's nothing against the law about me carrying a staff with an illusion on it."

"I should charge you as an accessory."

"It will never stick, and you know it."

The Inspector sighed loudly, and then blew a loose strand of her hair from her eye. "Fine."

"Always a pleasure, Constable Inspector." The halpbloed smiled and walked to the doors.

"Wait a minute," the underdressed female said. "We're the victims here. Arrest him!"

"There's no law against getting two groups of stupid adventurers to fall for his stories." The Constable Inspector crossed her arms as Pfastbinder walked out of New Port with a wave.

"So, we can go, too?" asked one of the adventurers.

"Oh, no," Lunaria said with a grim smile. "I'm still arresting all of you." She turned to Whitlocke as the two groups exploded with yells and curses. "Put them in cells across from each other. Maybe they'll gain some clearly needed experience from this."

Chapter 6

Aavril stood at the ship's wheel, eyes locked on the area ahead and to the port of the *Majestic Tern*. The mid-morning sun shone through broken clouds, and he used the gentle easterly breeze blowing in from Black Elf Bay to guide the *Tern* toward the dock in Tenyl. This was always a tricky task, requiring the ship to navigate waters that were congested with merchant ships, fishing boats, barges, and any idiot who thought that it would be a good idea to try out his new magical ring of water walking, in the busy port. It was a task that Aavril insisted on doing himself in order to make sure that they docked without running over some hapless crabber's rowboat.

Janish and Olwynn stood at the port rail, ready to toss the thick, half-hand ropes to the waiting halpbloeden. They'd pull the ship the last few paces into the dock and secure the lines.

The last week of the voyage had been filled with muted tension after the punishment that had been delivered to Erroll. Everyone knew that it had been justified, but it had thrown wet leaves on what had otherwise been a successful trip. As the *Tern* had rounded the Leaphii headland and entered Black Elf Bay yesterday, there had been a noticeable relief in the crew.

Erroll had been kept confined to his hammock after the punishment. Aavril had tried to avoid being cruel in the application of the lash; it was meant to be a serious punishment, not a death sentence. Aavril had heard of sailors being killed when punishments had been taken too far and the skin flayed from their backs. Aavril had been judicious, making sure that the whip hit Erroll's back at the very point of its crack, but to not drag it across and leave long wounds. It had been painful, but instead of long, bloody gashes in his back, Erroll had been left with twenty small, well-placed wounds.

Aavril wondered if he should have been that nice in his application of the punishment, as Erroll had continued to be surly afterward. Captain Sterna, feeling that the matter had been resolved, had at first ordered the young sailor to return to his duties, but Erroll had refused the Captain's orders, brooding and moping on the deck and just being a nuisance. He'd gotten in the way and was becoming a hazard to the crew, so the Captain had ordered him confined to his hammock. Erroll seemed to be content to stay there, sulking. He ate the food that Kelsey brought him and, other than trips to the head to relieve himself, he'd stayed put. But Aavril had noticed that whenever Loren was in his own hammock, Erroll would glare daggers at the *Isean*.

Aavril eased the *Tern's* wheel to port, allowing the ship to glide close enough to the dock for the Blueleaph brothers to toss their lines to the waiting halpbloeden. The ship was pulled forward and, within a few minutes, there was a slight bump and shudder as the *Tern* stopped and was tied up to the dock. Kelsey stood ready and dropped the gangplank when the ship came to rest.

Aavril's emotions were mixed. He was happy to be home, and he was looking forward to seeing Reva after being at sea for four months, but he was not looking forward to the conversation that he would have with her. She'd asked him to open a shop when he returned and not go back to sea so that they could spend more time together. He'd never promised that he would, but he wasn't sure if she'd under-stood him or misread his intentions. He'd wanted to spend time with Reva, but she never committed anything to him in return, especially not regarding her own job. Now he'd have to tell her that he'd accepted a promotion to *Isean* and would not only be returning to sea sooner, but he'd also be gone longer. He didn't see how that conversation could turn out good for him.

That conversation would have to wait, though. Captain Sterna was already heading down the gangway to meet with his backers. He passed a large gathering of halpbloeden and humans who were waiting on the dock to unload the ship and carry the cargo to waiting warehouses. Aavril and the rest of the crew still had a lot of work to do to make sure that the cargo was taken off in the right order and to work the winches to get the cargo out of the hold.

Still, despite his unease, Aavril was looking forward to seeing Reva. If the day went well, he should be able to meet her for dinner. Grabbing the navigation log, he tore out the last page. Inking a quill, he wrote a note to Reva, letting her know that he'd arrived and suggesting that they meet at a restaurant near Nymph Creek in River Grove.

Aavril went down the gangplank to find somebody to carry the message. *If I play this right,* he thought, *the topic of my plans for the future won't come up tonight. That will give me another day to figure out how to break the news to her.* He spotted a young halpbloeden boy who looked like he'd snap in half trying to unload the cargo.

"Boy!" Aavril called. The child stepped over to him, grimy breeches and a dirty, ill-fitting shirt hanging loose on his thin body.

"*Áree*, master."

"Two Acorns if you deliver a message for me."

The boy's eyes widened. "Sure, master. Where?"

Aavril knew that the two copper coins would be twice

what the boy would get for unloading the *Tern*. He was over-paying, but he wanted to make sure that the boy did the task. He handed the message and one Pfen to the boy. "Take this to New Port and make sure they give it to Constable Inspector Lunaria. You'll get the second coin when you tell me the task is done."

The boy nodded and started to turn when Aavril grabbed the boy by the shoulder. "And make sure that the duty Constable gives his mark and bring that back, so I know you did the job."

The boy nodded again, maybe a bit sullenly this time, but Aavril didn't care. He'd had messages supposedly delivered before, only to find out that Reva hadn't gotten them. Verification was simpler than trust. He released the boy, who ran off down the dock.

Aavril turned to head back to the ship and had to jump aside as Loren came running down the gangplank. "Where are you going?"

Loren smiled. "If we're going to turn the *Tern* around," he laughed at his own joke, "then I need to meet some investors and get funding."

"But what about our current cargo?"

"You can handle this, *Isean*." Loren gave him a large smile. He then waved to the waiting halpbloeden and humans. "Besides, you have plenty of help here."

"We still have to get the cargo out of the hold. That's easier with experienced hands."

"I know. I told Erroll that if he wants his pay before heading off—not that I think he deserves it—then he needs to help unload the cargo." Aavril understood. The Captain had told Erroll that he was no longer a part of the crew and would be leaving the ship with the pay he'd earned when they docked. Erroll had shown the same sullen insolence at that news as to everything else that had happened after the theft and punishment. Captain Sterna still considered the matter of the theft resolved, and he had a reputation that he wanted to maintain, even if he was retiring. Apparently, Loren was already putting his own mark on how the ship was going to be run.

Aavril wasn't sure how much help Erroll would be, but nodded. "Fine. But hurry back. We'll need our *Captain* if we are going to pull this off."

Loren smiled and turned to head up the dock. "Of course."

Aavril shook his head and went back up to the ship. "Kelsey, let's get everything ready."

"Aye, sir."

Aavril turned, catching movement toward the bow. He looked in time to see Erroll slip over the rail and jump the two paces down to the dock, then run toward shore.

"Damn it." He couldn't stop him, and now the task to unload the ship would be more difficult. He took a Pfen and said a small prayer, then tossed it over the railing. Even if they worked flat out, they would need a miracle from Demar to get everything done in order for him to make his dinner with Reva. He hoped that the sea god was listening.

Chapter 7

Loren whistled a nameless tune as he stepped off of the ferry and headed toward Embankment Road. He was in a very good mood. After leaving the ship, he'd met with two members of the Merchant's Guild: elves he'd been cultivating for the past year with gifts brought back from his voyages. It had been like courting a beautiful woman, but the time—and expense—in gaining their patronage had paid off today. Over an excellent bottle of Torollan wine Loren had brought along, they'd congratulated him on becoming Captain of the *Majestic Tern*, toasted his father's retirement, and discussed Loren's proposal to take the *Tern* to the Spice Islands.

The two elves were newer members of the Guild and were just as ambitious, and just as eager, as Loren to make their mark in Tenyl. Around his own age, they were determined to open Tenyl to new markets and agreed with Loren that the Sneveves Peninsula was not what it used to be with regard to trade. Too many merchant ships from Tenyl, Narris, and other, smaller, coastal ports were trading there now, diluting the market for their goods. The *Tern* fared better than other ships by rounding the cape and traveling up the west coast to trade with the Torollans, but even that market was quickly becoming too competitive.

Loren's plan made sense, as by sailing directly to the Spice Islands, they would cut out the Torollan merchants who marked up the spices they sold. This meant that, by buying directly from the Nephrinians in the Spice Islands, they'd be able to increase profits for everybody. They all agreed that Loren's idea would work, and they agreed that if they didn't act soon, this opportunity might be grabbed by somebody else. Making their move now would allow them to get in at the roots and possibly cut others out of the market. They'd have their own monopoly on the trade, at least until somebody else caught up with them, but by then, they'd have made their Crowns and could afford to let others in.

The merchants had agreed to finance Loren's trip, but only if he could sail within the week. Loren had expected this demand and had told them he was already preparing the *Tern* to do exactly that. Better to let them know that he was an excellent planner rather than somebody who would take orders from merchants. This would be a partnership, not a master/worker relationship. Drinking another toast to their venture, the merchants had agreed to deliver a cargo of wine, ironwood, and bales of fine Highland sheep's wool for Loren to trade with. They'd also deliver a strong-box of 5,000 Crowns to finance additional purchases.

Loren had left the Guildhall excited and filled with anticipation. As with most children, he wanted to show that he was just as good—if not better—than his father. He could imagine the additional ships that he'd buy on the success of this trip, allowing him to bring back even more cargo the next time. He was determined that, within five years, he would have a fleet of four or more ships, all under his command. He'd no longer be Captain Sterna, as his father had been, but Fleet Captain Sterna. Never again would he be in his father's shadow.

Now that business was completed, he wanted to take care of some personal matters. Loren knew that he should return to the ship and help unload their cargo. Aavril was

43

going to be bloody furious when he found out why Loren would be late, but Loren was so excited by the new partnership and his plans that he wanted to see Amber now. He wanted to tell her of his success, about becoming Captain, and how, in a few months, he'd be returning home as a hero. He knew that now was the time to ask her to marry him.

Amber Myosotis had struck Loren like a lightning bolt over a year ago. Loren had been with Aavril as he'd gone to buy flowers for Reva. He had been giving Aavril a hard time about having to work so hard to keep Reva happy.

"You see, Aavril," Loren had patiently explained, "you have thrown away your freedom. You spend every moment in port looking for gifts in order to keep your woman happy, and even when you get her a splendid gift—like that parrot—you still are under some compulsion to spend even more Skips on flowers."

"And you have it so much better than me?" Aavril had asked.

"Of course I do. I have no woman to moor me in place when I'm in port. I have the pick of any woman I want without having to worry about keeping them happy beyond a single night."

"You manage to keep them happy that long?"

Loren had cuffed his friend on the shoulder as they entered the flower shop. Voran must have been waiting in ambush as they entered, because the God of Love and Fertility had struck him hard.

Amber had been holding a bouquet of red and white roses that paled in comparison with her own beauty. Her skin was smooth and perfect, the color of freshly cut maple. Her long, golden hair glowed brightly in the sunlight. She'd smiled with a petite mouth and had batted her golden-amber eyes at him. Loren had never been at a loss for words around women, and, even now, he knew exactly what to say, but it hadn't been his usual, lewd pitch to try to pick up a strange woman in a pub who he just wanted to have sex with and be done with her. Instead, pure elegance had flowed from his lips.

"Under Yntalla's light do the night roses bloom. People say their beauty is unmatched anywhere in the world, but clearly, those people never saw you, for if they had, they would surely change their minds."

Amber had laughed. Not a mean laugh, but playful and inviting. "Many men enter my shop with lines of poetry on the lips, but none so unique as that."

"Please, allow a humble sailor the honor of dinner with someone whose beauty is unmatched in all the exotic lands of the world."

Aavril made an exaggerated gesture of rolling his eyes. Thankfully, Amber either didn't notice or thought that was part of the charm. Certainly, Aavril had never heard Loren speak like that to any woman before. The words had come to Loren unbidden as if Vyhan—the Goddess of Music—herself had placed them on his tongue.

"You are quite the charmer," Amber had said. "And I like the look of your eyes. Since you compare me to my favorite flower, I will accept your invitation."

After the first date, Amber had agreed to see Loren again. They spent every free minute he had together while he was in port. They went for long walks in Nuphar Wood, and Loren had listened as she named for him all of the flowers and trees. He took her to the port and gave her a tour of the *Tern*, pointing out the different ships and how to tell them apart. And they spent long evenings together, their bodies entwined. It had been a magical two weeks, and when it was time for the *Tern* to sail again, Amber had promised to wait for him.

And she had. When they'd returned to Tenyl, Amber had greeted him warmly. They picked up their romance where they had left off. They managed a trip out of the city to the Eoseen Forest and the famed red cliffs that overlooked Black Elf Bay. Loren was in love. He cherished every moment that he spent with Amber, and she had been overjoyed at the gifts he brought her: a gold bracelet from Oroma, an ivory and pearl hair comb, and the most prized gift of all, a book detailing the flowering plants found in the Kingdom of Cantull, exquisitely illuminated with detailed drawings of the flowers. Loren had spent a day searching booksellers in Cantull to find the book, and it had cost him a fortune, but it had been worth it to see Amber's face light up when she'd opened her present.

Loren knew that he wanted to spend all of his time with Amber. She filled a hole in his life that he hadn't realized was there. So now, as he walked up Embankment Road, he rehearsed in his head how he was going to ask Amber to marry him. Marriage was a big step, and a risk to take with him being a sailor and away for so many months of the year. He knew it had been a miracle that his parents had stayed together, and he understood why Reva had kept Aavril sitting on a branch about the subject. While he and Amber had never discussed the topic, he knew that it was the right decision. He ran his fingers along the silver chain of the necklace he'd bought in Cantull. It would be his engagement gift to Amber.

† † †

Erroll dashed across the road, keeping one eye on Loren as he headed up a side road. There was a metallic taste in his mouth as he followed the *Isean*. After jumping ship that morning, he'd wound his way through the port, intent on Loren's trail. Even though he'd not seen where Loren was headed, some inner sense had guided Erroll through the chaos of the port. He didn't know where the *Isean* was going, but Erroll knew where he was.

When Erroll arrived outside the Guildhall, he felt Loren's presence inside the building. He was almost pulled into the building, his feet heading up the short steps before two guards blocked his path. He mumbled some excuse and skulked away, turning into an alley behind a cheese shop. Although he *knew* Loren was inside the Guildhall, he watched the door with a burning intensity; he wasn't going to lose his quarry.

He sensed Loren leaving the building moments before the *Isean* stepped out the door. He had a smile on his face and walked down the steps and up the street with a jaunty gait. Loren didn't return to the port and Erroll followed, keeping the *Isean* in sight.

While waiting for the ferry, Erroll had caught sight of a silver chain around the *Isean's* neck and he'd felt his pulse quicken. The urge to step up and demand the necklace swelled in him, but there were too many people around, including a constable. He needed to get Loren alone.

They crossed the River Tenz together on the ferry. The *Isean* stood at the front, absorbed in his thoughts and completely unaware of Erroll's presence. As the ferry bobbed across the river, Erroll had stared intently at the back of Loren's neck, where a glint of silver could be seen between strands of brown hair.

Heading up the side road now, away from Embankment Road and the crowds, Erroll thought that he should make his move. He began edging his way closer to the *Isean*, ready to strike. Erroll was a pace behind Loren, his arm stretched out to grab Loren's shoulder and whirl him around, when the *Isean* abruptly turned and entered a flower shop. With a silent curse, Erroll crossed the road to watch the front of the building.

† † †

The pleasant scent of flowers and soil filled the small shop, bringing a smile of familiarity to Loren. It was a wonderful smell, the smell of love. He didn't see anybody, so he paused for a moment inside the door. He'd planned to surprise Amber as she walked from the back to see what this new customer wanted but, after a moment, Amber didn't appear. Loren stepped up to the large table that she used to replant customer's orders into decorative pots. Right now, a small mound of rich black potting soil sat on the table next to a colorful green and blue pot. A bunch of peonies sat in the partially filled pot, awaiting the last of the dirt.

Loren looked around, concerned and a bit irritated. *Why hadn't she heard the bell and come out to greet me?* A bubbling of fear started to churn in his stomach, along with a brief flicker of pain in his chest. He was about to call out when a noise from the back caught his attention. He stepped up to the curtain that separated the back room from the shop and paused. He could hear the faint sounds of laughter now, followed by a few notes from a lyre, or maybe a mandolin. *Who's playing music?* Curious, and with a seed of fear taking root in his mind, he parted the curtain and walked into the back room.

"I pray you learn to trust / my love for you is deep and just."

Loren heard the lyrics, sung to the accompaniment of the instrument. The voice was rich and melodious. *Not Amber's voice.* Stepping around a trellis filled with colorful flowers, Loren saw them. Shock and anger exploded like a wizard's fireball inside him, a deep burning flame of jealousy that consumed his thoughts and charred his broken heart.

Amber lay on several burlap bags of potting soil, her long hair cascading around her head in a nimbus of gold. She was laughing at the music, pulling the hem of her dress up seductively above her knees. The top of the dress had been untied and pulled down off her shoulders to expose her breasts. It would have been a welcoming sight for Loren had it not been for the male elf standing before her playing a mandolin.

He was about Loren's height with short-cut brown hair. He wore no shirt, his smooth skin a pale, golden oak color. He wore deep blue leggings, but they were untied at the front. He was playing and singing, and neither of them was aware of Loren's presence.

"Do you remember me / my love calling for you / on a string of dreams? My heart filled with my love for you / as I fill you with my love."

Amber giggled at the last line, and the singer gave her a lecherous grin and shook his hips seductively. They both started laughing.

"What in the hells is going on here?" Loren yelled. He stepped from behind the trellis and both Amber and her lover jumped.

"Loren!" Amber exclaimed. "You're here?"

"Shut up, whore!" Loren hurled the words at her, his fury hitting her like a physical force. Anger filled every part of his body, and he felt an intense pain in his chest, as though his heart was being gripped in a vice.

Pain...

The singer stepped up, his hand grasping the neck of the mandolin. "You can't talk to her like that! Who is this barbarous brute, my dear?"

"Lo...Loren. H...he's m...my...b...boyfriend." Amber was sobbing, trying to simultaneously pull the top of her dress up and the hem of her dress down to cover herself.

"So, you're the lout of a sailor who thinks that he's good enough for Amber. She deserves much better than you," the singer said. He gave Loren an appraising glance and clearly found him wanting. "She deserves an elf who's here for her, not traipsing around the oceans bedding any whore who'll open her legs for him. She doesn't love you. Now get out, before I summon a constable."

"No, Garwin. Don't say that, you'll only make it worse." Amber stood up and tried to pull Garwin back. She looked at Loren, tears filling her amber-colored eyes. "Loren, please. I didn't know that you were back."

Pain brings...

Loren didn't hear a word that they were saying. Blood boiled in his ears and his vision collapsed until all he could see was the two of them. It felt as though his chest was about to burst. Amber's eyes grew wide, the whites showing around the golden irises, and she tried to pull Garwin away from Loren. He and Loren stood only a few hands apart.

"Please, Loren! It didn't mean anything! Please, don't!"

Pain brings truth.

Garwin raised his hand. "That's enough! You're scaring Amber, and you need to leave." He stepped forward and put his hand on Loren's chest, ready to push.

Show him the truth!

Loren exploded into a flurry of activity. With a quick upward thrust of his left hand, he pushed Garwin's hand away from his chest while delivering a sharp blow with his right fist directly into Garwin's jaw. The singer and the mandolin both fell to the floor, the mandolin making the more musical of landings. Loren picked up the fallen mandolin and smashed it down on Garwin's head. The mandolin broke with the SNAP of splintered wood and the TWANG of broken strings. Garwin lost consciousness, blood flowing from his deep head wound. Loren raised the remains of the broken instrument and smashed it back down, again and again.

"No! Stop it, Loren!" Amber cried and grabbed his arm. "Stop! You're killing him!"

Loren shoved Amber away, causing her to fall onto the sacks of potting soil, her dress catching on something as she fell, tearing part of the fabric away and exposing one breast. He sneered at her and took a step forward.

Pain is truth. She must be shown!

Amber screamed and tried to get up, but Loren pushed her back. He climbed on top of her, putting his hands around her throat. She gasped, crying and trying to scream. Amber tried to pry his hands from her neck, but he was just too strong. A sound like a moan of pleasure escaped from Loren's mouth as Amber's nails dug into his flesh, rending a bloody trench through the tern skin art on his arm. Tears fell from Amber's eyes as she realized that this was a fight that she wouldn't win. Her struggles lessened as her consciousness began to slip away. Loren stared down at Amber as the life left her eyes.

As his hands continued to squeeze her neck, the Joy of the Widow's Tears slipped out from his shirt. It twisted in the air, the golden design turning slowly, the small tear-shaped gemstone catching the light.

Sound returned to Loren's ears and his vision regained focus on the scene before him. He pulled his hands from Amber's throat and stood up. He began to slowly shake his head, looking down at the two lifeless bodies. "What happened? Amber? What have I done?"

Bile and fear rose up from his stomach. His head swiveled around, checking to see if he was alone. Seeing no one, he took one last look at Amber and, with tears in his eyes, fled from the flower shop.

Chapter 8

Reva sat at an outdoor table at the Blue Asparagus, swirling a goblet of white wine and trying to contain her growing anger. She'd been here for nearly an hour; long enough that the sun was now setting, and the waiters were lighting paper lanterns around the patio. This was her second goblet and she'd been nursing it. She wanted a clear head for when she lit into Aavril once he finally showed up.

She'd received the note from him around lunchtime and had been excited by the news that he was finally back in town. These past four months had been difficult, especially since Gabii mimicked his voice so well that she sometimes thought that he was still around. She'd been doing a lot of thinking since they'd last seen each other, and she was almost ready to commit to him. *Well, at least to moving in together.* Once he had established himself as a merchant, things would settle down and they could discuss everything that might come later; things like marriage and children. But for now, they could be comfortable just being with each other. It was something that really hadn't been a part of their relationship before, and Reva wanted to see how it would feel.

But being late to dinner is not a way to impress me, she thought to herself. She leaned back in the chair, impatiently tapping a finger against the table as she tried to calm herself. Aavril had never been late before. In fact, he was usually the one waiting on her, since she often got tied up with a new case or some other disturbance. It wasn't like Aavril to pull a joke on her just to make a point, so there was probably a good reason for him to be late. *At least there had better be.*

She took a sip of the wine and looked out onto Embankment Road. Elves were heading home to their own meals, and couples strolled along the wide road, holding hands and laughing. She and Aavril had rarely had time to do something as simple as taking a stroll at sunset. When he was in town, they were usually too busy making up for all the time that they'd been apart to bother with romantic walks along the river. That is, when her schedule allowed them to get together. *Have I been the problem? He knows that my career is important to me, but have I given him enough reasons to know that I care about him too?*

"*Reis inellen,* Inspector."

Reva looked up to see Seeker Pfinzloab waving at her. "Hello, Norah." Reva smiled a greeting.

"Are you eating alone, Inspector?" Norah asked. "Would you like to join me and my husband?" She gestured to a table across the patio where her husband sat.

Reva shook her head. "Áeorias, but no. I'm not alone. At least I won't be in a bit. My boyfriend is just running late, is all."

Norah smiled and nodded. "Enjoy your evening, then, Inspector." Norah smiled again and returned to her own table. Reva returned to tapping her finger on the table. She was going to give Aavril a few more minutes before she started thinking of ways to skin him alive for being late.

† † †

Aavril slowed down a few buildings away from the Blue Asparagus to catch his breath. He was very late for his dinner with Reva, and had run all the way from the ferry. It wouldn't look good to run up to the restaurant like a mad-elf. *Though if I just stroll up, she might think that I didn't care about being late.*

Breaking into a jog, Aavril hurried the last few paces. As he approached the restaurant, he saw her immediately. Reva sat outside under a trellised canopy of ivy and hya-cinth. A nearby paper lantern cast a soft, warm yellow light that made her silver-red hair glow. She wore her hair loose, tucked behind the graceful point of her ear. She wore a sleeveless dress of light blue and silver that he recognized as the one that he'd bought her last year for the Bonfire Festival.

But her forehead was furrowed, and Aavril saw the scowl on her face and knew that she was angry. Reva was not the most punctual elf in Tenyl; her job often saw to that, but she hated to be kept waiting. Aavril had tried to point out the double standard, but she defended the times that she was late by saying that her job was important. *As if mine isn't?* Aavril shook the thought away. He hadn't waited four months for this reunion just to ruin it by being angry. With confidence, he opened the wooden gate for the restaurant and stepped over to Reva.

Before he could say anything, the scowl on Reva's face fell away like autumn leaves from a tree and a huge smile lit up her face. Standing up, she flung her arms around him, kissing him deeply. Aavril returned the kiss and embraced her in a tight hug. Her skin was cool and soft and felt won-derful in his arms.

† † †

After too short a time, Reva broke the embrace and stepped back, letting her hands slide down his arms, rest-ing in his hands. He looked so amazing to her, his straw-brown hair glowing in the lantern light and his hazel eyes twinkling. They smiled at each other. "That was for coming home," she said.

"One of the reasons I like coming home to you." He pulled out his chair to sit down.

Reva punched him hard in the shoulder as she took her own seat. "Ow!" Several diners looked in their direction.

"And *that* is for making me wait." Reva signaled for the waiter.

Aavril rubbed his shoulder. "I'm really sorry about that. See, things at the ship—"

Reva held up a hand. "No. Telling me about it will just make me mad again. So, where's my present?"

"Why do you think I brought you a present?"

"You show up late and don't bring me a present? You clearly want to sleep alone tonight."

The waiter's ears reddened at that as he refilled Reva's goblet. She smiled at him, and he quickly filled Aavril's goblet before scurrying off.

"Well, if you are going to make threats..."

"Sometimes, a girl just has to take charge."

Aavril smiled and pulled a pouch from his belt and set it on the table. Reva put a sneer on her face as she daintily picked up the pouch with thumb and forefinger. The sarcasm dripped from her mouth as she said, "Oh, good, you got me a ragged old pouch. How thoughtful. It's just what I wanted. I hope it wasn't too much trouble."

"Oh, stop it and just open it."

Reva gave him a mocking smile as she opened the pouch. She pulled out a round object like a ball, colored bright orange. Its texture was smooth and waxy. She raised one eyebrow. "What am I, a child? You got me an orange ball?"

"No. It's a fruit. They're called *raemalus* and we brought a bunch back from Torolla to sell."

"A sunapple?" She looked at the fruit warily.

"Now you're acting like a child. Try it, you baby."

Reva put the sunapple in her mouth and took a bite. Bitter flavor filled her mouth and she spat the piece out onto the table. Aavril erupted in laughter, causing the diners around them to turn and stare.

"You don't eat the skin," he said, between laughs. "You have to peel it first."

"Why didn't you say that?"

"Because I wanted to see you do that. The look on your face was perfect. It was all..." He screwed up his own face in crude mimicry of what Reva had looked like.

Reva made to throw the sunapple at him and Aavril flinched, but she decided not to waste the fruit. "For a sailor who's been away for four months, you are working really hard to not have any sex on your first night back."

Aavril grabbed the sunapple and began peeling it. "I'm pretty sure that won't happen. Your real present is still in there." He nodded at the leather pouch sitting on the table between them.

Skeptically, she pulled the pouch open and looked inside. Her eyes widened, and she couldn't suppress a smile. Reaching in, she pulled her present out. "It's lovely."

It was a chain of small gold rings linked together, about five hands long. On the chain was a pendant of gold wire with a multicolored gem set on the wire. The gem was carved to resemble a parrot in flight, and the play of color on the stone mimicked the bird's colorful feathers.

"I knew you'd love it." Aavril had finished peeling the sunapple and pulled off a couple of the orange-colored wedges of the fruit, handing them to Reva.

Reva put on the necklace, letting the pendant rest on her chest. She took the fruit and bit into it without hesitation. Sweet juice filled her mouth and the soft flesh almost melted as she chewed. She spit out some seeds into her hand. "That was wonderful. I guess I'll just have to forgive you." She leaned over the table, as did Aavril, and they kissed when they met in the middle.

A polite cough broke the kiss, but only enough so Reva could say, "We're not ready to order yet."

"Well, that's good, 'cuz I ain't your waiter."

Reva sat back down to glare at Senior Constable Ghrellstone. "Damn it, Senior Constable. Somebody better be dead, or I'll have your bracers." She was only partially jesting, but she knew Willem well enough to know that he'd not bother her like this if it weren't serious.

"Evening, Aavril," Willem nodded a greeting.

"Good evening, Senior Constable. I suppose this means that you are taking my lady away from me on my first night back."

"'Fraid so. Sorry." He gave an apologetic shrug and looked at Reva. "As the FC has oft said, 'This is a bad one.'"

"Murder."

"Two murders, as a matter of fact, Inspector."

"Damn."

"Yes, ma'am."

Standing up, Reva placed her hand over Aavril's. "You know I have to go."

Aavril patted her hand. "I know. I don't like it, though. Can't they find somebody else? Aren't there any other Inspectors? Why is it always you?"

She leaned down and gave him a lingering kiss, then looked him in the eye and winked. "Because I'm the best," she whispered.

Caressing her face, he looked into her turquoise eyes. "Just promise me that you'll punish the asshole extra hard for breaking this up."

"Sure thing." Letting her fingers trace a line up his arm, she headed toward the gate. "Let's go, Willem. I'll need to go change first."

Willem gave a polite wave to Seeker Pfinzloab and her

husband. Norah looked relieved that it wasn't her who was having her evening ruined. "Yes, ma'am." Together, they walked out of the restaurant.

Chapter 9

Erroll watched Loren as he left the flower shop in haste. He didn't know what had happened while the *Isean* had been inside, but he'd apparently been the only one on the street to hear the screams. And he'd felt...*something*. A tingling of expectant energy had danced around Erroll, like faerie fire around a ship's mast during a storm. Something important had happened, but he just didn't know what it was.

He wasn't drawn into the shop to see what had happened. Instead, he followed Loren, continuing to be attracted by the necklace. Loren moved quickly and erratically, dodging groups of people and avoiding the main streets. He didn't return to the ferry. Instead, he headed upriver, meandering aimlessly along side streets and alleys. He appeared to be talking to himself, and several times he'd pause, then shake his head and continue on his way.

A few times, Erroll thought about making his move and confronting the *Isean*, but each time something prevented him from acting—a couple walking down the road, a constable walking patrol. So, Erroll decided to hang back and watch where Loren went. He knew that, at some point, the right time to act would present itself.

Loren wandered across the city for over an hour, and he crossed the river a couple of times. Once, he seemed to be heading toward the top of Poplar Hill, and Erroll thought that the *Isean* was going to turn himself in to the Constabulary. That would have been a disaster for Erroll, and he'd almost run up to Loren to stop him, but at the gate of New Port, Loren seemed to change his mind and he turned around.

Loren was back on the north side of the river now, wandering through Marsh Grove. He headed toward Victory Bridge, which crossed over Mill Island and into Nul Pfeta. Erroll started to panic again. *He's seen me! He's trying to lose me in Nul Pfeta.* The panic almost overtook him, but then he remembered that he'd known where Loren had been all day, and not even the warrens of Nul Pfeta would hide the *Isean* from him.

The road heading to the bridge was filled with halpbloeden heading in and out of the grove. They all ignored Loren and Erroll. Loren headed across the bridge, but instead of heading into Nul Pfeta, he took a set of stone steps that led down to Mill Island.

The island bisected the River Tenz at the western end of the city. It housed several large grain mills that processed the grain into flour. The island was cut through with canals, sluices, and ponds to direct the waterworks that operated the mills. Normally the area would have been busy with mill workers, teamsters, and halpbloeden, but the day was ending, and most of the workers had gone home. The area was practically deserted.

Loren wandered to the south bank, heading toward the piers located under the bridge. Erroll smiled to himself. Now was the time for him to get his necklace back.

Erroll moved quickly, picking up a stanchion that was lying on top of some barrels. Looking around to make sure that he was alone, Erroll headed under the bridge. Loren stood at the water's edge, rubbing his hands together roughly like he was trying to rub something off of them.

"I need to get it off of me. *Why won't it come off?*"

A board creaked as Erroll stepped up behind the *Isean*. Loren turned as Erroll raised the makeshift club.

"Please, help me get this—" Loren started to say, but then his eyes widened as he recognized Erroll. "*You* did this to me! This is *your* fault!"

Erroll hesitated for just a moment and then brought the club down. Loren raised his left arm to block the blow and there was a loud CRACK in the air under the bridge as the club hit Loren's arm and broke the bone. Erroll expected Loren to cry out, or to at least pull back from the blow, but instead, a manic grin spread across Loren's face. Before Erroll could react, the *Isean* landed a punch in Erroll's stomach. Unprepared, it knocked the wind from Erroll.

"It was *your* fault!" Loren yelled. "*You* made me do it!" He then grabbed his head with both hands, ignoring the pain from his shattered arm, and cried out, "Stop yelling at me! If this is the truth, I don't want it!"

Erroll recovered from the punch. Ignoring the *Isean's* words, he said, "Give me my necklace!" He reached out, grabbing Loren's shirt by the collar, tearing it as he pulled to get at the necklace.

"Why did she do it?" Loren asked, staggering back. "I loved her. Didn't she know that I loved her? But she has become closer to *Him* now. She has seen the truth."

"Stop talking, you crazy bastard. Give me my necklace." Erroll swung the club again, hitting Loren's shoulder. Again, Loren smiled at Erroll, almost paternally. He seemed to look through Erroll, and then the *Isean* focused on him as if really seeing him for the first time.

"I will show *you* the truth. You, too, can become closer to *Him*." Loren stepped forward, grabbing Erroll's arm as he swung the club again, stopping the attack. The *Isean's* grip was harder than Erroll expected, and Loren twisted his arm back. Desperately, Erroll reached up, clawing for the necklace. He felt the silver chain in his hand, and he yanked hard, pulling the necklace off with a sharp TINK of broken links. Yelling, Loren smacked Erroll's hand, sending the necklace skittering across the damp wooden planks of the pier.

The two elves lunged for the necklace, tackling each other. They began rolling on the pier, clawing, punching, and biting each other. Each tried to grab the necklace, only to be pulled away, and hit or scratched by the other. Loren shoved Erroll, causing him to roll away, where he bumped into the stanchion that had fallen from his hand. He grabbed it again as Loren stood up, trying to get to the necklace. Erroll swung the stanchion, smashing it hard into the *Isean's* left shin. Loren yelled in obvious pain, and Erroll swung the club upward, catching Loren in the jaw.

Staggered, Loren took a step back, and Erroll stood up to continue his assault. He hit Loren in the face and across the head until he succumbed to the blows, falling to his knees. Erroll pulled back and delivered a massive swing, catching Loren in his temple. The *Isean* toppled backward and fell into the river with a black splash.

Erroll tossed the club into the river and then turned to look for the necklace. Panic rose as he didn't see it. *Did it fall into the river?* He turned in a circle, looking for it. *It's not here!* Then he felt it. He could sense the necklace as he had before when Loren had been wearing it. Walking to the spot, he knelt and looked into a gap between two planks. The necklace sat on the top of a wood piling, less than a hand's width from falling into the dark water.

Erroll reached down and gingerly grasped for it, his fingers squeezing into the small gap. They touched the necklace just enough for him to get a grip on it and pull it up. Holding it up, the gold twisted in the air, revealing the woman's profile. The gemstone glinted in the light of the setting sun. Erroll smiled.

Even though he had heard the necklace's chain breaking when he'd yanked it off Loren, Erroll saw that it was whole again. It confirmed to Erroll that the necklace was special, and it was rightfully his. He was destined to wear it. He placed the necklace over his head.

As the Joy of the Widow's Tears settled below his throat, a sharp, burning pain stabbed into his mind. He wanted to scream, but instead, he laughed at the joy that the pain brought him.

Pain is truth!

"And truth is enlightenment!" Erroll yelled. Erroll now knew what needed to be done. It was time to bring enlightenment to Tenyl.

Chapter 10

Seeker Ansee Carya sat at the small table in his living area. He'd just finished his dinner and was sitting with a small cup of *sloatii*—a strong alcoholic drink made from elderberries—and reading. The fire in the fireplace was dying down, and Ember, his pet fire salamander, was resting across Ansee's shoulders. *What a good way to end a hectic day at New Port.*

Ansee was reading a pamphlet about new detection spells that had been published by one of the wizard committees at Auros Academy. The wizards were attempting to more accurately determine the strength of a spellcaster and the length of time from when a spell had been cast. Ansee could appreciate the problem.

All magic left an aura that could be detected by even the most inexperienced of spellcasters. The aura's strength could tell you how strong the magic was, or how powerful the spellcaster was, or how long ago the spell had been cast. Knowing all three parameters with any degree of accuracy was nearly impossible. It was a problem first stated by a famed elven wizard—Ketoralac—nearly a millennium ago. Ketoralac's Uncertainty Principle stated that, for any given aura, a spellcaster can know the strength of the magic, the power of the spellcaster, or the time since casting with great accuracy, but to know any two properties reduced the accuracy of the spell by half, and to know all three properties reduced the accuracy to zero.

While this was a theoretical exercise for the fine wizards at Auros Academy, it had practical implications for spellcasters like Ansee. Seekers in the Royal Tenyl Constabulary used detection spells to determine if magic had been used during a crime. Knowing that magic had been used, as well as the type of magic, could narrow the search for a suspect and provide evidence when a suspect was arrested. And in cases like the one with the Fury Blade, it could tell the constables when they were dealing with a strong spellcaster or a powerful magic item.

Ansee wanted to know what the wizards were doing to alter their spells in order to better determine strength, power, and duration. This was hard—and very frustrating for him since he was not a trained wizard. Ansee was a sorcerer, and his ability to cast magic came naturally, without the need to study, perform intricate gestures, or recite complex incantations. The magic flowed in his veins and he could tap it and shape it to his will, usually with just a thought or a few meaningful words. When wizards discovered a new way to cast an old spell, they had to relearn the gestures and incantations. It wasn't that simple for Ansee. First, he had to understand what the end result of the spell would be—his expected outcome—and then shape the magic accordingly. This was easy for offensive and defensive spells, but for magic that required finesse, like detection spells, this was a lot more difficult. Since Ansee had no formal schooling, just being able to understand what the wizards were writing often gave him a headache.

Ansee was reading a particularly difficult and highly technical part of the pamphlet right now, for approximately the fifth time. "Damn it, Ember. Why do wizards have to make everything so hard?" Ember didn't reply, as expected. "You're a lot of help." Ansee took a drink of the *sloatii* and began re-reading the section yet again.

The knock on his door startled them both, and Ember let out a low growl, jumped off his shoulders, and scurried to the safety of the fireplace. "Boy, you're really fierce," Ansee said, as he got up to answer the door.

Constable Kai Gania stood in the hall, wearing his uniform. *Not a social call,* Ansee figured. *Too bad, I could have used the distraction.* "Good evening, Gania. What's up?" Ansee stepped back so that Gania could enter, closing the door behind him.

"Evening, Seeker. We have a murder over in Forest Grove."

Ansee sighed and turned to his wardrobe. "What do we know?" he asked, as he got his own uniform out.

"Not much. A double murder at a flower shop over on Sycamore Lane."

Ansee hurriedly put on his puttee and armor. "Has the Inspector been notified?"

"The Senior Constable went to go find her." Gania paused for a moment. "I heard she was on a date."

"Yep. Her boyfriend is a sailor and his ship docked today."

"Is he nice?"

"I don't know," Ansee answered as he finished tying on his bracers. "I've never met him." Grabbing his cloak, they headed out the door. "Don't burn down the place," Ansee called as he pulled the door shut. Ember poked her head from the coals in the fireplace with an annoyed croak.

† † †

It took them just over twenty minutes to get to the flower shop. They made small talk on the way, mostly speculation on what kind of person Reva's boyfriend was. A Birch stood guard outside the shop, and he saluted them as they approached.

"Is Constable Inspector Lunaria here yet?" Ansee asked.

"No, sir. You two are the first from Acer to arrive."

Ansee nodded and they walked into the shop. Multiple scents filled Ansee's nose as he walked in: the sweet perfumes of blooming flowers, the musty, earthy odor of soil, and, under it all, the slightly metallic smell of blood.

"Who reported finding the bodies?" Ansee asked, as they wove their way to the back of the shop.

"A customer came to pick up an order and found them in the back. He went and found a constable, who came and saw the bodies before sending for us."

They walked through the curtain of red cloth into the back of the shop. It was dark, and Ansee pulled out a quartz crystal, casting a light spell into it. The magical light gave off a bright, white light that filled the small space. Ansee and Kai walked around a trellis filled with flowers, prepared to see their victims. Instead, they found an empty storeroom.

"They said two bodies?" Ansee asked.

"Yes, sir," confirmed Constable Gania.

"So, where are they?"

Kai shrugged his shoulders. "I can see the signs of a struggle," he offered, pointing around the room. "There looks to be some broken wood, torn cloth, ripped bags of soil, and blood."

"But no bodies."

Kai shook his head.

"Good," Ansee said, "Because I want to make sure we both report the same thing to Constable Inspector Lunaria. Don't touch anything." He tossed the light crystal to Kai. "I'm going to see what our young Birch knows."

He walked quickly back through the shop. "Constable?" he asked as he stepped outside. The young elf turned toward him. "Where are our bodies?"

"Sir?" The confusion was clear on his face.

"The two victims that are supposed to be here. They're

gone. Did someone come and collect them already? We need to know where they went."

"The bodies are gone? Then why in the hells did I get all dressed up to come here?"

Ansee turned to see CI Lunaria and Senior Constable Ghrellstone walking up to the shop. He nodded his head in greeting. "There are clear signs of a struggle, blood and such; just no bodies. Constable Gania is in there now, making sure nothing else disappears."

Reva gestured toward the door and Willem nodded, heading into the flower shop. She rounded on the Patrol Constable. "You mind telling me where in the hells my victims went? Have you been sleeping at your post, or did you just turn the other way for a minute?"

"No, ma'am. I don't know what happened, ma'am." To his credit, the young constable didn't flinch under Reva's stern gaze. Ansee figured that made him Senior Constable material in and of itself. "Nobody but the Seeker and Constable has entered—or left—the shop through this door since my senior posted me here."

"Is there a back door?" Reva asked.

"I don't know. I was never in the back of the shop. Lynnus was the first one here. He went and told Senior Constable Hollbush, who brought me along for crowd control. There were a number of people in the shop when we arrived, and Lynnus and I had to get them out. Hollbush went into the back, then told me to guard the entrance while he and Lynnus went to notify somebody in Acer."

By the expression on Reva's face, it was clear to Ansee that she was mad that the scene hadn't been properly secured. "I'm going to have a few choice words with Hollbush," she said. The young constable merely nodded. It wasn't his place to question a superior officer.

"Tell the Alkies when they get here that they can go home. Without any bodies, we won't need them."

"Yes, ma'am."

Reva and Ansee entered the shop. "Nice necklace," Ansee observed.

"Thanks." Reva touched the necklace as it rested on the front of her armor. "It was a gift from Aavril."

"The dinner went well?"

"What dinner? He was over an hour late and he'd barely given me this before Willem interrupted us about this mess."

Ansee heard the slight bitterness in her tone, but he couldn't tell if it was from having her dinner interrupted or because Aavril had been late. "That's a shame," he said, purposefully vague. "Will you introduce me to Aavril?"

"Who are you, my father?" Ansee felt his cheeks warm and had started to apologize when Reva tapped him with the back of her hand. "I'm kidding. I don't know. We didn't have any time to really talk, so I don't know how long he expects to be in port. But they are usually here for a couple of weeks, so maybe you can come over later in the week to meet him."

"Is he going to compare me to Cas, too?" Reva's mother liked to bring up her former partner; it was a sport for her now, but Ansee thought it was mostly in fun. Mostly.

"As long as you don't put him under the threat of a scrying spell, or try to divine whether he has only good intentions toward me, then you and he will get along well."

"Cas did that?"

"She did scry on him for a few days until I found out and told her to stop. As far as I know, she only threatened him with the other spells."

Ansee smiled as they entered the back of the shop. The back room was a small space to begin with, and it felt even smaller with the plants, supplies, and now four constables crowding the space. Reva looked around the room quickly, but Ansee began casting his detection spell, putting a new twist on it from what he'd learned in the pamphlet earlier. He still kept an ear open to the conversation around him.

"There's a small door back here," Constable Ghrellstone said. He stood behind several sacks of dirt and gestured over his shoulder. "It has a lock, but it's not damaged, so either it was unlocked, or somebody was able to unlock it on their own."

Ansee began his examination of the room for auras, doing a casual examination at first.

Reva said, "Thieves are everywhere in town, so finding somebody with the skill to pick a lock wouldn't be that hard."

"Though why would anybody want to break into a flower shop?" Willem asked.

The air seemed misty to Ansee as he made his examination, and he couldn't understand what was going on. *Did I mess up the spell? Damn, I should have practiced it before trying it out at a crime scene.*

"Gania?" Reva asked.

"Definitely signs of a fight. I found pieces from a musical instrument," he held up the broken neck from a mandolin. The strings dangled haphazardly. "A mandolin, I think. There's also some torn clothing on the dirt and somebody's shirt is over in the corner."

Ansee was still trying to understand what he was seeing. There was no noticeable magic in the room except for the light crystal that Gania held, but it looked like there were golden dust motes hanging in the air everywhere. He continued to move, trying to find a way to see them better. There weren't very many of them. Although there were some small concentrations of the motes in a couple of places, he couldn't find a point of origin. Because he'd modified his spell slightly, he didn't know if what he was seeing was real, or what it meant. He knew it was strong magic to have affected the whole room as it did, but he didn't think that a spell had been cast. He wanted to recast his spell the way he normally did it, just to verify what he was seeing, but then he noticed that the room had gone quiet and that everybody was staring at him.

"Well, out with it!" Reva ordered. "What do you see?"

"I'm not really sure," Ansee admitted. He wasn't going to admit to Reva that he'd modified his spell. "There's some kind of aura here, but it's very diffuse. It's everywhere," he spread his arms, "but there are some small concentrations of the aura in a couple of places. There," he pointed to where the rest of the broken mandolin lay shattered. "And around the sacks of dirt. I'm pretty sure it's divine magic."

"Pretty sure?" Reva asked with a raised eyebrow.

"Well, the aura has a golden hue, it's just that there's not enough of it to be sure. It's like motes of dust floating in the air, even where it's concentrated." He knelt to get a better look at the mandolin parts. "Most likely it's divine."

"You're not instilling me with confidence, Ansee."

"Definitely divine," Ansee stated. He paused for a moment, and then added, "Maybe." He couldn't bring himself to provide a firm answer.

Reva seemed to ignore his leaf blowing. "Fine. It's divine magic. So, somebody raised our two bodies as undead."

"I don't think so," Ansee said, as he let the spell drop. Reva gave him the same glare that she'd given to the Constable outside. "Look, the aura is wrong for it to be a spell to create undead. That spell leaves a very distinct aura. And it's not from a spell to raise the dead, either," he added, to quickly cut off that line of inquiry. "That's a long and complicated ritual, and there would be a lot of magical evidence that it had happened. I don't see any of that here."

"I can't believe that I gave up my night for this," Reva muttered softly to herself. "Is it possible that they weren't really dead and just got up and walked out?"

Everybody shrugged.

"Wow, you all are a lot of help," Reva said.

"Why not tell somebody?" asked Constable Gania. "Or stay here? There had to have been people around since they were reported as being dead. People saw two bodies here and ran to tell a constable. If they were alive, why would they sneak out the back door?"

"Maybe they were afraid?" Ansee offered. "Or confused?"

"Hells, we don't even know who the victims were... are," said Willem in exasperation. "We think it's the shop owner and a second person, maybe a customer. Without the bodies, it could really be anybody."

"Shop owner and boyfriend," Kai said, holding up the neck of the mandolin.

"Her lover," Reva stated. "But we still don't know who he is. Who was the shop owner?"

Constable Gania fumbled for a scrap of parchment.

"Amber Myosotis," said Willem with a grin. Gania gave him a rude gesture that Willem returned with a blown kiss and tapping his head. "Memory like an iron box."

"Well, it's clear that she didn't live here," Reva said, ignoring them both.

Ansee nodded. This part of Forest Grove was filled with stand-alone shops with no attached homes. "Maybe if she was only injured, she just went home," he said.

Reva nodded. "We need to find out where she lives."

Everybody sighed. That was easier said than done. Ansee knew that they'd have to talk to all of the other shopkeepers along the street to see if they knew Amber. While there was a good chance that they did, there was no guarantee that they'd know where she lived. All of the surrounding shops were closed now, so they'd have to wait until morning.

"While we're doing that, we'll also see if any of the neighbors heard anything. Maybe we'll get lucky," Reva said. "Let's gather what evidence we do have here, and then get some rest tonight. We'll return in the morning to start our interviews."

"What if somebody did kill them and came back later to raise them?" Ansee asked.

"You said that there's no evidence of such a spell."

"Well, yes, but there is still an unexplained divine aura here."

"Then explain it," Reva said testily. "I'm not going on a zombie hunt until I know for sure that there's actually a zombie to hunt."

Chapter 11

Cedrus Deodara blew on the dying embers of the fire, and then stuck the wick into the coals until he had a guttering flame. The pounding on the door came again, louder and more insistent this time.

"I'm coming, already, I'm coming," he groused, standing up and yawning.

Brenna stuck her head out of her room. "What is it?"

"I don't know yet. Go back to sleep."

Ignoring him, Brenna grabbed her robe and went to sit by the fire while he answered the door. Standing on the stoop was an elderly elf with long, grey hair and a wrinkled face. He wore black leggings and a red tunic with a royal seal sewn onto the right breast. He had a short sword strapped to his left hip, and Cedrus wasn't sure that the old elf could have drawn it without injuring himself.

"Yes, sir. What can an ovate of Nera do for you?" Cedrus stifled another yawn as he tried to sound pleasant and grateful for the interruption. He and Brenna tended to a small shrine dedicated to Nera, the Goddess of Nature. The shrine sat at the southeast corner of Nuphar Wood and was a simple affair, a sanctified oak tree with a small altar shaped into it and basins that were carved from rock for offerings. All too few, since barely a dozen people visited the shrine on a good day—most of them lived nearby—and Cedrus and Brenna did their best to see to their spiritual needs. They lived in a small cabin near the shrine, and since they depended on the generosity of the few worshippers and their neighbors, it was always important to be polite. *Even when awakened in the middle of the bloody night,* thought Cedrus.

"*Reis inellen*, Ovate. I hope I didn't disturb you?"

Cedrus considered the absurdity of the statement. He'd been awakened from a sound sleep. *Of course, you disturbed me!* But instead of speaking his mind, he said, "Not at all. How can I be of service?"

"I'm Aaron. I'm the night guard at the library."

Cedrus nodded and briefly wondered about the idiocy that allowed an elderly elf to work all night to guard someplace. He knew that Aaron was referring to the Grand Library, which was located nearby. It was the only public library in the city—possibly the only one in the Kingdom.

"I wanted to let you know," Aaron continued, "That I was making my rounds on the library grounds, you know, making sure nobody was skulking about and up to no good."

Cedrus nodded again, though he was thinking, *Why would anybody in their right mind skulk around the library at night?*

"Well, anyway, while I was making my way along the north path, you know, the one near the woods..." Cedrus continued to nod. *Get on with it already.*

"Well, I spotted two people skulking about just inside the woods. Of course, I yelled at 'em to get going or I'd call the constables."

"A sensible thing to do."

"Yeah, but they didn't run off. They stayed in the wood, and so I shone my lantern on 'em and, well, damn me if they weren't two zombies skulking there."

Cedrus woke up a bit by that news. *Zombies?* "Are you sure that they were zombies?"

"Hells, yes. One had his head all bashed in and bloody.

There's no way anybody living would be walking about with a wound like that."

Cedrus was fully awake now. If he could destroy a couple of zombies that were threatening the area, when word got around that it was Cedrus Deodara, Ovate of Nera, who'd done it, then there'd be an increase in visitations to the shrine. *Maybe even requests to perform blessings.* That would mean more offerings and donations. Maybe even offers to handle other problems within the city, with commissions. Cedrus had no illusions about getting rich as a cleric. Had he wanted riches he could have gone into adventuring. But he was no Telenite, with their vows of poverty. It took Pfen and Skips to maintain the shrine and provide for him and Brenna; money that was constantly in short supply.

"How long ago did you see them?"

"Not long. I came here as soon as I saw them skulking about."

"Good, good." *They won't have had time to go far and chance somebody else dealing with them.* "Let me get my stuff and then you can show me where they were skulking at. I won't be but a couple of minutes."

Aaron looked relieved, and Cedrus knew why. Shooing away miscreants and halpbloeden was one thing, but dealing with the undead was something that few people cared to do.

Cedrus left the door open and returned to his room, setting the candle down on a stool. He started putting on his vestments. Brenna stood in the doorway.

"What'd he want?"

"He said that there are a couple of zombies lurking near the library. He wants me to deal with them."

"Really? Zombies in the city? If you can take care of them, people will know, and we can get more visitors to the shrine. This could be really good for us...and for Nera." She touched two fingers to her lips, then to her forehead.

"Exactly my thoughts." Cedrus finished tying his vestments and pulled an old mace out from under the bed.

"Do you want me to help?"

"No, it's only a couple of zombies. I think I can deal with them. But you should get ready to start getting the word out. As soon as I'm back, we should start spreading the news."

Brenna nodded as Cedrus placed his holy symbol—a silver eagle with outstretched wings—over his head. The heavy silver weight rested on his chest and felt reassuring. Finished, he walked out of the room. He paused by the door to pick up a vial of blessed holy water. He was sure that he wouldn't need it, but it was always good to be prepared. Besides, maybe he'd use it so that Aaron would get a good show as he dealt with the zombies.

With a goodbye wave to Brenna, he walked out the door, barely pausing to let Aaron catch up. Cedrus set a brisk pace toward the library. Ten minutes later, they were walking along the groomed garden paths that made up the grounds around the library.

The Grand Library had started life as a single, massive oak tree that had been magically enhanced, enlarged, and modified to house the library within its trunk. The upper branches had platforms and small rooms housing all sorts of minor collections of books, scrolls, tomes, and folios. Over the years, additional structures had been built in order to add more branches onto the ground level and other, less massive, trees had been grown and added to the building. Today the library was a small copse of trees in a roughly circular shape with buildings interconnected between the trees. The first tree stood the tallest in the front with crushed red limestone paths leading to massive double doors. The building was dark now, but in the early evenings, the library was ablaze with lights in the windows and colored paper lanterns.

Aaron led Cedrus around the north side of the library, passing the sculpture garden dedicated to Elven poets through the ages. Cedrus's palms were starting to sweat, and he wiped them on the hem of his vestments. He'd never actually encountered any undead before, and he was more worried about making a fool of himself in front of Aaron than dealing with the zombies. He focused on how he and Brenna should get the word out about what he'd done so that they could increase traffic at the shrine and increase their donations.

Aaron stopped and pointed toward the edge of Nuphar Wood, a spot just to the right of a dryad statue. "'Twas over there that they was skulking."

Cedrus nodded. "Very well. Stay here while I take care of them."

Aaron gave him a look that said, *I have no intention of getting any closer than this.*

Cedrus stepped forward, his feet crunching loudly on the gravel path. He grasped his holy symbol and held it, saying a small prayer to Nera. He then concentrated, trying to recall the prayer he needed. He'd never had to cast this spell before, and after a moment of panic, the words came back to him. "May Nera's sight reveal that which is an abomination to life and the living."

Nera's divine blessing filled his mind and he could sense, rather than actually see, the presence of two undead creatures. They were like two blocks of ice in a pool of warmth. The cold was coming from an area just to his right. Cedrus walked confidently toward the creatures.

Approaching the tree line, Cedrus couldn't see anything at first. The starlight and thin moon gave him plenty of light to see by, but the foliage of the trees and shrubs made it hard to discern any real shapes. Using the spell, Cedrus focused on the spot where he knew the two zombies to be and, after a moment, he could see them. They sat crouched behind a bush, their teeth chewing on the bones of some small creature. *Probably a squirrel.* A feeling of sadness threatened to engulf him as he thought about one of Nera's blessed creatures being killed by such a foul abomination.

As Cedrus approached, both zombies grew alert, as if they could also sense his presence. As one, they turned to look at him, standing up as they did so. Cedrus saw them clearly now. One had been male, with short hair. It was bare-chested, its head was bashed in and crushed, and dried blood covered its head. The other was female, its torn dress exposing one pale breast. It looked uninjured at first, but then Cedrus noted deep bruising on its neck, partially covered by tangled, long hair.

The two creatures stepped out of the shadows cast by the trees. In the starlight, Cedrus now saw that their skin had been peeled back around their fingers to reveal long, sharp claws. As they approached, he could hear raspy voices coming from the two creatures. *Zombies don't talk, do they?*

"Pain..." The word was faint, and Cedrus wasn't sure that he had heard it correctly. "Pain..." The second time he heard it clearly.

"Don't worry. I will free you from this unholy pain soon enough," Cedrus said.

"Dreen...Dreen..."

Cedrus had no idea what that word meant. It sounded somewhat familiar, but it didn't matter. They would soon be dealt with.

"Dreen...is...pain...Dreen is pain...pain is truth...Dreen is truth..."

By Nera, what in the hells is this? Cedrus had never heard of zombies that spoke. As the creatures continued to approach, slowly chanting the words over and over, Cedrus's mouth went dry and it felt like an alchemist's lab had exploded in his stomach. This wasn't feeling right. Sure, he'd never faced real undead before, but he shouldn't be afraid of a couple of zombies. He rubbed his fingers over the cool, reassuring weight of his holy symbol and felt his resolve strengthen. *Nera will protect me.*

Cedrus took a purposeful stance, spreading his feet apart. He took off his holy symbol and held it before him. "By Nera's will and grace, I banish the evil before me." The holy symbol glowed with a soft blue light, and a winged bird of pure light flew out, growing to fill the area in front of Cedrus, then flew to the two zombies and passed through them.

The zombies seemed to stop, growing silent, and Cedrus smiled. But his smile quickly faded as the two creatures resumed their chanting and seemed to pick up speed.

"With Nera's fury, I banish the evil in my presence." Cedrus began fumbling for the old mace at his side, holding his holy symbol protectively in front of him. The creatures were unaffected by his attempts to turn them.

Cedrus stepped back, placing his holy symbol over his head and finally freeing his mace. The creatures were almost upon him. *Even if my faith will not deter these monsters, my steel will.* Holding the mace low, Cedrus stepped up and swung upward toward the male zombie. The mace struck the creature in the head with a resounding SMACK of metal on flesh and the snapping of bone. As the weapon struck, Cedrus felt a sharp, biting pain in his own jaw and let out a cry. It felt as if his own jaw had just been broken.

What in the hells is this?

He brought the mace back in a strong backhand that struck the female in its side. Again, a sharp pain radiated through his own ribs, causing him to yelp with shocked agony. It was as if he had been struck by his own mace.

The two creatures now attacked, slashing at him with their long talons. They continued chanting as they raked Cedrus across his arms and chest, digging deep furrows into him. Each slash burned and his mace suddenly felt heavier in his hand. Cedrus staggered back a few steps, grasping for the vial of holy water. He pulled it free from his belt and pulled out the cork with his teeth, spitting it to the ground.

"By Nera's blessing, I anoint you with her righteousness!" He slashed out with the vial twice, a crisscrossing movement that splashed the holy water onto both creatures. The water smoked where it struck them, and both creatures hissed with...glee? *By Nera, they seem happy to be in pain.* Cedrus was not, as his own skin burned as if his body had been dumped in a vat of acid.

Real fear now enveloped Cedrus, a deep twisting knot in his stomach. *I don't know what these creatures are, but they are not zombies.* The two creatures moved toward him again, clearly burned by the holy water. *Well, at least that injured them,* Cedrus thought. *Too bad I only had the one vial.* Then he recalled his own burning pain when he'd used the holy water, and added, *maybe that's not such a bad thing.*

The creatures attacked him again, with quick slashes of their claws. Cedrus brought up the mace and managed to deflect the attack from the male zombie (he didn't know what else to call them), but the female's claws raked down his side. Again, the attack hurt, but more disconcerting was that the mace felt even heavier now. He gripped it with both hands and struggled to lift the weapon.

They struck again, easily slipping past his feeble attempt to parry the attack. Four sets of claws slashed through his vestments, slicing through skin and muscle. Cedrus fell to his knees, too weak to stand. He looked up at the cruel faces of the creatures in the moonlight as they continued their monotonous chant. "Dreen is pain. Pain is truth. Dreen is truth."

His own body was filled with pain and he found himself focusing on it, embracing it. The sharpness and clarity of the pain centered his thoughts, allowing him to see clearly for the first time.

Tears began to flow down his cheeks. "How could I have been so misguided?" As he spoke, the creatures continued to rake his body. As Cedrus's strength ebbed away, he finally saw the truth.

Aaron had watched, horrified, as the two zombies had attacked the young cleric. His attempt to turn them and his own attacks had seemed to cause him more harm than he'd done to them. Aaron had been rooted to the spot, unable to turn away from the brutal attack.

Now the cleric lay unmoving, and the two zombies turned to look at Aaron as if finally sensing his presence. His bladder failed, and terror gripped his heart as they began running toward him. He finally began to move, but in his haste, he tripped over his own feet and fell hard onto the gravel. He tried to get up, but the zombies were upon him and he felt deep, intense pain as they slashed at his back. Panic filled Aaron like an overflowing cup of cacao, but he couldn't find the strength to lift himself.

In less than a minute, Aaron ceased struggling, finally seeing the truth. The two creatures moved away a short distance, waiting. It took only a few minutes before Cedrus, and then Aaron began to stir and rise. They looked around for a moment, as if confused, and then all four creatures began walking toward the woods, slowly chanting. "Dreen is pain...pain is truth...Dreen is truth...Dreen is pain..."

Chapter 12

Reva sat at a corner table drinking a hot cup of cacao from a chipped mug. She sighed. This was not her usual cacao house, Iliam's place, the House of Theobroma. This place—the sign above the door proclaimed it to be Forest Glen Cacao House—was decorated with actual trees growing in the building, mostly maples and birches, their branches intertwining in the space beneath the roof. Reva idly thought that it was appropriate for meeting her team, as the trees matched the divisions of the RTC: Acer and Betula.

Reva's table, like all the rest, was a stump cut and polished to make a smooth surface. She sat on a wooden stool whose height was not an exact match for the table. Reva assumed that, at one time, the proper height stool was with each table. Not anymore. She'd managed to grab four stools—none of which were the same height—and was fiercely guarding them so that other customers didn't take them. Being in uniform meant that nobody gave her any trouble about it.

The cacao here wasn't bad, but it wasn't what she was used to. It was sweeter than she preferred and had some odd spices mixed in, but it was still cacao no matter how it tasted, and Reva's day didn't really start until she'd had a cup or two.

She spotted Ansee and Constable Gania as they entered

the shop, and she waved to get their attention. Ansee waved back while Kai got the proprietor's attention, held up two fingers, and pointed at the table. He then walked over and evaluated the remaining two stools before choosing one.

"*Reis hoestii*, Constable Inspector."

"Good morning, Constable."

"Were you able to salvage any of your date?" asked Ansee.

"No. Aavril didn't wait for me, and I didn't expect him to. He went and spent some time with my mother." She took another sip of her cacao.

"Is it safe for him to be alone with her?" Ansee wondered. He'd been over for dinner enough times now to know that Aeollas often prodded Reva about getting married so that she could have grandchildren to dote on.

"What? Sure. Mother loves to hear his stories about all the exotic places he visits."

"And nothing else?"

"And I'm sure she talked his ears short about why he hasn't proposed to me yet. You know, it's not like I don't have a say in the matter, too."

A server arrived and set down two cups of cacao.

"Áeorias," Ansee said. "How much?"

"Nothing, Constable. Our pleasure."

"No. How much?"

"No, really, it is with our compliments."

"Look, just tell me how much the cacao costs," Ansee insisted, his voice rising. He was getting irritated.

"Two Pfen each," the server said. He turned to go and nearly bumped into Senior Constable Ghrellstone. "Do you want anything, Constable?"

"No, thanks." The server nodded and scurried away.

"You antagonizing people again, Seeker?" Willem asked in greeting.

"It's not antagonizing to offer to pay for what we order."

Reva knew that this was an old argument for Ansee.

"They don't mind it," countered Willem as he sat down. He nearly disappeared from view as Kai had left him the shortest stool. The others had a good laugh, while Willem stood up with as much dignity as he could muster. "I sit too much as it is. Better to stretch my legs."

"I don't care if they don't mind it or not," continued Ansee. "It's wrong. It's stealing and makes us no better than a thieves' guild."

Willem bristled at that. "Hey, we're a hundred times better than any thieves' guild. We won't cut off fingers or ears if they refuse to pay. We don't threaten to burn down their businesses or kidnap their families to get them to accept our patronage."

"But we decide whether to patrol an area or not based on who's given us gifts. That just allows the guilds to step in."

"Which is why we should accept their gifts so that we can keep the low-lifes out."

"But we don't. The guilds just come in right after we walk out to demand their cut. As long as we accept bribes like this we don't have the moral authority to stop them."

"We have the legal authority," countered Willem, testily.

"Enough," Reva said. "I swear, if you two fight about this one more time, I'll demote you both to doing fire watch in Nul Pfeta." She gave them both her best commander's glare to let them know that she was serious, then smiled. "But since Ansee feels so passionately about this, then I suggest that he can always pick up the tab for all of us from now on."

"Hey! It's not like I'm earning a First Constable's wage here. Or even a CI's wage."

"But it's your *moral authority* to do this," smiled Willem. "Maybe I will have a cup of cacao, come to think of it." He started to turn and raise his hand to get the server's attention when Ansee kicked him in the shin. "Ouch." But he grinned at Ansee.

"Stop acting like children, you two, or I'll make Kai sit between you."

"Please leave me out of this, ma'am," Kai said, drinking his cacao.

Everybody chuckled at that. "Fine. If you two," she waggled her finger at Ansee and Willem, "can play nice, then you will work together today getting interviews from the shops north of the flower shop." Ansee and Willem nodded. "Constable Gania and I will hit the ones south of it."

Finishing their drinks, they all began to leave the cacao house. Reva saw Ansee place six copper Pfen on the table, and then place a cup over the coins. That would keep wandering eyes from seeing the money. Reva knew that whoever cleaned the table would find the coins, and she didn't know a shopkeeper in Tenyl who refused money that they found.

Chapter 13

"Is she in?" The voice was filled with condescending authority and dug its thorns into Lord Constable Inspector Nyssa Betulla.

She looked up from the parchmentwork on her desk toward the door. Since taking over after LCI Gania's death, Nyssa had spent her days trying to put her own mark on the Royal Tenyl Constabulary. The late LCI Gania still had many trusted officers within the RTC's ranks, and they all stubbornly refused to accept Betulla's promotion to LCI. None of them were blatant about disobeying her—they were too smart for that—but she knew they were conspiring to have her removed. Certainly, they were doing their best to make her look bad in front of the Mayor, which would amount to the same thing, as the Mayor technically had the authority to remove the LCI. Nyssa knew that wouldn't happen. Grand Inquisitor Agera would make sure that it didn't happen—he had his own plans for having Nyssa in command of the RTC—but Nyssa hated the thought of being beholden to Agera for anything.

"The Lord Constable is not seeing callers at this time, Magistrate," Nyssa heard her aide inform the uninvited person.

Nyssa ignored the conversation, knowing that her aide would deal with the intruder. She'd left strict instructions not to be disturbed. She'd assigned two of her closest friends—

elves she could trust—the task of collecting information about Acer and Betula Divisions (she knew that Nul Pfeta Division had no problems, having just been promoted from that hellhole). She was busy reviewing the latest reports that her friends had gathered, and they confirmed what Betulla had long known about the RTC: Acer and Betula Divisions were an unruly mob of prima donnas, rogues, and halpbloed-lovers. The individual constables were only loyal to the First Constables, not to the office of the LCI, and so, not to her. The Constables had no oversight, and FC's Aescel and Churlsleaf let them do as they pleased. If she was going to keep the Mayor from interfering and keep Agera at branch length, Betulla needed to get control of the divisions. They needed to know who was in charge.

There was a timid knock on the doorframe to her office, and Nyssa looked up to see her aide give an apologetic smile. "Forgive the intrusion, ma'am. Magistrate Syllaph is here to see you. I explained that you were not seeing anybody, but he's very insistent that he see you now."

Nyssa's first reaction was to have her aide throw the Magistrate out. Magistrate Syllaph had been one of the key voices urging the Mayor to promote Gania to LCI over Nyssa, even though she had more experience. Nyssa had been relegated to the eternal hell of Nul Pfeta Division, while Gania had lorded over everybody as LCI. Nyssa knew that, if she asked the Grand Inquisitor, he would find a way to get rid of Syllaph, but she refused to do anything that would put her more in Agera's debt. He had his plans, and Nyssa understood that she would have to play her part in them, but until then, she was going to rule the RTC as she wanted, not as Agera's pawn. Besides, if she threw Syllaph out on his arse, then he'd just go whine to the Mayor about it.

"Did he say what this was in regard to?" she asked.

Her aide bobbed his head. "It's in regard to constables overstepping their authority."

Nyssa kept her face rigid, but she lifted a metaphorical eyebrow at the news. *Really? Maybe this is something I can use to my advantage.* "Tell him I will see him."

The aide bobbed his head again and returned to the tiny outer room. Within a few moments, Magistrate Syllaph strode into her office, looking a bit huffy at having to wait. The Magistrate was a short and slightly plump elf, whose black and red robes of office did little to hide his large gut. His face was puffy, like a ball of baker's dough, with deep wrinkles creasing his mouth and forehead. He had long grey hair that was simply braided and tied together with a green silk ribbon. He liked the finer things in life, especially good food and wine, in ample quantities. Nyssa knew that he was nearing the end of his second century of life, but he was still healthy, and she could tell from the way his blue eyes were focused that he still had a sharp mind.

"*Reis hoestii*, Arwynn," Nyssa smiled and stood up to greet the Magistrate.

"Nyssa, my apologies for coming unannounced like this."

"It's nothing. You know that I am always happy to meet with you." The pleasantries were polite, but both knew that there was no sincerity behind the words. "Please, have a seat." She gestured to one of the two large armchairs before her desk.

Syllaph settled his bulk into the armchair and Nyssa asked, "What can I do for you today, Arwynn?"

Syllaph's face flushed, and she wondered if her assessment of his health was accurate, but then he said, "I demand that you get your officers under control! They are running amok and exceeding their authority!" His tone implied that he expected results, immediately, and Betulla did her best to not let her own anger show. *Nobody orders me around in my own office.* She considered whether she should still throw him out and risk the eventual complaint to the Mayor, but then she realized that somebody had to have really tugged his ears to force him to come to her for help—even if it was delivered as a demand.

"Is there any particular officer that is the problem, or has the entire Constabulary managed to upset you?" she asked, her voice even, but she didn't try to veil the sarcasm.

"Just one," Syllaph answered. "Constable Inspector Reva Lunaria."

Betulla forced herself to keep from smiling. *So, Inspector Lunaria isn't just a thorn in* my *side.* She shouldn't have been surprised. She had disliked Lunaria from the first time that she'd met her. Lunaria had managed to disobey Betulla's strict orders to close the Fury Blade case. Instead of being punished for her disobedience, she had been rewarded for it. Betulla had even been forced to give Lunaria and her idiotic Seeker a commendation, and had to thank them before King Aeonis. Lunaria had then managed to pull Constable Gania away from Betulla's influence, further eroding her authority. It was only later that Betulla had learned that the Fury Blade that Reva had shown to the King had been a fake. When Agera had told her that, after informing her that Senior Inquisitor Malvaceä had been punished for failing to secure the weapon, she had wanted to deal with Lunaria right then. Agera had counseled against any overt punishment—the events that had saved her and Agera's lives and stopped Locera's rampage—was still too fresh on people's minds. *Lunaria's blessings have protected her for too long,* Betulla mused, *but maybe that is about to change.*

"I find that hard to believe, Magistrate," Betulla put as much sincerity into the words as she could. "Constable Inspector Lunaria is one of the RTC's most capable constables. I don't see how she could have 'run amok.'"

Magistrate Syllaph let out a grunt of disgust. He was too shrewd—or too informed—to take Betulla's sincerity at face value, but he let it go. "This morning I was seeing cases like normal: petty thieves, assault charges, disturbing the King's peace. Then I had one case come in. Eight local adventurers who'd been arrested by Inspector Lunaria on a dozen trumped-up charges."

"I'm sure that she had her reasons to arrest them."

"Oh, she had one reason! She hates adventurers. And *those people* included my grandnephew!"

Ah, Betulla saw the foliage now. *This is personal for the Magistrate.*

"Their only crime was to be conned by a smooth-talking halpbloed. But Lunaria let the damn halpbloed go free, while my grandnephew and his companions had to spend the night in a damp, smelly, disgusting dungeon cell without food. It was completely uncalled for, and I have it on good authority that she did it just to spite them for earning an honest living as adventurers." Syllaph leaned forward in his chair. "If you can't control your officers, I will take my complaint to the Mayor. As I understand it, your position is still temporary, so maybe somebody else can provide some discipline to the rabble you have who are pretending to be constables."

Only Betulla's strong will kept her from throwing Syllaph out of her office right then. *How dare he threaten me in my own office!* It was true that the Mayor had not yet made Betulla's position as LCI permanent. It should have been finalized weeks ago, but the Mayor had been putting off the decision. He was making excuses for the delay. Betulla suspected that Agera was using his own influence to manipulate the Mayor, and thereby trying to get more control over Betulla. He'd made it clear that he expected Betulla to be his lapdog in the RTC. While she was committed to Agera and the greater cause of uniting the elves and dark elves, she was nobody's puppet. Agera was using the Mayor to apply leverage to Betulla to get his way, and she was just as determined to not have his roots in her affairs.

All of this meant that she couldn't just ignore Syllaph and his complaint. Letting him go to the Mayor would be the justification that the Mayor needed to not make her appointment as LCI permanent. That would force her to appeal to Agera to keep her position, and that would put her further into the Grand Inquisitor's debt. But maybe she could twist Syllaph's anger to do her a favor and nudge the Mayor onto her side without involving Agera. Being able to slap Reva Lunaria down several branches in the process only made it all the better.

"Arwynn," she soothed. "Certainly, I agree with you on this matter. You wouldn't believe the level of ineptitude and callous regard for the rule of law since I took over from Gania."

"I always thought that LCI Gania ran the RTC quite well."

"Oh, on the surface that was what she wanted people to think, but there is a considerable amount of rot in the trunk. CI Lunaria is just one symptom of that rot, and I have been keeping a close eye on her. She's gotten too many passes for her disrespectful actions, and I have been planning on severely disciplining her for some time."

"Then why haven't you done so already?" Syllaph huffed.

"You'd be surprised how many patrons she has in the underbrush. Even the Grand Inquisitor has counseled me against publicly reprimanding her because he fears how that might reflect upon the King."

"Really?" He raised one eyebrow.

Betulla nodded her head sagely. "You know how Agera likes to play his little games, but in this case, his actions are hurting the good citizens of Tenyl because I can't do my job. Maybe you and I can work together on this."

"How so?" There was a note of caution in his voice, but Betulla saw in his eyes that he was interested in what she had to offer.

"I will take severe action against Lunaria. She needs to

be properly disciplined for exceeding her authority—especially with such noble adventurers such as your grandnephew—but I need protection from Agera. He will certainly tell the Mayor what he thinks, and if I'm removed as LCI, then the chaos that Lunaria represents will not be dealt with."

"I am having dinner with the Mayor and his wife tonight. I may be able to drop a word or two to him," Syllaph offered. "If you can address the lack of discipline here by then."

"You know how much I value your friendship, Arwynn. Any words of support you can give the Mayor would be appreciated."

"And your unruly constables?" It was a general statement, but she knew he only cared about Lunaria.

"Oh, I'm sure you will learn about my decision before you go to the Mayor's dinner."

Syllaph repositioned his arms and levered himself out of the armchair. "It will be nice to see some much-needed order return to the RTC."

"On that, you and I are in complete agreement, Magistrate." Betulla rose and smiled as she escorted Syllaph out. "I'm sure that you and the Mayor will have a lot to discuss at dinner."

Chapter 14

"**D**amn it, Ian! You know Captain Sterna is good for the bill. Can't you just deliver the stuff so we can get our repairs done?" Aavril pleaded. He stood on the dock alongside the *Majestic Tern* arguing with Ian Thornberry, the owner of a mill that supplied timbers, wood, rope, pitch, and everything else that a ship needed to remain afloat and make repairs while at sea.

This last voyage had been blessedly uneventful, so there had been no major damage to the *Tern*, but every sea voyage caused minor problems that had to be dealt with before they became larger problems. That was even more important on a ship as old as the *Tern*. Captain Sterna's meticulous insistence on maintenance and repairs was the main reason that she'd stayed afloat for so long.

Ian shook his head. "Maybe Älaan was good for it, but the rumor around the docks is that he's tied up for the last time, living out his golden years with grandchildren climbing his rigging now." He gave a sympathetic smile as if he dreamed of someday being able to do the same thing. "Now, I think that giving the *Tern* to Loren was a good idea and one that was a long time coming. Loren will make a fine Captain, in time, but I don't extend credit to *any* new Captain. Period. Even somebody as skilled as Loren. This will be his *first* voyage and I won't risk my Skips on a virgin Captain."

"Virgin? Come on, Ian. You're being unreasonable. Loren has been the Captain of the *Tern* in deed, if not in title, for the last year. You know that. Captain Sterna—Älaan—has been grooming him to take over. Everybody knows that. That has to count for something."

"It might count for the moneylenders over at the Guild, but I have elves working for me that have families to feed. If I gave every Captain credit for a two- or three-month voyage, I'd go broke and my workers would go hungry."

Aavril rubbed a hand through his hair. He really shouldn't have to haggle and dicker with Ian about this. This was Loren's job. Well, it was Loren's job to make sure that the financing was secure. Loren knew Ian's rules just as well as Aavril did. *Where in the hells is he?*

"Look, Ian. Loren met with his backers yesterday. He got his funding for the trip. Part of his deal with his backers was that we set sail by the end of the week." He saw Ian raise his eyebrows at that news. "So, we need to get started on our work today. Loren's on his way to the ship now, and by the time you deliver what we need, he'll be here to pay you."

Ian nodded, but his eyes gave him a look that said, "Do you think I just walked out of the forest yesterday?"

Aavril sighed. This was not how he wanted his day to start. The truth was that he had no idea where Loren was. He'd never returned yesterday, he hadn't been on the ship when Aavril had returned last night, and he hadn't shown up this morning, either. Loren was letting Aavril, and the rest of the crew, down, and Aavril was getting mad. A Captain had to be better than this. He had to be there for the important things to make sure that the ship and crew were taken care of. Now, with Loren off doing who knew what—*probably with his girlfriend*, Aavril thought, jealously—all of the responsibilities were falling on Aavril's shoulders.

Aavril knew that being *Isean* would mean more work and more responsibility, but that didn't include arguing with vendors and provisioners—that was the Captain's responsibility. But if they were going to make sail when Loren wanted, they needed to have their supplies today.

Aavril opened his leather pouch and pulled out a few coins. Even though he'd had to pay for Reva's drinks last night—she'd conveniently run out and left the bill for him—he had some coin left, but not enough to cover all of the supplies that they needed. He hoped Ian would accept an initial payment to get the stuff here. "Here's ten Skips. It's all I have on me right now, but that should be enough for you to deliver our supplies. Loren will pay you the rest when he gets back."

Ian hefted the silver coins, closing his hand around them. He smiled. "Sure, this will get the supplies you need here." Aavril smiled, but Ian said, "But if Loren doesn't have the rest of my money, I'll take my goods back and keep your Skips for my troubles."

Aavril gritted his teeth. That was nothing better than robbery, but they needed the supplies. He nodded his head.

"Good." Ian folded the parchment on which Aavril had written down the supplies that they needed. "I'll be back in a couple of hours. Captain Sterna better have the rest of my money by then." He turned on his heel and walked up the dock where he got into a litter to be whisked away.

Aavril climbed the gangplank onto the *Tern*. He walked over to Kelsey and Donnel along the starboard rail. They were applying wood oil to the rail in order to protect it from the seawater. "How much have we got left, Sailing Master?"

"Just what's left in tha bucket there. We tapped tha last keg this mornin'. We can finish this rail, but we'll need more ta finish tha rest of tha ship."

"Well, Ian's agreed to bring us our supplies in a couple of hours."

"How'd ya manage that, Sir?"

"I gave him my own Skips to tap the sap. How much money do you have, Kelsey?"

"I dunna know for sure. Me an tha boys hit a few pubs last night after we unloaded tha ship."

"Six pubs," said Donnel. "And then up at dawn this morning." Aavril had noticed his bloodshot eyes but kept his thoughts to himself. He'd gone on more than his fair share of benders.

"Buncha lightweights. We had ta drag Janish ta tha last two places."

"Well, Sailing Master, when you finish here, why don't you and the others see what you have left, okay? If the Captain doesn't return, we may need it to keep Ian from taking our supplies back."

Kelsey and Donnel both scowled, and then Kelsey slowly nodded his head. "Can I speak freely, *Isean*?"

Aavril nodded, knowing what was coming.

"Sir, it ain't right. We's startin' out on tha wrong branch with this voyage, especially with tha Cap'n missin'. We'll do our parts, but it ain't fair."

Aavril patted Kelsey on the shoulder. "I agree, Sailing Master. I'm standing on the same branch with you. I appreciate you doing this for me, so while you guys go scrape out your squirrel holes for loose coins, I'm going to try to find our missing Captain." He turned away, heading for the gangplank. "I'll be back in a couple of hours," he called back. "If Ian shows up before I return, don't let him leave with our supplies."

Aavril left the ship and hurried through Tenyl's streets to North Gate Grove. That was where Amber lived in a simple flat. Aavril had been there with Loren a couple of times, and he figured that Loren would've gone to see his girlfriend after meeting his investors. Aavril didn't blame Loren for wanting to see Amber, but the thought that he was spending this much time with her, at the expense of running the ship, made Aavril seethe. Knowing that Loren was enjoying himself while he had to look after the ship and everything, and not get any time himself to see Reva, made Aavril even angrier. *Captain's prerogative be damned,* Aavril told himself. *Once I get Loren's ass back to the ship, I'm going to go see Reva, or Loren can just find a new* Isean.

Amber's flat was in a three-story building of stone and wood, one of the new buildings built in the past hundred years to house Tenyl's growing population. It had none of the old-growth charm of Old Grove, or even the beautiful aesthetics found in places like Reva's mother's home in River Grove. The flat's only redeeming feature was a nice view of Ilvalé Arena and Castle Tenz from its top floor.

Aavril entered the building and took the narrow stairs two at a time up to the top floor. Approaching Amber's door, he pounded on it, a bit louder than was polite, but he was in a hurry and angry. "Amber! Open the door!" He pounded again. "Come on, Amber! I know he's here. Open up!" More pounding, and then he tried the handle. The door was locked, and he was sure that nobody could have slept through his pounding.

"Shit." *If Loren isn't here, then where in the hells is he?*

Aavril headed downstairs and outside. He turned to-ward the river as he tried to figure out his next move. *If Amber isn't home, then she'll be at her shop. Is Loren hanging out with her there? Why would he do that?* Aavril didn't have an answer but headed toward the shop.

When he arrived, he found that the door to the flower shop was shut and locked. *What the hell? Did they run off someplace, together?* Aavril could understand Loren taking time to be with Amber, but going missing like this was completely out of character. *Loren is dedicated to the* Tern, Aavril told himself. *He was always reliable as* Isean. *Even when he spent all night carousing, he'd be the first one ready the next day.* Plus, Loren had been so excited about his plans that it didn't make any sense to Aavril that he'd be missing.

Aavril didn't have the time to figure this mess out now. He needed to get back to the ship. *Though I don't know how we'll pay for the supplies.* He turned away from the closed shop and headed back to the docks.

When Aavril returned to the dock, he saw a small group gathered at the base of the gangplank. Kelsey was speaking with two elves wearing fine cloaks, one blue and the other red, while two other elves wearing ringmail armor and carrying swords stood a pace back with a strong box between them.

Kelsey spotted Aavril. "Here comes *Isean* Paroth right now," he said, with a relieved voice.

The elves turned to Aavril. "*Reis se,* sirs. What can I do for you?" Aavril noticed that the two elves in the cloaks wore merchant guild chains of gold and silver around their necks. *These must be Loren's investors.*

"I'm Ghalen," said the taller of the two, who was wearing the red cloak. "And this is my partner, Vanya." The elf in the blue cloak bobbed his head in greeting. "We told Captain Sterna that we'd meet him today to deliver his finances for the voyage. Where is the Captain?"

Thank you, Demar. Aavril quickly decided how to best handle this gift. "The Captain is off the ship right now, meeting with our vendors to get us the best terms for our supplies. You know how Loren likes to leave nothing to chance and get the best deal." The two merchants nodded.

"The Captain instructed me to take delivery of the finances and to offer you both a drink by way of apology for not being here himself to greet you."

Ghalen and Vanya looked at each other and Aavril wasn't sure if they might have been communicating telepathically or maybe they just knew each other so well that they didn't need to speak. After a moment, Vanya looked at Aavril and said, "Very well, *Isean*. Please lead the way."

Aavril let out a breath he hadn't realized he'd been holding. He headed up onto the ship with Ghalen, Vanya and the guardelves following him. He led them into the Captain's cabin and offered them seats on the bench. As they sat, he knelt and opened the secret panel, pulling out the bottle of North Highlands whiskey that Captain Sterna (the elder) had left as a gift for his son.

Aavril set out three cups and poured the whiskey, which Ghalen and Vanya drank, each with an appreciative smile. Aavril made polite conversation as they each had a second drink, assuring them that, with the Captain's financing secured, they'd be sailing as planned by the end of the week. Ghalen said they'd begin delivering their cargo in two days and all three shook hands. Vanya left the key to the strongbox with Aavril, and then the merchants and guards left.

Aavril stood on deck watching them leave the ship. Kelsey stepped up to him. "Well, Sailing Master," Aavril said. "I guess your coin is safe for now."

"That's good, me boy. We barely had twenty Skips between tha five of us."

Aavril turned to look at the Sailing Master. "Just how much *did* you guys drink last night?"

Kelsey didn't say but just smiled by way of an answer. He pointed up the dock. "Demar seems ta have smiled upon us. There's Ian now with our supplies."

Aavril turned to see two wagons pulled by mules and loaded with their supplies. He breathed a sigh of relief. They'd be able to finish their repairs to the *Tern* and store away the other goods. They'd be ready when the merchants came back with their cargo.

But it still doesn't answer where Loren is. "Get everybody together, Kelsey," Aavril said. "Let's get our supplies on board."

Chapter 15

Reva and Ansee waved hello to Constable Whitlocke as they walked into New Port. Whitlocke jabbed a thumb towards the Stable upstairs. "You better hurry. The LCI is here, and it's not a social visit."

Reva sighed. "When is it ever?" She continued upstairs but didn't bother to hurry.

The Stable was quiet as they entered, with everyone standing at the back of the room near Aescel's office. Reva and Ansee made their way toward the group.

LCI Betulla spotted them, sneered, and said, "Now that Inspector Lunaria and Seeker Carya are finally here, I will begin."

There were a few snickers of laughter from the gathered constables, but Reva ignored them and Betulla's comment. Such a petty insult wasn't worth getting upset over. Reva stood at the back of the group and leaned against a table. First Constable Aescel stood next to the LCI, his hands clasped behind his back. Reva tried to divine what this meeting was about from Aescel's expression, but his face was like a wooden mask. If he actually knew what this was all about, he should have been on stage at Pfenestra's, but Reva had a feeling that the First Constable was just as lost in the underbrush as the rest of them.

"The RTC has become a disgrace among the good citizens of Tenyl," Betulla started. The comment was met by immediate murmurs of dissent and a few shocked exclamations. *So, it's going to be one of* those *talks,* Reva told herself. She wasn't surprised. LCI Betulla had been in command for about a month and hadn't yet attempted to prune the bushes.

Betulla ignored the comments. "I hear complaints daily from worried citizens about how you Constables behave," she continued. "You run about, arresting whoever you please, but our city is no safer for it. People are afraid, and frankly, I don't blame them."

What kind of hawkshit is this? Reva thought. She didn't know where the LCI was headed with this, and looking around at some of the other confused, and angered, faces in the Stable, she knew that she wasn't the only one.

"Magistrate Syllaph barged into my office this morning, demanding that I take action. He informed me that one of you brazenly took the law into your own hands, arresting a group of adventurers..."

Oh shit, thought Reva. Her stomach started a slow roll off a steep cliff.

"...while letting the real criminal go free." Betulla let her gaze run over everybody in the Stable. "This gross ineptitude and callous disregard for the law will not be tolerated. I insist on discipline from my constables, even if I have to force it upon you."

Betulla finally turned and looked directly at Reva. *Here it comes.* "Constable Inspector Lunaria."

"Yes, ma'am." Reva managed to keep her voice even, even though she could feel her anger rising. She knew exactly what was coming next.

"I demand to know why you arrested two noble adventuring groups while you let the real criminal, a known halpblooed con artist, go free?" Her voice was casual, almost conversational, but Reva knew that no answer she could give would satisfy the LCI.

In for a Pfen, in for a Crown. "Pfastbinder hadn't broken any laws, while the *noble adventurers* assaulted several constables and nearly set fire to several businesses." Reva hadn't been able to keep the sarcasm from her voice.

"It was your gross incompetence that led to that fight," Betulla retorted. "Had you arrested the halpbloed immediately, that fight wouldn't have happened."

"But the adventurers were already fighting each other before we even got there," Ansee blurted out, apparently unable to contain his own anger. Reva didn't blame him, because it was clear that Betulla had no idea what had really happened. Betulla looked daggers at him for interrupting her.

Reva put a hand on his shoulder to keep him from saying anything else. "We had to intervene in order to keep these adventurers from hurting themselves, or any innocent bystanders."

The LCI waved her hand dismissively. "You stumbled in like a clumsy and incompetent rookie constable. Your blunder forced the adventurers to defend themselves. You were unable to do your job." Reva could tell that the LCI was reaching her climax, unable to keep a vindictive smile from her lips. "Therefore, I am suspending you..."

Here it comes, Reva thought. Suspension for a couple of days was the usual punishment for breaking the rules. Reva had plenty of experience with that.

"...for one week without pay."

"What?" Reva was stunned. A week suspension—without pay—was unheard of in the Constabulary. Sure, it wasn't the first time that Reva had been suspended. Her habit of doing her own thing—often against her superior's direct orders—tended to rub Aescel and the others the wrong way, but she always knew when she'd crossed the line and could usually anticipate what sort of punishment she'd get. But a suspension for a whole week, delivered in front of the entire Division, was a new low. What galled Reva the most was that she hadn't done anything wrong.

Every constable in this room had done exactly what she'd done. They all considered adventurers to be pesky meddlers at the very least, and dangerous interlopers at their worst. Adventurers always had a disregard for the constables and the law, feeling that they were above it all. They took matters into their own incompetent hands and ended up destroying everything around them. *Hells,* Reva told herself, *just last week Olwyn arrested a group of adventurers who'd destroyed half of the Laughing Cockatrice to deal with a thief who'd managed to clean out their coin purses.* So, Reva knew that this had nothing to do with making some adventurers happy; this was personal for the Lord Constable Inspector. Reva had suspected that the grace period she'd gotten after the Fury Blade case was over, but she hadn't expected such a direct attack by the LCI.

Reva wanted to lash out, to fight the LCI—and the flinty look in Betulla's eyes showed that she was hoping for Reva to do just that. Any protest by Reva would give Betulla the justification that she needed in order to make Reva's punishment even harsher. She could give Reva a demotion or remove her from Acer Division. She might even kick Reva out of the Constabulary once and for all. *I love my job too much,* Reva told herself. *I won't give her the satisfaction of taking it away. I can climb above this. Besides, a week off with Aavril in port would be a nice change.*

Reva wanted to speak her mind, to tell the LCI where she could shove her suspension, but instead, she bit her tongue. Reva reflected that it was actually more satisfying this way, as the LCI's pinched lips spoke volumes.

"I will not have Constables in my command making false arrests and letting real criminals go free," she said, recovering her disappointment and giving Reva a triumphant look. "Make sure you all bear that in mind." The Lord Constable

Inspector walked out of the Stable without another word, leaving a stunned Acer Division in her wake. After a couple of seconds, the room exploded as everybody began talking at once.

"Shut up!" bellowed FC Aescel. "Get your asses back to work now. I don't want to hear any complaining." He looked at Reva and Ansee. "You two, in my office."

Ansee gently gripped Reva's arm. "Maybe Aescel can do something?"

Reva kept quiet and headed toward Aescel's office. A few Constables gave Reva consoling pats on her back as she passed them, while others seemed to be embarrassed and turned away. She held the door open for Ansee, and then closed it after she stepped in.

Aescel sat behind his desk, rubbing his hands over his face. "My bark is too gnarled for this shit, Reva." He put his hands down and gave her a fatherly look. "You have certainly twisted the manticore's tail this time."

"But sir," Ansee said. "We all know that this was an unjustified and vindictive attack by the Lord Constable. She can't do this. We can go to the Mayor and lodge a protest, or—"

Reva cut him off. "No. She's the Lord Constable Inspector. She has every right to do it."

Ansee looked at her, raising one eyebrow. "Did you get smacked in the head harder than I thought yesterday? Why don't you want to fight this?"

"Because," Aescel answered, "Reva loves what she does too much." Reva nodded in acknowledgment. Aescel continued, "If we tried to appeal to the Mayor, he might intervene and reinstate Reva, but that would just piss off the LCI even more. The next time, she'd probably just remove Reva from the Constabulary."

"But it's so unfair," Ansee said.

"So's life," Reva replied. "But I still have my job, and

some time off while Aavril is in town will be nice for a change. If Betulla knew that, she'd probably have waited or come up with another punishment, so I can get a small bit of joy from that." She patted Ansee on the shoulder, but he still looked like a child who'd been told that his favorite pet had just died.

"I have to take your current case from you," Aescel said, turning the conversation to business. Reva nodded, as she'd expected that.

"Who will you give it to?" she asked, out of curiosity.

"Pflamtael. He and Seeker Pfinzloab just finished a case."

Reva turned to look out Aescel's office window. CI Pflamtael and Seeker Pfinzloab were standing at Olwyn's table looking at the Stable. He knew that he'd be getting Reva's flower shop case and he couldn't keep from smiling. Reva idly wondered if Olwyn had had a hand in her suspension, but she knew that even he wouldn't stoop that low just to get a good case. He was an ambitious son of a succubus, but he had a perverse sense of honor. He'd consider getting the case like this as cheating. The smile on his face made it clear that he was happy to be assigned the case, but she was sure that he'd have preferred to have earned it on his own.

"Ansee will make sure that they get our notes and what evidence we collected. Not that we have a lot to give them."

"Not even bodies," Ansee added. "What about me? Will I continue to work with them?"

"No," Aescel said. "Something's bound to come up that you can work on. In the meantime, find something to keep yourself occupied."

Ansee nodded and Reva could see his shoulders relax. She knew that he didn't like working with the other Seekers. Reva turned to open the door and stopped when Aescel gave a polite cough. She looked back at him.

"I'll need your bracers," he said, "and your sword."

Reva nodded and untied the black bracers with their red maple leaf. She set them on Aescel's desk, quickly followed by her sword and scabbard. She kept her dagger since it was her personal weapon. She opened the door and said, "See you in a week."

Ansee followed her out and across the Stable. "Are you following me to make sure that I leave?" Reva put a bit of annoyance in her voice.

"I wasn't sure if I should say something. Or do something. I've never been suspended before."

"You aren't the one that was suspended."

"I know. It's just new for me, and the fact that you are taking it so well seems wrong. You shouldn't be happy. I'm so angry right now that I want to introduce Betulla to my shocking grasp spell."

Reva laughed. "If you do that, I can assure you that you'll learn what it's like to be suspended." They headed down the stairs. "Don't worry about me. I'll be fine," she said.

The doors opened and Senior Constable Ghrellstone and Constable Gania walked into New Port. They had missed the LCI's talk, and both of them gave Reva a quizzical look.

"Reva's been suspended," Ansee said before they could say anything.

"What'd you do this time?" asked Willem.

"Ansee can tell you if he wants. I'm going home." Reva walked out of the front doors and didn't look back.

Chapter 16

W illem stared at the doors after Reva left. A part of him wasn't shocked by Reva getting suspended— it had happened before, and Reva was so dwarf-headed at times that he was sure that it would happen again—but he couldn't figure out what would cause the First Constable to suspend Reva right now. He turned to look at Ansee. "Well, spill it. What in the bloody hells happened?"

Ansee moved a few steps away from the doors, past Whitlocke's table. "The LCI stripped Reva's bark for our arrest of the adventurers yesterday, and for letting Pfastbinder go."

"Wait," Willem interrupted. "The LCI suspended her, not the First Constable?" As shocking as Reva's suspension was, this news was more troubling to Willem. First Constables had nearly complete autonomy over their divisions. They decided who got what cases, who worked with whom, who needed to be disciplined, and what the punishment would be. Even when disciplinary action was ordered by the LCI, it was always delivered by the First Constable. For LCI Betulla to break from tradition was alarming, and Willem wondered if this also wasn't a threat to FC Aescel.

Ansee seemed to be unconcerned—or unaware—of this threat to their First Constable. He went on, "She said that Reva had been incompetent for not arresting the right person—"

"That's a cart of hawkshit," exclaimed Willem. Constable Whitlocke gave him a dirty look, reminding him to keep his voice down.

"Of course it's hawkshit," Ansee admitted. He shrugged his shoulders as if to say, "What are we going to do about it?" Aloud he said, "Betulla said that Reva had been inept and had made a rookie mistake by not arresting Pfastbinder before things got out of hand."

"Those two groups were already at each other's throats when we got there," protested Constable Gania.

Ansee nodded his head. "I said the same thing. Apparently, the truth doesn't matter."

"So, what are we to do with the Inspector out of commission for the next couple of days?" asked Willem.

"A week," corrected Ansee.

"A week?" Willem nearly yelled, earning him another glare from Whitlocke that he ignored. "Reva's never been suspended for a week before. Hells, I don't think anybody in the history of the RTC has been suspended for that long before."

"My mother used to say that a harsh punishment only serves to reinforce a mistake, not how to learn from it," Gania commented. Ansee's brow furrowed a bit and he quickly added, "Not that the Constable Inspector—or us, for that matter—did anything wrong. Those adventurers would've happily destroyed the whole city just to get what they wanted."

"Pfastbinder went too far with his joke," groused Willem. "Otherwise, it wouldn't have escalated to that point. Of course, had there been two Pfens worth of intelligence among those damn clerics, it wouldn't have gotten that far in the first place."

"Anyway," said Ansee, "Betulla didn't come out and say it, but she implied that Reva's suspension was a warning to everyone else to make sure that we do our jobs right."

The front doors opened and Ansee turned at the sound. Willem looked over the Seeker's shoulder and saw a woman walk up to Whitlocke's table, streaks from tears clear on her face. He could see a large silver eagle hanging from a chain around her neck.

"What are we supposed to do now?" asked Gania.

Ansee turned around to answer. "Aescel pulled us off the flower shop case. We're to give our notes over to CI Pflamtael. Otherwise, we wait until something else comes up." Ansee turned again toward Whitlocke's table. Willem could tell that the woman was a cleric, as she wore a white and silver vestment in addition to the holy symbol, though Willem couldn't place which deity.

"...he'd been called over to the Grand Library..." They could hear part of the conversation.

"I guess we had better get our stuff to Pflamtael before he starts screaming for it," said Willem. He started to head toward the stairs, Gania and Ansee following him.

Passing Whitlocke's table, Willem heard the cleric say, "...it was only a couple of zombies. Cedrus should have had no trouble dealing with them."

"Look, Ovate," Whitlocke's weary, but still polite voice said, "We really aren't set up..."

Willem headed up the stairs, but stopped when he heard the Seeker stop. He turned and saw Ansee staring toward Whitlocke and the cleric, his forehead furrowed in thought. He tugged at Kai's sleeve to get him to stop. Ansee went back down the steps and up to Whitlocke and the cleric.

"Did you say zombies?" asked Ansee.

What in the hells are you doing, Seeker, Willem thought. The cleric was giving Ansee an expectant look while Whitlocke sighed audibly. Willem knew that she hated it when constables butted in on her turf. "Seeker Carya, this is Ovate Hedgewill—"

"Brenna, please," the cleric interrupted. "We're not big

on titles at the Shrine."

Whitlocke continued, clearly miffed at being interrupted. "Ovate Hedgewill was explaining that her fellow priest was summoned last night by a guard at the library. He said that he'd found two zombies lurking about the grounds there."

"Cedrus went to deal with them," Brenna interrupted again. "It was only zombies, and if we could show the grove that we had dealt with them, it would have been a boon for the Shrine."

"He didn't return, though," said Whitlocke, taking control of the conversation again. "The priest is now missing, as is the guard from the library. I was about to tell the Ovate that she would be better off seeking help from one of the larger," Whitlocke stressed the word, implying that larger definitely meant better and more capable, "temples, like the temple of Basvu. They are better equipped to deal with zombies than we are."

"I'm certain we can help out," offered Ansee. Willem muttered a curse under his breath. *Why is he getting involved?*

Whitlocke raised one eyebrow. "It's been Constabulary policy to let clerics deal with any undead in the city, and I'm sure that you have a lot of other cases that you are dealing with." She was doing her best to get the cleric out of her waiting room and to take her problem with her.

"No, Constable," Ansee said cheerfully. "I happen to have nothing growing at the moment, and we shouldn't turn away anyone who's looking for help." He turned and smiled at Brenna. "I'd be happy to help you out."

Whitlocke's ears smoked and she bit her lower lip. After a moment, she shrugged, apparently deciding that it wasn't worth it to argue with Ansee. She inked her quill to make an entry into her logbook.

Ansee touched Brenna on her elbow and motioned to

the door. "Let's go outside and talk. Constable Gania," he motioned for Kai to follow them. The younger constable had a confused expression, but Willem knew exactly what Seeker Carya was doing. He could feel his forehead furrow as he scowled at the Seeker.

Brenna headed for the door, along with Gania. Ansee started to follow, but Willem grabbed his arm. "What in the many hells are you doing, Seeker?"

"I'm helping somebody with a missing person case. FC Aescel said that I should keep myself occupied."

"Uh-huh. And this just wouldn't have anything to do with our two missing bodies from the flower shop, does it? A case we are no longer supposed to be working on?"

"Why, I don't know what you mean, Constable," Ansee said with mock formality. "I told you yesterday that there was no proof that a raise dead spell had been cast."

"You also said there was an unknown divine aura in the room, too." He gave Ansee a stern, fatherly look, the same look that he used on his children. "If you're thinking that this is somehow going to help Reva, you're mistaken. It's likely you'll just get in trouble since this is now Pflamtael's case."

"Look, I really don't know what happened to our victims, but if they *did* become zombies by some unknown means, then there is a bigger problem here than Reva, Pflamtael, or anybody else would be ready to handle. I just want to confirm whether these zombies are our victims or not. If they aren't, then we can just get rid of them ourselves or let one of the churches deal with them."

"And what if they are?" Willem asked.

"I'd rather not think about that possibility right now." Ansee glanced up the stairs, and then back to Willem. "Please go take care of our notes for the case and get them to Inspector Pflamtael."

Willem stood with his arms crossed for a moment. He

knew that no other constables would give a kobold's ass to help this cleric, and the churches would just slay the creatures and burn them, destroying any evidence. Reluctantly he said, "Fine. Just don't do anything stupid."

Ansee smiled and did a passable impression of Reva's "Who me?" look, and then walked outside.

Chapter 17

The madness that had been driving at his mind had subsided the instant that Erroll had placed the Joy of the Widow's Tears around his neck. He'd been filled with an inner calm unlike any that he had felt in his entire life. He'd left Mill Island and wandered back into the city, meandering through the streets until he finally arrived at a lonely rock cliff overlooking the Bay Grove beach. The night air was cool, but his skin felt like it was on fire, and he found a spot to sit and reflect. The necklace had called to him from the moment that he had spied it in that vendor's stall, but now he wondered why. A need had been fulfilled by killing Loren and getting his necklace back, but something still felt empty, like something important was missing. He fell asleep watching the waves roll against the beach under the moonlight.

Erroll found himself bound to a stone pillar in a strange land. The air was hot and dry on his skin, and strange smells lingered in the air. The pillar that he was tied to was in the center of a square plaza, with pillared buildings and ornate archways lining the four sides. He saw men—humans—with swarthy skin and wearing loose, flowing clothes of a sky-blue color. They had cloth of the same color wrapped around their heads and they held large, curved swords. The ache in his arms told him that he'd been here for some time, and the caked blood at his feet told him that he was being punished for some sort of crime. The similarity to his pun-ishment on the *Majestic Tern* was not lost on him.

At that moment, there was a sharp, biting pain across his back. Erroll gave a loud cry, letting the pain flow into his soul. He then called out, in a voice that was not his own, but yet somehow strangely familiar, "I will not repent! Only my pain will redeem the Lord Ados, absolving Him of His sin! Lord Ados, I suffer to forgive your failure!"

As he said the words, Erroll could feel a cooling sensa-tion, a tingling on his back where the whip had struck him. The pain was eased, though its memory was still sharp, as the wound was healed. This went on for a dozen more times, each time the whip biting into his back, each time he exclaimed his resolve to not repent, to suffer so that Ados's sin would be absolved.

There was a pause in the punishment, and Erroll heard booted feet walk toward him across the stone cobbles of the square. "Check him!" A rough voice commanded. The language was foreign to Erroll, although he could understand it clearly. "It is clear that the heretic has an enchantment upon him that prevents his punishment from being carried out."

Rough hands pawed at him, and he could hear spells being cast. He could see a man with a dark goatee and thin mustache lean toward him. "I will break you, heretic," the man whispered. "You will be punished for your crimes against Lord Ados. When I am done with you, nobody will ever recall the name of Dreen or the heresies you spout."

Dreen. The name was like a fresh breeze through a sum-mer glade, blowing away the old leaves.

"There is nothing on him, Alguacil," said another voice. "The heretic has no magic cast upon him either. We cannot explain the mira—"

There was a loud smack as the goateed man slapped the speaker. "You will not utter that word. There is devilry about the heretic. Ados's punishment will be dealt." The men moved away and Erroll could hear additional commands being given.

Who is Dreen? When did this happen? What did he say about Ados that got him into so much trouble?

He didn't have time to think about his questions or to see if this Dreen would give him guidance. A deep, incapacitating pain seared his back as six whips struck him nearly simultaneously. He felt his skin and muscle being carved from his body, the last whip scraping across the bone of his spine. His scream came from the very bottom of his soul, a primal cry as the pain nearly caused him to lose consciousness. But then he could feel the gentle tingle, the cooling breath as he was healed again. "Ados's sin is my sin!" Erroll yelled. "My pain releases Him of His sin! My suffering redeems his suffering!"

The crack of the whips sounded, again and again, their bite flailing the skin from his back, only to have new skin replace the wound. The pain was overwhelming and Erroll screamed again, finally startling himself awake. He looked around in confusion, the dark and cool beach seeming very out of place at first. He blinked a few times and started to stretch when a pain ran up his spine. He twisted an arm and touched his hand to the spot. When he held up his hand in the moonlight, he could see blood staining his fingertips.

What just happened? He looked around the deserted beach. Most of the night had passed, and the dawn was starting to color the eastern sky. Had his sleep reopened his own wounds that he'd received on the ship? Or had his dream been real? It had certainly felt real.

Dreen is pain...

The voice was soft, a gentle whisper in his head. He focused on the pain in his back, letting it focus his mind.

Pain is truth...

The pain cleared his doubts. It was as if a hidden path

had been revealed to him.

Dreen is truth.

"Dreen is truth," Erroll said, his voice sure and full of conviction. Dreen had spoken to him in the dream. The shared experience of the lashings bound him to Dreen, and Dreen's message was simple and pure: life is full of pain, but through that pain you can find truth. Erroll knew that he needed to share this message. He needed to get others to understand what he now knew.

But how? I am a sailor, not a cleric. How do I spread your message? He waited for a moment, expecting Dreen to answer him, but no voice sounded in his head to give him guidance. *Typical deity.*

How does one start a church? I know the truth, but how do I tell others about this truth? Do I stand along the Grand March and call out to all the people passing by? What do I say to them? Surely, if I do, the other churches will react. They will see me as a threat, as I steal their blind herds by giving them the truth. They will set the Green Cloaks on me or send an assassin to martyr me. I cannot be open about Dreen and His truth too soon. I need to start small, but how?

He leaned back to stare at the stars and a sudden sting from the wound on his back jolted him upright.

Gather my Disciples.

Of course. I cannot be the only one. There must be others. He felt a stirring in his gut, similar to the feeling he'd had as he'd followed Loren. He had always known where Loren was because Loren had the necklace. Now Erroll knew that there were others. There was somebody else out there who was a follower. Somebody else who knew the truth. He could feel them. He would find Dreen's Disciples. They would provide him the base from which he would start spreading the truth of Dreen's message.

Erroll stood up and touched the necklace. It brought him comfort, and the pain in his back brought him clarity.

He made his way slowly, but purposefully, toward the river. He was no longer confused or unsure of himself. The sun rose as he walked through Tenyl's early morning streets. He silently pitied the few people that he passed, knowing how troubled their lives must be without knowing the truth as he did.

Crossing King's Bridge, he walked north along the narrow streets until he stood before the trees of Nuphar Wood. He started along the Wood's paths, confidently turning to head toward the thickest part of the forest. As the trees thickened, he stepped off the path. Here, the trees grew so close together that they screened out the morning sun. It was still twilight here. Erroll pushed his way through the thick undergrowth and brambles, traveling deeper into the wood. Branches tugged at his clothing and roots tried to trip him up. He ducked under low branches and circled tall trees before coming upon a small clearing. A tree had died and fallen here many years ago. Larger trees grew around the clearing, shading the area in perpetual twilight.

At the far end, he could see them: four creatures crouched in the dimmest of the shadows. All four had the pallid skin of the undead; thin, bloodless, and blotched. He saw that two, a man and a woman, were only partially clothed, while the third wore a cleric's vestment and the last one looked ancient and was dressed in a guard's outfit. Between the four creatures lay a dog, its body motionless and blood matting its fur. One of the creatures drew a clawed finger across the dog's body, gently tracing the wound. The dog whimpered and kicked, and pain rolled off the animal like a wave. All four creatures shuddered as if in ecstasy, and even at this distance Erroll could feel the joy as the pain reached him. He let out an involuntary gasp of pleasure and, at the sound, all four creatures turned to look at him.

As one, the four creatures rose up and began shuffling

toward him. "Dreen is pain...pain is truth...Dreen is truth..." The mantra was spoken by all four creatures, though slightly out of synch. They continued across the clearing, spreading out to encircle Erroll.

Erroll should have been afraid, but instead, he felt calm; he was unconcerned by the undead that were approaching him. These were Dreen's disciples...his disciples. He smiled and held up his right hand, closing it to make a fist, digging in his nails until he drew blood. The pain was sharp and inviting, and he said, "Dreen gives us pain to sharpen the mind. Pain brings enlightenment and truth."

The four creatures stopped moving but continued their slow mantra. Erroll knew that they were now his to command. Four disciples would not bring about Tenyl's enlightenment, but it was a start.

Chapter 18

Reva walked out of New Port feeling as if a heavy branch had been lifted from her shoulders. She'd known that the King's commendation had given her a little protection from Betulla's wrath, but she also knew that the LCI had been furious with her. Yes, Reva had managed to stop Roya Locera during his murderous rampage, even saving Betulla's life in the process, but she'd defied Betulla's orders to do it and had embarrassed her among the First Constables and the Grand Inquisitor of the Sucra. Betulla hadn't been able to do anything to Reva while the Fury blade case was still fresh grist for the gossip mills, but the case had been closed for nearly a month, and Reva had expected something to come from the Lord Constable Inspector.

I certainly didn't expect this, she thought to herself as she walked out of the main gate. *Still, I plan to make the most of it. If I can have a good time, maybe Betulla will hear about it, and it'll piss her off.*

Reva walked along, enjoying the feeling of not having to constantly look for the LCI's attack. Reva knew that this would only mollify Betulla for a little bit; as soon as Reva returned, she'd have to keep her ear to the foliage again. She hated having to play politics, and that was one reason why she never planned to rise beyond her current rank. She dreaded the kind of ass-kissing and ego-stroking that FC Aescel had to do.

Reva paused in her walk and realized that she'd uncon-sciously wandered to the intersection of Ferry Road and Circle Road at the base of Poplar Hill. Somehow, her body knew that she didn't want to be home right now. Mother would want to know why she was home so early, and Reva would have to tell her. (The thought of lying didn't even cross Reva's mind. Mother seemed to always be able to sniff out Reva's lies as if she'd been born with a lie-detecting dowsing rod embedded within her. Of course, Gale always seemed to get away with telling lies.) That would mean tell-ing Mother that she'd been suspended. Again. And Mother would bring up (again) how Reva's father had never been suspended when he'd been in the Constabulary, and how he'd be so disappointed with her.

No, Reva decided, *I just don't want to deal with Mother right now.*

She continued up Ferry Road past the guild houses, pubs, and shops that catered to the travelers that infested Port Grove. She turned off of the main road into the warren of side roads and paths, her hand automatically moving to rest on the hilt of her dagger. She didn't trust half of the people she saw in Port Grove, and she was always alert for thieves. She threaded her way toward the waterfront, pass-ing dive pubs, brothels, trading houses, and storehouses both big and small.

The port was a busy, chaotic place. Large ships were tied to the piers, sailors, and longshore-elves (most were halpbloeden) walking up and down gangplanks carrying cargo. In between the large ships were smaller, coastal ves-sels that served the cities and towns that ringed Black Elf Bay. Scattered everywhere were even smaller boats, loaded with gill nets or crates stacked for trapping crabs and lob-sters. The area was filled with a loud, constant cacophony of noise and smelled of brackish water, dead fish, and un-washed bodies.

Reva threaded her way through elves and halpbloeden as they carried goods or pushed carts. She paused at the bridge that led over to Dock Island. To her right was South Fort, its stone walls and tall keep looking out to the bay. Several tall ships were tied to the piers to the left and right of the bridge. She didn't see the *Majestic Tern* among them, and she didn't know where Aavril's ship might be docked.

She grabbed the shoulder of a halpbloeden—a human in fact—carrying a large coil of rope. He paused but didn't bother to hide his irritations. "Do you know where the *Majestic Tern* is docked?" she asked.

The human shook his head and said, "No," then walked on.

It took three more tries before Reva stopped an elf who was leading a mule that was hitched to an empty cart. "Aye," drawled the elf. "Da *Tern's* docked o'er da udder side." He vaguely waved in the direction he meant. "She's in number six."

Reva thanked him and headed across the bridge and onto the island. Surprisingly, the island was less chaotic than the rest of the port. People here moved with a purpose instilled with a seaelf's discipline. She walked to the other side of the island and, after a moment, spotted the *Majestic Tern*, its distinctive winged figurehead proclaiming her presence. Reva had only been on board the *Tern* a couple of times with Aavril, and had always been struck by the figurehead: a beautiful woman, naked from the waist up (of course), her arms—which were actually wings—outstretched to wrap the prow in a protective embrace.

She headed along the dock, passing another mule and cart that was heading away from the ship. An elf with weathered skin that was a deep bronze color from so much time spent at sea was heading up the gangplank. It took Reva only a moment to remember his name. "Kelsey," she called out.

The elf turned at the sound of his name, the scowl that had been on his face quickly turning into a broad smile. "Aye, me lady." He looked at her briefly, appraisingly, before adding, "And if'n I do recall, you'd be Reva. The *Isean's* lady friend."

Reva wondered at the title—Aavril was only the Quartermaster—but ignored it. "I'm glad you remember me."

"Oh," Kelsey's smile widened even more. "I always remember a lovely lady."

Reva actually felt herself blushing a bit. She'd only met Kelsey once before and recalled that he'd been just as full of flattery then as well. "Is Aavril on board?" She started to put a foot onto the gangplank, but Kelsey held up his hand to stop her.

Irritated, Reva snapped, "This had better not be some superstitious hawkshit about me not being allowed on the ship because I'm a woman." She glared up at Kelsey—giving him her best 'irritated commander' expression—who looked unfazed by the look that could wilt young constables.

"Aye. There be plenty o' superstitions 'bout women and ships. Some'r good, some bad. 'Tis important ta knows tha difference." Reva felt her ears going red. "But that's not why I'm stoppin' ya."

"Oh." Reva let her irritation fall away.

Kelsey gave a chuckle, clearly happy with having tweaked her ears. "Nah. The *Isean* stepped off for a moment."

Reva's irritation came back with a vengeance. *Have you spent so long at sea that your brains are addled?* she thought. Aloud, she said, "I don't care about the *Isean*. I want to see Aavril. You know—your Quartermaster."

Kelsey folded his arms and gave Reva a condescending look. "I knows who I am speakin' of, ma'am. I think you're tha one who's confused." Reva started to speak, but Kelsey held up his hand. "Look. 'Tis not fer me ta do the 'splainen. Aavril is not on board right now. He went ta look fer tha Cap'n."

"Oh," Reva stepped back, confused. "I'm sorry. I didn't know," she managed to say, but her mind was running. *Aavril got a promotion to First Sail? And he hasn't told me! Why? Was he keeping it a secret? Was he afraid to tell me? Why would he not say anything?"*

"S'alright, ma'am," Kelsey continued, unaware of Reva's thoughts. "I don't know when he'll be back, but I'll be sure ta let him know you was lookin' fer him."

"Áeorias", Reva said absently and turned away from the ship. *What in the hells is going on? Aavril never said that he wanted to become Isean. Before his last trip, he'd even agreed to stop sailing and open his own shop. Was he lying to me then? He said he wanted to spend more time with me. Was that a lie, too? Has everything he's ever done been a lie?*

Aavril seemed happy when they'd discussed him leaving the ship. He could make good money as a merchant, especially with his contacts among the captains. He talked about getting a house together, getting married, and raising a family. Reva liked the idea of moving out of her mother's place, but she wasn't ready to start a family. She'd been adamant about that with him. She wasn't ready to give up her job to start a family.

But now she wondered if all of Aavril's talk had just been an illusion. *Why had he changed his mind? Why hadn't he wanted to discuss this with me?* It meant spending even more time away from her. *Why would he do that?*

As she left Dock Island, the thought came to her. *Did he become Isean to spite me for wanting to keep my job?* She paused to look at the ships in the harbor. *Well, if that's how he wants to play it, then he can just stay at sea forever!*

Chapter 19

"Áeorias, Senior Constable," Constable Inspector Olwyn Pflamtael took the small stack of parchment from Senior Constable Ghrellstone.

"I'd be happy to give you a rundown on what we know about the case," Ghrellstone said.

"Don't bother. If Reva's parchmentwork is in order, then I'm sure that I can scry what I need from it."

Ghrellstone bristled at the comment, but he nodded, "It's in order."

"Good. If I have any questions, I know where to find you," Olwyn said, in dismissal.

The Senior Constable nodded and walked back to the cluster of tables shared by Reva and her team. *He's a decent enough constable,* Olwyn thought, *but he's not inspector material. But I suppose that every great inspector needs a good subordinate to handle the legwork.* Olwyn recalled that he'd tried to get Willem to join his team several years ago, but he'd said no at the time. He'd thought that the Senior Constable was daft to want to work with a green inspector rather than with him.

Olwyn should have been happier with the current situation. He'd just snagged one of Reva's cases away from her, which was something that always made him happy. Maybe it was due to *how* he'd gotten the case. Having the case handed to him took the pleasure out of the challenge since he couldn't tweak Reva's ears about it. There was a strange feeling in the pit of his stomach, and it took him a moment of reflection to realize that it was guilt. It was not a feeling that he had a lot of experience with. He knew, even cherished, the fact that he was egotistical and self-serving—that was the price to pay for advancement. But Olwyn also had a strong sense of honor that was instilled in him by his faith and his family. It was honorable to do anything and everything in his power to take a case away from another inspector, but having it taken away from them and handed to him on a platter was wrong.

Olwyn blamed LCI Betulla for this blotch on his honor. Her dislike—hatred, really—for Reva bordered on the pathological, and that had been clear to everybody in the Division after Reva had stopped Locera's homicidal spree. Reva had made the cardinal sin of embarrassing a superior officer; an officer that was known to hold grudges. The Constables in Acer Division had a pool going for how long and when the branch would fall on Reva's head. *That cost me five Skips*, Olwyn thought with chagrin. He'd figured that Reva would have been punished long before now, though he'd been just as surprised by the manner and severity of Reva's punishment as she had.

Olwyn didn't like the way that Betulla was taking everything so personally. LCI Gania had never been this petty and malicious. She'd let the First Constables run their divisions with little oversight from her. Gania had also been more amenable to listening to suggestions from her constables, something that Olwyn had used to his advantage numerous times.

He'd taken Gania's death hard, not so much because of the death itself—which was tragic—but because it had practically ruined Olwyn's career. He'd been courting LCI Gania for years, planting little seeds that he'd hoped to bring to fruition when Aescel finally retired. Olwyn was sure that his time with Gania would be rewarded and he'd be named First Constable. Now all of that hard work was nothing but leaves in the wind.

Olwyn didn't know how his chances for the First Constable position stood now. He'd tried to feel Betulla out once since she'd taken over as Lord Constable Inspector. He'd tried to get the LCI to talk about her vision for the RTC, what sort of elves she wanted to lead the Constabulary. Olwyn realized, after the fact, that he had overplayed his hand. Betulla had been non-committal in her response, and now she knew that he was eager for the First Constable's position. Looking eager would, at best, make it harder for him or, at worst, put him in a position to owe a debt to the LCI. Olwyn didn't like being in debt to anybody.

A wadded-up ball of parchment hit Olwyn in the shoulder. "Material Plane to CI Pflamtael," chided Norah.

Olwyn had been gathering moss and turned to look at his Seeker. She stood with her arms crossed, a look of irritation on her face. A lock of her reddish hair hung down over her eyes. It often did that when they made love and he smiled at the pleasant memory. "Hmm?"

"I said, 'Are you ready to discuss our situation?'"

"Sure. When are you and I going to get together again?"

"I meant about the case."

"The case can wait. It's more important to me to know when you and I will have our time alone."

Norah tried to suppress a smile. "Inspector," she said formally and quietly, "You know I won't get together when my husband is home."

"Why does he have to be home so much, then? It's been nearly two weeks since his last trip. Doesn't he have a farm to go inspect or something?"

"He's supposed to travel to meet with the breeders in a few days. You'll just have to wait until then."

"It's about time," Olwyn huffed. "Ever since Cas left for

Narris, I've not had anybody else to share my bed with me."

"You're a big elf, I'm sure you'll get over it." Norah patted his arm but there was a tinge of anger in her voice. "I, for one, am glad she's gone. I never liked sharing you with her."

"There was that one time..."

"Yes. And Cas and I could hardly look at each other after that. How you convinced us that it would be fun is beyond me." She held up the parchments. "Now, can we focus on doing our jobs?"

Olwyn nodded. "So, what did Reva leave us?"

"Not much. Not even bodies."

"Really? I thought that was just a rumor." He crossed his arms and began to tug at the laces on his right bracer. It was a habit that he wasn't even aware that he had.

"Apparently it's true. The Birches were first at the shop and reported finding two bodies, one male and one female, dead in the back room. The elf that found them also swears there were two bodies. But when Reva arrived, the bodies were gone."

"Were they raised, or did somebody take them away?"

"Unknown." Norah flipped to a parchment filled with tiny, neat script. "Seeker Carya reported finding a diffuse divine aura at the scene, but no evidence that a raise dead spell or other divine magic was cast." Olwyn noted her clearly skeptical tone.

"You don't believe him?"

"I believe him. I just don't trust him."

"Oh, that again."

"Come on, Inspector. I've seen him cast spells and I've spoken with some of the Seekers over in Nul Pfeta Division. If he's a wizard, he was never trained in Tenyl."

"There are good wizard academies in Narris and other places in the Kingdom."

"No. I mean he wasn't trained *at all* in the Kingdom."

She leaned over conspiratorially. "I swear that he's one of *them*."

"*Them*?" Olwyn mocked. "You mean a sorcerer."

"Yes," she hissed. "And if he is, then it's dangerous to have him around. He might become enthralled by his demon master and summon it here to kill us all."

Olwyn didn't bother trying to suppress the laugh that came out. Norah glared at him. He'd only worked with Seeker Carya on one occasion, and he seemed safe enough. Not very competent—certainly not to Norah's or Cas's level—but not a threat.

"Go ahead and laugh. He sold his soul to a demon to get his magic. We're playing with fire by letting him stay in the Constabulary."

"Hellfire?" Olwyn couldn't help himself.

"Screw you," Norah shot back.

"You said I'd have to wait a couple of days. Did you change your mind?"

Norah reddened, the points of her ears almost going crimson with anger. Olwyn knew that he'd stepped over a line, though he thought it was funny. "Fine," he said in a consoling tone. "You can check his auras again yourself. What else do we know?"

Norah calmed down a bit. "That's about it. There was a fight, but the bodies disappeared. Reva's team spoke to the elves who own businesses around the flower shop hoping to find out where the owner, and possible victim—Amber Myosotis—lived. They didn't have any luck."

"I guess that's where we'll start then. Shanna," he called. Senior Constable Shanna Rhosa looked up from her table. "We'll need a couple of Constables to help us canvas the area. Go grab some warm bodies, and meet us outside."

Chapter 20

Ansee, Brenna, and Constable Gania stood on the grounds of the Grand Library. The library grew up behind them, while in front were the library's gardens and paths, with the mass of Nuphar Wood beyond. People were strolling along the red gravel paths and enjoying the afternoon.

"Do you know where the watchelf would have taken Cedrus?" Ansee asked.

Brenna shook her head. "No. I wasn't paying much attention when he showed up."

"Well, I doubt it was out in the open," Ansee commented. "Nobody has come forward about finding a body or seeing any undead." He pointed to all of the elves enjoying the gardens. "If a body or zombie had been out in the open, somebody would have seen something."

"We should check near the tree line," said Gania. "The library abuts against the Brambles, so there aren't many paths or easy ways into the woods from here. The library doesn't have any paths near the wood for just that reason."

They headed down a path to get closer to the woods. The day was warm, and high clouds drifted across the sky. Ansee saw several birds—bright red cardinals and dun-colored swallows—flying around, but no crows that might have signaled a dead body. He hoped that was a good sign.

They paused by a bronze statue of a dryad standing

atop a stone plinth. They were closest to the wood here, and there were fewer people around. Ansee held up his hand against the sun and looked into the wood. He couldn't see much, as the trees became thick and tangled a few steps from the edge. It was certainly a good place for undead to hide out during the day, as the trees grew so close together that little sunlight reached the ground.

Ansee turned to Kai and Brenna. "Let's spread out and start looking between here and the wood. Maybe Cedrus dropped something." The others nodded, and they fanned out to search the grass.

Ansee wondered what they would find. He'd rarely dealt with undead. The RTC let the churches deal with any undead that cropped up in the city. The clerics and priests were much better equipped to handle the creatures. He'd only ever once encountered an undead while on patrol; a skeleton that somebody had animated and sent into Nul Pfeta to stir up trouble. The Constables had laughed and found it funny to watch the halpbloeden cower and run from the shambling skeleton. Ansee had dealt with it with a single spell. They never did catch the person who'd animated the damn thing.

As Ansee scoured the grass looking for clues, he thought about the possible outcomes from this search. They might find Cedrus's dead body, or what was left of it. A pair of zombies shouldn't be able to kill an elf, especially a cleric with strong faith in his deity, but Ansee had seen the after-effects when a normal person was unlucky enough to encounter a zombie. It wasn't pretty. But Ansee only had Brenna's word that these were zombies. It was possible that these were ghouls or even ghasts, which could be very dangerous.

Another possibility was that Cedrus had dealt with the zombies and had decided to not tell Brenna. Ansee had no idea why the cleric would do that, but it was still something he had to consider.

The last possibility was that Cedrus had dealt with the zombies but had been seriously wounded in the effort. He could be unconscious and unable to heal himself. Again, that didn't seem likely to Ansee, but he didn't want to rule it out.

Ansee looked up to check on the progress of the others. He was near the edge of the library grounds, which were bordered by a low hedge. Constable Gania was on the far side of the dryad statue, head bent as he walked a slow pace over the grass. Brenna was in the middle, walking hurriedly and stopping often to kick at something in the grass. Ansee continued his search, walking between the gravel path and the woods several times when Brenna gave a shout. Looking up, he saw her bending down to pick up something in the grass.

Ansee and Kai walked over. "What did you find?" asked Kai.

Brenna held up a small object, no bigger than Ansee's thumb, which was a sandy-brown color. "It's a cork from a bottle of holy water," she said.

Ansee knelt to look at the cork and the area where Brenna had picked it up. Constable Gania asked, "How do you know that? It could be from somebody's wine bottle left after a picnic."

She held it up and tapped a mark on the edge. "That's Nera's symbol. I mark all of the corks with it before sealing the flasks."

It was difficult to tell if the grass here had been flattened or not, but Ansee was sure that his spell would tell him what he needed to know. Touching the grass, he began to incant, "*Bana burada atilan adimlari ortaya koymaktadir.*" A green mist formed over the grass and swirled around his fingers, up his arm, and then around his head. He blinked a couple of times and his eyes took on a soft green glow.

Ansee stood up and looked around. He could see sharp prints from where he, Kai, and Brenna had just walked. The grass was not the best surface to capture the prints, but among their sharp tracks, he could make out faded, almost ghostly impressions of footprints. There were gaps in the tracks, but enough remained that Ansee could put together what had happened.

"Somebody came this way," he pointed from the statue to the woods. "Probably Cedrus. Two other people came out of the woods over there," he pointed toward a dense cluster of trees. "Their prints are clumsy, so they probably belong to the zombies. Cedrus appears to have stopped briefly there," he pointed to a spot a few paces in front of them. "He seems to have taken a few steps back, dropped the cork here, and then continued to back up. The zombie's prints continue toward Cedrus the entire time."

Constable Gania began walking a spiral out from where Brenna had found the cork. He paused a few paces away and pointed to the ground. "There's blood here, and a mace." He picked the weapon up from the grass.

"That's his mace," Brenna said.

Ansee walked over to Kai. From what he could see, Cedrus's tracks stopped here, and there was a large depression made in the grass as if somebody had fallen. *That's not a good sign.* But the zombie tracks seemed to move past that spot and it looked like Cedrus had then stood up and walked toward the woods. *Why would he do that?*

"Cedrus fell here," Ansee said.

"Fell?" Brenna scowled. She held out her hand and Kai gave her the weapon. "Then where in Nera's name is he? Where's his body? Where are the zombies?"

"I don't know," Ansee admitted, trying to remain calm. "The tracks are hard to read, but it looks like after he fell, the zombies went past him, then he got up, and headed into the woods."

"Why would you do that without your weapon, Cedrus?" Brenna asked.

Ansee shrugged. "The tracks are really confusing here. The zombies head to the path, and then there are three sets of prints that come from that direction, and all they all head toward the woods. They overlap each other, and the other prints, so it is hard to make out what really happened." Ansee ended his spell, his eyes returning to their normal color.

"Maybe the zombies were just wounded and Cedrus and the guard followed them," Kai suggested.

"Well, whatever happened," Ansee said, then pointed toward the woods. "The answer is in there."

Brenna stood up and gripped the mace tightly in her hand. "Then that's where we need to go." She began to stride purposefully toward the woods.

"He could be anywhere in there," Kai said.

Ansee nodded agreement. "And we don't know if he's alive or dead."

"Or undead," whispered Kai.

"You had to say it?"

The young constable gave him a look that said, "You were thinking it too." Ansee sighed and they followed Brenna into Nuphar Wood.

Chapter 21

It took Constable Inspector Pflamtael, Seeker Norah, and the other Constables just over an hour to reach the flower shop. They spent a few minutes looking at the back of the shop. Nobody had yet cleaned it up, and it was clear that a fight of some kind had happened. Norah insisted on checking the room for magical auras, even though Seeker Carya had already done it. Plus, it was nearly a day after the crime had happened. Even Pflamtael knew enough about magic to know that the chances of finding a good aura would be difficult at best, but he shrugged, not wanting to hear another tirade about Seeker Carya. He headed outside to talk with the neighboring shopkeepers.

Olwyn split up his team and he walked across the street to start his interviews. Unsurprisingly, he encountered some anger and complaints about constabulary incompetence as the shop owners didn't like having to repeat what they'd already told somebody that morning. What Olwyn learned matched Reva's notes, and that didn't surprise him either. Reva was a pain in the ass a lot of the time, but she wasn't incompetent. (Despite the LCI's opinion on the subject.)

Olwyn entered the fourth shop, presumably a cobbler based the sign over the door and the boots and shoes on display. The shop smelled of leather and boot polish and was small, with no back room. The front half had finished footwear on display, while the back half was filled with dozens of wooden lasts, sheets and strips of leather, bundles of cloth, and several different tools hanging from the center of the far wall.

The cobbler sat on a stool in the center of the room. A workbench sat in front of him, while a bucket of water with several pieces of leather soaking in it sat to his right. He held several tacks in his lips and was hammering a leather sole to a boot. The cobbler looked up as Olwyn entered and he removed the tacks from his mouth. "I see the Constabulary wised up and finally sent a man to handle this."

"Well, of course," Olwyn answered. He had sized up what kind of elf the cobbler was by just that one sentence. "Why we bother sending women out to handle crimes is beyond me. I mean, look how much of a mess the Constabulary has been with a woman as the LCI." Olwyn smiled, and the cobbler softened his expression. "My job would be a hundred times easier if I don't have to go behind these damn female constables to do their jobs. They should just stay home where they belong."

The cobbler nodded his head thoughtfully. "Aye. They've no place tryin' to do a man's job. That's why when that lady constable come 'round this morning, I kept my mouth closed. Answerin' questions would just encourage her that she belongs in that uniform you wear."

Olwyn nodded thoughtfully. He could just imagine the kind of words Reva would use to describe this elf. "So, do you have any information that might help me find Amber's killer?"

The cobbler nodded. "There's another woman who was tryin' to be more than she should've been. Thinkin' she could own her own business. B'ah! See where that got her."

"Did you hear anything yesterday that might have sounded like a fight?"

"N'ah. I didn't hear nothin' yesterday morning and I was

out makin' a delivery in the afternoon."

Olwyn sighed inwardly at another dead end. But then he thought that maybe this cobbler might know more about Amber herself. None of the other shopkeepers had admitted to knowing anything about where she lived. "You know, at New Port, I'm constantly asking the women why they are there. Why aren't they taking care of their husbands instead of pretending to be constables? I'm guessing you may have done the same thing with Amber, trying to find out why she wasn't home raising a family."

"Dozens of times," the cobbler nodded. "Not that she ever listened to me. I could tell she didn't have a head for runnin' a shop."

"Why did her husband let her do it then?"

"Oh, she wasn't married. All the more reason she should've stayed away; to find herself a good husband. How her parents could let her humiliate them by workin' just boggles my mind."

"Do you know if Amber lived with her parents?"

"No. She was *independent.* She had a flat in North Grove. I followed her home a few times—"

I bet you did, thought Olwyn.

"—thinkin' I'd give her parents a good tongue lashin' for not controllin' her." He held up his small tack hammer and pointed the handle at Olwyn. "I blame her parents for her death. Had they raised her properly, she'd not have gotten it into her head she should be anythin' more than a wife and mother."

Olwyn managed to keep his face a mask as he thought, *Gods, I wonder what kind of woman ever married this man?* Aloud, he said, "Amber's death is tragic. However much blame for it belongs with her parents, I'm trying to find out who actually did the deed. Can you tell me where she lived? There might be clues there that will help me find her killer."

The cobbler nodded and gave Olwyn detailed instructions to get to Amber's home. Olwyn thanked him and started to turn away, then paused. "If Amber wasn't married, do you happen to know if she was seeing anybody?"

"She was seein' lots of guys," the cobbler said in a voice that bemoaned the fact that he wasn't one of them. "You know how loose *independent* women are." Olwyn nodded, preferring his own women that way. "Over the past few months," the cobbler continued, "I know she was seein' a bard or minstrel of some sort. Before that, I think she'd been datin' a sailor or dockworker. Just the sort that those women attract."

Olwyn thanked the cobbler again and left the shop. He saw Norah exit the flower shop and he walked over.

"And do Seeker Carya's auras match yours?"

"Yes," she said, managing to sound upset. "There is still a faint divine aura nearly a day later, and that has me puzzled."

"Well, you'll have to puzzle it out later. I've learned where Amber lived. Let's head there now to look it over."

Olwyn found Senior Constable Rhosa and told her that she and the rest of the team could return to New Port while he and Norah headed toward Amber's flat. It took them only fifteen minutes to reach the building, which was located on a busy side street just off North Road. It was three stories tall and rather ugly looking, with warping wooden planks making up the top two stories and rough-cut, grey colored limestone blocks and crumbling mortar coursing the ground floor. At one time, Olwyn guessed, the wood had been whitewashed, but it had mostly peeled away. The building looked cheap, and Olwyn figured that had attracted Amber to it.

The cobbler had never followed Amber into the building, so he'd not known which flat belonged to her, so they started knocking on doors as soon as they entered the building. Nobody answered at the first door and, before they could move on to the next, a door opened down the hall. A stooped, elderly woman with long white hair stepped into the hall. She looked to be well over 250 years old.

"*Reis sei*, Constable," she greeted. "Nobody on this floor is home now, except for me."

Olwyn gave her his best smile, the one he used so effectively to charm women. "Constable Inspector Olwyn Pflamtael, ma'am. This is my Seeker, Norah Pfinzloab. Actually, I think you may be able to help us. Do you happen to know which flat belongs to Amber Myosotis?"

The old woman nodded and licked her lips. "Áree. Though I don't think she's home now, either. I haven't seen her since yesterday morning."

"I understand, but we really need to look at her flat." He was afraid that, if he told this woman that Amber was dead, she'd die of shock.

The woman paused, chewing on her lip. She seemed to know that Olwyn was keeping something from her, but then she said, "Her flat's on the top floor. Front right."

"Áeorias." Olwyn and Norah turned to take the stairs.

"Amber is missing, isn't she?"

Norah paused, "Why do you ask?"

"Her boyfriend came by this morning, running up the stairs like an orc brute. He pounded on her door yelling for her to open up."

Olwyn had stopped on the stairs. He leaned over the banister and asked, "Her boyfriend?" The few facts that he knew about the case strongly implied that the elf responsible for Amber's murder was her boyfriend.

The old woman nodded. "Yes. He's a sailor, I think. I stepped out here to tell him to not be such a halpbloeden, pounding on the door like that. I heard him yelling for her."

Olwyn and Norah exchanged a look and he stepped back off of the stairs and approached the woman, "What did he say?"

The woman tilted her head a bit in thought. "He said, 'Open up. I know he's with you. Open the damn door.'"

"Did he say anything else?" asked Norah.

The woman shook her head. "He banged on her door some more, and then ran downstairs. He went by me so fast that I don't think he even saw me."

"And this was this morning. Not last night?" asked Olwyn.

The woman gave him a glare that could kill weeds. "I may be old, but I still know my morning from my night."

Olwyn beamed his smile at her again. "Of course. I had to ask, just to make sure of the events. You see, the reason we are here is that Amber was found murdered in her shop this morning."

Norah slightly raised one eyebrow, so subtly that only he'd notice, but she remained quiet. The woman gave an audible gasp and put one hand to her mouth. "By Basvu's Tree. The poor child. And you think her boyfriend did it?"

"That's what we're trying to determine," said Olwyn. He tapped Norah on the shoulder and pointed upstairs. She nodded and headed up to Amber's flat.

The woman looked straight at Olwyn. "I'm sure he did it. I told you he's a sailor. They are such a brash bunch, ill-mannered, rude, and always drinking and starting fights."

"Did you ever meet Amber's boyfriend? Could you describe him for me?"

"She never introduced me to him, so I don't know his name, but I saw them together on several occasions. He had straw-colored hair that fell to his shoulders and he was about your height, or maybe a bit shorter."

Hells, thought Olwyn. *That describes most of the male population in Tenyl.* "Can you remember anything else?" he prompted. "Anything like a scar, or something else that might help identify him?"

The old woman shut her eyes briefly and then opened

them wide. "Oh, yes! He had skin art on his arm, of a bird in flight."

Olwyn nodded. It wasn't a lot to go on, especially without a name, but it was better than nothing. *I've solved cases with less information.* He glanced up to see Norah walking back down the stairs, a subtle green light shimmering around her eyes. He turned back to the woman. "I am grateful for your assistance, ma'am."

"I hope you catch her murderer, Constable Inspector. Amber was the sweetest of girls. She would give me flowers that would always brighten up my flat."

Olwyn nodded but dropped his smile. *I've learned all that I can from her, and if I let her keep talking, I'll be here all day.* Norah was already outside. "Áeorias," he said curtly and followed her out of the building. Looking around, he spotted her several paces away, walking toward North Road. He hustled to catch up to her.

"You have something?"

"Yes, but the tracks are almost lost out here. There's too much traffic on the road and they've been too disturbed. They were very strong inside the building, but out here," she stopped at the intersection with the main road and waved her hand dismissively. "I've lost them completely." She let the spell end and her eyes returned to their normal blue color. "Do you want to go back and check out her flat?"

Olwyn shook his head. "No point. We know she's dead and, while her body is missing, I doubt that her murderer brought it back to her flat." He started heading down North Road back toward the river. "We know Amber was killed along with another man. Reva thought that it was Amber's lover, and I'll admit that fits with what we know. Amber's boyfriend is a sailor, according to the old woman. So, he gets back from the sea and goes to see her at the shop. He finds out that she has a lover and, in a fit of jealous rage, kills them both."

"But Amber was killed yesterday. Whoever the old woman saw this morning probably didn't do it. Not if he was looking for Amber today."

"She was clearly confused. You saw how old she was. No, when we find this sailor, we'll have found Amber's murderer."

Chapter 22

Constable Kai Gania leaned against the trunk of an elm while he pulled off one of his boots. "How much longer are we going to keep at this?" He tried, unsuccessfully, to rub the soreness from his foot.

"Just a bit longer," urged Brenna.

Kai sighed loudly. It had been getting darker in the woods the longer they searched, especially here in the Brambles. Kai had lost track of the time but guessed that it was late afternoon, at least. Kai could barely make out Ansee's form from just a few paces away. They hadn't expected that it would take them this long to look for Cedrus.

"We haven't seen anybody since we came in here," Kai complained, not trying to hide the irritation that he felt. "And if there are any undead out here, I'd rather come across them during the day."

Ansee remained quiet, but Brenna said, "But we haven't found him yet. I'm not leaving without Cedrus."

Kai was growing weary of this. "You want to know why we haven't found anything? He was eaten by the bloody things." Brenna let out a gasp, but he couldn't really see her in the deepening darkness.

"Seeker Carya. Ansee," Kai pleaded as he put his boot back on. "We're risking our necks by staying out here. We've traipsed through this area a dozen times and we haven't seen a damn thing." He let out another loud sigh. "Look, the Brambles are difficult to navigate in the day. It's almost impossible to do it now. If we stay out here any longer, we won't be able to find our way out until morning."

Ansee stood still, apparently deep in thought, for several moments. "We need to find the zombies," he said, mostly to himself, but loud enough that Kai could hear him. "I know they are our missing victims from the flower shop."

"That's not even our damn case anymore, Ansee. Why do you care?"

"Why don't you?" Ansee shot back. There was a pause for a moment, then he said, "Look, I don't care whose case this is. I don't like not knowing what happened to the bodies."

"And why do you think they became zombies?" Gania asked. He was tired of dancing around the leaves and let his anger show.

"I don't know that they did, but until I find them, I don't know that they didn't."

"My mother always said that a good constable keeps an open mind about a case until the facts tell them what happened. But keeping an open mind doesn't mean that we need to spend the night in the forest."

Ansee let out a tired chuckle. "Very well. Brenna, we need to call it a night. We can start again in the morning. I promise you, I won't give up until we've found Cedrus."

"Fine," she said in resignation. "I just hate the thought of Cedrus spending another night out here alone."

"Do you know the easiest way out of here, Kai?" Ansee asked.

"I think there's a footpath a few hundred paces in that direction." Kai pointed to his left.

"Lead on, Constable."

Kai led the way, working around a thick bramble of bushes and fallen trees. It was hard to imagine that they were in the middle of the city, that something so wild could be found here. The woods blocked out any of the usual sounds of the city. They could have been in the middle of the Highlands.

The going was slow, as they had to detour around a thick growth of trees and silverthorn bushes. As they moved along, Kai thought he heard movement, as if somebody was walking with them. It was hard to tell, as Brenna and Ansee sounded like a pair of dwarves stomping around. He paused a moment to try to get a better listen but heard nothing. He shrugged and continued. *I must be imagining things,* he told himself. *Who in their right mind would walk through silverthorn?*

The branches overhead were starting to thin out and let in the faint light from a waxing crescent moon. *Have we been out here that long? No matter.* The light was enough to allow him to see more clearly now and he could pick out more details. He realized that he had gotten ahead of the others, and he paused to let Ansee and Brenna catch up. He was about to start off again when he heard the unmistakable sound of a twig being broken. The sound had come from the silverthorn thicket on his left, and he turned toward the sound.

"We are not alone," he whispered. Gania saw four creatures emerge from the thicket, ignoring the sharp thorns that tugged and scratched at their skin. They moved with a slow, purposeful gait that he mistook as shuffling at first, but as they cleared the thicket, they became more sure-footed. As they approached, Kai could hear a slow, steady chant coming from the four creatures.

"Dreen is pain...pain is truth...Dreen is truth...Dreen is pain..."

Gania swallowed and felt his throat go dry and his palms begin to sweat. Butterflies shot through his gut and he had to steel himself to keep from running. *What's wrong with me? I didn't feel this way when I fought Roya Locera,* he chided. He grabbed the hilt of his sword and pulled it from its scabbard.

"I think we just found Cedrus," Ansee said.

Kai saw that one of the creatures was wearing the same vestments that Brenna wore. Two of the other creatures—a man and a woman—were only partially clothed. Though the night robbed everything of color, Kai thought that he recognized the pattern of the woman's dress from the torn piece of cloth that he'd found at the flower shop.

"And your missing murder victims," Kai said.

Brenna yelled, "Cedrus!" and rushed forward, pulling out a silver eagle pendant from her vestments. "By Nera, what happened to you?"

"Brenna, wait," shouted Ansee. "We don't know what these creatures are, or if anybody is controlling them."

Brenna ignored him. She raised her holy symbol above her head. "With Nera's blessing and will, I banish the evil before me!" She was crying as she spoke, tears rolling down her cheeks as she spoke the prayer. A bright eagle, glowing with a silver light, rose up from her holy symbol. It spread its wings and the small area near the thicket was filled with its brightness. Ansee and Kai blinked and had to turn away from the sudden brilliance.

The creatures paused for a moment, as if something was pushing against them, then they moved forward again, their chant growing louder. "Dreen is pain...pain is truth... Dreen is truth...Dreen is pain..."

Brenna stared at the four creatures, tears falling from her eyes. "Why, Nera? Why? How have I failed you, Nera?" Cedrus and the woman were almost on top of Brenna, their hands raised. Kai could see that the skin of their fingers had peeled back to expose long, bony claws. Kai raised his blade and he heard Ansee incanting a spell.

The Cedrus creature raised one clawed hand and was struck in the chest by a red bolt of magic. Kai swung his sword at the woman, thrusting it into her belly. Both creatures seemed to cackle in glee and, at the same instant, Kai grabbed his belly as a sharp, hot pain suddenly struck him. He cried out and heard a similar sound coming from Ansee.

"What in the hells?" Kai stumbled back, pulling the sword from the creature. He felt a tickle of pain in his own gut. He didn't have time to think, as he blocked a clawed hand from striking at Brenna. But the other creature managed to slash Brenna's side and she gave a sharp yell.

Kai could see Ansee reacting quickly. The other two creatures were moving toward them, and Ansee thrust out his left hand at them. Blue-white light crackled between his outstretched fingers, and then a bolt of lightning lanced across the small clearing, forking out to strike them both. The impact knocked them back half a pace, and lightning skittered across their bodies, but Kai was amazed to see them both looking like they were laughing. At the same moment, Ansee let out a loud scream, and Kai turned his head to see the Seeker's body jerk and spasm before falling to the ground.

"Ansee!" Kai stumbled back, forgetting about Brenna. He picked up Ansee's unconscious body and draped him over his shoulder. Then he began to run as fast as he could away from the creatures. He didn't look back. He only cared about saving Ansee. But then he heard Brenna give a cry and his training slowly returned. His mother's voice scolded him, "Never leave a fellow constable to face danger alone. When others flee, we run toward danger to protect the citizens of this city." Brenna needed his help.

Kai set Ansee down and ran back to the clearing. He could see the four creatures surrounding the cleric. They lashed out at her, her cries stabbing at him directly. He had failed to protect her. Her knees buckled under the assault and she collapsed. "Brenna! No!"

One of the creatures turned and stared at him. It began

walking forward, arms outstretched. "Dreen is truth…"

"Oh, shut up!" Kai swung his sword, aiming for the creature's exposed neck. The blade sliced in but slowed on the hard sinew and bone. Kai felt a corresponding pain in his own neck and nearly doubled over. *Basvu, what in the hells are these creatures?*

The creature was on him before he could react. It slashed at him with both hands; long, wicked claws that raked at him. One slid down the armor on his chest, leaving long marks but not breaking through. The other claw sliced his arm above his bracer. The wound hurt, but not as badly as the strange pain that he'd felt when he'd attacked the creatures. He stepped back and lifted his sword. *Why does it feel heavier? I can't be that tired from this fight yet.* He lifted the weapon and blocked the next attack. *I need to get out of here. I don't dare attack these things again.*

Two other creatures tried to flank Kai and he began to defensively swing his sword to fend off their attacks. A part of him wondered why he didn't feel anything when he struck their arms with the blade as they attacked him, but he was too busy parrying their claws to give it much thought. *That's a question for when I get out of this.*

Just then, one of the creatures slipped a claw under his sword and slashed his chest, digging through his armor. Kai yelled a curse and he stumbled, his knees wobbly.

Footsteps sounded behind him and he panicked, fearing that one of the creatures had gotten around him. He saw Brenna move and slowly stand up; all the color and life had drained from her. He flinched as a hand touched his shoulder, and then he heard Ansee say, "*Bizi eve götür!*"

A brilliant yellow light enveloped Ansee and Kai. There was a double popping noise as the spell gated them away from the clearing.

Chapter 23

Reva lifted her empty goblet to signal the barkeep. It took a moment before Burl Pfletcher noticed and nodded his understanding. She put the goblet down and waited for him to bring her refill.

Pfletcher's pub—nobody called him Burl—was called The Beehive and was located in Merchant's Grove, next door to Pfenestra's Playhouse. It was because of the latter that Reva knew The Beehive—and Pfletcher—so well. She always stopped into The Beehive whenever she saw a play next door.

Tonight, she sat near the front door and gazed out the smoky, but still translucent, windows onto the street. It gave the scene a surreal feel as if she was seeing the city but was apart from it, like looking at it through a seer's crystal ball. She watched now as theatergoers were heading to Pfenestra's to catch the late performance. (Pfenestra was starting a new play called *Talia* that Reva had thought about taking Aavril to see. That idea was now chopped down.)

The Beehive was—buzzing. Reva smiled at her little joke. Pfletcher had named his pub aptly. She'd never been here when there wasn't a crowd. It was always filled with people getting ready to go to, or coming from, the theater. And Pfletcher always had musicians, bards, or other entertainers to perform songs or humorous skits on the small stage in The Beehive's back room. Tonight, there was a troupe of musicians playing upbeat Highland music; a mandolin player, a drummer with a bodhrán, and a woman who sang and played the flute. The music reminded Reva of her brother Gale, who was currently serving in the Highlands. Right now, they were playing a fast-paced reel and several patrons were attempting to dance to it; a task made difficult by the tables in their way.

"Here you go, Inspector." Pfletcher stood next to her with a clay bottle of wine. Pfletcher didn't look like the typical barkeep—or at least not how the playwrights always liked to portray them—as burly, overweight, and bearlike elves. Pfletcher was nineteen hands tall and as thin as a sapling. His brown hair was braided in a simple braid that easily touched the small of his back, and his bright green eyes always lit up when he served Reva.

"Thank you, Pfletcher." Reva held out her goblet and he poured in a generous helping of a deep burgundy wine.

"Oh, damn. Looks like I gave you too much." He'd poured the wine so that it nearly overflowed the goblet. "Well, why don't you just pay me the normal price?"

Reva smiled even though this was an old game between them. There were just a few places where Reva refused to accept any gifts or services for being a Constable. The Beehive was one. It had never been in her patrol area when she'd been a Birch and she'd been frequenting the pub for several years before Pfletcher had learned that she was a Constable. He'd tried to give Reva her drinks for free, but she'd insisted that she continue to pay. She knew that a couple of other Constables already regularly visited The Beehive and she hadn't wanted to become a burden on Pfletcher. Too many Constables tapping the tree for sap might dry up the source and get Pfletcher upset. They'd reached an agreement where Reva paid for her drinks, but he always served her. He always gave her a generous portion.

Reva placed three Acorns on the table and Pfletcher picked up the copper coins, putting them in the pouch at his belt. "You better hurry if you are going to catch the start of the play," he said.

Reva carefully lifted her goblet and took a drink. "I'm not going to the play." She realized that there was more bitterness in her words than she'd intended, and by Pfletcher's expression he had noticed it, too. She shrugged, "Maybe I'll see it tomorrow," she said airily, trying to cover up her anger at Aavril. She had really wanted to see this play and she wasn't going to let him ruin that.

"It's pretty good. You'll enjoy it. There's a nice plot twist at the end, and the writing's better than most."

"Isn't it a new writer?"

"Yes, her name is Christy King, from the Retoca area." He managed to make it sound like he wouldn't hold that circumstance of her birth in the southern part of the country against her. "And they have a new, young actress playing the lead. She's perfect for the part."

In addition to being a pub owner, Pfletcher was also an amateur theater critic. A recommendation from Pfletcher to his patrons could make a play be a rousing success or a dismal flop. Pfenestra had realized the importance of getting Pfletcher's opinion and had started inviting him in to see shows before they opened in the hopes that Pfletcher would give them positive reviews. "I'm sure others will say it's not as good as *Dirty Deeds* was, but I think *Talia* will draw a good crowd."

"Which is always good for you."

"Naturally," Pfletcher smiled. There was a loud crash from the back room, followed by raucous laughter. Reva and Pfletcher both turned to see what had happened. "Excuse me, Inspector, while I go see if I need to throw anybody out." He stalked toward the back of the pub.

Reva carefully lifted the goblet to take another drink of

the wine. This was her fifth generous goblet and the wine's effects were tickling at her mind. Her plan was to get drunk and forget about the Constabulary, LCI Betulla, and *Isean Paroth*. After how they'd all treated her today, she figured that she had the right to get drunk.

"How do I get a serving like that?"

Reva looked up at the elf standing next to her table. It took her a moment to recognize Inquisitor Rhus Amalaki. (She told herself that it was due to him being in civilian dress and not the wine that had dulled her senses.) His hair was loose, hanging in a wavy mass of light brown around his shoulders. He wore tan leggings and a bright green shirt.

"Special dispensation," Reva said.

"Ah. So, I don't have to sleep with Pfletcher then."

"I don't think you're his type."

"Oh, I don't know. I might surprise him."

Reva raised one eyebrow. "So the Green Cloaks *do* know everything about everybody."

Amalaki shook his head. "Far from it. But I spend a lot of time at Pfenestra's, and here. It's hard to not learn things when you sit quietly and listen to the people around you." He gestured to the open seat at Reva's table. Reva kicked the chair out with one foot so he could sit.

"How come I've never seen you there before?" She took another drink of wine.

"Probably because you sit up front, nearest the stage. I prefer to sit in the balcony."

Reva wagged a finger at him. "So you *are* spying on everybody."

"Well. It's my duty to be a spy. And I am quite good at it."

"And are you rooting out traitors to the King right now?"

"No. I have a rare night off. But one is never really off duty. You should know that."

Reva leaned back in her chair and picked up her goblet. "For once I have no cares or worries."

"How fortunate for you. But why are you not spending it with your boyfriend? Didn't I hear that his ship docked yesterday?"

Reva felt her brow furrow as she took a long pull on the wine, draining the goblet. She set it down on the table with a loud CLUNK. "I wanted a bit of time alone."

"Would you like a refill?" Amalaki gestured to the goblet.

"You buying?"

In response, he picked up her goblet and headed to the bar. Reva's head was starting to swim with the wine. Something was tickling at the back of her mind, but she wasn't sure what it was. Amalaki returned a few minutes later carrying two goblets. Her goblet was short a couple of fingers worth of wine.

"They shorted me."

"Apparently I don't have your charm." He took a drink, his eyes searching her face for something.

"What?" she asked, testily. She didn't like how he was looking at her.

"Why do you continue to work for the Constabulary? It's clear that they don't appreciate your talents."

"I suppose you'd have me become a Green Cloak."

"You avoided my question."

Reva drained the goblet and set it down. She had avoided the question because right now she wasn't sure why she was still working for the RTC. "I love my job," she said quickly, hoping to avoid a longer discussion.

"And yet you get treated no better than a common criminal. Certainly, what happened to you today wasn't fair."

"Life isn't fair."

"Come now, Inspector." Amalaki drew out her title. "We both know that's a crock of philosophical hawkshit. You are the victim of a personal vendetta, and you know that it will continue. Betulla will not be satisfied until she has gotten rid of you."

"I can deal with the LCI. She won't beat me."

Amalaki paused for a moment as he took a slow drink. He set the goblet down and ran a finger along its rim. "I just wonder why you are even giving her the opportunity. There are other jobs where people will appreciate your skill."

Reva laughed. "You *are* trying to recruit me."

"You would make a good Inquisitor, but I think you'd chafe under our own regulations just as much. But you could work for the Royal Guard, or even freelance."

Reva shook her head. "I'm a Constable, just like my father. It's in my blood. I can deal with whatever Betulla does. I won't give her the satisfaction of beating me."

"Have you seen the new play?" Amalaki finished his wine.

Reva wagged her finger at him again. "Don't interrogate me." She'd used the technique enough herself to know what he was doing. "You'll have to be satisfied with knowing that I won't be leaving the Constabulary any time soon."

He shrugged as if conceding something but said, "I thought it was a very good performance, considering King is an unknown playwright around here. With the right patron, she could go far."

Reva eyed Amalaki. She was usually really good at reading people, but she didn't know what he wanted. And she'd had too much wine already to give her a clear head in the matter. *Damn it, all I wanted to do was get drunk.* He was still talking about the play, being careful to not give away any details, which meant that he was just blowing leaves around as far as Reva was concerned, but she knew he was digging for something else. He had to be. She didn't know a Green Cloak who didn't stash away every tidbit of gossip or observation like a squirrel storing nuts for winter. With Malvaceä, she'd have an idea of what he wanted, but she hadn't worked with Amalaki long enough to know his intention.

Amalaki paused in his description of how great the sets for *Talia* looked and Reva said, "This has been nice and all, but I need to get home." She stood up to leave.

Amalaki touched her arm and she narrowed her eyes, a look that he ignored. "Be careful, Inspector."

"I'm a big girl. I think I can find my way home."

He gave a gentle shake of his head. "Betulla hates you. She lost a lot of face with the Grand Inquisitor over the Locera murders. I don't know the details or why, but I know that not all is right in your house."

Reva pulled her arm away. "Like I said, I'm a big girl." She walked out of The Beehive without looking back. The air outside was cool and little pricks of gooseflesh tickled her skin. Her mind was swimming as she made her way toward Queen's Bridge, and it wasn't all from the wine. Amalaki had clearly warned her, not that he needed to. Reva knew that Betulla was a succubus, and she knew that the LCI had been mad about how the Locera case had turned out. She also knew that Betulla and Grand Inquisitor Agera had a secret connection that wasn't related to their official duties. She'd pieced that together after seeing her family tree in the secret room under Pfeta fey Orung. She suspected that Agera had used his influence to get Betulla the LCI position because she'd have never gotten it on merit.

Was Amalaki warning me, or had he been fishing for his own information? He'd repeatedly said that he wasn't anything like Malvaceä, but Reva didn't trust any of them. *Is he trying to investigate Betulla? Or even his boss?* Reva laughed at that, a dark, ironic laugh that scared a couple that had been strolling along ahead of her.

If Amalaki looks too hard, he's liable to uncover something that will shake him to his roots. That is, if he lives to learn the information, Reva thought. She didn't think that Agera would allow anybody to know his secrets. The Grand Inquisitor hadn't had to resort to violence with Reva since he'd threatened her with revealing her father's family tree. She'd not been able to destroy the illuminated parchment, even though it was a lie. Reva knew that—or at least thought she knew that. She only had Locera's word that it had been a fake, and he was dead. She figured that Agera would have a copy of the family tree somewhere, able to produce it at any time to implicate Reva of being a dark elf halpbloed if she ever tried to expose his secret. It was a stalemate that she could live with. For now.

Still, she had to wonder as to what exactly Amalaki's intentions had been tonight.

Embankment Road near Mother's shop was quieter—and darker—than The Beehive or Queen's Bridge. The shops were all closed up for the night. Reva pulled out a key from a pouch and was surprised when an elf stepped out of the shadows at the corner of Mother's shop.

"Good evening, Reva."

"Shit!" Reva jumped at the elf's sudden appearance and dropped her key. Instinct and training propelled her back a step and she grabbed for her dagger.

Aavril raised his hands. "Whoa, Reva. It's just me, Aavril. I'm not a thief in the night."

"Damn it! You scared the shit out of me." She relaxed her posture and bent down to pick up the key. She swayed as she did so, putting a hand out against the side of the house to steady herself. At the same time, the anger that had been simmering all afternoon toward Aavril boiled over.

Aavril reached down and put a hand on her shoulder. "Are you alright?" he asked as he helped her to stand.

Reva shrugged him away. "I don't need your help."

Aavril sniffed loudly. "Are you drunk?"

"Maybe I am." She glared at him. "What are you going to do about it, *Isean*?" She put as much disgust and contempt into his title as she could. Aavril's face went pale and Reva gave a bitter laugh.

"What, *Isean*? Nothing to say, *Isean*? You certainly didn't say a damn thing yesterday, *Isean*!"

"I was going to tell you. But *you* got called away on another of your precious cases." Aavril's face started to flush.

"Oh, so it's *my* fault that I didn't know about *your* promotion. It's *my* fault that you aren't going to stay here with me. *Like. You. Promised.*"

"Damn it, Reva—"

Reva cut him off. "Shut up! You don't have the right to say anything to me."

"The hells I don't!"

Reva shook her head. "No. You don't." She jabbed a finger accusingly at Aavril. "You went and made a decision about *our* life without me! You decided that you didn't want me to be a part of it anymore!"

Aavril grabbed for Reva's arm but she slapped his hand away. "You don't know what you're talking about," he said. "Of course, I want you to be a part of my life."

"Oh, so I get to be a part of *your* life," Reva snorted. "Why can't you be a part of *my* life?"

"Stop sorting moss."

"Fine. Why did you take a promotion that will keep you at sea? You promised me that you'd leave the ship. You said you'd open a shop here so that we could be together. Were you lying to me then, too?"

"I never promised I'd do any damn thing! But maybe I'd be willing to stay here if you'd commit to getting married. But since you're already married to your damn job, that'll never happen!"

"Again, it's my fault that you want to stay away from me. My job is a hell of a lot more important than yours." She poked her finger into his chest. "And I won't give it up for any damn sailor, no matter his rank. If you can't get that through the bark around your skull, then you can just leave!"

"Fine!" Aavril huffed. He started to leave, and then turned around, pointing his own finger at Reva. "I'm glad I took that promotion. It finally showed me what kind of person you really are, you ungrateful succubus."

The slap of Reva's palm against Aavril's face reverberated across the silent road. The chill in Reva's voice was palpable as she said, "Go back to your precious ship, *Isean*."

Aavril's hand went to his cheek and the shock was clear on his face. He started to say something, then shut his mouth to form a tight line. He turned and stalked off into the night.

Reva watched him leave, her blood boiling and her heart aching, and then turned to the door. Her hands shook as she unlocked the door, and she was surprised to find that her legs felt weak. She wiped away a single tear that had slid down her face as she stepped into the shop.

Chapter 24

Ansee's command for the teleportation spell had been instinctive. "Take us home." The small clearing in Nuphar Wood and the undead creatures had disappeared in a flash of yellow light, the scene instantly replaced by Ansee's flat. There was a loud popping noise that shook some of the smaller lizard statues on the shelves, and Ansee and Kai found themselves in the middle of Ansee's living area. Ember, who'd been dozing above the door—a favorite spot from which she could drop down onto Ansee when he came home—gave a startled hiss as she jumped nearly three hands into the air. She landed with a dull THUD and scurried into the safety of the fireplace.

"Damn it, Ansee! Warn me next time before doing that. I think I left my stomach back in the woods."

"I can send you back if you want."

Kai narrowed his eyes, "Hells, no."

"I'm sorry that saving our lives was more important than upsetting your stomach." Ansee started to shake, the terror of the encounter finally hitting him.

Kai sheathed his sword. "I'll forgive you this time." He sounded relieved and Ansee saw the beginning of smile. Kai then wobbled a bit and he threw out a hand.

Ansee reached for Kai and now noticed the blood flowing freely from the wounds on his arms and chest. "Are you going to be alright? My sister is a healer. We can go see her."

"These are just scratches," Kai said, dismissively. "You're the one who lost consciousness." Kai swayed some more and started to fall. Ansee caught him and guided Kai to the armchair by the fireplace.

"You need to sit down before you fall down."

"What in the hells were those things?"

Ansee grabbed a chair from the kitchen and sat down. "I don't know. But I know they weren't zombies."

"When I hit them...It was strange. I could actually feel my blows. Here." He touched his stomach and then rubbed a hand across his neck. "I mean, I felt the pain as if I'd been the one that had been stabbed or had somebody try to cut my head off. It felt real."

Ansee's hand automatically rubbed his own neck at the spot where Roya Locera had tried to sever his own head less than a month ago. He hadn't told anybody—not even Reva—that he'd been having nightmares about that attack, reliving it several times a week. In the nightmares, he always moved too slowly, his attempts to block the Fury Blade sluggish, while the blade moved in a blur as it sliced off chunks of Ansee like a butcher carving up a hog. In no time, Ansee was nothing but a collection of body parts and a head that stared up at Locera behind the Basvu mask. As Locera swung the blade toward his head, the mask would gape open to reveal long rows of sharp fangs and Ansee would jerk awake in bed, a sheen of cold sweat covering his body.

"Ansee? Hello," Kai snapped his fingers. "Seeker Carya."

"What?"

"You were staring off into the void there. Are you sure you're alright?"

"Sorry. I felt the same thing. The pain, I mean. When my spells hit those creatures, it felt as if I'd been struck by my own magic. I don't think I like knowing what it feels like to be struck by a bolt of lightning."

"Why did it happen?" He paused for a moment, and then added, "And if we'd kept attacking them, could we have died?"

Ansee shuddered. He didn't want to think about that possibility, so he stood up and adjusted the position of a pair of green soapstone lizards perched on the mantle. "I don't know the answer," he finally admitted. "For either of your questions. Since I went unconscious, and the pain felt real—"

"It was real."

"Then I'd have to guess that, yes, you could die if you continued to attack them."

"That's not a comforting thought." He stared into the hearth of the fireplace for a few moments. "I'm positive that two of those creatures were our missing cleric and the library watchelf. The other two were probably our missing bodies from the flower shop. I recognized the woman's dress."

Ansee nodded. He'd been able to get a good look at the cleric before Brenna had rushed forward but hadn't been able to see the others clearly. He trusted Kai's eyes, though.

"We need to tell CI Pflamtael," Kai said.

Now that he was home and the stress of battle was gone, sleep was coming on fast. "I'm exhausted. I'll tell them in the morning." Ansee stifled a yawn as he spoke.

Kai stood up. He looked a bit uncertain on his feet, but he remained standing. "I'll see you in the morning, then." He walked to the door and Ansee followed.

"*Reis naeht*," he said, closing the door with a wave. He then walked to his bed and fell into it, still fully clothed. He was asleep as soon as his head hit the pillow.

Ember finally poked her head out from the fireplace and scurried over to the bed. She climbed up and circling a few times, curled up next to Ansee, her warmth giving him comfort as he slept.

Chapter 25

The rustle of leaves and the snap of branches brought Erroll's head up. He could sense his disciples coming and smiled to himself. *Our numbers continue to grow.* He watched the disciples enter the small clearing through the thick underbrush, their slow gait and methodical chanting gave Erroll the feeling that they were all truly blessed to have been touched by Dreen's divine grace.

He approached his newest disciple, commanding her to stop with a simple thought. She stopped moving but continued her slow, patient chant. She wore a cleric's vestment identical to the other disciple, though she appeared to be older. The long claw marks in her chest and arms showed him how she'd received Dreen's blessing. Already, her own fingers were changed, the skin pulled back and the bone grown into sharp claws. Her face was starting to lose its color. Soon she'd be as pallid as the other disciples.

Erroll nodded in greeting. "Welcome, fair disciple of Dreen. Rejoice in Dreen's truth and share in our enlightenment."

The new disciple continued the slow mantra. "Dreen is pain...pain is truth...Dreen is truth..."

Erroll's jaw clenched and his ears flushed. "Say something different for a change. Share His enlightenment with me!" He lashed out and slapped the disciple on the cheek. He instantly felt a comforting sting in his own cheek. The other disciples turned to face him, and he sensed their excitement, their lust for pain. He quieted them with a thought, and all five clustered together to continue their endless chant.

My disciples are just a tool, Erroll told himself. *They only understand Dreen's truth on the most basic level. I need somebody that I can speak to, somebody who can understand Dreen's love as I do, and who can share in His enlightenment.*

Erroll walked to a fallen tree and sat down. He leaned back and let the sting of the pain in his back focus his mind. He stared off into the darkness of the forest, and as he listened to the unending chant from the disciples, the trees gave way to the hot stone of the plaza. He was still bound to the pillar, and his lips were cracked from the sun, though he noticed it was starting to set. The whips had stopped, but Erroll could now hear the sound of horses and men approaching him. The voice of the goateed man shouted for the men to hurry, to deal with the heretic.

Erroll smiled and continued his prayer to Ados, absolving the god of His sin; that he, Dreen, was suffering for Him. The men roughly pulled him from the pillar and laid him on the hot stone. Erroll didn't bother to resist, or to try to make an escape. He felt rough ropes tied tightly about his wrists and ankles and saw that the ends of the ropes were tied to the pommels of the saddles on the horses.

"Do it! Now!" yelled the goateed man, and Erroll knew what was coming.

"My pain redeems Ados!" he yelled at the top of his lungs. The men whipped each of the horses. "My suffering absolves His failure!" The horses bolted, the ropes quickly going taut. "My pain redeems Ados! My suffering—"

Erroll couldn't contain the loud scream that escaped his mouth as the horses reached the ends of their tethers. The ropes bit hard as his body was pulled and, within a second, he felt the searing pain as all four limbs were torn from their sockets. The scream he gave echoed around the plaza as blood flowed freely from the jagged holes where his arms and legs had just been detached.

Erroll's scream ceased as the pain consumed him, and he stared, unblinking, at the goateed man, who turned away, a satisfied smile on his face. Then Erroll felt it again, the gentle cooling and tingling sensation. He could see one arm, several feet away, but he could feel it as though it was still attached to his body. He could even feel the fingers twitch. He started to laugh, a proud, joyous laugh. "My pain redeems Lord Ados! My suffering absolves His failure!"

The goateed man spun around quickly, the cloth of his blue turban fluttering with the sudden motion. Erroll could see his arm melt, like a wax candle left in the sun, and then it seemed to flow out of his body, once again whole.

The goateed man's face was red with rage. "The heretic continues to blaspheme our Lord! Marak," he yelled to one of the other men. "Send for the others. We have no choice but to burn the heretic until only ashes remain!"

Suddenly, the scene changed and Erroll found himself on the *Majestic Tern*, his arms bound to the mast. A biting pain gnawed at his back, and he felt the sting of the whip, followed by Aavril's voice calling out, "Five."

Each lash of the whip was placed with exquisite care. Delivering the necessary punishment, but not with cruelty. Another painful sting and Erroll realized how the pain focused him, cleared his mind. Aavril had a gift that brought clarity with the punishment. The pain brought knowledge.

Pain brings enlightenment.

The crack of the whip again sounded, Aavril's voice calling out "Seven." The crack and sting lifted his spirit.

Enlightenment is the first step to rebirth.

"Eight." Erroll could feel his spirit lift, his past failures absolved.

Pain brings rebirth. Reborn, our sins are forgiven.

"Nine."

Yes, I see it now. I know what must be done.

Erroll started awake, the cool of the clearing replacing the muggy heat of the ship. The pain in his back was fresh, and he could feel blood seeping from the old wounds. The pain brought the clarity that he needed.

Erroll would need more than just his disciples to convert the citizens of Tenyl. They served a purpose, but he needed something more. He needed people who understood pain and how it could be delivered to clear the mind. They needed to be disciplined in order to convert to Dreen's truth. Only then would they understand and become closer to Dreen. Erroll knew he wasn't the one to apply this discipline. He needed somebody skilled. He needed the elf who'd awakened his own mind. *I need Aavril Paroth.*

The Quartermaster of the *Majestic Tern* had been carrying out the Captain's orders, but the way he did it had tended to Erroll's absolution. Aavril had known exactly when to apply the next lash just as the pain from the previous one was receding. He'd helped Erroll see the truth then, cleaned him of his past. The Quartermaster had been part of Erroll's transformation, part of his awakening to Dreen's enlightenment.

Yes! Erroll now knew how he needed to proceed. *Aavril is the key. I will be able to speak about Dreen's enlightenment with him, about His purpose for us. Together we will spread Dreen's message to all parts of the Kingdom. We will gain willing converts who will know Dreen's truth.*

Erroll smiled to himself in the darkness of the small clearing. His disciples sensed his mood and they began to chant louder, their voices rising up to the stars. *Yes. Aavril is the key to spreading Dreen's message.* With that, Erroll closed his eyes, falling asleep to the disciples' comforting chant.

"Dreen is pain...pain is truth...Dreen is truth..."

Chapter 26

Aavril stared across the mouth of the Tenz, watching the sunrise over Black Elf Bay. The morning air was cool, and he soaked in the salt air along with the first rays of the sun. Fisherelves were raising their sails to head out to the bay for the day, their decks filled with nets. Smaller boats rowed past the docks, wooden lobster and crab pots stacked neatly around the rowers.

The docks were bustling as well. A large, two-masted merchant ship—the *Golden Aspen*—was preparing to leave on the morning tide, and her crew was busy reeling in the lines and setting her sails. Aavril clearly heard her captain's shouted orders, the crew moving quickly to carry them out.

Aavril envied them. He wanted to be at sea right now. To feel the roll of the deck and the sea spray as the ship moved through the waves. He wanted to climb to the top spar on the mast to scan the horizon for other ships and possible dangers. *Out at sea, I only have to worry about the ship and the crew and what awaits us.*

Aavril lowered his head and stared at the brown water lapping against the *Tern's* stern. *Things are so much simpler at sea. Why can't they ever be as simple on land?* After last night's fight with Reva, he figured that he now had two problems: finding Loren and patching things up with Reva.

As to the latter, Aavril tried to tell himself that Reva hadn't meant to say the things that she did. She'd obviously been drunk, and clearly not herself. *So? It's hard for a drunk to lie. She was obviously telling me how she really felt.*

Besides, where does she come off blaming me for making my own decisions? Sure, he'd accepted the promotion without talking to her about it. *Why shouldn't I? It's my life.* And yes, he hadn't been able to tell her about the promotion at dinner, but that wasn't his fault. *If she hadn't fled dinner for one of her damn cases, I'd have told her everything. How is that my fault when she's always working?*

He didn't know how Reva had learned about his promotion, but that didn't matter now. She'd not heard about it from him first. So, to Reva, that meant that he was clearly trying to hide it from her.

She's being stubborn, Aavril told himself. *She doesn't want to discuss my plans or my feelings about leaving the sea.* She certainly didn't want to talk about the future—marriage and children—that they might have together. *She's always changing the subject, refusing to discuss it. Her job is too important.* She'd said before that she wouldn't give it up for a family. *But she doesn't even want to discuss how we could make a family work.*

Aavril spit into the water. *If she won't talk about a future with me,* he thought grimly, *why should I give her one? Why would I give up the sea just to make her happy? Everything has to be about her. She always has to have everything her way.*

Aavril looked back at the rising sun, letting the warm rays bathe his face. He did a few navigational problems in his head to calm himself and clear his mind. He needed to think clearly.

After a few minutes, he thought, *Am I the one being stubborn? Am I being selfish?* He thought about it a bit more and finally told himself, *maybe.* He'd certainly not considered her feelings when he took the promotion. He'd known from their first date just how important her job was to her. And how much she valued the truth. She was a constable, and the daughter of a constable, after all. *And I've been so distracted with the promotion and Loren's disappearance that I've not really given any consideration to her.*

He watched the *Golden Aspen* cast off from the dock. The ship glided easily through the water, and a feeling of emptiness overcame him. *I don't want our relationship to end.*

But that wouldn't matter if Reva really had trimmed him. He needed to talk to her, to try to clear things up, to let her know that he'd made some mistakes and that they needed to talk things through. But he needed to wait until she sobered up and her head had cleared. Besides, he had a more critical problem to deal with right now. *Loren.*

Aavril had been concerned yesterday by Loren's absence, but not worried. Mad as hell, yes, but not really worried. He'd been too focused on getting the supplies and being able to pay for them. But when Loren still hadn't shown up by nightfall, Aavril's anger had turned to worry.

That's why he'd gone to Reva's last night, to tell her that Loren was missing. He'd been surprised to find out that she wasn't home and that Aeollas didn't know where she was. He'd thought she'd been on a case and decided to wait outside, but when she'd staggered home, reeking of wine and out of her uniform, he'd been shocked. He'd completely forgotten about Loren at the time.

Now Aavril was thinking that something ill had befallen the Captain, and it was time to get the constables involved, even if it meant going to somebody other than Reva. He wasn't sure what had happened to Loren, but he suspected that one of the thieves' guilds was involved. They made demands on the ships that used the port and, if they learned that Loren had become Captain, it was possible that they'd made a demand for payment from him. The elder Captain Sterna had made his deals years ago, but with a new

Captain, Aavril was sure that the guilds would see a chance to renegotiate. That would have been trouble, as Loren hated the guilds and their fingers getting into everything. And he could be quite stubborn. Aavril didn't know what the guilds could have done to Loren, but it wouldn't be good.

After his fight with Reva, Aavril didn't have easy access to the Constabulary, and making a general report about a missing elf would probably get tossed to the upper branches where nothing would be done. Missing elves were not a high priority for the RTC. *No, I'll need to find Loren on my own.*

Aavril turned from the stern rail and walked down to the main deck. He gave a quick look at the deck and saw that everything was in place, ready to receive the cargo that the merchants would deliver tomorrow. The crew still had some minor repairs to make, but they would be done by the end of the day.

He headed to the stairs and down to the hold. The space directly under the quarterdeck was reserved for the crew, and he found Kelsey and the others preparing breakfast. At sea, it was usually dried and salted fish or eel, hardtack (with or without weevils), dried mushrooms, and pine needle tea to fight off scurvy. Since they were in port, though, the crew could splurge, so they had fresh fish, grapes, and some goat cheese. Somebody had even found some ground cacao beans, which were steeping on the small stove. It wasn't what you'd get at a fancy cacao house, but it was better than pine needle tea.

Kelsey looked up from his plate, "Mornin', *Isean.*"

"Good morning, everyone. Are we looking forward to caulking a few holes today?"

"Oh, aye," Janish said with an exaggerated roll of his eyes. "We love spending our days in the bilge." Everybody laughed good-naturedly.

"Well, I'll treat everyone to a round—one round only,

mind you—at the Knotty Leg tonight. After you've all had a good bath, of course." They all laughed and cheered. "We have cargo arriving tomorrow and we won't be able to reach those spaces once it's on board."

"Sir," Kelsey said. "Any word on tha Cap'n?"

Aavril shook his head. The whole crew knew that Loren was missing. It was impossible to hide the fact. "No. I'll be going to see Captain Sterna this morning and tell him. Maybe he knows something, and if not, then he deserves to know."

"Finishin' tha repairs an' loadin' our cargo would be easier with a full crew. We're down three with Erroll gone, no replacement for you, an' tha Cap'n missin'. If we're leavin' at tha end of tha week we shoulda had a new Quartermaster signed on yesterday." Kelsey didn't bother to hide his irritation.

Aavril understood Kelsey's frustration. The captain decided who to hire for ship's officers. The *Isean* could hire other crew, but with Loren gone and Aavril busy trying to find him *and* make sure that the necessary work got done so they could sail at the end of the week, he'd not had time to think about filling either position.

"Send Donnell around and let folks know we're hiring for a deckhand," Aavril said. "Have them here at dinner and I'll get one hired. If the Captain hasn't been found today, I'll hire a quartermaster tomorrow."

Kelsey nodded and stuffed several grapes into his mouth. Aavril could tell that he wasn't happy about any of this. *Neither am I, but we have no choice.* They needed to get the *Tern* ready if they were going to sail on time. If Loren was found and was upset about any of it, Aavril would just tell him that it had been his fault for leaving them in this position.

Aavril grabbed some grapes and cut into the cheese. "I'll be back as soon as I can to help with the repairs." He headed back to the main deck.

Kelsey followed him and waited until they were on the deck before asking, "Aavril, lad. What happens if'n we can't locate Loren? Or if somethin' has happened ta him?"

Aavril looked out at the receding form of the *Golden Aspen* in the bay. "I don't know, Kelsey. I don't know."

Chapter 27

Seeker Ansee Carya awoke with a start. He'd had another nightmare, though thankfully this one didn't involve Locera and the Fury Blade. Instead, he'd dreamed about zombies that could turn any person into an undead at a single touch. Ansee had been helpless as his friends and family were consumed by the undead tide. Each time he'd tried to stop the horde, he was punched in the chest by some invisible force. Ansee had been standing in the middle of King's Bridge, the zombies approaching from both ends, when he woke up.

Early morning light filtered through the windows, and Ember gave a croak from the cold hearth. Ansee got out of bed and completed his morning routine. As he got his tea and Ember's crickets ready, he kept recalling the encounter in The Brambles last night.

"I have no idea what these creatures were," he told the fire salamander. Ember looked at him expectantly, but only because Ansee was still holding the crickets. "They weren't zombies, though they did look like them. How can I convince CI Pflamtael that they are real, and our murder victims are with them?"

Ember gave an annoyed croak.

"Well, I can't take this to Reva. She's been put on suspension."

Ember cocked her head and let forth another low croak.

"I know, Reva will want to know about this, even if she can't do anything about it. Maybe I can tell her this afternoon once Pflamtael's dealt with them."

Ember jumped onto the low bookshelf by the fireplace. With a flick of her red and black tail, she shoved aside a wooden lizard and started pulling out a random book from the shelf. Smoke began curling from the pages gripped in her mouth.

"Hey! Stop that!" Ansee rushed over and grabbed the book, dropping the crickets on the floor. "Fine, I'll go see Reva this morning. You don't have to be destructive."

Ember ignored him and chased down her breakfast.

† † †

"Reva, wake up! Reva, wake up!"

It sounded like her mother, but the sharp caw between sentences told Reva that it was Gabii, sitting at the foot of her bed.

"Go away, bird," Reva mumbled, kicking out with a foot and pulling the blanket over her head.

There was a flutter of wings, then, "Reva, wake up!" sounded loudly in her ear. Sharp pain spiked itself between Reva's closed eyes and she waved a hand, trying to swat at Gabii. The bird deftly avoided her feeble attempt.

The parrot gave a shake of its blue and green feathers, making a sound like she was clearing her throat. "I'm up, I'm up," Reva moaned, dragging herself into a sitting position. Gabii cocked her head, and then walked to the edge of the headboard, clearly disappointed that the game was over.

Reva rubbed a hand slowly over her face, and then decided that the headache would probably be the same whether she was sitting or standing. Her mouth was as dry as her mother's kiln and she really had to pee. With a deliberate motion, she stood up, closing her eyes to steady the churning motion of the room, and then walked to the water closet.

After relieving herself and splashing some water on her face, Reva walked into the kitchen. It was too damn early to be up, and she contemplated stuffing Gabii into a sack and going back to bed. Her mind was still a mush of wine-induced haze and she slowly poured water into a cup, adding powdered willow bark for the headache.

"My gods, you look like hell," said a voice behind her.

Reva jumped, spilling some of the willow bark powder, and turned to see Ansee standing at the top of the stairs. "What in the hells are you doing here?"

"Are you hungover?"

She didn't say anything and just gave him a rude gesture instead.

"It's just that I've never seen you get really drunk before." He stepped over to the table and pulled out one of the chairs.

Reva took a long drink, finally removing some of the pottery dust from her mouth. "Who gave you permission to make yourself at home?" She tried to glare at her partner but that just made her headache worse.

Ansee ignored the comment. "I know that Betulla suspended—"

"Shhh." Reva tried to quickly shut Ansee up, but it was too late.

"What was that? Reva?" Aeollas called from downstairs. "Why aren't you ready for work yet? Why is that dragonspawn partner of yours here?"

"It's none of your business, Mother."

"Well, you don't have to act like a halpbloeden about it," Aeollas yelled from downstairs. "But if you're gonna come home drunk and have fights on my doorstep, I'm gonna kick you out."

"Fights?" Ansee asked.

Reva ignored him. Her headache throbbed through her temples and she massaged her forehead. "I can't deal with this."

She walked into her room, leaving Ansee at the table. She returned a minute later, having thrown on a blue-green dress, leather boots, and a plain brown cloak. "Come on," she called to Ansee.

Reva ignored the stern looks and questions fired at her from her mother. She didn't want to deal with her this morning. Too much had happened in the past day. With her suspension, the strange encounter with Amalaki, and the fight with Aavril, there was too much grist for her mom to work with. It would all crack open soon enough, but Reva wanted some good cacao before she had to deal with it.

Reva was thankful that Ansee kept quiet as they walked to the House of Cacao. Twenty minutes after leaving the pottery shop, the beautiful aromas of percolating cacao and warm sweetbreads greeted Reva. Most of her headache instantly evaporated.

Although Reva was late this morning, her usual table was sitting vacant, despite the fact that it was standing room only in the shop. Reva held up two fingers to Ilium as she headed toward her seat, exchanging pleasantries with familiar faces. A second seat materialized for Ansee, and they both sat down.

Two large cups of hot cacao appeared as if by teleportation spell, along with two sweet rolls covered with cranberries and drizzled liberally with honey.

Reva made no move to pay, though she saw Ansee reaching for his coin pouch.

"No, no, no," Ilium said with an emphatic shake of his head. "Your hard-earned Skips are not necessary, Constable."

"I insist," Ansee replied.

Ilium's face contorted into an expression of shock and anger. "You would besmirch my gift and insult me?" He turned to Reva. "I thought you had this one trained?"

Reva shrugged her shoulders and smiled as she picked up her cacao. "Seeker Carya has 'principles.'"

"So do I." Ilium turned with a huff and headed back to his counter.

Reva saw the look in Ansee's eyes. "This isn't about graft or corruption—at least not to elves like Ilium." She tore off some sweetbread. "To him, it's about honor and tradition."

"Is this why we came here? So you could give me an object lesson in how the leaves of business blow?"

"No, although it is a nice side benefit. I wanted my morning cacao and to get away from Mother."

"You haven't told her about being suspended." It was spoken as a statement.

Reva kept quiet, eating the sweet roll and drinking her cacao. How she handled things with her mother was none of Ansee's concern.

"Why aren't you at work?" she asked. "Don't tell me that Betulla suspended you, too?"

Ansee leaned forward and whispered, "I have a break in our case."

"You mean Pflamtael's case."

"I'm going to tell him, too, but I knew that you'd want to know about this." She could hear the excitement building in his voice.

"You found the bodies." It was a statement. There was no other reason Ansee would be this antsy and bothering her this morning.

Ansee nodded. "And some more."

"More?" Reva's curiosity was more than just peaked now. *Do we have a serial killer on our hands?*

"After you left yesterday, a cleric came to report a missing person. Her fellow Ovate. He'd gone to deal with *two zombies near the Great Library*." He added emphasis to the end of the sentence.

Reva had been about to take a drink and slowly set her cup down. "So, our victims were raised after all. But you said there was no evidence of a raise dead spell at the flower shop. What are we dealing with then? A necromancer, or something else?"

"Kai and I didn't see any evidence of a necromancer. And these things didn't behave like any zombie I've ever dealt with."

"And just how many zombies *have* you dealt with?"

"Well, none. But I've read about them and heard stories."

Reva rolled her eyes and then asked the important questions. "Where did you find them?"

"In the Brambles."

Reva nodded. The Brambles was close to Amber's shop in Forest Grove. "So, you and Constable Gania stopped them."

Color rose on Ansee's cheeks and it wasn't from the hot cacao. "Not exactly." Reva raised one eyebrow, and he quickly added, "These things, they look like zombies, but they act differently. They are dangerous. Gania and I almost died last night."

Reva couldn't keep her eyes from going wide. *While I was drowning myself in wine, they were trying to fight undead. At night.* She didn't feel any guilt, only a slowly building anger. "You'd better tell me everything."

Chapter 28

Constable Inspector Pflamtael ducked his head as he entered the pub. The Roots was literally a hole in the ground, the space dug out from around the roots of a massive oak tree that made up part of Noeht Copse in Old Grove. Being built so close to the cemetery kept most of the more respectable clients from patronizing the establishment and, over the centuries, The Roots had become a refuge of illegal gamblers, prostitutes, fences, and assorted ruffians from the Corpse Tenders, one of Tenyl's few thieves' guilds.

Olwyn's eyes adjusted to the dim light in the pub. He wore normal clothes, nothing that would announce that he was a Constable. That was part of the agreement with his informant.

It was early morning, so The Roots was as dead as the neighboring cemetery; there were just a few dedicated punters nursing drinks or sleeping off hangovers. Olwyn walked around the benches and tables toward the back of the pub. A few eyes followed him, sizing him up as a possible mark, but as he approached the occupied table at the very back of the room, they quickly returned to their normal business.

Two huge humans—they stood over 19 hands tall and their muscles strained against their leather armor—stood with their arms crossed in front of the table. "She's not seeing anybody right now," said the human on Olwyn's left.

"Scram, pixie," said the other bodyguard.

Pixie? "Are things so bad, Caelyn, that you have to hire human fungus?"

"Olwyn?" called a mellifluous voice. "Go toss out the trash or something," she said to the two guards. They glared at Olwyn, but followed their orders and headed off.

Caelyn Silverfrond sat at the back table, a plate of fruit, cheese, and bread spread before her, and a small pot of cacao warming over a candle. She smiled at Olwyn, flashing perfect teeth, and set her cup down.

"Why, Olwyn," she purred. "How is my favorite Constable Inspector this morning?" She leaned back in the chair, giving a toss of her amber-colored hair. Flashes of purple and red light rippled over the hair as it moved.

"That's new," remarked Olwyn.

"It's the latest fad," Caelyn said, running her hand through her hair. More colors flickered across it. "All the young kids are getting illusions cast on their hair. It makes me feel young again."

"Why do you need to feel young? You can't be a day over one hundred." Olwyn gave her a seductive smile. In truth, he knew that Caelyn was at least 150, or maybe she was closer to 160 now. Nobody really knew—not even Caelyn—but she looked younger, and Olwyn knew that she was vain about her looks, so a little flattery was always called for.

"Why, Inspector," she traced a red-painted nail down her smooth, acorn-colored cheek. "You always know the right thing to say. Please, have a seat."

Olwyn pulled out the chair opposite Caelyn and sat down. With the pleasantries done, they could now get down to business. "You still have your contacts down at the docks?"

Caelyn smiled as she picked up a slice of cheese, "You know I do." She narrowed her green eyes. "Is there something that I should be concerned about?"

Olwyn shook his head. He kept Caelyn aware of any raids or crackdowns planned for the docks. The city's three main thieves' guilds all operated around the docks, an arrangement that was tenuous at the best of times. Occasionally, the guilds would get too greedy, or too violent, and then the merchant's guilds or the ship's captains would complain to the Mayor. Then the Mayor would order the RTC to go clean up the port. When that happened, Olwyn would let Caelyn know so that she could protect her people and assets. In exchange, she gave Olwyn tips about the other guilds or information about petty thieves and criminals. As long as they weren't part of her guild, she had no problems cutting the branch out from under them.

"I just need some information of a nautical nature," Olwyn said.

"Do I look like a sailor?" she tittered.

"You are prettier than any sailor I've ever seen," Olwyn beamed. "And you keep a lot of information behind those pretty eyes."

Caelyn smiled and bit into an apple slice. "If I have the information you want, I will be happy to share it."

"I'm looking for a sailor."

"Why, Olwyn. I didn't think your branches twisted that way."

"There's a lot that you don't know about me, Caelyn." He flashed her a coy smile. He was decidedly heterosexual, but a bit of mystery never hurt. "A ship docked a couple of days ago. I'm looking for one of its sailors."

"Ships dock every day. Even I can't keep all of them straight."

Olwyn knew that was a lie. He knew that she kept close tabs on every ship that entered the port. If she didn't, she'd lose income. "The sailor from this ship has skin art on his forearm," he tapped his own forearm to indicate where, "in the shape of a flying bird."

"Sailors love birds." She picked up her cacao, taking a long sip. Olwyn wasn't sure if she was just stalling for time, or if she actually had to think about his question. "But if this ship arrived within the last few days, then it might be Captain Sterna's ship. The *Majestic Tern.*"

Olwyn nodded, and started to get up. Caelyn's hand reached over the table to rest on his own hand. "Leaving so soon?" She widened her eyes and gave him a small pout.

Olwyn took her hand and deftly brought it to his lips, giving it a chaste kiss. "The new LCI has expressed concern over the amount of crime in our fair city."

"Things seem pretty quiet to me."

Olwyn gave a shrug. "Well, she is of the opinion that criminals are running rampant through the streets. She's planning to crack down on criminal activities."

"How very noble of her." Olwyn could see the clockwork mechanisms start to turn behind her beautiful eyes.

"Well, having so many criminal elements in the city is bad for everybody. The LCI is still learning the ropes, so she's not given us any specific orders. Yet."

Caelyn plucked another apple slice off the plate. "And I'm sure she'll listen to you when the time comes."

"Naturally." Olwyn secretly hoped that would be the case. He moved to stand up again and Caelyn didn't stop him this time. He gave her a slight bow. "Until next time."

"Always a pleasure, Inspector."

Olwyn headed toward the exit, passing the two body-guards who were dragging another drunk out of the pub. As he ducked his head through the entrance, he let a small smile form on his lips. *The Majestic Tern.* He now had a ship to go with the sailor. A quick arrest would be a nice bloom in his garden, and well worth the price he had paid.

Chapter 29

Ansee hustled up the stairs at New Port and walked briskly to his table. He felt better after telling Reva everything about the undead. She'd been tight-lipped about what she was going to do with the information. Ansee figured that she was doing it to protect him should she get caught by LCI Betulla. Ansee still planned on giving the news to CI Pflamtael, but he was glad that Reva had the same information.

Norah glared at him from her table where she was studiously preparing her spells. Ansee had a good idea why she hated him; she'd made enough veiled threats about him being something other than a proper wizard, but for some reason, she'd never acted on them. He wasn't sure why.

CI Pflamtael was not at his table, but Senior Constable Ghrellstone walked toward Ansee from the tea nook, a mug of tea in his hand. "You're a bit late this morning, Seeker." Willem grimaced as he drank his tea. Bitter as usual. Ansee was glad he'd had cacao with Reva earlier.

"Overslept," Ansee lied, trying to avoid Willem's eyes.

"Out late last night? I didn't think you were one for pub-hopping."

"We weren't hitting the pubs." Ansee realized his mistake too late.

"We? Did you go on a date? Good for you." Willem gave him a slight nudge in the shoulder.

"It wasn't a date."

"Oh, I gotcha." Willem gave him a conspiratorial wink.

Ansee felt his ears flush. "No, Kai and I—"

Willem held up a hand, waving it frantically. "Whoa. I don't want to—" Ansee cut him off with a rude gesture and Willem laughed. "I'm just twisting yer branches, Seeker." Then his face hardened and he looked pointedly at Ansee.

"This wasn't anything to do with that missing cleric and those zombies?"

Ansee nodded and he saw the Senior Constable's eyes widen. He lowered his voice. "We found the cleric and guard in The Brambles. They'd been turned into undead."

Willem swore under his breath.

"We also found our missing victims," Ansee said.

"You don't mean...?"

Ansee nodded. "They were undead as well."

"Son of a succubus. I hope you put them down."

Ansee shook his head. "We tried, but these weren't regular zombies. There was something wrong about them. Kai and I barely got out with our lives."

"And the Ovate you were helping?"

"She didn't make it."

"Shit, Ansee." Willem's voice was loud, and several constables turned their way. Ansee saw Norah give him a disapproving look before turning back to her spellbook.

"Have you told anybody yet?" Willem asked.

Ansee wasn't sure if he should tell Willem that he'd already told Reva. She hadn't told him to keep it to himself, but he felt that she wanted to keep her involvement quiet. He knew that the Senior Constable wouldn't give a kobold's ass whether Reva knew or not, but he wondered if he should try to protect Willem the same way Reva was trying to protect him.

"Who'd you tell?" Willem persisted.

"Nobody."

"Hawkshit. You make a face when you're thinking about lying."

"I do not."

"Yes, you do," Willem nodded. Ansee kept his mouth shut. "Fine. Are you going to tell CI Pflamtael?"

"Tell Olwyn what?" Norah seemed to materialize at Reva's table. Her arms were crossed, and she was looking daggers at Ansee.

"Morning, Norah," Ansee greeted her politely. She continued to glare at him, and Ansee finally said, "There was a missing person case yesterday. It's connected to the flower shop murders."

Ansee could tell that Norah wanted to tell him to leave their case alone, but his statement had apparently piqued her curiosity. "Connected how?"

"We found the missing person, but he'd been turned into an undead. He was with three other undead creatures at the time, two of whom looked like our flower shop victims."

"Looked like?" Norah asked derisively.

"It's not like I could ask them," Ansee bristled. "But it was a man and a woman. The woman fit the description we have for Amber, and her clothes matched the scraps that we collected at the scene."

Norah put her chin in her hand, tapping one finger on her cheek. "It could be connected with that divine aura at the shop. It was still there when I searched the scene yesterday, so it had to have been a strong spell."

"You double-checked my auras? What in the hells?"

"I wouldn't have to verify your work if you were a *real* spellcaster."

"If our victims have become undead," Willem interrupted, "what does that mean for the case?"

"I don't know," Norah admitted. "But I'll discuss it with Olwyn." She returned to her own table.

Ansee glared after her, still mad that she obviously didn't trust him.

Willem cleared his throat. "Are you still up to give the dagger training tomorrow?"

"Hmm...oh, yeah. There's nothing else really important going on. I'll be there." Ever since Ansee had held off Roya Locera using just a dagger, Willem had been pushing Ansee to show him what he knew."

"Good. We'll be there."

"We?"

"Sure. A couple of the other Seniors want to come, too."

"Great. The more the merrier."

Willem smiled, in a way that Ansee could only describe as predatory, and went over to his own table. A feeling of impending doom started to settle into Ansee's gut. The elaborate practical joke with the gingerbread cookies came to mind, and Ansee started to wonder what Willem might be plotting.

"Seeker Carya!" First Constable Aescel stood in the doorway to his office. "Get in here!"

Ansee stood up, his mind immediately shifting to wondering what Aescel wanted. *Great, just what I need now is to be on Aescel's shit list.* He walked into the office and shut the door.

"*Reis hoestii*, sir," he said, coming to attention.

"Where in the hells were you yesterday? I don't recall Betulla suspending you along with Reva."

"You told me to keep myself busy, so I took a missing person case that came in."

"It wasn't connected with the flower shop murders? You were supposed to turn that case over to CI Pflamtael."

"No, sir," Ansee quickly lied. "It was unrelated to the murder investigation."

Aescel furrowed his brow as if he didn't believe Ansee, and then dismissed the issue with a wave of his hand. He leaned back in his chair and picked up a parchment. "With Reva out, I can't have you working major cases alone." Ansee nodded, glad that he wasn't in any real trouble.

"Nobody needs any help right now, either," the First Constable continued. "There's the usual petty stuff, but the Senior Constables can handle those. I have a floater that came in early this morning." He gave the parchment to Ansee. "Somebody dragged it out of the river. Go see if you can fill out the foliage so we can put the sorry soul to rest."

Ansee nodded, but sighed on the inside. A floater wasn't how he wanted to spend his day. Cases like this were almost impossible to close and were always disgusting. It was their job to find out who the victim was, determine the cause of death, and notify the next of kin, if possible. Most floaters were suicides, sometimes accidental drownings, and the rare murder. But without a crime scene, little could be done except to collect as much information as possible.

Ansee looked at the parchment, noting the basic details: male elf found under King's Bridge by some kids. Brown hair, about 18 hands in height. No obvious cause of death, but wounds were found on the body. *I've had less to go on,* Ansee thought.

"Alchemist Bromide has the body."

"Anything else, sir?"

"That's it for now."

Ansee saluted and turned to leave.

"Oh, and Seeker," Ansee paused in the doorway. "I'm looking forward to your training tomorrow."

Ansee managed to stammer out a reply and quickly left. *Who all did Willem invite to this training?*

Chapter 30

The late morning air was still cool as Reva walked along the road, one of the first heralds that summer was finally over. *Good riddance*, she thought. The summer had been hotter than normal, and she was ready for the relief that autumn would bring.

She entered the tea shop that was located at the corner of Narris Highway and Blackthorn Road. She was surprised that a tea shop still existed in Tenyl. Tea had been the primary drink in the Kingdom for centuries until the traders had brought in the first shipments of cacao. Cacao houses had sprung up like mushrooms after a rainstorm and, within a year, the tea houses had all but disappeared. Tea still ruled in private homes, and there were the ubiquitous tea nooks in most shops and businesses—even at New Port—because it was cheaper and easier to make, but cacao now ruled the marketplaces.

Reva figured that the only reason this shop still existed was because it had been forgotten. There was no bell to announce the presence of a customer, and the shop was no bigger than a breadbox—barely five paces wide and maybe seven deep. It was squeezed between a tavern and a yarn shop. Eight tables were stuffed into the room, so close together that they nearly touched, and there was no space for chairs. An earthy, herbal smell mixed together in the tiny shop, reminding Reva of a flower garden.

Only three customers were in the shop, and Reva wove through the tables to the person standing at the back. He wore the same yellow vest he'd had on the other day, but today his leggings were a horrible mismatch of one leg in black and red stripes while the other leg was actually baggy black jodhpurs. His shirt was a similar monstrosity of different styles, fabrics, and patterns that had been haphazardly sewn together. The ensemble was causing her headache to begin throbbing again, right behind her eyes.

Coleus Pfastbinder set down his cup of tea and gave Reva a broad smile. "Why, Inspector," he gushed. "What a pleasure to see you. Have you come to make an offering to Lord Banok, or is this an official visit?" He gave Reva's own outfit a quick look and lowered his voice. "Or maybe this is an unofficial visit. The word among the undergrowth is that you've been suspended. Again." He raised one eyebrow and gave an approving smile and Reva had to wonder who Pfastbinder's sources were that he was so well-informed.

The shopkeeper—an aging female elf—walked the two steps to their table. "Are you ordering or are you like this piker and brought your own?" She turned to Pfastbinder. "I'm gonna start charging you for the hot water."

Pfastbinder gave her a hurt expression, while still managing to smile. "But, Ellanna, my dear. Think of all the business my flock brings to you."

Ellanna sneered at him. Reva pulled out some Acorns and said, "I'll have a mint-cherry tea and some honey." Ellanna took the copper coins, apparently surprised that anybody who associated with Pfastbinder would pay for anything. She left to brew Reva's tea.

"This is a semi-official visit," Reva said to the cleric.

"As in there might be a stipend involved?"

"I thought you made a fortune duping clueless adventurers."

Pfastbinder put his hand to his chest with a "who me?"

expression. "Do you fault me, a man of faith, from trying to earn a decent living? I'm not some Telenite, you know, and being halpbloeden, my other earning opportunities are somewhat limited."

"I can't promise anything," Reva hedged. "I'm not here in an official capacity. But if you can help me, I will see what I can do."

Pfastbinder nodded, taking Reva at her word.

"I need some help identifying some undead."

"Since when do you bother with undead? Are you moonlighting as an adventurer?" He gave her a conspiratorial smile and wink.

Reva grimaced. "Never. My Seeker encountered some undead while looking for a missing person." A cup of tea was set on the table, along with a small pot of honey. Reva nodded politely and started to spoon in the amber liquid.

"Seeker Carya. I do like him," said Pfastbinder. "Do you know if he's seeing anybody?"

"Weren't you involved with a woman at The Red Otter?" She hadn't known that Pfastbinder's branches leaned that way, and she wasn't sure if Ansee's did either.

Pfastbinder gave a dismissive wave. "She wasn't really right for me. Besides, I'm a leaf on the wind, I don't care who ends up in my bed."

Reva shrugged, drinking her tea. "About the undead?" she prompted, returning to the reason she was here.

"What about them?"

"Two of them were murder victims and somehow became undead."

"Do we have a necromancer on the loose?" he asked excitedly.

Reva shook her head. "I don't think so. Seeker Carya said there was no spell to raise the dead at the scene, but there was an unusual divine aura."

Pfastbinder tapped a finger on his chin. "You said 'two

of them.' There are more now?"

Reva nodded as she drank her tea. "According to Ansee, there are at least five of them now. He said that a cleric had tried to turn the creatures but failed, and had somehow become one of the creatures, as did others."

"Seeker Carya has seen them, then?"

"Yes. He said they look like zombies, but they act differently."

"Differently?" Pfastbinder picked up his tea.

Reva shrugged. "I've only ever come across a couple of undead, so I don't know what he means. He said they chanted the whole time, some kind of phrase about pain and truth."

Reva saw Pfastbinder's eyes widen just a bit at that. "Anything else?" he asked, trying to sound casual.

"Only that physical and magical attacks didn't seem to harm them. In fact, he said that when they attacked the creatures, that they felt the pain of the attacks themselves."

Pfastbinder drained his tea and set the cup down. "Sorry, Inspector. I can't help you."

"Hawkshit." Reva crossed her arms and glared at the cleric.

He managed to withstand the look. "You're right. I won't help you."

"Why?"

"Self-preservation." He started to gather up his multi-colored cloak from a hook on the wall. The slap of a hand on the table drew his attention. Reva removed her hand to reveal a Crown, the gold metal shining bright in the dim light of the shop. Pfastbinder reached out hesitantly to take the coin, but Reva jabbed her index finger down on it.

"Down payment for you to consult with the constabulary."

"You're on suspension. Will anybody at the RTC agree to this? I'm not exactly welcome there."

Reva shrugged. She was spending her own money (again) and defying the orders of the LCI (again). There was no guarantee that Aescel would agree to pay her back.

"My life is worth considerably more than a single Hawk," Pfastbinder said, but he was still eying the coin.

"If you can give me useful information, we can arrange for more. Besides, I'm not asking you to fight them. Just tell me what they are and how to deal with them."

Pfastbinder deliberately picked up Reva's finger and grabbed the coin. "Well, Inspector," he said with a smile. "That's the problem."

Chapter 31

Ansee wrinkled his nose as he walked into the Feedshed. The Alchemist's lair had a perpetual odor that clung to it like foul dungeon slime. It was a combination of alchemical elixirs, earthy minerals, and dead bodies. It was bad enough that Ansee's stomach always curdled when he walked in.

The Feedshed had originally been a wooden shed that stored sacks of grain when New Port had been a stable. At some point, an alchemical accident had caused the original building to explode in a purple and blue fire (that was still talked about by the locals) and had fused parts of the building to the two alchemists who were working there. Neither had survived for very long. The building had been rebuilt from stone; the added expense was determined to be worth every Acorn to contain any future mishaps.

Several tables sat in the front half of the building so that the Alkies could do their work. The walls were lined with shelves that were straining under the weight of jars, glass bottles, clay pitchers, and the occasional thick tome. Loren Uldfoester stood at one of the tables, mixing two liquids into a copper kettle that was sitting over a candle flame. He waved to Ansee as he walked toward the back room, passing through the flimsy wooden door.

The odor of death was stronger here. They kept the room scrupulously clean all the time, but no amount of cleaning could remove the stench of death that had been accumulating like falling leaves for centuries.

Two stone tables sat in the center of the room; each table had grooves carved into them to drain away blood and other fluids into the buckets that sat under the tables. A light wand set into a metal bowl hung above each table to provide bright, magical light to each work surface. Tables, cabinets, and washbasins were shoved against the walls.

One table was currently empty, while Alchemists Bromide and Rianna stood at the other, a naked body lying on the table.

"Seeker Carya," Thea called out cheerily. "Did you draw the short twig?"

Ansee stepped forward, trying not to get too close. The body on the table gave off a sickly, fruit-like odor mixed with the cloying stench of wet clothes, dead fish, and sulfurous river mud. *I should come up with a spell that removes the sense of smell.*

"FC Aescel assigned it to me since Reva's been suspended."

"That's a bunch of hawkshit," Thea said, as she picked up a rectangular-shaped saw.

"No disagreement from me. Maybe you can tell the LCI how wrong she is."

Thea gave Ansee a rude gesture with a blood-covered hand. "Step closer, Seeker. You won't see anything from back there."

Ansee stepped forward. The body on the table was male and, judging by the lack of animal bites, it hadn't been in the river for too long. "Did he drown?"

"I don't know yet," Thea held up the saw. "I'm about to cut out the rib cage. We'll see if he has any water in his lungs. But even if he does, it may not be a suicide."

"Oh." Ansee took another step forward, his curiosity overcoming his squeamishness. Most floaters were suicides and it was rare for them to be the result of something else. A murder would at least be interesting.

"Our victim has several other wounds that appear to have been made before death." She pointed at the body. "He's got a broken arm with some bruising. Maybe a defensive wound. There's bruising to the left leg," she gestured to the limb in question, "and lots of cuts and abrasions."

"So, he was in a fight?"

Thea shrugged. "Then there's this." She motioned for Ansee to come around to the head of the body.

Ansee could see that the face was swollen and bruised. The swelling could have been from the river, but the other damage suggested that he'd been in a fight. "Parts of his skull have been broken and his temple has been crushed in," Thea said. "It's possible that he hit something in the water, but I'd wager my Skips on him getting this before he went into the river."

Ansee continued to look at the body. The victim—that's how Ansee thought of the elf now—had golden-brown hair of a moderate length. He was well-built, his arms and legs quite muscular. His skin was also well-tanned, still evident through the mottled blue-grey color of death.

"Anything else about him?" he asked.

Rianna spoke up. "His hands are well callused, and he has some skin art." She folded the skin from the chest back over and pointed to a coiled nautilus shell inked in faded blue ink on it. She then pointed to his forearm where Ansee saw a long scratch, but under the wound, he could see a bird in flight, wings stretched and with a scissored tail.

Ansee nodded, taking in the details. "Well, that's more than we usually have to go on for a floater." He took a step back and looked to Thea. "When will you know the cause of death?"

"If he drowned, as soon as I cut out his lungs. If it was something else..." She shrugged.

Ansee nodded again. "Áeorias. You can send your report to me." He turned to leave the room, already anticipating the clean air outside, when a new thought struck him. He wanted to be thorough, to show FC Aescel and Reva that he was able to handle a case on his own. He should do everything he would normally do, even for a floater. He turned around just as Thea was starting to cut the dead elf's ribs.

"Just a moment," Ansee said. "I should check the body for auras."

Thea raised one eyebrow up dramatically. "Really? He's just a floater."

"Just being thorough."

"Somebody's looking to climb the branches," Rianna said jokingly.

Ansee ignored the remark. "*Bana sihirli işiği göster.*" A cat-like eyeshine illuminated his eyes with a golden light. He looked over the body, not really expecting anything. It was just a floater, and he wasn't trying for a promotion, but it wouldn't hurt to be able to tell Aescel that he had checked for auras.

The body showed no auras along the arms, legs, or trunk. Had he worn any magic rings or other magic items their aura would have left a trace, even after a day in the water. Thea had cut open the chest, pulling the skin back to get to the ribs and organs. Part of the skin covered the victim's face. Ansee motioned with his hand, "Can I see his face?"

With an exaggerated sigh, Thea grabbed the skin and pulled it down. As she did so, Ansee let out a gasp. "By the gods."

Around the victim's neck were small gold specks forming a thin line. Ansee traced the aura to a spot on the chest where a pendant or necklace would rest. There, Ansee saw a strong concentration of the golden flecks. It was as if somebody had spilled gold dust on the body.

"What?" asked Thea. "Do you see something?"

Ansee nodded and pulled a quartz crystal from a pouch on his belt. He pointed to the spot. "Divine magic. Maybe from a necklace or something."

Rianna gave a low whistle, while Thea said, "He wasn't wearing anything except for his clothes." She pointed to a pile of wet clothes that Ansee had originally taken as rags.

"Maybe he was killed for it," Rianna said. "A robbery gone bad."

Thea gave a disapproving look. Ansee knew that she didn't like to speculate about the bodies that came through the Feedshed. She dealt with the facts and let the Constables draw their own conclusions, but Ansee figured that Rianna probably wasn't wrong.

"Could be," he said. He set the quartz crystal on the victim's chest where the greatest concentration of the magical aura could be seen. "*Bu aura taklit edin, sihrinizi paylaşin.*" The crystal glowed briefly with a golden light. Ansee picked up the quartz.

"Anything else?" Thea asked, all trace of annoyance gone from her voice. Ansee knew that most Seekers didn't bother to check for magic on a floater. He wondered how many cases might have turned out differently if they had.

Ansee shook his head. "Áeorias, again."

"I'll get you my report as soon as I'm finished." Thea moved the flap of skin and started cutting out the rib cage.

Ansee left to start his own report, though his mind wasn't really on the floater. His mind wandered back to the undead lurking in Nuphar Wood and he wondered how Reva was doing in her own investigation.

Chapter 32

A slight breeze came off of the bay and ruffled Constable Inspector Pflamtael's hair. The wind carried the odor of the sea, clearing the more fetid smell emanating from the docks for a brief moment. He strode down the dock, navigating around coils of rope, boxes, and halpbloeden who were carrying heavy loads. Seeker Pfinzloab walked a pace behind him, and both were trailed by Senior Constable Shanna Rhosa and a couple of constables. Olwyn didn't expect any trouble for the simple reason that he'd brought enough assistance to make sure that there would be no trouble.

The Majestic Tern was tied up exactly where he'd been told it would be. He didn't see anybody on the deck, but the gangplank was down. Olwyn stopped at the bottom of the gangplank and turned to his elves.

"This sailor has already killed two people," he said. "He may be willing to kill again to keep from having to answer for his crimes." He unsheathed his longsword. "Be ready for anything, but I want to take him alive if we can."

Shanna and the two constables nodded, each of them unsheathing their own longswords.

"He may have a magic item as well," Norah added. "He used it to turn his victims into undead."

Pflamtael nodded to Norah, who held up her staff as she began to incant the spell. When he'd returned from

The Roots, she'd told him about Seeker Carya's suspicion that some undead he'd encountered in Nuphar Wood may have been connected to their case. Olwyn had recalled the strange divine aura that both Seeker Carya and Norah had found at the flower shop. Plus, he figured that if Reva hadn't dumped him after being saddled with the new Seeker when Cas had left, then he must have some talent. He'd accepted the new information as fact, and had easily woven it into the narrative that he had made for this murderer.

Norah's eyes glowed softly as she looked over the ship. With a shake of her head, she dropped the spell, her eyes returning to normal. "There are no undead on the ship." She sounded disappointed.

"Then we'll make sure he tells us where they are. After we arrest him," Olwyn said. "Let's go."

He turned and walked up the gangplank. Once on deck, he strode to the cabin door at the aft end, while Senior Constable Rhosa and another constable moved forward. One constable stood guard at the gangplank while Norah followed Olwyn. She readied her staff and nodded. Olwyn gripped his sword and pushed open the door. He entered in a rush, only to find the tiny cabin empty. With a shake of his head, he headed back to the main deck.

Senior Constable Rhosa waved to him. She pointed toward an open hatch and then to her ear. Olwyn nodded his understanding; she'd heard something below deck. He walked with a light tread to the hatch.

Muffled voices and laughter came from below. A narrow, steep set of stairs dropped from the deck into the darkness below. He considered for a moment whether to have Norah cast a defensive spell to shield them from attack. It was the smart thing to do with a potentially armed and dangerous criminal, but he decided that surprise was a better defense.

He pointed at himself, then Shanna, Norah, and the constable, then pointed to the hatch. Everybody nodded, and

Olwyn rushed down the stairs. They were steeper than they looked and he almost lost his footing—which would have been embarrassing—but he managed not to fall.

The hold was a large, open room, with stout crossbeams that supported the deck. Hammocks stretched between the beams in places, and an iron stove and cabinets were tucked along the back wall. To Olwyn's right (carelessly behind him as he came down the stairs) stood a group of sailors who were crowded around a hatch in the floor. They talked good-naturedly and helped a crewelf lift a bucket from the hole. A dank, fetid odor—a cross between a latrine and a marsh on a hot day—filled the hold.

Olwyn had tried to be quiet, but his near stumble had made some noise. One of the sailors—a grizzled, sun-tanned elf with greying hair—turned to see Olwyn and the others come down. He cleared his throat loudly. "We 'ave vis'tors, *Isean*."

A younger elf with medium length brown hair turned to face them. Olwyn heard a sharp intake of breath from Norah.

"Constables, what can we do for you?" He was polite, but he eyed the drawn longswords warily.

"Who here knows Amber Myosotis?" Pflamtael asked.

"You've found Amber?" asked the *Isean*. "Does she know where Loren is?"

"Aavril, isn't it?" asked Seeker Pfinzloab. Olwyn kept his face impassive, though he wondered how Norah knew this sailor.

Aavril nodded. "Yes." He gave her a closer look with a slight narrowing of his eyebrows.

"You're Reva's boyfriend, right?"

The leaves parted for Olwyn. *Reva's boyfriend? How interesting. And how tragic for Reva when she finds out that he's a cold-blooded murderer.*

On an impulse, Olwyn sheathed his sword. "Yes, we've

found Amber. And we could use some assistance." He looked at Aavril closely, noticing the skin art of the bird on his right forearm. He noticed that the other sailors had similar skin art, but Reva's boyfriend was the only one with brown hair. "Can your crew spare you to help us out?"

Aavril hesitated, but the older elf spoke up. "Go, lad. If'n this'll help tha Cap'n, then go. We can finish 'ere."

Aavril nodded and said, "Sure. Anything I can do to help." He started for the stairs, the two constables heading up first. Olwyn and Norah followed.

† † †

Erroll had been surprised to find a constable guarding the ship when he'd arrived, and he had taken a position by some boxes to keep watch. Now, he watched the constables lead Aavril off the ship as he made himself look busy and coiled some rope. He made sure to look down as the *Isean* passed him. Aavril was asking about Loren and some woman named Amber, but the constables were tight-lipped as they walked up the dock.

Erroll watched them lead his future disciple away. "What do the Constables want with him?" he asked himself. He tossed the rope to the dock in irritation. *More importantly,* he thought, *how will I get him away from them?*

Chapter 33

Pfenestra's Playhouse always looked different to Reva in the daytime. It seemed a bit more run-down and drabber than it looked for the evening performances. Maybe it was the anticipation of seeing a play that allowed Reva to look past the cracking plaster and peeling paint when she came to see a show. She walked past the empty payment kiosk, and the burly doormen were absent, but the front doors were unlocked. The polished wood floors and walls in the foyer glowed from the sunlight coming through the high windows. Red and black carpet runners headed up the two curved staircases that lead up to the balcony, while the cloakrooms and refreshment stands stood silent.

After her meeting with Pfastbinder, Reva had formulated the beginning of a plan. She knew from Ansee that there were undead in Nuphar Wood. Pfastbinder had been unable to enlighten her about the undead and what had caused them to reflect any damage back to their attackers. He'd offered to help study one if they could capture it—he'd seemed almost gleeful at the thought—but he'd been unable to tell her anything other than to avoid damaging them.

He had been able to give her some information about which god was involved. There were many gods throughout Ados, and Reva was too practical to bother with any sort of formal religion. She really only knew about the important ones like Basvu, Cralde, Demar, Qurna, and Ados, but when Reva had told Pfastbinder the phrase that the undead had kept repeating, and he'd finally agreed to help, he'd told her what he knew. The cleric admitted that it wasn't much, third-hand information that he'd gleaned from some passing adventurers, but it was better than nothing.

The strange mantra the undead had uttered was linked to a minor deity called Dreen. This minor god was considered by some to be the god of pain and cruelty, though his followers said that Dreen was a god of enlightenment, who used pain to reach a mental plane where they could know the truth of all things. Reva thought that just made them crazy, but she'd seen religion do a lot of crazy things to a lot of normally sane people.

Pfastbinder didn't have any more information other than that the Dreenists were usually found in the far south, near the Kingdoms of Cantull, Torolla, and Oroma. He'd never heard of any members of that faith being here in Tenyl. Those were the Kingdoms where Aavril's Captain usually sailed to, so Reva figured if Tenyl imported the exotic spices, foods, and cacao from there, why not strange religions too? How this weird faith had gotten here didn't matter. She needed to figure out how to stop it from getting out of hand. It was clear that whatever cultist was in charge was going to fill his ranks by killing people and turning them into zombies. That was something that she couldn't allow to happen in her city, even if she was suspended.

Reva passed the staircase and the empty cloakroom. A short hallway led toward the back offices and the entrance to the playhouse's basement. Reva took the stairs down and worked her way through the narrow and twisting halls until she found the right room. The door to the room stood open. Within was a cluttered mess of half-assembled costumes, a plethora of wigs, and dozens of jars of makeup and face paint. It looked like a chaotic mess, but Reva knew that if anything was out of place, the room's occupant would know.

Reva leaned against the door jamb and said, "I thought theater people always slept all day."

A male elf was bent over a dressmaker's dummy, sewing frantically along the hem of a costume. At Reva's voice, Amaryllis spun around and beamed a broad smile at her. "Reva!" he said in a high, singsong voice, "Dear. It has been too long." He stepped forward and quickly placed a kiss on each of her cheeks. "Why have you been avoiding me? You haven't been to a show in how many weeks? And what has happened to your partner? I haven't seen Cas in nearly as long." He brought his hands together right under his chin. "Please tell me that nothing bad has happened to Cas."

"I've been busy with work. Cas had to move home to take care of her mother, so I've been breaking in her replacement.

"Cas moved away and didn't tell me! How dare she do that?" Amaryllis said with an anger that Reva couldn't tell if it was feigned or real. He lanced a look at Reva that pinned her in place. "And you, training Cas's replacement is no excuse to avoid me. This new partner of yours must be some kind of strange dwarf freak if you've not been able to get away for even one night." Amaryllis stuck out his lips and widened his eyes in an effective pout. "You must promise me you will come to the next show. Tonight!"

Reva couldn't help but smile. "I'll come." Amaryllis smiled. "But not tonight," she finished.

His pout returned with a vengeance. He pointed to the door. "Out! You are not a friend of mine if you tease me like this. Out!"

"If you feel that way." Reva straightened up with a shrug and turned away. "But you'll be missing out on helping me with an important case." She took a slow step down the hallway.

"A case?" Amaryllis grabbed her arm and pulled her into the room. "You didn't tell me you were on a case. And you need my help?" His hands fluttered as he drew them to his chest in excitement. "What is it? A murder? A kidnapping?" A light wand went off and he smiled, "Oh, you're going undercover. You're smart to come to me. I will disguise you so well that even your dear mother won't recognize you!"

Reva considered that offer. It would make not having to explain about her suspension a lot easier.

Amaryllis flittered about the small room, still talking rapidly. "Are you going to infiltrate one of the thieves' guilds like in the *Thieves of Lankhmar*?" He pulled out a black thief costume and shook his head. "Maybe you need to get close to royalty like from *Castle Amber*?" He pulled a regal gown of pink satin and a thousand inlaid pearls out of a cupboard, and then put it back with a shake of his head. "Maybe," he turned and gave Reva a conspiratorial smile, "you're going to infiltrate the Sucra like in *The Veiled Society*." A thick, hooded cloak in a dark green color seemed to materialize in his hand.

"None of those," Reva said, smiling. "I'm thinking more along the lines of *Destiny of Queens*."

A sparkle lit within Amaryllis's eyes. "Ah, something along the lines of Queen Aeroth, then!"

"No, more along the lines of Sarah."

"The chambermaid's daughter?" He shook his head. "No. That will never do for you."

"I need something anonymous," Reva explained.

Amaryllis continued to shake his head. "No. You insult me. I had an understudy do those outfits and they were horrendous. I will find something much better."

"But nobody will see the outfit because of the scars."

"Scars?" Amaryllis lifted his head like a dog that had caught the scent of a juicy bone.

"Several of them, on my arms," Reva indicated with a

cutting motion across her forearm.

"Short, shallow cuts, like you've been punished for some transgression and not allowed to see a healer?" The spark had returned to his voice.

Reva nodded. "Yes. Can you do it?"

Amaryllis puffed out his chest. "Why do you insist on insulting me? Of course, I can do it. They will be so real that you'll think you've always had them. Now, sit," he gestured to a stuffed armchair. "I will find something like your Sarah outfit, and then we will disfigure your pretty little body."

†††

Inquisitor Amalaki approached the small outdoor café that rested along the south bank of the River Tenz. The café sat directly across from Pfenestra's Playhouse, where currently there was a decent group of people enjoying a late lunch. Amalaki's own stomach gave an audible growl to remind him that he had foolishly skipped his own breakfast and lunch, but he would not have a chance to relieve his hunger right now. He passed the café, and the enticing aromas from the various meals, and walked down a short alley between the café and a flower shop.

Within the shadows between the two buildings, a form moved, resolving itself into a cloaked figure, the dark green of the cloak blending in nearly perfectly with the dark alley. The figure saluted, applying his fist to his heart, and whispered, "Hail, King Aeonis."

Amalaki returned the salute and greeting. "What news do you have, Novice Whalen?"

The young Sucra officer looked confident and spoke clearly while keeping his voice to a whisper as he'd been trained. "I spotted Constable Inspector Reva Lunaria entering Pfenestra's about an hour ago. Your briefing this morning had been quite clear, and I figured that this was important enough to warrant using the sending gem." The novice licked his lips, "This is such a time, right?"

Amalaki nodded, and he saw the Novice relax noticeably. The sending gems were a new magical item that had been developed by the wizards at the Red Keep. The idea was simple, to use two (or more) gemstones—in this case, well-formed quartz crystals—and allow them to function in the same manner as a scryer's crystal ball. Amalaki knew the basics of it, but the actual arcana was lost on him. He only knew that the sending stones could send short communications between the crystals. He also knew they were expensive, not only to craft, but also to use since each gem had a limited number of uses. The wizards assured everybody that they were improving the magic that went into the gems but, for now, their use was restricted to only the most sensitive of cases. Amalaki had bent the truth a bit in his requisition of the sending gems for this morning's patrols, but his decision had paid off, and results were always looked upon more favorably within the Sucra than failure.

"You did as you were instructed to do, and that is as it should be. Now, what did you observe?"

The Novice licked his lips again. Amalaki knew that Whalen was trying to get a promotion to Inquisitor, and to do that, he had to demonstrate his knowledge and proficiency in the basic skills all Sucra officers had to employ. This was the first patrol that Whalen was performing on his own, and Amalaki could understand his nervousness. That didn't mean that he would make it any easier for the young officer. He still had to prove himself to the Sucra's—and Amalaki's—standards.

"I first spotted the Constable Inspector walking up Merchant Road, heading toward the bridge. As you cautioned us in the briefing, she was out of uniform, but I recognized her from the description you gave."

Amalaki nodded, but remained quiet.

"She turned onto the road here and headed straight to Pfenestra's. Because there are no plays scheduled to be performed during the day, I knew that this was unusual. She entered the playhouse and I made sure that nobody else was following her before I took my position here." He pointed toward the road. "From here, I can see the front entrance and the side entrance that the actors use. I know from my own visits to Pfenestra's that there is no rear entrance, and that the other side of the building abuts directly against The Beehive." Even as they spoke, Amalaki had noticed that the Novice had kept his eyes on the target.

"Did you consider a secret passage between Pfenestra's and Pfletcher's pub?"

The color drained from the Novice's face. "I did not. Is there one?"

Novice Whalen had done a good job, so Amalaki decided to go easy on him. "Not that I am aware of," Whalen relaxed at the words, "though this is Burl Pfletcher we're talking about, and who knows what sort of secrets he's hiding. Never make any assumptions unless you have verified things with your own eyes."

Whalen nodded his understanding of the lesson. "Nobody else has entered the playhouse since I took my watch, and the Constable Inspector has not left."

"You have done a good job, Novice Whalen. I will be sure to let your instructors know. I will take over now, so you can continue your patrol."

Whalen saluted again, which Amalaki returned, and both gave honor to King Aeonis. Whalen slipped out of the alley, using the shadows as he'd been trained so that he seemed to appear among the people traveling along the road. Amalaki liked what he saw in the Novice.

He took up his own position within the alley to watch Pfenestra's. He hadn't been lying to Whalen about Pfletcher's pub, but at the same time, he'd never had the chance to do a thorough examination of The Beehive. *That is something that should be addressed*, he realized, making a mental note to get that done. Instead, he positioned himself in such a way that he could see the entrance to The Beehive in addition to Pfenestra's.

As he observed the buildings, he wondered what Reva was up to. After their chance encounter at The Beehive last night, he had decided that he needed to speak with Reva more thoroughly. She'd been too drunk last night, and while that may have loosened her lips, she'd been too surly, too upset at something, that she'd have given him false information or misled him just out of spite.

His investigation into the threat against King Aeonis had stalled, but he'd learned some information about the Constable that he thought was involved in the conspiracy. He needed to have it confirmed, and Reva was the one who could best provide him that information. She hadn't understood that last night. Amalaki wasn't sure how credible the threat was against the King, but he took all threats—real or not—seriously. It was his duty to protect the King, and he took that duty most seriously of all, but what he'd been learning scared him more, and he needed to discuss it with somebody. Reva was that somebody, and it galled him that he was hesitant to discuss it with anyone within the walls of the Red Keep.

The doors to Pfenestra's remained closed, and the afternoon drifted by. Amalaki was beginning to wonder if there *was* a secret entrance to the playhouse that he was unaware of, when the side door opened up. A woman with dark brown hair who was wearing servants clothing walked out. He almost dismissed the servant, but then took a closer look. The woman walked with a determined gait, very sure of herself. She walked like a Sucra officer—or a constable. As the woman passed the alley, he got a closer look at her face. It was smudged in places, but nothing could hide those turquoise eyes.

Reva. What is she doing? As she headed up the street, he thought that he recognized her outfit as one of Amaryllis's costumes—possibly from the *Destiny of Queens*. He needed to talk to Reva about his case, but even though there was a threat to the King that he needed to address, his curiosity had been peaked. *Where are you going dressed as the chambermaid's daughter?*

Chapter 34

Reva walked into Nuphar Wood wearing her new disguise. Amaryllis had lived up to his reputation as the best costume designer in Tenyl, and Reva was sure that even her mother would not recognize her. She wore a dirty blouse of undyed linen that was stained and spotted from harsh lye soaps, and a green skirt that was faded and patched from years of use. She'd traded in her soft leather boots for wooden clogs, and her hair had been covered by a dark brown wig. A cotton shawl of bright blue was wrapped around her shoulders because Amaryllis had insisted that even a poor maiden would need a spot of color in her life.

Under the long sleeves of the blouse were the scars. Amaryllis had spent the most time on them, getting them just right. Reva wasn't sure how he did it, or what materials he used—he insisted that they were a trade secret—but they had come out better than she'd expected. Half a dozen scars lined the inside of both forearms. Each was about a hand long and looked like she'd been making these scars for years. One looked raw and red as if she'd just drawn the knife across her skin last week.

Reva headed along the paths toward The Brambles. Several people were enjoying the afternoon, and Reva was already in character, stooping her shoulders, and dropping her head. She looked like a halpbloed and everybody ignored her.

The afternoon sunlight gradually dimmed as she headed off the main path and into the dense thicket of trees and bushes. Ansee had tried to describe where they had encountered the undead last night, but he admitted that it had been dark, and trying to identify any specific location in The Brambles was nearly impossible. So, Reva headed toward the center of the area, figuring that anybody hiding out here would want to try to avoid any accidental contact.

Branches caught at her clothes, and roots seemed to take pleasure in leaping out of the ground to try to trip her. She should have been quieter—she could have been quieter—but that was not the kind of person that "Sarah" was.

She stumbled on a root near a dense thicket of silverthorn and landed on her hands and knees. That had not been intentional—walking through the woods in the cumbersome wooden clogs was hard—and Reva silently swore under her breath. As she started to stand up, a sound caught her attention; somebody was walking through the silverthorn. She stood with the tree to her back and scanned the thick bush with its long, sharp thorns that jutted out everywhere. Movement caught her eye, and she turned to see several figures walking out of the bush, the long thorns tugging at their clothes and digging into their skin.

The light filtering through the trees was dim, turning the late afternoon into early twilight, but Reva was able to tell that the creatures emerging from the bushes were no longer alive. Their skin was pallid and grey in color, pulled tight and sunken into their bodies, while long claws protruded from the tips of their fingers.

There were five of the creatures, two wearing the vestments of clerics. They fit the description that Ansee had given her of Brenna and her partner Cedrus. One was an elderly elf wearing the uniform of a royal guard, and the last two were partially clothed, so Reva assumed that they were Amber and her boyfriend, her missing murder victims. *The gang's all here,* she thought.

All five creatures moved directly toward her, their arms raised in anticipation. They spoke in a low, crackling voice, each a bit out of synch with the others so that the effect was grating on the ears. "Dreen is pain...pain is truth...Dreen is truth..."

Ansee hadn't told her how disconcerting their mantra really was. Its slow cadence and asynchronous speech worked to worm a sliver of fear into Reva. She stood straighter and caught sight of another elf walking out of the bushes to her right. There must have been a hidden path through the silverthorn, as he was not covered in scratches. He wore the simple clothes of a sailor, although around his neck a glint of gold reflected off a beam of sunlight. He stood watching the five undead creatures approach Reva, unconcerned that they may cause her any harm.

Reva swallowed, not having to try to pretend to be afraid. She only had her dagger on her, and she was afraid to use it after listening to what had happened to Ansee and Kai. The unrelenting mantra coming from the creatures was unnerving. They were about two paces away and would soon be able to rake their sharp talons across her.

Reva collected herself, standing a bit straighter and sticking her chin out fearlessly. She prayed that Pfastbinder hadn't been full of hawkshit when he'd told her about the cult of Dreen.

She stuck her arms forward, letting her forearms show as the sleeves pulled back. "Dreen is the truth. He brings enlightenment from pain," she said in a clear voice. The five creatures didn't seem to be phased by her words, but she saw the elf out of the corner of her eye stand up straight. He took several quick steps forward.

Reva stood still, but turned her head to look at him. She could see the image of a bird—a scissor-tailed tern—inked onto his forearm and she did her best to suppress her shock. *Aavril has the same skin art on his own arm.* She pulled back the sleeve on her right arm to better show the scars, including the "fresh" one. "Pain sharpens the mind and strengthens the will. I know the truth," she said, letting an earnest tone fill her voice.

The elf smiled and the five undead stopped, barely a pace away from Reva. They lowered their arms but continued their mantra. Reva took the opportunity to move a few steps away from them. The elf was clearly wearing the breeches and shirt that she associated with every sailor she'd ever seen. He had shoulder-length brown hair. His oak-green eyes sparkled, and Reva knew it wasn't from the play of the light. She'd seen the same, manic glee in many other elves over the years. She knew that seeking out a cult leader and his undead minions alone was a foolish and dangerous mission, but adding crazy to the mix just made it that much harder.

Reva did her best to ignore the undead behind her. She looked at the elf, a timid smile playing across her lips. She nervously stuck a strand of hair behind an ear. "Were you drawn here as well?" she asked.

"You've heard Him, too?" he asked excitedly.

Reva nodded. She didn't want to lead this conversation, worried that, if she displayed too much knowledge, this elf might become suspicious.

The elf brought his hands together and smiled. "This is wonderful. Dreen has heard my prayers. You, my child, are the first of our new church."

"But who is Dreen? I get frustrated and can't think straight sometimes. But when I do this," she pointed to the scars, "things become clear. And I hear a name in my head, but who is he?"

She wanted to sound naïve, like somebody who was looking for guidance. It seemed to be working.

"Dreen is the savior of Ados," he said. "He suffered to

remove the sin from Ados, and through that act, he spread the truth. A truth that Dreen knew because of the pain he suffered. We follow in his footsteps, gaining truth and enlightenment through pain."

Reva had to force herself to not roll her eyes. *What sort of hawkshit was this?* She wasn't that religious, and beyond saying the odd prayer to Basvu to keep her brother safe, and the occasional curse in one or another god's name, she had no time for most religions. It took all of her willpower to not slap this elf and laugh in his face. *Though he'd probably like that*, she thought, knowing what little she did about this Dreen. The mumbled chant coming from the five undead behind her reminded her that it was probably not a good idea to get on this guy's bad side.

"Who are you?" she asked.

"I am the one who will bring a new age of enlightenment to Tenyl."

† † †

A thin roll of parchment tapped the edge of Ansee's table, getting his attention. He looked up from his own parchmentwork to see Thea standing next to his table.

"Here's my report," she said. "But to get to the sap, he was dead before he hit the water." She tapped the side of her head. "Massive blow to the head."

"Thank you." Ansee took the parchment. "It might be useful if we knew who he was. Any chance of a Speaking Ritual working?"

Thea gave Ansee an odd look. "I thought you didn't believe in the Speaking?"

"I don't. It's a cruel punishment on the soul, but if we can learn something about our victim, I'm willing to try."

"Well, it would take approval from one of the First Constables to even perform the ritual. They would never justify the expense of doing the Speaking for a floater, and even if they did, it wouldn't work anyway. Your victim has been dead for over a day. The Speaking only works when a person's been dead for less than a day. The theologians and clerics say that time flows differently in the spirit realms so, after a day, it's nearly impossible to call a soul back. Besides," she added, "I need a person's true name to even make the attempt."

Ansee nodded. He'd known that. He held up the parchment. "Well, this will at least give me something to put into my own report. Thank you again."

Thea nodded and headed toward the back stairs. Ansee returned to his own work, finishing his write-up on the floater. He had a lot of information: a magical aura, skin art on the arm and chest, and a cause of death. What he didn't have was a name, the scene of the crime, a murder weapon, a motive, or a suspect. "No problem."

After a quarter of an hour, Ansee finished his report. He placed it and Thea's report into a parchment tube, writing the case information on the outside. Without some new information, that would probably be the end of it. Thea would keep the body for another day, and then take it to Alnua Copse. It was the only cemetery that took in Tenyl's poor and forgotten.

Ansee picked up the small quartz crystal in which he'd collected the aura. He wondered if it was worth the time to transfer it to a larger crystal for safekeeping. The large crystals were expensive, and he'd have a hard time justifying the cost to FC Aescel. This was still a floater, after all.

After some hesitation, he put the crystal into a small cloth bag. It had a tag of parchment sewn to it—something Ansee had done at his own expense—and he filled out the particulars. He put the bag into the tube and stood up.

New Port's massive front doors opened as he walked down the stairs. Constable Inspector Pflamtael and several constables walked in, leading an elf that caused Ansee to do a double-take. He looked almost exactly like his floater, with gold-brown hair and a similar physique. As Ansee stared, he noticed that the elf had skin art on his right forearm. A bird in flight.

Senior Constable Rhosa and two others headed upstairs, nodding a greeting to Ansee as she passed. Pflamtael and Seeker Pfinzloab led the stranger past Constable Whitlocke's table.

"Why are we heading this way?" asked the elf. His voice had a wary edge to it.

"It's too crowded upstairs," said Pflamtael. "We'll be more comfortable down here."

They headed toward the stairs that led to the cells. Instead of heading to the storage room to put up his case notes, Ansee followed them down the stairs.

CI Pflamtael was holding open one of the cell doors, gesturing for the elf to enter. "We can get started while Seeker Pfinzloab gets us some tea."

"What about Amber?" asked the elf. "You said you have her. Is she all right? What about Loren?"

Amber? Ansee asked himself. *The murdered shop owner? Have they found her murderer? Who's Loren?*

The elf started to turn when Pflamtael shoved him hard in the back, pushing him into the cell. Before the elf could react, Pflamtael slammed the door shut, flipping down the iron latch to lock the door.

Screams of protest came from the cell. "Hey! What are you assholes doing? Let me out! Let me speak to Reva!"

Reva? Is that... Ansee stepped up to Norah as more shouts of profanity were hurled out of the cell. "Who's that?" he asked.

"His name is Aavril."

"Wait. You don't mean..."

She nodded. "Reva's boyfriend. And we're arresting him

for murder."

"Of Amber and her lover?" Ansee asked, sounding shocked.

Norah noted his tone and narrowed her eyes at him. "Of course."

"What evidence do you have?"

"Somebody at Amber's apartment identified him. Well," she admitted after a slight pause, "they identified his skin art and described him." She turned to head upstairs as Inspector Pflamtael walked over.

"Wait," Ansee said. "My floater has the same skin art."

Pflamtael looked at Ansee. "Maybe he killed him too. Looks like I solved your case for you."

"But what if my floater is your killer? He looks exactly like Aavril. How do you know you have the right elf?"

"I always catch the right elf, Seeker," said Pflamtael coolly.

"But you can't believe that Reva's boyfriend would resort to murder, do you?" Ansee realized that he was walking out on a branch here, as he'd never met Aavril. He assumed that Reva was a good judge of character.

"I don't solve my cases based on belief." The condescending tone caused Ansee's ears to redden.

"Are you at least going to inform Reva?"

"Why would I do that? It's not her case anymore. And she's suspended." Pflamtael turned and headed up the stairs.

Aavril continued to pound on the cell door and hurl curses at anybody within earshot. Ansee gave a long look at the cell and then trudged back up the stairs.

Chapter 35

Erroll sat in the clearing with Sarah seated on the ground before him. She continued to cast furtive glances over her shoulder to the disciples standing at the other end of the clearing. The five creatures stood in a circle as they repeated Dreen's prayer in an endless loop.

"You understand Dreen's first three tenets?" he asked. He'd been explaining the foundation of Dreen's faith to her. Sarah had been scared at first, afraid of the disciples, until he'd shown her that he could control them completely. She had kept quiet, not saying anything or asking any questions, and Erroll was afraid that he was doing this wrong. He was a sailor, after all, not a cleric. He had always preferred action over words and he was afraid that he was going to mess this up. He was going to drive away his first convert.

But she'd begun to show signs of understanding and then started asking her first questions. They had discussed Dreen for a bit before Erroll realized that he needed to make this simpler. He had stated what he already knew— and what the disciples endlessly repeated—as the basic laws of Dreen's faith. The tenets—a term he'd heard some cleric speak about at one time in his youth.

Sarah nodded her head and stuck up her fingers as she repeated what he'd told her. "Dreen is the embodiment of pain. Only by experiencing pain can we learn the truth. And from this truth, Dreen will show us enlightenment."

Erroll smiled. "Exactly. It is very simple. So simple that even the disciples can get it, and they are merely vessels. They get the basics, but they don't fully understand it as you and I do."

Sarah slowly nodded, chewing on her lip. "But why do I feel compelled to hurt myself?" She pointed to the scars on her arms. "The healers said there's something wrong with me. That hurting myself is dangerous."

"My child," Erroll took her hands in his. "The healers are ignorant of the world as it really is. They think too much and are not open to the truth." He traced one of the scars with a finger as he began, "When you anoint yourself with pain..." He smiled at his choice of words (*Maybe I am a priest.*) He continued, "you are allowing Dreen to speak to you directly. The pain clears the mind and focuses your thoughts to a single point. This opens you to hear Dreen's message."

"And what is his message?"

Erroll smiled, wondering how he should respond. He wanted to sound like the priests who seemed to always know everything, even when it was clear that they didn't. They spouted dogma, called it enlightenment, and spoon-fed it to their followers. He didn't want to be like that, and he realized that he didn't have to be. Dreen's message was about truth, so honesty was the best response. He spread his hands and gave a slight shrug of his shoulders. "I do not know."

Sarah's eyes widened and her mouth opened in surprise.

"But I am learning. Every day I learn more about Dreen and his message. What he expects from us." He stood up and pulled his shirt over his head. "Like you, I have newly come to Dreen. I was awakened through this." He turned around to show her the scars on his back. "I received each of these as a punishment, but they were an awakening. Each one allowed me to see clearly, to better understand the world."

He turned back around and saw Sarah's eyes drawn to the necklace. He reached up and touched the gold form. "The Joy of the Widow's Tears."

"You named your necklace?"

"That's what the merchant in Cantull called it." He held it out for Sarah to see. "See the profile of the woman, and here is her tear." He tapped the small gemstone, and then let the necklace rest on his chest. "The necklace is a portal to Dreen. Through it, I receive Dreen's message of enlightenment. It has helped me understand what my purpose in Tenyl is. I have been blessed with this." He touched the necklace again.

"And what *is* your purpose?" Sarah asked.

"To convert the people of Tenyl to the ways of Dreen. Dreen's followers are few and scattered across Ados, but I can change that. I can make Tenyl into the center of Dreen's faith. Followers will come from across the world to worship here, and that will increase Dreen's power. As His power increases, our power will increase. We will be able to cast out the false gods as we show the people the truth. And you! You will be a part of it!"

Sarah sat still for a moment, her eyes wide with the realization that she was a part of something monumental. "How will we accomplish this? Aren't there too many followers of Basvu, Demar, and the other gods? How can we get people to understand Dreen's message?"

Erroll slipped his shirt back on and let the slightest frown of concern crease his face. "I asked myself that very question just yesterday. The simple answer is that those who are not like you, who are not already receptive to Dreen's message, will become disciples. They are simple creatures, unable to fully grasp Dreen's truth, but followers, nonetheless. But I want more. I want people like you who can understand Dreen's message. Who will see the deeper meaning and rejoice at their new enlightenment."

"How will we do that?"

Erroll held up a finger. "You saw the scars on my back." Sarah nodded. "The elf who gave them to me—he is the secret. His skill at delivering pain was the key that I needed to unlock Dreen's truth. With him at our side, we will be able to baptize people in Dreen's touch—as you have done to yourself."

"We will hurt them?" She gave a slight shudder.

"The truth may be hard to bear for some, but for others, the pain will awaken them to Dreen's message, just like you have experienced. That is why I need to find the elf who awakened Dreen for me. His skill was not a punishment. The care with which he delivered each lash sharpened my mind. That is what we will need to convert the good citizens of Tenyl."

"Who is this elf?"

"My former shipmate, but he may be lost to me."

"Why is that? Has he gone back to sea?"

Erroll shook his head. "Worse. He was taken away by constables this morning."

† † †

Erroll leaned against the trunk of the tree, looking up at the stars through the few breaks in the foliage. Sarah lay resting a few paces away, and his disciples stood at the other end of the clearing, their mantra a gentle song on the night air. He was thinking about how he would get Aavril away from the constables. As he'd explained to Sarah, Aavril would be the key that he needed in order to convert others to Dreen, but if he'd been arrested by the constables, what could he do? How could he get Aavril away from them?

He pushed his back into the rough bark of the tree, letting it dig into his scars. The sharp kiss of pain cleared his mind of all thought. He closed his eyes, opening himself to

Dreen's message. Dreen would show him the way.

He drifted into a sort of half-sleep, his mind clear as the pain caressed his back. Then he felt rough flagstones under his body, radiating the heat of the day. Several hands grabbed him and roughly dragged him back to the central pillar, binding his hands yet again. Erroll—Dreen—continued his invocation to Ados, absolving the god of His sin, of His failure. One of the guards cuffed him roughly across the head, cursing Dreen for his continued blasphemy. The blow stung, but the cut was quickly healed. The guards finished and stepped away.

Dreen could see the goateed cleric standing at the edge of the plaza. He stared at Dreen with hate and contempt. Dreen raised his voice to show that he had not been beaten.

Much time had passed, the sun had set, and Dreen knew that a crescent moon would be rising in the east. An auspicious sign, he thought, the symbol of the sinner god rising over his own enlightenment. Three blue-robed clerics entered the plaza and hurried over to the goateed man. With the arrival of more Crescent Defenders, Dreen knew that his time was coming. He was anticipating the climax that would come.

He could hear the commanding voice of the first cleric, who pointed at Dreen. "This heretic is possessed by a powerful evil. He refuses to recant, and his evil has prevented us from delivering Ados's will. Our only course is to purge the heretic with the blessed fire of Ados."

The other Crescent Defenders nodded solemnly, and the four of them took up positions around the plaza. Each of them drew forth their holy symbols from within the folds of their robes: crescent-shaped lapis lazuli in polished silver settings. Holding their symbols of office before them, they began to chant, drawing power from each other, weaving their spell.

Night turned into day and Dreen's skin was suddenly

ablaze as a pillar of blue-white fire fell down from the sky. He tried to continue his invocation to Ados, but the pain was too great. He let out a powerful scream, the noise tearing his very soul apart. Before the flames burned his eyes from their sockets, he could see his skin melting. Abruptly, the pain ceased, and he stopped screaming. He opened his eyes in surprise and he looked in awe at his unblemished body. The heavenly fire still burned and raged around him. The four clerics continued their incantation, but the fire no longer hurt him. All was clear to him now. Ados had heard his prayer and had rewarded him.

Dreen turned in the flames, holding his arms outstretched and smiling as he learned the truth. "His sins are absolved!" he yelled over the roar of the flames.

He could see the four clerics, their brows furrowed in concentration. Sweat streaked down their faces. The goateed man's eyes bored into Dreen, the hatred and fury evident. Dreen stood there, arms outstretched, realizing that he had been right. Ados's sins had been absolved through Dreen's effort. He saw everything clearly now. It was time to share this new insight with the others. With a twist of his wrists, he added to the four clerics' power, causing the circle of fire to grow.

The holy fire melted the stones of the plaza as it grew, and the sand fused into small grey-green gemstones. The expanding pillar reached the four clerics and they were consumed by the fire. In the Crescent Defender's final moments, Dreen shouted, "I am enlightened! I am Dreen, and I have become a God!"

The goateed cleric's eyes widened in sudden realization and Dreen smiled. He could feel his body finally give into the flames. It seared his flesh from his bones in a blissful, glorious instant of pain. He ascended to heaven on a column of ash along with the four clerics.

Erroll gave a cry and started awake, his skin glowing

with an inner fire that burned with a blissful radiance. In a moment, his skin had returned to its normal color, but the pain continued to dance across his skin. He felt whole and complete, having witnessed the ascension of Dreen. He understood now how Dreen had to embrace the pain of torture and death in order to remove the sin that Ados had borne since his defeat by Cralde. Erroll and his followers must welcome the pain, a reminder that Dreen freed Ados from His sin.

His cry had apparently not disturbed Sarah, but Erroll couldn't sleep anymore. He was too excited by the vision he had been shown. He stood up and began to pace the small clearing, his mind filled with thoughts and ideas, glorious visions of how to bring Tenyl into Dreen's embrace. But it still all hinged on Aavril. He was the key. If Aavril was still in the hands of the constables, then freeing him would take more than the five disciples that he had. They were powerful, but if he attacked the constables directly, they could overwhelm his disciples. He couldn't risk the future he saw on failing to recover Aavril. He needed more disciples, and he knew exactly where to get them.

Chapter 36

Aavril lifted his head from the foul-smelling mattress at the sound of the bolt being drawn on his cell door. He had to blink at the sudden brightness of a candle that filled his dark cell. All he could see was the silhouette of an elf standing in the doorway.

Since his entrapment and arrest yesterday, he'd only interacted with the constable who had brought him his single meal. Aavril had pleaded with him to get a message to Reva, but the guard had been stern-faced and quiet, leaving behind a few slices of bread and a wooden mug of water. Aavril had drained the water to relieve his aching throat, but had left the bread untouched. It still sat by the door.

He expected the guard with the candle to take the bread, or maybe to deliver another meal. He'd lost track of time within the dark cell. He had expected Inspector Pflamtael to return at some point to question him, but the Inspector never showed up. He didn't know if that was a good sign or not.

Aavril's eyes finally adjusted, and he could make out a thin elf wearing an Acer Division uniform. He was neither Pflamtael nor the cell guard. Aavril waited, not saying anything.

"My name is Ansee Carya," the constable said. "I'm Reva's Seeker. Her partner."

Despite the circumstances of his last meeting with

Reva, a sudden warmth of anticipation and hope grew in his stomach. He had planned to let the constable do all the talking, but he blurted out, "Is Reva here? Can she help me?"

The Seeker shook his head. "Reva was suspended two days ago. You didn't know?"

The hope inside Aavril was snuffed out like a candle. *How typical,* he thought. *When I need her the most, she isn't here to do a damn thing.* "No, I didn't know." He didn't try to hide the bitterness that he felt.

"Reva doesn't know about your arrest," Carya said.

"Why would she bother?"

Carya looked at him with narrowed eyes. "I tried to tell her last night, but she wasn't home."

"You should have tried the pubs." Aavril laid down and placed an arm across his forehead.

"What is your problem? This whole thing is really complicated right now, and we need your help."

"Everything Reva does is overly complicated. She isn't happy if she's not neck-deep in hawkshit."

Aavril heard an exasperated sigh come from Carya. "You don't get it, do you? Reva's out there, in violation of the LCI's orders, trying to stop some crazy necromancer from attacking Tenyl."

"Once again, Reva's job is more important than me."

There was a long silence. Finally, Carya said, "Somebody killed Loren."

Aavril sat up suddenly. "Loren's dead?"

"We have a dead elf over in the Feedshed who looks a lot like you, including your skin art," Carya tapped his forearm. "Actually, until yesterday we didn't know who he was." Carya pointed a finger at Aavril. "You helped me there."

"Me?"

"When you were brought in, you were asking—yelling, really—about somebody named Loren. Since you looked so much like the body, and you have the same skin art, I realized there was a connection. I was able to do a little bit of digging and found out our victim was Loren Sterna. We contacted his father last night, and he was able to identify Loren for us."

Aavril put his head into his hands. "Loren is dead?" Everything over the last few days, all of the problems and difficulties with getting the ship ready, came rushing back to him like a rogue wave crashing on the ship. All of his frustration and irritation at Loren for hanging out with Amber; leaving the hard work to him and the crew. All of his anger that had been building up as Loren continued to let them down. All of that became an anchor of guilt that hung around his neck. *How could I have been so stupid? Loren would have never abandoned us like that. Sailing had been his life. He had talked of nothing but his plans for the rest of our return trip, and I thought he had abandoned us for a woman? I should have gone to the constables the first day instead of trying to do everything myself. This is all my fault.*

"I think Loren ran into somebody who killed him and dumped his body in the river. He...he fought back, but he suffered a blow to his head..." Carya's voice trailed off. "Look, Reva doesn't know that you are here, and I wasn't lying when I said that this is complicated. If you can't help me, then Inspector Pflamtael is going to pin at least two murders on you."

Aavril continued to stare at the floor, not really hearing what Carya was saying. *Loren is dead. I don't believe it. How could somebody kill Loren? Everybody liked him. He was the one we all looked up to. How is Captain Sterna taking this? I should have been the one to tell him. It's my fault. I was too interested in seeing Reva that I didn't bother to learn what had happened to Loren. Loren would never have abandoned us all day when getting back to sea was so important to him. Instead of running around like a fool, I should have let some-*

body know. I waited too long to try to tell Reva, and by then, it was too late.

He looked up as Carya shoved his shoulder. "Are you listening to me? Pflamtael is going to charge you with two murders."

Aavril sighed and leaned back against the wall. "What does it matter?"

"It matters because Reva is out there risking her career, and her life, to save this city. And I think that whatever she is dealing with may be related to Loren's murder. I don't think that you're involved, and if we can't convince CI Pflamtael of this, then not only will you be sent to your death needlessly, the real killer will go free, and may hurt Reva in the process."

Aavril leaned forward. Despite what had happened with Reva, he didn't want anything to happen to her. "How are these cases related?"

"Loren had a necklace or something stolen when he was killed. It was magical and had a unique aura. After Pflamtael arrested you for Amber's murder, I learned that he had done it because he had a witness who said that a sailor had killed her—a sailor with your skin art," he tapped his forearm again, "So I decided to compare the aura that I collected from Loren to the one that we collected at Amber's flower shop. They matched."

"Loren's necklace?" Aavril thought back to the stupid necklace that Loren had bought right out from under Erroll. "Erroll," he whispered.

"Who? Do you know who killed Loren?"

"I don't know. But Erroll was...obsessed with a necklace that Loren bought on our last voyage. He tried to steal it while on the ship. Maybe he followed Loren to try to get it back."

"What sort of necklace?"

Aavril shrugged. "It was a plain gold necklace with a

small, ugly gemstone. It didn't look like much except from a certain angle, and then it looked like a woman's profile, with the gem placed as a tear coming from her eye. The Cantullian merchant said that it was called the 'Joy of the Widow's Tears.'" Aavril looked at Carya. "We didn't know that it was magical. Hells, for what Loren paid for it, I don't think that the merchant even knew."

Carya put a hand to his chin. "There are still a lot of things that I don't know, but based upon the auras, the necklace was at Amber's shop, and I know that Loren was in possession of it."

"Are you suggesting that Loren killed Amber?" Aavril gave an indignant laugh. "Loren loved Amber. He wouldn't kill her."

Carya looked up, "Even if she was cheating on him? There was somebody else in her shop. A boyfriend, we think."

"What? No...I knew Amber. They were in love." Aavril thought about him and Reva. *Just like Reva and I were? Are we still in love? Does Reva still love me? Do I still love Reva?*

Carya shrugged, as if to say that women have been known to change their minds. Just then, he looked over his shoulder as the cell door was pulled open all the way. Aavril could make out Constable Inspector Pflamtael and his Seeker standing in the hall.

"Seeker Carya," Pflamtael said acidly. "What are you doing with my prisoner?"

Aavril saw Carya stand a bit straighter. "Getting confirmation about the identity of my floater. You may not want to believe it, but our cases are linked, and I know that Reva's boyfriend didn't kill Amber."

"Loyalty to Reva is not evidence of innocence," Pflamtael said.

Carya's ears reddened. "This has nothing to do with Reva. The auras confirm what I am saying. The one from the flower shop and the one from my floater. They are the same." He waved a hand angrily at the other Seeker. "Hells, let Norah check my work if you don't believe me. Loren was killed for a necklace, and that necklace was in Amber's shop."

The Inspector was silent, and Aavril saw nothing but a cold glare from the other Seeker. Finally, Pflamtael said, "Get out of here, Seeker Carya, before I decide to report this interference to Aescel. You'll be lucky to continue to investigate floaters."

"Will you at least look at the auras, Norah?" Carya pleaded.

She continued to give Reva's Seeker an icy stare, and Aavril felt his hope being snuffed out again. After a moment, Carya turned and walked out of the cell, letting his shoulder hit the Inspector. Pflamtael let the petty insult go and turned to look at Aavril. "Now let's find out why you killed Amber and her boyfriend."

Chapter 37

The morning air had a slight chill to it as Reva followed Erroll through the empty streets. He had awakened her before dawn, explaining that they needed to get moving in order to implement his plan to bring about Tenyl's enlightenment. The five disciples walked ahead of them, their chant never ceasing.

Erroll had been excited, explaining that he knew what they needed to do in order to save Aavril from the constabulary. Reva had been surprised last night when Erroll had mentioned that Aavril had been arrested. She had no reason to think that Erroll would be lying to her, and besides, it sounded like the kind of knee-jerk action Pflamtael would take just to be able to close the case. Aavril had been behaving like a total halpbloed since he'd returned, but he didn't deserve to be accused of murder, and she had no doubt that Pflamtael would find a way to make the charges stick to be able to close his case.

Their little caravan reached the bank of the river, and Erroll had them stop in a dark alley between two shops. Reva put Aavril's predicament on an upper branch and focused on the problem at hand. Erroll had been very forthcoming—clearly passionate—about what he wanted to do. It was clear that he had become a fanatical follower of Dreen. She'd learned that he'd never heard of Dreen until after returning from his recent trip aboard the *Majestic*

Tern, and hadn't even been all that religious, even to Demar. Now he was proselytizing for a god he'd never heard of before. It was clear that the Joy of the Widow's Tears was a magical talisman, and it was quite dangerous if it could make somebody like Erroll into a mouthpiece for a strange god.

Erroll spoke in a hushed tone to the five disciples. Reva didn't think the undead creatures understood his words, but after seeing him demonstrate his power over them last night, she knew that he could control them. *Probably another gift of the necklace.*

The disciples turned as a group and walked into the river. Reva nodded to herself. Erroll may be a fanatical follower of a deranged god, but he was not stupid. She wondered what kind of sailor he had made, and whether Aavril had taken him onto his branch to teach him the proper ways of running the ship.

"Let's go, Sarah. We need to get to the port." Erroll waved her on and turned toward the ferry.

Reva knew that she would need to make her move soon if she was going to save Aavril's crew. Her best hope of ending this quickly was to get the necklace away from Erroll. Without the ability to control the disciples, he would be powerless and could be arrested. But to have the best chance, she needed to keep Erroll away from groups of people. It wouldn't do to have an innocent bystander injured or taken hostage. She knew this part of Tenyl quite well, and a plan quickly developed.

She called out tentatively, "We need to get to the port quickly, don't we? The ferry will be too slow. Too many people crowd it in the mornings and it always runs late."

Erroll paused and looked at her. She licked her lips and added, "It may seem unwise, but taking King's Bridge in the morning is actually faster. It's how I was able to serve my mistress so well."

Erroll stood still, looking first at the ferry, and then at the bridge upriver. He finally turned and gestured toward the bridge. "Lead on, daughter of Dreen."

Reva bobbed her head and hurried along the path. They were right next to the river, along a narrow footpath that ran along the riverside of the embankment. Embankment Road was to her right, up the small slope, but she didn't want to take the main road. It would lead directly to the bridge and still had too many people around, even this early in the morning. Instead, she knew where there was a smaller set of stairs that led from the bridge's piers along the river and up to the main span. It was little used, and the bridge would hide any action that she decided to take.

The path was muddy after the night's tide receded, so she picked her path carefully. During her search for the Tenz River Troll, she and Cas had spent many hours walking along the river in order to find its lair. That would have been a good spot to set an ambush, but the troll's abandoned lair was on the other side of the river. Her best opportunity would come as they reached the bridge on this side.

She had only walked a few minutes when the bridge came into sight. The massive stone pier was set into the mud along the riverbank, part of the stone embedded in the soil and part dug into the river. Reva turned to Erroll and pointed to the bridge. "There's a stair on the other side of the bridge that we can use."

Erroll nodded, but she could tell that his mind was focused on his plans, not thinking about what was going on here and now.

They walked under the massive stone edifice of the bridge. The ground was muddy, with small pools of water, and smelled heavily of dead fish. Reva stepped aside, pointed again at the stairs just on the other side of the bridge, and allowed Erroll to go past her. She reached behind her back and took a grip on her dagger, sliding it out silently.

She turned it around so that the pommel pointed forward, and started to lift it as Erroll ascended the first step of the stairs.

Suddenly there was a commotion from above. "Maybe we'll find another body today!" said a voice. Two young boys came into view, hurrying down the steps. One of them stared wide-eyed at Reva and cried out, "What are you doing?"

Reva tried to react, slamming the dagger down hard toward the base of Erroll's skull, but he reacted surprisingly fast, leaning forward and to the right so that her blow glanced off of his shoulder. It still had to have hurt, but instead of a cry of pain, he laughed with pleasure.

Suddenly Reva felt her body stiffen, her limbs unable to move despite her best efforts. "Betrayed so soon?" Erroll purred. "You have the spirit of Dreen within you, child, but there can only be one who leads."

With a gesture of one hand, Reva felt herself being flung backward, hitting the stone pier hard, the wind knocked from her lungs. She hit the muddy ground and her dagger slipped from her hand. Before she could react, she felt herself being lifted again. She struggled against the magical bonds and managed to limply flail her arms. The pounding of feet sounded as the two boys ran back up the stairs.

"I trusted you. You felt Dreen's presence just as I have. It is a shame that you want my power so much that you cannot know your place."

Again, Reva was flung back violently, this time hitting her head as she struck the stones. Stars swam in her eyes from the blow, and she landed hard on the muddy ground. A pair of boots appeared in her vision. "You could have served Dreen at my side and rejoiced in his enlightenment. I should send for one of my disciples. I wonder how your spirit would react to serving Dreen in that fashion."

"You don't serve Dreen," Reva said, trying to keep

Erroll's attention on her face. "You only pretend to know what it means to serve Dreen." Reva was blowing leaves, trying to make Erroll angry. While he was focused on her words, he wouldn't see Reva's hand move to grip the hilt of her dagger.

"Pretend?" Erroll laughed. "Silly girl." He tapped the Joy of the Widow's Tears. "I am the embodiment of Dreen."

Reva was getting annoyed with him. She took the dagger and swung it in an arc, slicing across Erroll's shin. He let out an angry exclamation as she rolled away, but she stopped in mid-roll, again bound by Erroll. *Damn it, I hate this!* Reva felt her throat being constricted, unable to get air into her lungs. Blackness started to rim the edge of her vision. With an effort, she drew her arm back.

"You are a willful one. Maybe I shouldn't convert you into one of my disciples. Who knows what sort of danger you could do even from the grave?"

The sound of stomping boots sounded on the stairs, and Erroll turned at the noise. Reva took advantage of his distraction and flung the dagger toward him. Her arm was stiff from the magical binding, and so her aim was off, but the dagger still managed to stick into Erroll's thigh. He gave a grunt and with a thrust of his arm, he sent Reva flying out over the river.

† † †

Amalaki stood impatiently at the railing of King's Bridge, letting people walk around him as he watched the stairs on the opposite side of the bridge. He was tired and very hungry and getting more than a little angry.

He had followed Reva from Pfenestra's Playhouse yesterday afternoon to Nuphar Wood. He'd paused when she'd headed into The Brambles, knowing that if he followed her into the thick undergrowth that he would have to risk being spotted by her to keep sight of her. He knew from the way that she had gotten into the character of her disguise that she was working a case and not just dressing up, but he couldn't figure out what sort of case would take Reva to The Brambles, especially since she'd been suspended.

He knew that if he let her go in there that he would never find her again. She could easily come out in over a dozen places inside or out of Nuphar Wood. He had to take the risk to follow her.

He'd crept into the wood after her, careful to stay hidden. Luckily, Reva had made a poor choice of footwear—Amaryllis had probably insisted that she wear them to be 'authentic'—and Amalaki was able to hear her tripping over roots. Then, he had heard other movement and had stepped into the deep shadows provided by the trees. The scene that he had watched had confused him at first and scared him a little bit. The undead that he saw were clearly threatening, even though the elf that Reva spoke to seemed to be able to control them. When the entire group passed through a silverthorn thicket to a spot well protected within The Brambles, Amalaki knew that he couldn't get any closer. At least, not without the undead noticing his presence.

So, he had settled in to wait. It had turned out to be a stupid decision as the sun soon set. His stomach had protested the lack of any meal, and he had forced himself to stay awake, should Reva and her mysterious companion decide to leave in the night. He'd been startled awake by a cry coming from within the silverthorn. He'd chastised himself for falling asleep and thought about risking an approach through the silverthorn, but after a minute, there were no other sounds, so he'd continued his vigil.

Dawn was breaking over the horizon and, with the new morning, Amalaki began to seethe. He had a pain in his neck and his stomach felt like it was going to start feeding upon itself. He was stiff, cold, and mad at himself. He'd wasted an entire afternoon and night chasing after Reva when he could have been tracking down more relevant— more real—leads in his own case. The Kingdom, and the King, deserved better from him, and his stupid desire to get Reva's opinion on some rumor that he had overheard had been selfish. It was a novice mistake, and he may have put the King's life in danger because of it.

He was about to leave, deciding to cut his losses, when he heard movement coming from the silverthorn. His training and duty pulled him behind the tree to watch the procession of the elf, Reva, and the undead heading out of the shrubs. They took a slow path through the wood, taking them to a spot that would let them exit near the Great Library. With resignation, Amalaki followed them.

He'd watched them head through the empty streets toward the river, and then was surprised when the elf had commanded the undead to enter the river. He and Reva had then headed toward King's Bridge. Amalaki had kept to Embankment Road and rushed ahead of them. He knew that if they were going to cross the river, they would take the stairs from the river's edge to the bridge. He'd arrived and took up his position.

It seemed like an eternity before he spotted Reva leading the elf along the footpath below the bridge. *Finally.* Amalaki turned to watch the steps that led up from the river. He watched as two boys ran down the stairs, and he'd expected Reva and the elf to appear shortly after them, but they hadn't appeared. Then the two boys had come back up at a run, heading toward a pair of constables standing in the middle of the bridge.

Amalaki moved quickly, sliding his way through the people on the bridge and headed down the stairs, his back to the wall. Stealth was an important weapon, and he needed to ascertain what was going on before jumping in like a halpbloed. He could hear talking, and then the sound of something—somebody—being thrown against a wall. He drew his hand crossbow and pulled back the string, nocking a bolt, and then headed down the stairs.

He saw Reva below him, her clothes covered in mud, being lifted off the ground, bound by a spell or magical item. Despite being immobile, she had managed to free one arm—Amalaki was impressed by her strength of will—and threw a dagger at the elf. The dagger struck the elf in the thigh and, at the same time, Reva was flung out over the river. She landed with a splash about a dozen paces away from the riverbank.

Amalaki let his training take over. He took aim with the crossbow and pulled the trigger. The small bolt found its mark, hitting the elf in the back, right between the shoulder blades. Amalaki gave a start because instead of crying in pain, the elf seemed to laugh. Also, quite discouragingly, the poison that should have dropped him like a stone seemed to have no effect. The elf had a distant, glazed expression and a smile grew across his face. He was starting to lift his hand when the thud of boots and yells came from the stairs behind Amalaki. The elf seemed to pause, then grabbed Reva's dagger and pulled it out, letting it fall to the mud. He then took off, limping less than Amalaki would have expected from somebody who had a leg wound.

"What's goin' on here?" asked the constable coming down the stairs. Amalaki ignored him and rushed to the river, tearing off his cloak and pulling off his boots.

"Hey, what are you doing?" called a second voice.

Amalaki jumped into the river and swam to the spot where he had seen Reva hit the water. He was thankful that the current was not very fast at the moment and when he reached the spot, he took a breath and dove under. The River Tenz was not known for its clarity—certainly not here at its mouth—but he could see about a pace or two before the mud and silt blocked his view. He dove toward the bottom, heading a few paces downstream.

He picked a spot and started swimming in what he hoped was an expanding circle, his eyes straining to make out shapes in the water. His own lungs were starting to burn and Reva had been in the water longer, and possibly without the ability to hold her breath.

Suddenly he saw a shape move in front of him, a person kicking their way to the surface. Amalaki kicked upwards as well and broke the surface just after Reva, and received a spray of water in his face as she spit out the water that she had taken in.

"Amalaki?" she sputtered. "What in the hells?"

Amalaki tried to grab her in order to help her reach the shore, but Reva knocked his hand away and started swimming. He rolled his eyes at her bravado and followed her. The two constables stood on the riverbank and one of them helped pull Reva out of the water.

"You can't go jumping in the river, lady. It's against the law to kill yourself."

Amalaki shook his head as he climbed out of the river, shivering a bit as the breeze hit his wet skin.

"Come on," said the other constable, pulling Reva away from the water, "Maybe a day in the cells will sober you up."

Amalaki reached for his boots and cloak and shook his head at the mistake the two constables were about to make. One of them turned toward him.

"And you, what were you doing down here—" His voice cut off as Amalaki held up his cloak. Despite the mud, the dark green color and unique cloak pin were quite recognizable. "Oh, Inquisitor...umm..." The constable went pale and turned back to dealing with somebody that he could control. Or so he thought.

"Let's go, lady," the first constable said, grabbing Reva's arm.

Reva jerked her arm out of his grasp. The constable started to go for his dagger as she pulled the wig off her head, letting the silver-red strands of her hair fall free. "Idiots," she said, using what sounded to Amalaki like her best command voice. "I'm not the one you should be arresting."

The second constable stood with his mouth open. "Inspector Lunaria?"

The first constable tried to put his dagger back without being seen. "What were you doing in the river, Inspector?"

"Going for a morning swim, what does it look like?" she said. She turned to glare at Amalaki. "And what in the hells were you doing here? You just happened to be wandering by?"

Both constables swallowed, clearly taken aback by Reva's tone with an Inquisitor. Amalaki ignored her comment and moved toward the stairs. The mud was oozing between his toes.

"Did something happen, ma'am?" asked the first constable. "Do you need any assistance?"

"Weren't you suspended?" asked the second constable. Amalaki smiled as Reva's glare wilted the constable where he stood. "Not that it's any of my business," the constable stammered. Again, Amalaki realized that Reva would have made a good Inquisitor.

"I don't need any help," she said. She looked around on the ground for her dagger. Amalaki bent to pick it up where the elf had dropped it and handed it to Reva. She took it with a small nod of thanks and cleaned the blade before sheathing it. She turned to the first constable.

"Look, Constable…"

"Lonicera, ma'am."

"Constable Lonicera," Reva's voice had taken on a softer tone. "I appreciate your offer, but I recommend that you stay away from me, and you probably don't want to report that you saw me here. When the shit from all of this lands, you don't want to be standing too close."

Constable Lonicera gave her a quizzical look, but then nodded. He motioned to his partner and they both climbed the stairs. Amalaki took a seat and tried to clean the mud off of his feet.

"You haven't answered my question," Reva said.

"Hmm..."

"Oh, screw you and your secrets. You've been following me. It's the only way you could have been here at the exact moment that all of this happened."

Amalaki managed to get most of the mud off of one foot by transferring it all to his hand. *Figures.* He looked at Reva. Water dripped from her in a small shower and, for the first time, Amalaki noticed how attractive she was. He pushed the thought aside and looked into her eyes, his face taking on a well-practiced mask. "You are lucky that I happened to be here."

"I didn't need any help."

"So being magically bound and thrown into a river is your way of having everything under control?" He started cleaning his other foot.

"Why were you following me?"

"Was I? I just happened to see you when I was crossing the bridge."

It was clear that Reva didn't believe his lie, but he didn't care. Telling her that he'd been following her would reveal too much about his own skills and the methods of the Sucra. He met her gaze and continued to clean his foot.

Reva threw up her hands. "I see the Sucra is still willing to share everything they do." She started to move past him and head up the stairs.

"And I see the Constabulary still isn't teaching manners to its constables." He let the anger and frustration of the past day and night fill his words.

"I didn't need your help."

Amalaki pulled on one of his boots. "Are you always this stubborn? No wonder Malvaceä hates you. How is it that nobody has slit your throat while you sleep?"

Reva nostrils flared at his words and she took an almost imperceptible step back, then she softened ever so slightly. "Thank you for pulling me out of the river," she said, the words still hard but no longer filled with the venom from before. "I'm a lot more civil when people stop lying to me."

Amalaki heard something more in her words. Something that was directed not just at him. He stashed that bit of information away for later. Reva was looking up the stairs, trying to edge past him. He considered what had happened and made a decision that would hopefully pay off later.

"I was following you. Ever since you left Pfenestra's yesterday."

Reva reached for a strand of her hair and stuck the end in her mouth as she considered what he'd said. He'd noticed that this was a habit of hers whenever she was thinking about a problem. After a moment, she released the hair and said, "Whatever. I need to go."

"Going after the elf?" Amalaki pulled on his other boot and stood up.

"I told you that I don't need any help."

"That may be the case, but you should consider some protection from his magic. Otherwise, you'll end up in the river again." He gave Reva a nod as he headed up the stairs. "And remember what I told you the other night. I don't want to have to break in a new liaison officer for the Constabulary."

Chapter 38

Erroll's heart finally started to slow down as he reached the crowded ferry. He'd been surprised by what had happened at the bridge, even more so when the Green Cloak's dart had struck him with no effect. The potency of their darts was legendary, so clearly this was a sign of Dreen's divine protection.

Facing the traitorous Sarah had felt good. He'd decisively dealt with the first threat to his church. He'd been surprised that the threat to his new church had come so soon, and he wondered if maybe she had been sent by Dreen in order to test his resolve. If that was the case, then he was sure that he'd proven himself to Dreen. He was committed to bringing Dreen's message to Tenyl.

At the same time, he was disappointed. When Sarah had shown up yesterday, he had been excited to have a true convert join him in sharing in Dreen's enlightenment. Her presence had validated his belief that he was doing the right thing. If there were people like Sarah already in the city, people who were already close to Dreen, then finding converts would be easier than he thought. This made it more important for him to get Aavril away from the constables and reinforced his idea that Aavril's skill was needed. Maybe if he'd had Aavril with him earlier, Sarah would have seen that she would have been better off as one of Dreen's new acolytes. Apparently, her own views of Dreen's message had led her to seek the power, rather than the truth. He would make sure that the proper message would be given to new converts from now on.

Erroll moved onto the ferry, more determined than ever that his path was the right one. When the ferry reached the far side of the river, he walked into the warren of roads that twisted through Port Grove. His next task was more complicated now, without Sarah to assist with this part of his plan, but he would find a way to make it work. It might take a bit longer, but his disciples would patiently wait for him.

While it was early in the day, the port was already busy. The tide was turning, and the ships that were planning on sailing today would be getting ready to leave. That meant that last-minute supplies and cargo would be unloaded. It took Erroll some time to find what he was looking for: a ship loading last-minute cargo and an empty wagon. The situation was perfect, with the driver seeing to the loading of the cargo. Erroll just had to walk up and mount the driver's seat. He gave a gentle swish of the reins and the two mules began to walk forward. There were a lot of people around the dock, so Erroll couldn't go fast even if he had wanted to, but the crowd of dockworkers, halpbloed, and sailors helped to hide his theft of the wagon. By the time a cry of alarm went up behind him, he was already several hundred paces away and heading further into the docks.

It took several minutes for Erroll to reach the pier where the *Majestic Tern* was moored. The area here was less crowded since the ships along this dock were not planning on sailing this morning. Erroll drove the wagon along the dock and stopped along the gangplank leading to the *Tern*. He had a moment of worry that somebody would do the same thing that he'd just done and make off with the wagon, but he had to trust that Dreen would not let that happen.

Erroll stepped down from the wagon and looked up at

the ugly little ship. He couldn't believe that, just over three months before, he had stood in this same position and looked longingly at the ship. He'd been so young, so naïve at that point, so sure of his skills as a sailor, developed over many years of work in Black Elf Bay and along the coast. He was determined to prove himself as a sailor on a real merchant ship and looking back now, he almost laughed at himself for ever thinking that the *Tern* was anything but an old scow. It was certainly not majestic; he knew that now. Captain Sterna had been too old, and too blind to the rot that had developed within his crew. The old Captain had been distracted, his mind already sitting on the beach in retirement, and so he'd pampered and indulged his son.

Loren had been a bully; a goblin drunk on the power of his position. That's why he had bought the necklace from the Cantullian merchant. He'd not cared one bit about the necklace: it had only been about his power over Erroll. But that was all in the past now, and Loren was dead. There was certainly no love lost between himself and the rest of the crew, as they had all laughed and partaken in the petty games and punishments that Loren had doled out. None of them—save for Aavril—had the least capacity for the higher calling that was Dreen's message of truth, but that didn't matter. They would all become His disciples anyway.

Erroll brought his attention away from the ship to his disciples, waiting patiently for him. They were close by, but not exactly into position yet, so he urged them on with a thought. He then stepped onto the gangplank and walked up to the ship's deck.

He looked at the pitiful deck and couldn't help letting a sneer of disgust flicker across his lips. A gruff voice called out, "You gotta lotta nerve comin' back here."

Erroll turned to see the Sailing Master jumping down from the quarter deck. "Get yer arse offa this ship," Kelsey flung his hand dismissively toward the gangplank.

Erroll held out his hands as if he was a beggar. He put a pleading, whiny tone to his voice, saying, "I've come to apologize. I want to make amends for my actions."

The Sailing Master glared at him suspiciously. "You had time enough ta have made amends when we was at sea. I don't want you on my ship." Kelsey stepped forward and tried to grab for Erroll, but he quickly took a step back.

"Please, is the Captain on board? Let me at least talk to him and apologize. I've had time to think and I know that what I did was wrong." Erroll tried to sound as meek as he could. "You know that it's bad luck to sail with things left unresolved on land."

Erroll knew that he had struck the right chord. Kelsey was a superstitious son of a succubus, and this made him hesitate. "Tha Captain's busy, getting us ready ta sail. He can't see you right now."

Erroll knew this was a lie since Loren was probably feeding the crabs and fishes in the river right now, but he was glad that Kelsey wasn't willing to just toss him off the ship. He needed to delay the Sailing Master just a little bit longer.

Erroll hung his head, and asked, "What about Aavril then? Is he on board? Maybe I can talk to him?"

"The *Isean's* busy, too." Kelsey crossed his arms across his chest.

Erroll briefly wondered if something had happened that he wasn't aware of. *Did the constables release Aavril last night?* Maybe his task would be easier than he thought. "So, Aavril came back from the Constabulary?"

"How in tha hells did you know tha Constables have him?" Kelsey exclaimed, his mouth gaping open like a pufferfish. His reaction was enough to crash Erroll's hope against the rocks. His plan would remain unchanged.

Kelsey seemed to realize his mistake and stepped forward, coming chest-to-chest with Erroll. "You need ta gets off tha *Tern* before I throw you off."

Erroll stood straight, letting all pretense of ever apologizing go. He stared hard at Kelsey as he withdrew the Joy of the Widow's Tears from under his shirt. At the same time, the sound of mumbled, chanting voices came from behind Kelsey.

Kelsey's mouth fell open again. "What in tha hells! How'd ya get tha Cap'n's necklace? You thief!" He moved to grab Erroll's arm, but he froze in mid-grab, his body unable to move.

Erroll took a step back and nodded, allowing two disciples, seawater dripping from their bodies, to step around and face the Sailing Master. Kelsey's face went pale as he saw the disciples.

"Kneel," Erroll said, as he released the magic that was holding Kelsey in place. Instead of kneeling, the Sailing Master took a step back and bumped into another of the disciples that was standing right behind him. With a casual flick of his wrist, Erroll commanded the disciples to attack. Each of the creatures slashed out with their long, bony claws, and Kelsey gave a cry as they dug into his flesh. He immediately dropped to his knees, no longer strong enough to stand.

Erroll held up his hand and the disciples gave a distinct hiss of displeasure at having been ordered to stop. Erroll grabbed Kelsey's throat, giving it a tight squeeze. He could see the pain roll across Kelsey's face, and he heard three disciples break up their mantra for the briefest of moments in a hiss of pleasure. "This is for all the shit that you put me through on this worthless ship."

He let go with a jerk and stepped back to allow his disciples to do what they loved to do. The Sailing Master's cries echoed across the deck, and Erroll sent the other two disciples to the stairs leading below decks. They met the scrambling forms of the rest of the crew as they charged up the stairs and came on deck. They had no time to give a cry before the disciples slashed into them. After a minute, all was quiet again on the deck of the *Majestic Tern*. Then, five new voices joined in, adding to the slow, methodical chorus of his disciples.

"Dreen is pain...pain is truth...Dreen is truth..."

Chapter 39

Reva hustled through the narrow streets of Port Grove, cursing every plodding wagon, every group of halpbloeden laden with goods. She cursed Amalaki and his interference. She had to put the fact that he'd been following her since yesterday on an upper branch. She'd deal with it after all of this was finished. She'd also cursed Amaryllis and his disguise. It had been perfect to get her close to Erroll, but in giving chase, it had left a lot to be desired. The wooden clogs had been a hindrance, and she'd contemptuously kicked them off after crossing King's Bridge. Running in bare feet was easier, but the rough cobbles, trash, and other detritus of Tenyl's streets had not been kind to them. Several times she'd stepped into something that had been a bit too warm, and a bit too soft for her liking.

But she'd pressed on, trying to reach the *Majestic Tern* in time to stop Erroll. She knew his plan, and she had to get to him before he could carry it out. She didn't want to think of the consequences if she failed.

Reva crossed the bridge separating the port from Dock Island. She dodged around more workers and sailors, and then slowed as she approached the *Tern*. The ship was quiet, but an unattended cart sat next to the gangplank. She padded forward and stood next to the mules, her hand resting on the neck of the closest animal. She was about to head up the gangplank when she heard screams coming from the deck. Without hesitation, she drew her dagger and headed up the gangplank, but she paused before she reached the top and looked onto the deck.

Five crewelves were rising from the deck, their bodies torn and shredded from the claws of the disciples, who stood nearby, each of them repeating that annoying mantra. Standing in the middle of the deck, arms outstretched as if basking in the adulation of a standing ovation at Pfenestra's, was Erroll. *Not good.*

The sight of ten disciples caused acid to bubble up from Reva's stomach. She didn't know how to stop one of the creatures, let alone ten of them. And Erroll was a very serious threat as long as he had the necklace. This fight was lost, and if she couldn't get away, she would turn into one of Erroll's pets. She shuddered, not liking the idea of becoming an undead minion. She was trying to figure out the best course of action when Erroll turned and looked in her direction. She didn't know if he'd seen her or not, and she didn't relish the idea of being bound and at his mercy. She turned and jumped off the gangplank, diving into the brown water between the hull of the *Tern* and the pier.

Reva swam down and paused near the base of one of the barnacle-encrusted piles. She looked up, the outline of the ship and pier simple dark shapes against the bright sky. There were no other splashes, which meant that Erroll had either not sent his disciples after her, or he'd not seen her at all. After a count to ten, she relaxed and pushed off away from the *Tern*, swimming under the pier. She stayed underwater until her lungs felt like they would burst, and she finally drifted up to the surface, gulping in the putrid, fishy air. She swam a few paces to a ladder that was set along one of the piles and climbed out of the water.

A halpbloed dockworker was coiling a rope and stared at her as she stepped onto the pier. "Ring of water walking gave out," she quipped, as she walked toward the shore.

She gave a glance toward the *Majestic Tern* and was relieved to see no disciples walking down the gangplank. Stopping Erroll now seemed an impossible task. He could increase his horde of minions at will; nothing seemed to be able to stop the creatures. But she knew from their conversation last night that he wanted more. He wasn't just trying to build an army of undead creatures. *He wants to make his own church. He wants—he craves—followers who can understand Dreen in the same way that he does.* And the only way that Erroll could see doing that was by getting Aavril. Reva didn't understand it, even after Erroll had shown her his scars—from a lashing that Aavril had given him—and tried to explain how the pain had freed his mind. To Reva, anybody who professed to like pain was either a fool or cursed with a head illness.

She didn't have to understand Erroll's motives to know what his next move would be. He needed Aavril, and Aavril was currently in custody. That meant that Erroll would try to break Aavril out of New Port.

Looking around at the number of dockworkers and sailors, she thought (hoped) that Erroll wouldn't make his move until later in the day. He'd stressed the need to move unseen through Tenyl this morning, and that had been why he'd sent the disciples ahead under the cloak of the River Tenz. He might have been able to throw a cloak or robes over the creatures to hide their forms, but nobody could miss their incessant chant. It was sure to alert somebody, who might tell a constable, or a Green Cloak, or a cleric. Despite their seeming invincibility, Erroll was smart enough to know that he couldn't stand up to a combined opposition to him. By waiting until this afternoon, a lot of the workers would have either gone home or drifted into the many pubs. It would then be easier to sneak the disciples out and make it to New Port undetected.

Reva was likely to be thrown into one of New Port's cells

if she showed up, but she knew that's where Erroll would be heading, so she would need to be there, too. Eventually. Amalaki's caution from the bridge blended with the conclusion that she had reached while bound by Erroll. She had a couple of stops to make before she could confront Erroll.

Reva headed through the narrow streets, casting murderous glares to any elf or halpbloed who thought that she might be an easy mark. After about ten minutes, she approached a battered door under a sign hung with four brass acorns and fading letters that said "Lombard". Rhoanlan's pawn shop was dim, with untold ages of grime coating the windows into a yellowed haze that kept out most of the daylight. The tall piles of junk that were seemingly stacked haphazardly around the tiny space helped to block the rest. Rhoanlan himself sat at a square table currently stacked with a pile of yellowed parchment, his large body looming over the documents.

Reva stood in front of the table, water still dripping from her clothes and onto the floor in slow, steady plops.

"Whoever you are, if you get my documents wet, I will have your innards pulled out to make a garland for my door."

"Somebody is testy today. What's the matter, fencing not paying enough these days?"

Rhoanlan looked up, pulling a jeweler's loupe from one eye. He was about to say something, but then a smile spread slowly across his mouth. "Funny, you look a little like a Constable Inspector I know, but since she's on suspension right now, you can't be her. Get out of here before I throw you out."

Reva laughed. "Have you ever lifted anything heavier than a gold necklace in your life, Rhoanlan?"

He shrugged, "I think a pint of ale counts."

Reva pointed to the collection of parchment he was leaning over. "I didn't know you were a *Pfedai fey Urlak.*"

Rhoanlan tilted his head, his mouth pinched.

"A magical collector," Reva pointed at the parchment. "Those appear to be rare magical scrolls, based on their illustrations. Cas liked to collect scrolls like those, and she would show them to me."

Rhoanlan made a harrumph sound and moved to stack the parchments, "I am cataloging these for a client."

"Did your client tell you where he had gotten them from?"

"Why do you care?"

"Well, maybe they want to part with some of them. I could get a Bonfires gift for Cas."

Rhoanlan's shoulders sagged a bit. "I might be able to make an inquiry with my client to see if they are interested."

"I'm only interested if these are the scrolls your client stole from Auros Academy last week," she gave him a predatory smile.

"There you go, accusing me of being something that I am not, Inspector." He quickly slid the scrolls off of the table and made them disappear somewhere behind his wide girth. "You know that I do not deal in stolen goods."

"Of course. My mistake. So, setting up a meeting with your client..."

"Is out of the question. I take the privacy of my clients very seriously." He narrowed his eyes, "Besides, you *are* on suspension, and I doubt FC Aescel or LCI Betulla would like to learn that you are working cases."

They held each other's gaze for a few beats, and then Rhoanlan leaned back with a smile. "Now, if you are done bothering me." He made a gesture to shoo Reva out of his shop.

"I need something, and I'm sure that you may have what I need buried somewhere in this midden."

Rhoanlan gave her an appraising look, and then spread

his hands. "What can a humble Lombard do for you?"

"I need something that can protect me from magical bindings."

"I didn't know that your love life was that kinky," he said, with a lecherous grin. Reva returned his comment with a rude gesture and he gave a hearty laugh. "Are we talking just a protection from becoming mute, full paralysis, or something in between?"

"Full paralysis."

Rhoanlan rubbed his chin and swiveled his head to take in the room. After a minute, he stood up and walked around to a cabinet that was bowed under a dwarf's hoard of junk. He opened a narrow drawer and pulled out a small box. He returned to his seat and set the box in front of him. "This is a ring that will give you protection from all magics that might bind or hold you against your will."

Reva held out her hand and he gave her the box. She pulled it open and saw a simple silver ring that was etched with what appeared to be dwarven runes. She would have to trust that the ring did as he said, but he had never given her wrong information, or a defective item, in the past. She moved to pull the ring out, but Rhoanlan quickly grabbed the box, his hand moving faster than a viper's strike.

"And how are you planning on paying me, Inspector? I am not running a charity shop."

"I don't want to buy it. I just need to borrow it for a while."

Rhoanlan raised one eyebrow. "I am also not in the habit of loaning out my inventory, at least not without the proper collateral."

Reva gestured to her outfit. "I am currently without any funds."

"There are more ways to pay for something than with common coin." He reached over and pulled one of her sleeves up to reveal the scars on her arm. Reva had actually forgotten about them. "From what I know about you, Inspector, I know that those are not real, despite how convincing they look. I also know that you are more tenacious than a hawk tick when it comes to a case, even if you've been suspended. Any constable worth his sap has many contacts that they can go to for assistance." He made a slow study of Reva's outfit.

"There is considerable damage, I'm sure that Amaryllis will scold you for damaging one of his creations."

"I'm not giving you the clothes I am wearing." Reva placed her hands on her hips.

Rhoanlan gave a little laugh. "My dear, I have no need for the clothes—although there are a few collectors who'd pay top branch for an Amaryllis original. No, my dear Inspector, like you, I'm a passionate follower of the arts, but I have been denied entry to our fair city's best playhouse for several years now."

Reva raised one eyebrow, but Rhoanlan did not give her an answer. Whatever his transgression, she was sure that it had to have been related to light fingers and a missing possession of Pfenestra's. She was starting to see where this was going. "So what can I do for you?"

Rhoanlan laced his fingers together and placed them on his ample stomach. "I want to see a play."

"A play?" Reva turned her head and glared at him.

"Well, the current play that is running at Pfenestra's."

No way it's this simple, Reva told herself. "What else?"

"And I want to be given backstage access, both before and after the performance. I want to meet the actors and see the costumes that Amaryllis has created."

Reva stared at Rhoanlan. Even if he'd been banned from Pfenestra's, this was too simple. Reva would be able to get Rhoanlan in—Pfenestra would take Reva's word that the Lombard would not cause any trouble.

Rhoanlan gave another laugh. "I can see the artificers

working away behind those pretty eyes of yours, Inspector. You are trying to figure out what my ulterior motive is for this. But I assure you—I give you my word of honor—that I only want to see a play and meet those responsible for putting on the performance."

Reva managed to give him her best *I still don't believe you* look, but said, "Sure. I can make that work. It might be a week or so until I can make the arrangements."

"But I thought you were on suspension?" He gave a little pout.

Reva just smiled and held out her hand. With some reluctance, Rhoanlan placed the ring on her palm. After she had closed her fingers tightly around the ring, she said, "Oh, but you are buying the drinks after the play."

He inclined his head, concluding the transaction. "I look forward to our date."

Reva slipped the ring onto her left hand and headed out of the small shop. *That's one task done. Now I need to get into some more appropriate clothes and find Pfastbinder.*

Chapter 40

Ansee walked across the New Port courtyard toward the training area. His mind wasn't on the upcoming training but was still rooting through the conversation that he'd had with Aavril that morning. Ansee was sure that Reva's boyfriend was telling the truth, at least about Amber's murder, and if they could have a longer conversation, he might be able to part the leaves on Loren's death as well. After the brief encounter with Inspector Pflamtael, Ansee had given up any hope of convincing him to listen to Aavril. As far as Pflamtael was concerned, everything was settled except for picking out the length of rope.

He hadn't given much thought to the training that Senior Constable Ghrellstone had asked him to give until Willem had reminded him about it at lunch. As he turned the corner of the Feedshed and approached the training area, his mouth fell open. There must have been twenty constables waiting in the training area. Sweat immediately slicked his palms, and any thoughts about Aavril and the two cases fled from his mind. Every Senior Constable—at least those who were not on duty—stood in small knots around the training area. Ansee even spotted First Constables Aescel and Churlsleaf standing among the group. All of them turned to look at Ansee as he approached the small field.

Senior Constable Ghrellstone had a broad smile carved on his face and waved Ansee forward. "What a great turnout for your class, Seeker."

Ansee walked through the group of his fellow constables, greeting everybody. When he reached Willem, he whispered, "You did this on purpose."

"I don't know what you mean," Willem's smile seemed to grow broader. "I merely suggested to my friends that it might be useful to come to your training."

"And this isn't an attempt to haze me, to get me to fall off a branch in front of every senior constable in the RTC?"

Willem actually looked hurt. "That's the furthest thing from my mind, Ansee. Besides, not every senior constable is here."

Ansee glared at the Senior Constable, who still managed to look sincere. "Very well." He picked up one of the wooden training daggers from a basket at Willem's feet. "Let's get started."

† † †

Two hours later, Ansee was feeling a lot better, happy with how the training had gone. It had been a bit shaky at first. Most of the Senior Constables had been reluctant to think that a mere Seeker could teach them anything about combat, but a few demonstrations—disarming Willem and besting Senior Constable Rhosa—had shown them that Ansee knew what he was doing.

Ansee had then paired everybody up and began teaching them the basic moves. He'd demonstrate with Willem first, then have everybody do the moves as he walked around to observe and correct their technique.

"That's good, everybody. Let's take a break," Ansee called. "I think that's enough for today."

A few of the students looked relieved, although Ansee noticed that most of the constables looked disappointed. Willem stepped up. "If it's alright with the First Constables,

I think we should have this become a weekly training."

Churlsleaf nodded, wiping sweat from his brow. Aescel added, "That's a good idea. I'm sure that Seeker Carya has more that he can show us."

Ansee nodded. "I've only really covered a few of the basics. There's a lot more to learn."

"Until next week, then," Willem said. He moved off to collect the training weapons. Ansee noticed that several of the Senior Constables were still practicing the moves that he had shown them. A warm glow flowed out of his stomach at the sight.

First Constable Aescel walked over, with Churlsleaf right behind him. "Where'd you learn to wield a dagger like that?" The question came from the Betula Division First Constable.

"I learned from a weapon master over in Marsh Grove. After my first days of being a constable, during Senior Constable Jurasee's sword training I realized that I needed to learn something other than the sword. Had we been using anything other than training blades, I probably would have killed myself in that first class. I couldn't get the hang of the sword, and I was sure that Constable Jurasee would kick me out of the Constabulary." Ansee managed to smile at the memory.

"I found somebody willing to give me lessons in wielding a dagger. I figured that if I couldn't use a sword, I had better get really good at using a dagger."

"Who's this master you went to?" asked Aescel.

"Her name is Kalo Lunthana and she was originally an adventurer from the Arisport area."

"Arisport?" Churlsleaf's eyes widened.

Ansee nodded. "Apparently she decided to retire from adventuring and opened a weapon school here. She knows a lot of different fighting styles with daggers, swords, and other blades. I learned everything I know from her. Well enough that I eventually bested Constable Jurasee with my daggers. That's why she let me graduate without a long-sword proficiency."

"Well, you certainly taught me a few things," said Churlsleaf.

Aescel nodded his agreement.

"I told you it would be worth coming," Willem said, as he walked up to the group.

"Are you okay?" Ansee asked. In one of the demonstrations, Willem had been a bit too aggressive, trying to catch Ansee flat-footed. Ansee had managed to drop the older constable hard onto his hip.

Willem rubbed the spot. "I'll be a little stiff tomorrow, but I'll live."

"If this becomes a regular class," said Aescel, "then we might be able to give you a raise since you'd be teaching a class in addition to your regular duties."

Ansee was surprised. He hadn't expected that. "Áeorias, sir."

"Excellent," added Willem. "Especially if you're always going to be buying our drinks."

"What?" asked the two First Constables at the same moment.

Ansee wasn't able to explain as, at that moment, a green bolt of light exploded with a loud BANG. All four turned toward the sound. It was a signal flare, and it meant that a constable was in danger.

"That came from within New Port," Ansee said, fear tingeing his words.

Chapter 41

Ansee, Willem, and several other constables drew their weapons and raced toward the front of New Port. Cries and yells could be heard coming from the courtyard. Running between the main building and one of the annexes, Ansee was shocked as he entered the courtyard.

A wagon sat in the center of the courtyard, with two mules hitched to it, moving aimlessly in a small circle. Near the wagon and moving away from it in a growing ring were several walking corpses. Ansee instantly recognized the cleric Brenna and the two victims from the flower shop.

The undead? Here?

He didn't have time to think. The creatures were cackling gleefully, chanting their insane mantra. Several constables were attempting to attack them and suffering the consequences as they staggered back from unseen, but very real, blows. One constable was being raked savagely by one of the creatures; he struggled to remain on his feet. The doors to the main building stood wide open.

"What the...!" exclaimed Willem. "What are bloody zombies doing here?" He hefted his sword. "We'll clear them out and then find the necromancer responsible."

"No!" Ansee yelled and grabbed Willem by the arm. "They aren't zombies. We need to fall back. Get our people to safety."

Willem pulled his arm free. "Fall back?"

"Trust me, Willem," Ansee pleaded. He pointed at the Brenna creature. "Recognize her? That's the cleric that came here looking for help. Kai and I encountered these creatures two nights ago. They were unaffected by her attempts to turn them, and they nearly killed Kai and me. We have to fall back, or everybody will be killed and turned into them."

At that moment there came a scream from another constable across the courtyard. He was staggering back from one of the creatures, grasping his shoulder. The creature's ghastly face was grinning wildly, almost erotically, with pleasure. It raised its claws to strike the constable.

Ansee thrust out his left hand, yelling, *"Onu savun!"* A swirl of red light raced toward the constable, enveloping him in a reddish mist. The undead claws slashed down and skittered away, deflected by the shield spell.

"Get everyone to the wagon shed!" commanded Willem, his voice rising over the din of combat in the courtyard. "Gather our wounded and protect them. Don't attack unless you need to."

The half-dozen constables that had come from the training area gave a cry and moved into the melee, trying to push back the undead and save their fellow officers. Attacks were unavoidable and there were surprised yells of pain as constables received reciprocating wounds when they struck the creatures. Ansee knew that direct attacks would be pointless, so he focused on aiding the others. He cast two more protection spells and gated a severely wounded constable away from one of the creatures. Ansee knew that there was something wrong about this attack, something was jiggling one of his branches, but he couldn't focus on the problem as he focused his attention on saving as many people as possible.

A cry of alarm came from across the courtyard, and Ansee turned to see a young constable flanked by two of the undead. The creatures lashed out before Ansee could react, four sets of claws raking across the constable's body. He collapsed in a heap and the undead paused, looking down at the fallen elf.

Ansee felt his ears redden and his body shake uncontrollably with anger. He'd failed, and a constable had fallen. Ansee knew that, within a minute, one of his fellow officers would rise up as one of these unstoppable creatures. He'd seen it happen with Brenna. It was a fate he would not wish upon his worst enemy. So with cold, calculated thought, Ansee brought his hands together, holding them slightly apart as magical energy built up between them. *I won't let you monsters claim another innocent life.* "*Yildirim yanmasi!*" A ball of blue-white lightning exploded from his hands and struck the fallen constable. Fingers of lightning jumped over the body, the skin burning and cracking, then burst into flame. The sound of thunder echoed around the courtyard.

Ansee was surprised to feel nothing from his attack and all of the undead in the courtyard turned their eyes on him, each of them hissing and screeching in fury. Ansee swallowed, "Well, I guess that's one way to get their attention."

A shrill whistle came from Willem, signaling that everybody was safe. Ansee waved back. Three of the creatures were between him and the wagon shed, plus there were two behind him. Another three were moving toward him from other directions.

"Dreen is pain...pain is truth...Dreen is truth..."

Their mantra grew louder with each step toward Ansee. Their numbers had grown since the forest, and Ansee still wondered why they were attacking here. *How did they even get here? Who's controlling them?*

He looked at one of the creatures, one that had not been in Nuphar Wood. It was a sailor by his dress, and Ansee noticed the skin art on the creature's forearm. A bird with wings outstretched. The same skin art as Aavril and Loren. *Aavril!*

As the undead closed in, forming a circle that was quickly closing with him at its center, Ansee yelled, "*Oraya git*" and disappeared in a pop and flash of yellow light. He appeared a dozen paces away, right in front of the doors to New Port, and ran inside.

† † †

"How is she doing?" asked Constable Inspector Pflamtael. He referred to the unconscious form of Constable Whitlocke, who was lying on the floor.

"Not good," replied Seeker Pfinzloab. "Whatever those creatures were, they seemed to drain away her strength with their attack. She's holding on, but only by a thin branch."

"What about you?" Olwyn asked, with genuine concern in his voice.

"It hurts, but I'll live." She'd tried to stop one of the creatures by casting a force bolt spell—her only offensive spell—at the creature. It had struck true, but she'd been surprised as searing pain had erupted on her own chest. She'd staggered back from the strange effect, wondering what in the hells had happened.

Olwyn flexed his right arm and Norah saw him wince. He'd also struck one of the creatures in the arm and Norah knew that he'd also experienced a similar phantom injury.

They had been heading to the cells to continue their interrogation of Aavril. He had been uncooperative in their earlier session and Olwyn had decided to try again with some more persuasive interrogation techniques. Norah had questioned the need—this was Reva's boyfriend, even if he was a murderer—and Olwyn didn't need a confession to make his case stick. She realized that this was more about sticking the arrest to Reva rather than catching a murderer. That thought had been bothering her like a piece of food stuck between her teeth as they'd headed to the cells.

Constable Whitlocke had been speaking with an elf with two hooded companions, telling him that he couldn't visit any prisoners as it was against the regulations.

"The only law that applies to me is Dreen's law as I spread his message of truth!"

The outburst had caught Norah's attention and she turned to see him snap his fingers. His two companions flipped off their hooded cloaks. They caught Constable Whitlocke by surprise, slashing at her with long, cruel claws.

She and Olwyn had sprung into action even as cries of alarm and combat could be heard coming from the courtyard. Olwyn had tried to intercept the elf as he'd headed toward the stairs, but the strange creatures—zombies by their appearance—had managed to block Olwyn's way. She and Olwyn quickly learned that these zombies were full of nasty surprises. Unable to follow the unknown elf, Olwyn had managed to hold off the undead as Norah had picked up the prone body of Constable Whitlocke. They'd retreated down the hallway to a storage room, barring the door.

Now that Whitlocke was safe, Norah saw Olwyn's ears redden and his nostrils flare. He wasn't just mad, he was seething. "That bloody elf had skin art that matched our prisoner. He's here to rescue his master."

Norah nodded, as it was the only thing that made sense right now. "If we go back out there, I won't be much use."

"Didn't you prepare your spells?"

"Of course I did," Norah snapped. Olwyn's tone had been accusatory. It may have been due to the stress, but it didn't excuse him. "But I only prepared the standard spell set. I've got limited offensive and defensive spells. And I'd rather not hurt them again—if they can even be hurt. Whatever magic is upon them that reflects our attacks is painful."

"Whatever you can do will be helpful. I won't let that murderer be rescued without a fight."

Norah's staff was upstairs, but she could manage without it. She spoke an incantation and a red nimbus of light surrounded her hand. She touched Olwyn and the light flickered over his body. "That will give you some protection from their claws. It won't last long though, and I don't know if it will protect you from whatever it is that hurts us when we hurt them."

Olwyn nodded and gripped his sword, pulling open the door. The short hallway was empty, and they quickly moved toward the stairs and down to the cells. A loud POP and the sound of running feet caused them both to turn toward the entrance.

"Seeker Carya," Olwyn said, "How's the fight going outside?"

"Not good. Everybody is safe in the wagon shed, but these creatures are still out there. They are here to get Reva's boyfriend."

"Yes, we already figured that out," Olwyn snapped. "I won't let Aavril make his escape." He hefted his service sword, and a quick look of disappointment flashed across his face. "I just wish I had *Aconitu* with me." He shrugged and headed down the stairs, with Norah and Ansee following him.

The cell block was a corridor three paces wide with six cells, three on either side of the corridor. Aavril's cell was the last one on the left, and Norah saw that it stood open. One of the undead stood in the corridor and turned to face them. Norah recognized the uniform of a royal guard and she wondered how this unfortunate elf had been turned into this creature.

"Dreen is pain...pain is truth...Dreen is truth..."

"Who in the hells is it talking about?" asked Olwyn.

"Some unknown god," answered Ansee.

"Another one?" complained Norah. "What is that, like twenty of them now?"

"I've lost count," said Olwyn. "It doesn't matter." He charged down the corridor, sword raised.

"Wait, don't—" Ansee called, but Norah cut him off.

"We know."

Olwyn feinted a strike and jumped around the creature as it tried to slash him with its claws. The undead turned to follow Olwyn and that's when Norah ran up, pulling off her cloak. She flung the garment over the creature's head, blinding it. The creature struggled wildly, and it was much stronger than it appeared, as she almost lost control of the creature.

"Open it!" she yelled at Ansee, nodding to the cell door right next to her. He immediately moved and opened the door, and Norah pulled hard on the cloak, steering the undead like a stubborn mule until it was facing the open cell. There was a ripping sound as the creature started to free itself, and she and Ansee quickly shoved it into the empty cell. Ansee closed the heavy door and threw the bolt behind it.

A wild cry and the sound of more tearing fabric came from the cell. "Damn it," Norah said, "That was my best cloak."

A cry came from Olwyn and she and Ansee turned to see him pinned against the wall. An elf walked out of Aavril's cell, his hand raised. Aavril stood behind the elf, and Norah noticed that he looked stunned and frightened, not elated or happy at being freed. The other undead stood behind Aavril and prodded him out of the cell.

"Save me!" Aavril yelled. "Don't let him take me!"

"Halt!" Norah commanded. She started weaving a spell, cursing that her staff was upstairs. *It would have made this so much faster to do.* Before she could complete the spell, the elf gave a flick of his wrist. Suddenly she couldn't move, her hands and arms refusing to follow her brain. She could hear Ansee struggling next to her and knew that he was also trapped by the binding magic. With a contemptuous flip of his hand, the elf flung all three constables down to the end of the corridor.

Norah and Ansee fell into a tangle on the floor, and then Olwyn landed hard against the wall above them. The binding magic had been lifted, but the wind had been knocked from Norah's lungs and she struggled to regain her focus.

The elf commanded the creature to prod Aavril down the corridor, stopping at the cell that was holding the trapped undead. Norah heard Ansee struggle to free his hands and call out an incantation, one that she had never heard before. *That is not one of the standard spells!*

"*Bu kapıyı şok edici bir sürprizle kilitleyin.*"

A ball of red and blue light leaped toward the cell door. It struck the door with no apparent effect, but as the elf tried to open the door, the bolt refused to move, and a cascade of sparks shot up the elf's arm. His hair stood out from his head and he let out a yowl that was part cry of pain and part laughter.

The elf turned to glare down the corridor, smoke rising in a thin wisp from his hand. Suddenly Ansee was lifted off of the floor, grabbed by the same binding magic. Norah heard a raspy gasp for air come from Ansee and his eyes started to roll back into his head. A small part of her—a very small part—was pleased that Ansee had met somebody that he couldn't handle with his demon magic, but she struggled to free herself out from under Olwyn's body. He may be enthralled to a demon, but Ansee was still a Constable. She wove her spell quickly, nearly without thought, and called out, "*Sihirli füze!*" to power the magic. Three scarlet bolts of light shot from her outstretched fingers and struck the elf, breaking his concentration. He yelled, more from anger than any pain, and Ansee dropped to the floor.

"You will not escape Dreen's truth!" He turned from the cell door and fled up the stairs, the undead creature forcing Aavril along ahead of it.

"After them," Olwyn cried. He climbed to his feet and took off at a run, Norah and Ansee following him. By the time the trio reached the front doors, Aavril and his liberator had climbed onto the wagon. The other undead had already climbed into the bed. They rolled out of the courtyard before anybody could give chase.

Chapter 42

After leaving Rhoanlan's shop, Reva had headed home so that she could change out of her wet clothes and grab her personal sword. She wasn't going to try to stop Erroll without something better than a dagger in her hand. Mother had been busy with setting a new batch of pottery into the kiln and hadn't heard Reva come in, though Gabii had. That had ruined any chance of Reva getting out without her mother knowing that she'd been there. It had taken half an hour for Reva to pry herself away from her mother's questions and looks of disapproval.

She'd headed toward Nul Pfeta wondering where she'd find Pfastbinder. She was going to need the cleric's help to figure out what to do about the disciples. Nul Pfeta had always had a run-down look to it as it had been the poorest part of Tenyl long before it had been converted into a ghetto for halpbloeden and humans. Shoved against the city's western wall, and bordered on the north by the river and to the east by Cicata Creek and Salicae Wood, Nul Pfeta formed a roughly triangular grove that had no place to expand except for downward and upward. Because of this, Nul Pfeta had some of the tallest buildings in the city—many three or four stories tall—and a set of sewers, catacombs, and underground passages to swell the heart of any dwarf, if there were any living in the city. The growth upward had been cobbled together so that most of the upper stories leaned precariously over the narrow streets. Reva had even seen a couple of buildings where their tops actually touched over the road.

Reva stepped off of Victory Bridge and past the gate-house that served as the RTC's garrison in the grove. Most of the grove's inhabitants were at their jobs right now, so the streets were relatively empty, although there were still plenty of people that were around. Reva had only ever been to the run-down shack that Pfastbinder called his temple once before, and she had to pause for a moment to get her bearings. A couple of halpbloeden kids watched her tentatively from the shadow of one of the buildings. Reva wasn't sure if they might just be beggars or if they were sizing her up as a potential mark for a robbery. Reva gripped the hilt of her sword and narrowed her eyes, and the two kids ran off.

She headed off, careful to keep one hand resting on the hilt of her sword. After about fifteen minutes, she approached the small shack that was jammed between two larger buildings. A jester's hat was crudely painted over the door. Reva pushed the door open and stepped into a smoke-filled room that was maybe four paces wide and barely ten paces deep. Tapers guttered along the walls, giving off a grey smoke, and a brazier burned at the front that released even more smoke. Reva was not surprised that the room smelled of *canab*. Pfastbinder and two others sat around the brazier as Pfastbinder was animatedly telling them some gospel of Banok or other hawkshit. Reva had little use for any of the major faiths, but she really couldn't stand the idiocy that Pfastbinder peddled in.

She stood as close to the door as she could, her arms crossed, and waited for him to finish his story. When it looked like he would ignore her and launch into the next tale, clearly enjoying the euphoric feeling that the burning *canab* was imparting, Reva grabbed a pitcher of "holy" water from its spot by the door. She walked over and dumped the pitcher onto the brazier and a cloud of steam and smoke erupted from the iron pan.

"Are you sure you are not Banok's own avatar here on Ados, Inspector? You are so good at creating chaos wherever you go."

"I'm just a constable who's tired of everybody's hawkshit. I found our friends."

"Who?" Pfastbinder's eyes were still a little glassy from his 'ceremony.' He was either playing with her or he didn't remember their conversation from the day before.

"The ones camping out in Nuphar Wood who played with Ansee."

"I see," he said, his eyes going wide with understanding. He jumped up and kicked the two elves who were trying to waft the faint smoke from the drowned *canab* into their noses. "Out! Out! You lazy goblins! Go see if you can spread Banok's gospel or something."

The two halpbloed stumbled to their feet and wove a meandering path to the door. When they had gone, Pfastbinder sat down on an overturned barrel that served as a chair. He seemed alert, and the far-off stare of a heavy *canab* user was gone.

"You recover rather fast from that," Reva gestured to the soggy leaves.

"I am a cleric in faithful service to my god," Pfastbinder huffed. "He rewards those of us with faith." Then he leaned forward and said conspiratorially, "Plus I have a lot of experience at praying."

Reva snorted, "That's what you call prayer?"

"You should come by for services sometime. Your senses will open up to the wider world that Banok offers." He spread his arms and lifted his head to the ceiling.

"No thanks. I like to keep my senses close to home."

Pfastbinder's smile seemed to say, *Fine, more for me*

then. Aloud, he asked, "So, what did you learn about our friends?"

"Quite a bit. They are controlled by an elf called Erroll. He's a former sailor who's become a fanatical follower of Dreen."

"Who is he? Is he a cleric? Or a necromancer? How does he control them?"

"He wears a necklace called the Joy of the Widow's Tears. He said he found it in a market in Cantull. He says that Dreen speaks to him through the necklace and it gives him power over the disciples, plus a few other things."

"Disciples? Interesting..." Pfastbinder stood up and started to pace the small temple. "You remember that I told you some things about the creatures: that they could reflect an injury, and that they had a thirst for pain as if they fed on it. But I didn't know they were called disciples. Interesting." He continued to pace, tapping a finger against his cheek.

"I spent a long night with them."

"Really? What was it like?"

"Creepy. They never shut up. They speak that mantra of theirs continuously. I thought that Gabii was a pain in the ass, but I'll take her yammering over the ravings that came from the disciples. At one point, they managed to catch a squirrel and they spent nearly an hour playing with it, poking it so that it would feel pain. Each time they did, it was like they were all drinking from a fine wine."

"So, this Erroll controls the disciples with the necklace?" Reva nodded.

"I wonder how many he can control with it?"

"Well, the last time I saw him, he had the five I met and it looked like he'd just added another four or five."

"Ten of them?" Pfastbinder stopped his pacing. "Well, that's it. I'm out of here." He started turning in a circle as if he was searching for something.

"What? We had a deal?"

"Sorry. Something just came up. Cleric of the God of chaos. You know how unpredictable we are. I've got to leave." He grabbed his multi-colored cloak and started to pull it on.

Reva grabbed his arm. "The hells you are. You said you'd help me."

Pfastbinder pulled his arm away and headed to a corner to collect his other possessions. "That was before."

"Before what?"

He turned, his eyes wide. "Before that crazy Dreenist brought down the end of Tenyl."

"Oh, come on," Reva crossed her arms. "You're exaggerating. It's just ten undead."

"Ten undead that I don't know how to stop. They feed off of our pain. You've seen how easily they can create more of their kind. And we can't hurt them. Your partner found that out the hard way."

"There's got to be a way to kill them. Everything dies."

Pfastbinder shook his head. "Maybe. But to kill these creatures you may have to kill yourself to do it. Are you willing to commit suicide to save the city? What about your friends and fellow constables? And how many will you have to sacrifice to stop them? There could be two dozen or more by now." He picked up a satchel and started to stuff things into it.

"What if we could capture one?"

"What? You want to try to catch one?" He tried to stuff things into the satchel faster.

"Sure. Everything has a weakness. If these creatures couldn't be stopped, they'd have spread across the entire world by now. Since they haven't, that means that there is a way to stop them."

"Good luck finding it, I wish you all the best," Pfastbinder said over his shoulder as he blew out the candles and stuffed them, hot wax and all, into the satchel. He started toward the door.

"Think of the converts you'd gain if you were the one to find out how to stop them?"

Pfastbinder paused, his hand on the door.

"I mean, if word got around that Tenyl's only cleric of Banok had found a way to stop a group of undead from overrunning the city..."

"A horde."

Reva shrugged. "Right, a horde. I'm sure a cleric who did that could get a few converts. Spread his message."

Pfastbinder turned, "And shove it in the faces of those pompous priests of Basvu."

"Sure," Reva chuckled. "Just don't start a holy war over it, or I'll have to arrest you." She looked around the room. "Do you need anything to be able to test one of these disciples?"

"I've got everything here," he patted the satchel. "Cleric of the God of chaos, always ready to be on the move."

They headed out of the temple. "So, how do we capture one of these disciples?" Pfastbinder asked.

"I thought you'd have an idea."

Chapter 43

Reva and Pfastbinder hustled the last several paces up the hill to New Port. She'd seen the signal flare as they had left Nul Pfeta and had raced toward the signal. It had still taken them nearly fifteen minutes to get across town. The whole time, Reva worried about what the flare meant. It had clearly come from New Port, and it was a sign that the constabulary was under attack, but by who? She was afraid that it was Erroll and his disciples, come to rescue Aavril. She was too late to give them any warning, and when they got to New Port, she expected to have to face dozens of her friends and co-workers who'd been turned into undead.

A wagon pulled by two mules almost ran her down as they neared the gate. Reva thought that she saw Erroll whipping the animals, but she was too busy dodging their hooves to be sure. The wagon was already fifty paces down the road when she tried to get a better look. With a frustrated sigh, she turned away and walked into New Port.

Inside the gate was pure chaos. She saw at least one dead body and several others who were injured. Senior Constable Ghrellstone stood by the wagon shed, checking on the injured. Near the main entrance, she saw Ansee, CI Pflamtael, and Seeker Pfinzloab.

Pfastbinder stepped up next to her and gestured to the courtyard. "What in Banok's name happened here?" He didn't wait for an answer and headed toward the nearest injured constable.

Reva walked over to Ansee and the others. "What happened?"

"I'll tell you what happened." Pflamtael snarled. "Your bloody boyfriend's partner attacked us with undead so that he could make his escape."

"Aavril may be many things," Reva said. *Liar and oath-breaker being two of them,* she didn't say. "But he'd never willingly work with undead. His sister was killed by undead. He loathes them."

"I know what I saw," Pflamtael said.

"No, you're wrong," Ansee said. "He was afraid. He didn't want to go with them."

"Do not reprimand me, *Seeker.* Our suspect made his escape with the help of his partner."

Seeker Pfinzloab cleared her throat. "You're not seeing things clearly, Olwyn. I saw the fear in Aavril's eyes. He didn't want to go with them. He yelled for us to save him."

Pflamtael bit his lip, his brow furrowed. He was about to speak when a new voice bellowed from the doorway. "What in the many hells happened here? Constable Inspector, report."

The group turned to see Lord Constable Inspector Betulla stride through the open doors. She took in the aftermath of the battle and continued to shout questions. "Who attacked us? Were they after anything? Where are the attackers?"

Betulla's gaze finally fell on Reva. "What are you doing here, *Inspector*?" The odd stress that she put on Reva's title implied that Reva might not hold that rank for much longer.

"My *duty*, ma'am." Reva held Betulla's gaze, daring her to question Reva's loyalty to the RTC. "I came per the regulations when I saw the flare."

"I don't think that the regulations apply to officers who

are on suspension." The LCI turned back to Pflamtael. "Well, who did all this? Where are they?"

"This was all a distraction as an attempt was made to free a prisoner."

"An escape? Who tried to escape?"

Pflamtael gave a side look to Reva for the briefest of moments, a flicker of a smile that Reva was sure that she'd been the only one to see, touched the corner of his mouth. "It wasn't an escape, ma'am."

"Are you saying that they got away? We no longer have a prisoner in our custody? How is that not an escape?"

"The prisoner was taken from his cell against his will by the attacker. In fact, he tried to resist the attempt to free him. I would call this a kidnapping."

The LCI glared at Pflamtael. "Kidnapping?" The word dripped incredulity.

Pflamtael nodded.

"So, who was the prisoner?"

"He was the one we'd arrested for the flower shop murders. However," Pflamtael added quickly, "based on my interrogation of the prisoner, and new evidence provided by Seeker Carya related to his floater, I'm convinced that we had the wrong suspect."

Reva saw Ansee's eyes go wide at the statement. *You sly bastard,* she thought. Based on Ansee's expression, Olwyn was telling the truth, but he was apparently twisting it to his own advantage. *Like he always does.* He was giving a plausible explanation to the LCI and forcing Reva and Ansee into a position to owe him a favor at a later date. She both admired and hated him for the move.

The LCI turned her warhawk gaze on Ansee. "What floater?"

"A body pulled from the river yesterday. He was the captain of the same ship as Inspector Pflamtael's prisoner." Reva could see that Ansee wanted to say more but wisely kept his other thoughts to himself. It wasn't wise to verbally spar with Pflamtael, especially in front of the LCI.

Betulla started to ask another question but was interrupted by Pflamtael. Reva had to admire his nerve at that. "I will explain everything in my report, ma'am. This is a very complex case and, with respect, I have a murderer and kidnapper to locate and arrest."

Reva smiled inwardly. Olwyn had just told the LCI to piss off and let him do his job so tactfully that Betulla looked like she'd just been stunned by Ansee's shocking grasp. LCI Betulla's mouth pursed briefly to hide her annoyance and she looked around the courtyard.

"Get this mess cleaned up. And make sure that all the *civilians*," at this, she shot a glance at Reva, "leave." Betulla turned and walked back into the building.

"Go home, Reva," Pflamtael said before Reva could say anything.

"Hells, no."

"Damn it, this is my case. I don't need your help. Besides, you're too close to this."

Reva laughed. "You couldn't find your own ass without Norah's help." She saw Norah's ears go red as Pfastbinder walked up and stood to Reva's right.

"Get out of here before I have Rhosa arrest you."

"What about the disciple we captured?" Ansee asked, apparently trying to weave the conversation along a different path.

"You managed to capture one?" Pfastbinder asked, the excitement clear in his voice.

"Yeah," Norah said, "Not that it will do us any good. Nobody will want to get near it, and we can't do anything to it without hurting ourselves."

Reva put a hand on Pfastbinder's arm. "I know who kidnapped Aavril and where he was taken."

Pflamtael narrowed his eyes. "I'm sure I will be able to

find a mad necromancer and a horde of zombies."

"Disciples," Reva and Pfastbinder said at the same time. Pflamtael waved the distinction away.

"You just admitted that you don't know how to stop those things without dying in the process," Reva said. "We can tell you how to defeat them." She gestured to Pfastbinder and herself.

"And how do you know that?" Pflamtael asked, his words filled with a mix of annoyance and anger.

"Pfastbinder will be able to test the disciple that you captured to find out how to defeat them."

"Then I don't need you." Pflamtael made a shooing motion with his hands.

"I don't work without Reva being there," Pfastbinder said. "And proper payment for my consultation with the RTC," he added, smugly.

Pflamtael glared at the two of them, but it was Norah who spoke. "Nobody else will go near that thing. If we can find out how to hurt them without killing ourselves in the process, it's worth it."

"I'd rather use a cleric from the Basvu temple," Pflamtael said. His tone made it clear that he thought they would be better than Pfastbinder.

"Sure," Reva snorted, "if you want to ruin our only chance to learn anything about these creatures. Basvuans have a standing policy to destroy all undead they encounter, no matter what, if that can even be done with a disciple. Bringing them into this will waste our time, put Aavril at risk, and it won't answer anything. It may even put the entire city at risk if Erroll sends those creatures out to attack people. He thinks he's doing his god's will, wanting to convert people to become followers of Dreen. That's why he wants Aavril, and if he can't get Aavril to cooperate, he will send the disciples out to do it."

Pflamtael looked at Pfastbinder. "You can find a way for

us to destroy these...things?"

Pfastbinder smiled and patted his satchel. "Certainly."

"Let's go," Reva said, but Olwyn held up a hand.

"I can't let you do this, Reva. The LCI—"

"Screw the LCI," Reva shot back. "If I'm not on the case, then neither is Pfastbinder."

"Damn it, Reva, the LCI will bust me back to constable if she finds out." He jabbed a finger at her. "And she'll fire your sorry ass."

Reva shrugged. "If we can stop this religious nut, then it will have all been worth it."

Olwyn raised a hand to his face and pinched the bridge of his nose.

"Look, if it's about credit for the case—"

Pflamtael shot a hurtful look at Reva. "Do you really not know me, Reva? Constables have died from this elf's actions. If we don't stop him, more innocent people will be hurt. You may think I'm a cold, callous son of a succubus, but I will do whatever is necessary to protect this city."

Reva tried to look chastised, but inwardly she smiled. She'd just played Olwyn as easily as he'd played the LCI.

"I'll let you be a part of this," Olwyn said, "but you'll take orders from me. This is still *my* case."

Chapter 44

Pfastbinder finished drawing the last symbol on the circle and stood up. "That will do it. You can let it out whenever you are ready."

"Are you sure that this will work?" Norah asked, skeptically. She stood behind a large tower shield that came up to her chin.

"Why do you wizards think that all magic has to be done your way in order for it to work?"

"Because it does," she replied. "My magic doesn't rely on faith or the whims of capricious gods."

Pfastbinder was about the reply when CI Pflamtael cleared his throat. "You two can argue about your magic later. Let's get this done."

Everybody nodded and got into position. Everybody, except for Pfastbinder, held large tower shields. Reva and Ansee stood at the far end of the corridor, and Olwyn and Norah stood near the stairs. Pfastbinder had drawn a circle on the corridor's floor in multicolored chalk. A small table stood next to the cleric with most of the contents of his satchel laid out on it.

Once everybody was ready, Pfastbinder opened the door to the cell. He stood back and, within a minute, the sound of shuffling feet and a slow mantra of, "Dreen is pain...pain is truth...Dreen is truth..." could be heard. The disciple walked out of the cell and quickly caught sight of

Pfastbinder. It started moving toward the cleric.

"It's the guard elf from the Royal Library," Ansee whispered to her. She remembered seeing him in the clearing in The Brambles.

With a flourish of his hand, he said, "*Leku honi lotu egingo zait.*" The air between him and the circle shimmered, and the creature abruptly stopped, unable to move beyond the boundary of the circle.

Ansee and Norah set their shields aside and picked up coils of thick rope. With nearly identical gestures and words of command, the two ropes slithered forward and wrapped themselves around the undead. Within a minute, the disciple was tightly bound, its arms pinned to its sides. It lost its balance and fell forward, leaning against the invisible surface of the circle's power. Pfastbinder made a gesture, and the disciple landed on the floor.

The cleric quickly got to work. He pulled out a weapon —a thin dagger—and proceeded to slice the creature, giving a curt cry of pain as he did so.

"I told you that would happen," Ansee said.

"The process of discovery requires the application of tests and responses," Pfastbinder said. He set the dagger down and looked over the items that were laid out on the table.

"A cleric of Banok being methodical?" Norah laughed. "Now I've seen everything."

"Laugh all you want, Seeker, but there is a madness to my methods," Pfastbinder said. He picked up something from the table, looked at it quizzically, and then tossed it aside.

Reva watched from the end of the corridor. She leaned on the shield and held a strand of hair to her lips. As Pfastbinder experimented on the disciple, she thought about Aavril. She hoped that Erroll had stayed true to what he'd said in the woods last night; that he didn't want Aavril hurt or converted. Erroll needed him mortal, not tainted as an undead disciple, for his plan to work, but how long would Aavril be able to resist Erroll, and what would he do if Aavril refused to help? She hoped that they could get to him before it came to that.

She didn't want anything to happen to Aavril, but that was because she wanted him alive so that she could tell him to go to hell. In the past couple of days, she'd shoved her anger at him onto an upper branch, but now, while Pfastbinder applied one test after another to the disciple, she could think back on everything that had happened. The facts were clear to her. Aavril had lied. He'd lied and hadn't cared that he'd lied to her. He only thought about himself, and Reva was angry at herself for falling for it for so long. She should have seen the signs sooner, should have seen that he wasn't being truthful when he said that he wanted to leave the ship and open a shop here. That he had so quickly jumped at the chance to become *Isean*, without bothering to talk to her about it, made it clear that he had never seriously considered his offer.

She didn't want any harm to come to Aavril, but it was over. There was no way that she would take him back now, not after the lies. How could she trust anything he said ever again?

Reva looked up as Pfastbinder gave a cry of delight. He'd just thrown some liquid on the disciple, and the liquid had sizzled and popped. The disciple's odd cry of pleasure was tinged with something else, not really pain, more like anger.

"Something we can use?" Olwyn asked.

"Only if we are desperate. That was holy water, and the creature was hurt by it, not that you could really tell. But I felt the same pain as if somebody had dropped a pot of alchemical acid on my face." He tossed the small flask to the side and rummaged around on the table.

"If he can't find anything that will hurt these things,"

Ansee said, "then we will be in trouble. Anything we do to them is liable to kill us in the process."

Reva nodded, thinking back to the Joy of the Widow's Tears. The necklace gave Erroll control over the creatures. *Is it limited to just him, or can anybody who wears the necklace command them?*

"There may be another way if it comes to that," she said.

"Why do I think I won't like it?" Ansee said.

"Because it's dangerous."

"Even more dangerous than fighting undead that are immune to attacks and can reflect the attack back to you?" Ansee asked.

"Well, maybe not more dangerous than that, but certainly more difficult. But it won't come to that. Pfastbinder will find something that we can use. He has too."

Ansee gave her a sidelong glance with a curl of his lips. He then went back to watching the cleric. Pfastbinder was rummaging around the table again, picking up objects at random, and then tossing them aside. After a moment, he started patting his body as if he had misplaced something.

"Inspector," he called, looking toward Olwyn. "Can you spare a Skip?"

"You are one greedy son of a succubus," he said. "You will get your consultation fee when this is over."

"Oh, I know you'll pay me. Just consider this an advance."

Olwyn looked to the ceiling, and then, with an exaggerated sigh, he dug a silver coin from a pouch and flicked it to the cleric. Pfastbinder caught it deftly out of the air. He picked up the dagger and used it to shave off some of the coin.

The constables all stared at him, but it was Norah who voiced the question on everyone's mind. "What in the hells are you doing?"

Pfastbinder looked up, gave a quick wink, and then went back to trimming the coin. Finished, he rubbed it across the rough stones of the corridor for a moment and then approached the bound disciple. With the coin held in his hand, he gave a long slash at the creature. Black blood welled up from the wound, and the disciple gave another hiss of pleasure that was mixed with anger. Pfastbinder made a curious sound and then slashed the creature again.

"Did that work?" Reva asked.

Pfastbinder nodded. "It seems that silver does the trick. I felt nothing and it is clear that the creature has been injured."

"Great," Norah said, "we can go break into the coin box in the tea nook and pretend we're throwing alms to beggars."

Pfastbinder seemed distracted by the results since he had clearly missed the sarcasm. "Any silvered weapon will do. You don't need to use your tea fund."

Olwyn seemed to be lost in thought, so Reva asked, "Anybody have a silver weapon?"

Chapter 45

Aavril sat huddled in the back of the wagon, trying to keep himself as far away from the undead as he could. It was hard, as there was little space and the creatures didn't seem to understand the need for it. They sat in a huddled mass and mumbled their ceaseless mantra under their breath constantly.

The fact that most of the creatures were his friends—people he had known and considered as family—tore at his heart. All of the members of the crew of the *Majestic Tern* were in the back of the wagon, and Aavril had even spotted Loren's girlfriend, Amber, among the creatures. *Had Loren been involved in her death and turning her into this creature?* He wasn't sure, but after Reva's Seeker had told him about finding Loren's dead body, he didn't know what to think.

He looked for some sort of recognition, remorse, or even fear coming from the *Tern's* crew. He stared into Kelsey's eyes for any sort of sign, but there was nothing behind them. No spark of the elf that Kelsey had been remained. They were creatures of pure evil now, and Aavril felt tears run down his cheeks as he realized that he had failed his crew. He had not been able to protect them from Erroll.

The pain of this ate at his soul and, as the tears flowed, he noticed that all of the creatures had turned their heads toward him. There was something in their eyes now—hunger, and maybe something else—and they seemed to strain against an unseen leash that held them back. *They want to tear into me,* Aavril realized, *but something is holding them back.* He realized that it was probably Erroll. He glanced up to the elf sitting on the driver's bench. Erroll wanted something from him; that was clear because he was still alive. *But what?*

When the cell door had opened back at New Port, Aavril had thought it was Inspector Pflamtael, come to perform another interrogation. When the elf wearing a torn cleric's vestments had entered, Aavril had been shocked at first. Then he'd been able to see the elf better and realized that this was not a cleric at all, but something far more insidious. The zombie had shuffled into the cell and Aavril had scrambled away from the creature in a panic. Then the undead had stopped moving, though it spoke a slow, sickening mantra that drove a wedge into Aavril's mind. "Dreen is pain...pain is truth...Dreen is truth..."

As much as the sight of the zombie had startled him when Erroll stepped into the cell, Aavril was sure that his mouth had hit the floor.

"By Dreen's suffering they have not harmed you," Erroll said. "You and I are about to do great things, Aavril." He held out his hand. "You've awakened Dreen's faith in me, and now we will do that for the rest of Tenyl."

Aavril had no idea what in the hells Erroll was talking about, and the presence of the undead was making him nervous. He had a deep hatred for the creatures ever since his sister had been killed by a ghoul. "Wh...What?" he managed to stammer out. Erroll made no sense and the zombie kept distracting him with its damn chant.

"Come with me, Aavril. I want you to become my disciple in the church that I will form here in Tenyl. Together, we will show everybody the Truth."

"I'm not going with you," Aavril said. "Not for any church

or faith, and not with any undead."

Erroll's features seemed to cloud over; he gave a glance over his shoulder, and then gestured to the zombie, who moved quickly to herd Aavril out of the cell. The rest of the journey out of the cells and to the wagon had been a blur of panic and fear as Aavril saw the constables pinned at the end of the cellblock. Everything had happened so fast and Aavril hadn't been sure what he could do to resist.

Now, the wagon bumped along the rough cobbles and Aavril could smell the peculiar odor that defined Port Grove. After a few more minutes, the wagon came to a stop, and the zombies all stood up. Aavril thought about making a run for it, but the creatures surrounded the wagon, not giving him any place to jump to. Aavril knelt in the back of the wagon and looked out to see the *Majestic Tern* rising above the dock. He was surprised at first, but then shook his head. He shouldn't have been surprised that Erroll had brought him back to the ship. All of the *Tern's* crew had been turned into undead, and somehow Aavril knew that the *Tern* was an important symbol to Erroll, for some strange reason.

Erroll turned to Aavril. "Come, Aavril. When I have explained everything, you will understand. You will see Dreen's truth for yourself." Erroll gestured toward the gangplank and Aavril hesitated for a moment, long enough that a flash of anger crossed Erroll's face and two of the zombies moved toward Aavril. He moved then, jumping down off the wagon and heading onto the ship.

The *Tern* rocked slightly from the waves in the harbor, and Aavril felt a pang of guilt and sorrow strike as he took in the ship. *How did all of this happen? How did everything go so wrong at the very moment that our future had seemed so bright?*

Erroll gestured toward the hatch leading to the hold and, with a resigned sigh, Aavril headed down the steps. The large space was dark, and he hesitated for a moment to let his eyes adjust. Erroll and several of the zombies followed him into the hold and Aavril instinctively walked aft to where his hammock hung. Erroll followed him and busied himself with lighting a lantern. The warm glow it gave off did not lighten Aavril's mood.

"What do you want?" Aavril asked, letting his irritation finally show. Now that they were back on the *Tern*, Aavril felt more sure of himself. He was the ship's *Isean*, and he wasn't going to let this poor excuse for a sailor dictate anything to him on *his* ship. "I will see you pay for what you did to Kelsey and the others."

Erroll was silent and busied himself. He returned to the zombies and seemed to confer with them in some manner. Two of the creatures ascended to the main deck and the rest huddled together in a circle, their voices low, but their incessant mantra echoing in the empty space. Erroll started making a fire.

"What is going on here, Erroll?" Aavril grabbed Erroll's shoulder and turned him around, shoving him into the bulkhead. A hiss of excitement came from the zombies, and then Aavril found himself unable to move: some unknown force held his body in place, and he struggled hard against the invisible bonds. Belatedly, he realized that some magic or spell had affected him, and he wondered how Erroll was doing it.

"Your first lesson will be about discipline," Erroll said. "I am the master of the *Tern* now." Aavril felt himself be flung backward. The room went dark as his head hit the opposite wall.

†††

Aavril came to with the smell of hot cacao filling the hold. He felt a lump at the back of his skull and a dull, throbbing pain when he touched it. He looked around, seeing the zombies still huddled in the far end of the hold. Erroll sat at the small table that was used by the crew, stirring a mug. He noticed Aavril moving, and he gestured to a pot sitting on the stove. "Would you like something to drink?"

Aavril felt the roll of the ship. It had changed since they had arrived, and he realized that the tide was flowing out of the harbor. *I was out that long?* He wondered what the constables were doing now after his escape. *Do they think I wanted to escape? Do they think that Erroll broke me out of the cells on my orders? Will they realize that we are here, and if they do, will they save me or arrest me?*

"I think the cacao was Kelsey's since I found it in his seabag, but he won't miss it now."

The mention of Kelsey brought Aavril back to his current situation. He stood up and went over to the table. "What did you do to the crew? How did you kill them and then raise them? How are you controlling them?"

"I showed them Dreen's truth," Erroll said, lifting the mug to his lips and taking a satisfying slurp.

"By killing them and turning them into zombies?"

"They are not zombies, Aavril." He set the mug down carefully and looked at Aavril with patient eyes. "They have each become one of Dreen's chosen, His disciples here on Ados. They will help me spread Dreen's message to the rest of Tenyl."

Aavril shook his head. "Disciples. Zombies. You killed my friends and made them into *that*." He gestured to the creatures huddled in a group at the other end of the hold. "I will see you hang for that."

"That will not happen, and I hope that, by the end of the night, you will come to understand just how important you are to what I want to do. Then you will see that what I have done to Kelsey and the others has been what is best for them."

Aavril snorted. "I doubt that."

"You are blinded to the truth, but when I explain Dreen's message you will understand. You will become enlightened like me."

"Who in the hells is Dreen?"

Erroll gave him a pitying look. "Dreen is the true god who suffered under the flames and persecution of non-believers so that he could absolve Ados of His sin."

Aavril couldn't help but laugh. "My gods, what sort of drivel is that? This Dreen must be crawling among the dung heap of the gods to have chosen you to represent him. Demar and Basvu are the gods that are good enough for me."

"All other gods are false before Dreen. The world is filled with constant pain so that we can experience the same suffering that Dreen went through. That pain brings us closer to the truth."

"The only truth that I can see is that you are several oaks short of a forest. What made you so crazy?"

"I am far from crazy," Erroll said, draining the cacao in his mug. "And as to how I received my enlightenment to Dreen's message, I have you to thank for that."

"What?"

Erroll smiled. "The punishment you gave me for taking back what was rightly mine." At this, Erroll reached into his shirt and pulled out his necklace. The gold flickered in the lamplight and the necklace twisted so that Aavril could see the profile of the woman with the single gemstone tear.

"The Joy of the Widow's Tears," he whispered. "You killed Loren and stole it from him."

"I cannot steal what was rightfully mine in the first place. Besides, after what Loren had done to his girlfriend and her lover, he begged me to kill him. He couldn't handle the truth that Dreen had shown him about himself."

Aavril was stunned and shook his head. *Loren killed Amber? Why would he do that?* But as he thought about it, piecing together what Seeker Carya had told him, along with Loren's disappearance the night that they had docked, the fog started to lift for Aavril. "Loren would never willingly hurt anybody, let alone Amber."

Erroll gave a shrug, as if 'what might have been' didn't really matter to him. He set the necklace against his chest, not bothering to tuck it back into his shirt. "The Joy of the Widow's Tears allows me to speak directly to Dreen. Loren was not meant to have this artifact, and he couldn't handle the truth that Dreen showed him."

"But how did the punishment I gave you do anything?" Aavril was confused.

Erroll stood up. "Because you have a talent, Aavril. You know exactly how to inflict pain to a person so that they will be receptive to Dreen's enlightenment. When you were carrying out the Captain's orders, however misguided they were, you allowed me to see the truth. Each lash you gave me was purposeful, methodical. Each one focused my mind and allowed me to see the truth."

"What? Methodical? Purposeful? I gave you a punishment for stealing Loren's necklace. There was nothing more to it."

Erroll gave him a coy smile. "Don't be so modest. You knew exactly how to apply the whip so that the pain of each lash would be felt and remembered, applying the next at just the right moment to heighten the experience and sharpen my focus. I saw the truth that night, and it was because of you."

"The truth is that you are crazy." Aavril took a step around the table, closer to the bow. It also put him closer to the tools that they'd been using to repair the *Tern*.

Erroll seemed to ignore the remark. "That is why I need you. If I am to spread Dreen's message, I need to convince people of Dreen's truth, to lead them toward their enlightenment."

"I thought that's what *those* things were," Aavril pointed toward the undead.

"The disciples only understand Dreen's message at the most basic level. They are his vessels here on Ados, but they do not grasp the deeper meaning of the truth they now know. For my church to grow, I need people to join us, to understand what Dreen's enlightenment means to them."

"And you want me to whip people to join your church?" Aavril asked, surprised.

"I want you to baptize people with pain so that they can focus on the truth of Dreen's message. That his suffering absolved Ados of His sin of losing to Cralde. That by this one act, Dreen released Ados from His duty to us and took on the mantle of our lord and savior. The truth is that there is only one god and that god is Dreen."

Aavril shook his head again. Erroll was clearly crazy. And Aavril wondered if somehow he wasn't part of the reason. He had been there when Loren had interfered with Erroll's purchase of the necklace. Had he stopped Loren there, then Erroll wouldn't have stolen the necklace and been punished for it. Clearly, some kind of mania had gripped Erroll around the necklace.

"I can see in your eyes that you don't believe me. You think I am crazy. They thought Dreen was crazy, too, when He preached His message about Ados. They punished Him for His sermons. The Joy of the Widow's Tears told me this; it allowed me to relive Dreen's suffering. It allows me to control Dreen's disciples, and to control people, too." He held his arms wide, and Aavril realized that Erroll was mimicking what he'd probably seen priests do during their sermons. "With it, I am Dreen's messenger here on Ados. And together, you and I can spread Dreen's message to others."

Aavril shook his head. "I have no desire to join your crazy religion, and I will not whip people for you." He edged closer to the wall, his foot near the wooden spade that they used to help muck out the bilge. "The only thing that I will do is make sure that the constables put you away until you can hang for killing everybody."

Erroll hung his head for a moment, a slow sigh escaping from his lips. "I thought surely—"

Aavril didn't let him finish the sentence. He jabbed his foot under the spade and jerked his leg upward, catching the spade in mid-air. He started swinging the spade toward Erroll's head but suddenly found himself held fast, unable to complete the swing. Erroll looked up from behind his bangs, a slow smile spreading on his face. "That's the passion I was looking for." He lifted his head. "Anger is one step toward acknowledging the pain that affects us all." He closed his hands into two fists. "When you have done that, the pain will allow you to focus and see the truth." He let his hands fly open and a strange light flickered over his eyes.

Aavril struggled, trying to make his arms move, to complete the swing, but the magic that was binding him held him immobile. Then he and Erroll both heard a noise coming from the deck above; the sound of a fight.

Erroll smiled. "More sheep come to join my flock. Maybe I will let a couple of them live so that you can try your skill with the whip to give them the chance to see the truth as I did. But for now, I can't have you interfering."

Aavril was flung toward the front of the ship, striking the wall of the hold hard, the spade snapping in two. His world went dark as he collapsed on top of the broken spade.

Chapter 46

It was after sunset and the docks were as empty as they ever got. Work on a ship never really ceased, but most of the crews and dockworkers were out enjoying watered-down beer and expensive liquor in the dozens of pubs in Port Grove. It meant that there would be fewer people around to accidentally get caught in the fight that was about to happen.

Reva and Olwyn stood together looking toward the *Majestic Tern*. Their Seekers stood at their sides and, behind them, stood Senior Constables Ghrellstone and Rhosa. Coleus Pfastbinder stood at the rear looking ridiculous when compared to the constables, in his multi-colored cloak. Constable Gania and three other constables formed a perimeter around the group to keep the curious and the occasional drunk from interfering.

CI Pflamtael held a spyglass to one eye as he looked at the ship. Reva adjusted her armor—she'd changed into her *ezustacél* armor for the assault—and asked Seeker Pfinzloab, "Do you see anything?"

Norah's eyes gave a soft green glow and she stared off into space, apparently not looking at anything. "There are two of the creatures on the main deck, near the cabin. The rest are down in the hold. Erroll and Aavril seem to be arguing at the back of the room. Two of the disciples are near them, and the other five are clustered together near the hatch." Her eyes returned to normal as she dropped her scrying spell.

"Did they see you?" Olwyn asked.

"No. The undead didn't look at anything and Erroll was too busy with Aavril to notice."

"So, what's the plan?" Ansee asked.

"You two get us onto the deck," Reva said, pointing at Ansee and Norah, then at herself, Olwyn, and Pfastbinder. "I'll be the distraction while Olwyn deals with the disciples on deck. Pfastbinder will block the stairs with his circle of protection, and then you can gate Willem up to lower the gangplank. Then you guys protect Olwyn as he takes out the rest of the disciples while I deal with Erroll and rescue Aavril."

Olwyn lowered his spyglass. "I should be the one to arrest Erroll. It *is* my case, plus you are still on suspension."

Reva held out her hand. "Fine, give me your sword and I'll deal with the undead."

Olwyn gave an emphatic shake of his head. "*Aconitu* is a family heirloom. No one but me gets to wield it."

"Fine, we'll do it my way then." Reva tapped the ring on her finger. "Besides, this will give me the edge against Erroll's binding magic."

"You don't know what else he might be able to do," cautioned Pfastbinder.

Reva shrugged. "It won't be the first time I take on a crazed elf with a powerful magic item." She drew her sword. "Let's get this over with before Erroll decides to do something stupid."

"Just make sure you capture this one alive, Reva," Olwyn said as he drew his own sword. The silvery metal almost glowed in the moonlight. "You have a habit of having suspects die on you."

Reva just stuck out her tongue at him. Ansee and Norah readied their own weapons—a pair of daggers for Ansee and a stout oak staff for Norah. Pfastbinder pulled his own dagger and retrieved a rod that seemed to have been cobbled together from a dozen different pieces out of his satchel. The Senior Constables had each drawn their service swords and picked up large riot shields.

"Remember," Pfastbinder cautioned the group. "Let CI Pflamtael deal with the disciples unless you want to feel like you've been cut by your own weapon."

"Let's go," Olwyn said.

The group headed quickly toward the ship. As they maneuvered around the stacks of boxes and crates on the dock, Norah began uttering an incantation. Her staff took on a green aura and she touched a hand to Pflamtael. He took a small skip, then planted both feet and jumped, the spell enhancing his leap and allowing him to bound over the railing on the ship's prow.

At the same time, Ansee spoke his own spell, a yellow mist swirling around his hands. With a flick of his wrists, the mist flew out to encircle Reva and Pfastbinder. Both disappeared with an audible POP. A moment later, there was a brief flash of yellow light over the deck of the *Majestic Tern* as the pair arrived on the ship.

Reva faced the two disciples who'd turned to her, while Pfastbinder headed toward the hatch leading to the hold.

"Remember me?" Reva asked. The two creatures were the ones that she'd spent the night within Nuphar Wood, but they gave no indication of whether they recognized her or not. They both hissed, interrupting their mantra, and headed toward Reva. The one on Reva's right didn't make it two paces before the tip of a silvery sword pierced through its chest. It gave a strange cry of delight, its eyes going wide. As Olwyn withdrew the sword, Reva caught a flash of yellow light coming from behind the other disciple. She prepared to block the creature's attack, but it turned to face Olwyn.

He took a powerful swing, *Aconitu* tracing a broad arc and cleaving the head from the body of the first disciple. It fell to the deck with a dull thud, and Reva heard a loud cry of anguish coming from below decks. The disciple on Reva's left also let out a bellow of anger and hatred. It turned to face Olwyn and he didn't hesitate, flicking his sword in two quick slashes that dispatched the second disciple.

"So far, so good," he said. He nodded to Senior Constable Ghrellstone, who'd been gated onto the ship by Ansee. "Everything is going according to plan."

A thump came from Reva's right, and she turned to see a disciple standing next to the large open cargo hatch. It was immediately followed by six more, all jumping from the hold and landing on the deck. The seven creatures gave a collective cry.

"You just had to say it," she said.

Chapter 47

The seven disciples jumped again, like *Hoaralle* players leaping to their branches at the start of a match, splitting up to deal with the different threats. Reva didn't know if the disciples were smart enough to think this tactically on their own, or if Erroll was controlling them, directing their actions. Whatever was happening, they were not advancing like a mindless horde. Three of them had leaped to Pfastbinder, standing next to the hatch, two landed before her and Olwyn, and the remaining two jumped toward Willem. Per the plan, Willem was trying to shove the heavy gangplank into position so that the rest of the constables—and their magic users—could get onto the ship. He didn't see the two disciples that were about to slice into him.

Reva ran forward and kicked out with one foot, buckling one of the disciple's knees. It fell to the deck, knocking its head against the hard wood. Reva had heard Ansee and the others describe the strange sensation of feeling their attacks reflected back to them, and she'd even heard Erroll explain their strange ability in the dark clearing in The Brambles, but the pain was still a shock. Her own knee nearly collapsed from the pain, and she felt a dull pain from the back of her head. *Son of a succubus*, she thought. *That is really a pain in the ass. And the head. And the knee. Ow!*

She didn't have time to think, though, as Willem was still

in danger. She lunged over the fallen disciple and thrust her sword into the side of the second creature. A deep, burning pain pierced through Reva's own side and she could feel a twisting pain in her lung. She didn't try to hold in the cry of pain that escaped from her lips.

Willem grunted as he slipped the gangplank into place. He picked up his riot shield and turned to face Reva. "Careful, Inspector," he said, "those things don't really play nice." He stepped up, the shield at the ready.

"Yeah, thanks for the advice." She took a step back and tightened the grip on her sword.

Booted feet sounded on the gangplank and Senior Constable Rhosa, Seeker Pfinzloab, and Ansee were soon standing on deck.

"What'd we miss?" asked Norah.

"Just the usual," Reva replied.

"Things have gotten that bad already?" Ansee asked. He gave Reva a quick grin.

Reva caught sight of Pfastbinder by the hatch. He had something that looked like a tangle of junk held before him and was barely keeping the two disciples at bay. Suddenly, a ray of scorching yellow-orange light lanced up from the hold and struck Pfastbinder in the chest. Flames erupted on his body and he staggered back in noticeable pain.

The two disciples started toward the fallen cleric, but they stopped in mid-step. Erroll appeared on the stairs and, with a gesture, he directed them toward Olwyn.

The creature that Reva had stabbed turned toward Reva, and she now realized that it was Kelsey. The realization that the old Sailing Master had been turned into a mindless, undead creature did more damage to her than the pain of her sword strike. The Kelsey disciple slashed out at her with sharp, wicked claws. Reva tried to parry, but the attack was blocked by Willem's shield.

"I told ya to be careful, Inspector."

"Go help Olwyn," she said. "He can't destroy these things if he's busy defending himself." Olwyn had been trying to get in attacks on the disciples, but they were coordinating their attacks so that he couldn't get in a decent attack without risking a counter-attack from the creatures' claws. He'd been able to hold three disciples at bay, but the two new ones heading toward him would overwhelm his defenses. They were boxing him in against the port side railing.

Willem nodded and, with a jerk of his head toward the Constable Inspector, he and Rhosa ran to help Olwyn. Behind her, Reva could hear Norah casting a spell. She had to hope that Norah and Ansee could handle two disciples alone. She ran around Kelsey, and the other disciple now getting back to its feet, toward Erroll.

"Give it up, Erroll. I won't let you convert anybody else to your stupid religion."

Erroll cocked his head, and his eyes widened in surprise. "Sarah," he said, and then gave a cackle of laughter. "I thought I saw you trying to sneak aboard earlier. You had me fooled that you were seeking Dreen, but I see that you were merely spying on me. It doesn't matter. Dreen's ascension came from his own persecution, and I, too, will be cleansed of you. Dreen's enlightenment starts tonight! Like I told you last night, there is more to pain than just being physically hurt. You'll see Dreen's truth. His blessing will be burned into you!"

Reva caught a flash of golden-red light flickering from the Joy of the Widow's Tears around Erroll's neck. Suddenly, the ship was engulfed in light and Reva briefly saw her own body casting two shadows on the deck. She risked a glance and saw two pillars of red-orange fire strike the deck of the *Tern*, each pillar centered on where her friends had been standing.

"No!" Her scream erupted from the depth of her soul as the deck burst into flames behind her. The planks exploded and fell with a crash into the hold below. The ship lurched from the impact, and Reva struggled to keep her footing.

"Your loss will bring you the enlightenment you said you were seeking, Sarah." Erroll laughed. "Bask in the majesty of Dreen's truth!"

Reva gripped her sword tightly, the pain from seeing the two pillars of fire immolate her friends still raw. "All I see is an elf about to die." She used the pain tugging at her heart and stepped toward Erroll.

He gave her a pitying grin that turned into a sneer of disbelief as she continued to stride toward him. She held up her hand and tapped the ring. "I gave myself a bit of insurance against your little trick. Nobody holds me against my will."

"Had you stayed with me, Sarah, you would know that I can do more than that. Dreen's truth has filled me with enlightenment."

"My name is Constable Inspector Reva Lunaria, and I'm going to take great pleasure in taking you down. Your disciples have been destroyed by your own flames. You are all alone. Please, don't give up. Give me the excuse that I need to make you pay for my friends' deaths."

Suddenly, from the hole in the *Tern's* deck came a cry of vindication from Seeker Pfinzloab. "I knew it! I knew it! Nobody would listen when I told them, but now I have proof!"

Erroll and Reva both stared at the hole wide-eyed, neither one of them believing what they were seeing. A few burning timbers tumbled aside to reveal Ansee, singed but very much alive. "You're welcome," he said, a mixture of irritation and relief in his voice.

Reva looked back to Erroll who continued to stare at the two Seekers. "I guess Dreen isn't all that powerful after all."

Erroll's face contorted as he clenched his jaw. "So be it. You will all become disciples at my command." With a wild, sweeping gesture, he waved his hand at Reva, and she was punched in the side by a loose timber, apparently flung at her by Erroll's magic toy. The blow pushed her over the edge, and she fell through the hole in the deck. She struck hard and felt shards of wood skewer her arm and shoulder, and blood streamed down into her eyes.

She felt hands grab her, followed by calls coming from Ansee and Norah. With their help, she struggled to her feet. Her left calf burned from the large splinter jutting from her leg, and her right hand was growing cold and numb. Blinking through the blood, she could see two disciples slowly walking out of the smoke in the hold.

"Shit."

Chapter 48

The disciples were naked, their clothing having been burned off by the pillars of fire, but they otherwise looked uninjured by either the fire or the fall. As the smoke continued to clear, Reva saw the other five disciples stepping away from a similar collection of fallen timbers and smoking deck planks where Olwyn, Willem, and Rhosa had been standing. She thought that she could see a blackened boot sticking out of the debris, and a glint of silver. From the deck above, Erroll stood and cackled with joy.

"Either of you two got anything that will help?" Reva asked.

"Maybe your demon-spawn partner does, but I don't have anything that can deal with them," Norah said, not trying to hide the bitterness in her voice.

"Nothing that will be useful against undead that will hurt us just as much as we hurt them."

"Then we'll have to do it the hard way," Reva said. "I'll take anything you got that will help me get Olwyn's sword. Then, you two try to keep them from turning me into one of them."

Reva prepared to move, wincing as she put weight on her left leg. *This is going to hurt.* Then she felt a pair of hands touch either shoulder. She heard an incantation coming from Norah and felt magical energy flow through her body. Some of her fatigue evaporated and she felt a newfound strength. From Ansee, she heard another spell and could see a soft shimmer of red mist envelop her body.

"That will give you some protection from their claws," he said.

"My spell won't last long," Norah said, "but it should allow you to get to Olwyn's sword and pull it free. Now go, we'll distract them."

This is still going to hurt, Reva knew, *but it's better than nothing. I won't go down without a fight.*

The disciples were closing in and Reva darted forward. Her calf yelled in protest, but she ignored the pain, weaving between two of the creatures. They each lashed out with their claws, but Ansee's spell kept their attacks at bay. Reva grabbed a still burning timber and tossed it aside with little effort, biting her lip to fight through the pain in her shoulder. Underneath, she saw the bodies of Willem and Rhosa draped protectively over Olwyn. Their riot shields were only ash and cinders and both Senior Constables were severely burned.

Reva had no time to check their condition or to mourn their loss. She tossed another timber and grabbed for Olwyn's sword. Miraculously Olwyn groaned and tried to hold onto the weapon.

"Family...heirloom..." he managed to croak through charred lips. Almost all of his hair had been burned away.

"If we live through this, I'll give it back," Reva promised. She pried *Aconitu* from his grip with her left hand and turned to face the disciples.

The hold was lit by the still burning deck. Reva saw Erroll standing on the stairs, joy and excitement shining on his face. Above him, and unaware to Erroll, she saw Pfastbinder climbing to his feet. In front of her, five of the disciples had turned to face her. The other two were attacking Ansee and Norah. The two Seekers were struggling to keep the creatures at bay with fallen timbers and hastily cast spells.

Reva slashed with *Aconitu*, driving the weapon into the side of one of the disciples. The weapon made a satisfying sound as it drove into the creature's flesh. It was followed by a howl from the undead and, suddenly, all of the disciples turned to face her.

Reva pointed up at Pfastbinder and shouted at Ansee. "Get him down here!" She pointed with her wounded arm behind her, and jabbed the silver sword forward, piercing the heart of the first disciple. The creature staggered and fell to the deck as she pulled the sword back.

Erroll yelled in fury and ran down the stairs. Reva spotted a flash of yellow light from the deck and heard a POP come from behind her. Three of the disciples lunged at her, raking her with their claws. She managed to parry one attack, feeling the pain in her own arm, and Ansee's spell deflected another attack, but two claws managed to slash across her stomach, rending through Ansee's spell, her armor, and her flesh. She felt the strength that Norah's spell had delivered drain from her body, and she staggered under the pain in her leg. She angrily lashed out with the sword, missing the creature that had struck her, but driving it back a step. *They know enough to fear the sword,* she thought.

Blood continued to flow into Reva's eyes, and through it, she saw movement in the smoky darkness behind Erroll. Suddenly, a jagged piece of wood was rammed through his body, the bloody tip protruding through his stomach. Erroll's eyes widened and his hands gripped the wood. He turned in time to see Aavril step out of the darkness and swing the long, flat blade of a spade. The makeshift weapon caught Erroll in the temple and he fell to the deck.

Each of the disciples straightened up, their unending mantra changing in pitch. The six creatures each turned to face different people, and they moved in to attack.

Reva tightened her grip and made two quick slashes at the disciple in front of her. As the second swing struck the creature, it stopped moving, seemingly frozen in place. Reva looked over at Ansee and Norah. The disciples facing them also stood still. She threw Ansee a questioning glance, and he pointed toward the stairs. Reva turned and saw Aavril standing at the base of the stairs, the Joy of the Widow's Tears hanging around his neck.

"Make it quick, Reva," he called, his voice husky and hoarse from the smoke. "They're fighting me."

Reva nodded and grimly set about the task. With the disciples immobile, it was quick work to decapitate all six of the remaining undead. When the last one fell, she saw Aavril pull off the necklace and drop it onto Erroll's prone figure. He then spit contemptuously on the body and turned, slowly walking up to the main deck.

Chapter 49

Ansee stepped out of the pile of timbers and moved toward Pfastbinder. As soon as Aavril had taken control of the disciples, Norah had rushed over to see what had happened to Constable Inspector Pflamtael. She stood near the pile of debris, biting on her knuckles. Pfastbinder held his hands gently on Olwyn's forehead, a golden nimbus of light surrounding the prone Inspector.

Senior Constable Rhosa lay motionless, a jagged piece of burning timber having sliced through her neck. Ansee hadn't really known the Senior Constable all that well, other than that she'd been magnanimous about being bested by him during his dagger training. There was still an ache in his heart from her death, though, and he was afraid to look at Willem. The Senior Constable had been a pain in the ass in so many ways—the smell of gingerbread suddenly filled Ansee's senses—but Willem had also been a good and supportive friend. Dreading what he would find, Ansee knew that he had to look, and so he turned his gaze on the other body. Willem appeared to be just as dead, his body severely blackened and one leg noticeably broken.

But as Ansee watched, he saw soot move from under the Senior Constable's nose and Ansee knelt down, checking for a pulse. It took him a long, panicked minute before he felt a very faint beat. "He's still alive!"

"I'm a little busy here," Pfastbinder said calmly. "Look

in my bag."

Ansee stumbled over the fallen debris and yanked open the leather and cloth satchel. There were a number of odd objects and knickknacks in the bag, but Ansee spied a small glass vial buried among the junk. He lifted it out and saw a paper label scrawled with the word *Palt*. A healing potion! Ansee didn't know how potent the potion was, but he didn't care. He hurried back and pulled out the cork stopper. He gently lifted Willem's head, pried open his charred lips, and poured in the magical elixir. Willem's breath became stronger and Ansee had to force himself to go slow and not cause Willem to choke on the potion.

As the last of the potion passed Willem's lips, his eyes fluttered open. He gave Ansee a critical look. "Maybe you should teach a class in magic instead of daggers," he managed to say.

"I don't think I can teach you what I know." He saw Norah give him a sidelong glance, but she didn't say anything. He wasn't sure how she'd treat him now that she knew his secret.

"Did we win?" Willem asked.

"Yes." Ansee left it at that, figuring that telling Willem about Rhosa's death wouldn't do him any good now. He'd find out soon enough.

A cough came from CI Pflamtael followed by a ragged breath. "Where's my sword?" he asked, his hand patting the debris around him.

Norah knelt down, "Don't worry about your stupid sword," she said. She then gave him a long kiss. Ansee stared for a moment then looked away. *I guess the rumors are true*, he thought.

Reva stepped up to the smoldering debris. "Is he going to live?"

Pfastbinder nodded. "The Inspector and the good Constable will both survive to harass criminals again.

Unfortunately, Constable Rhosa didn't survive."

Reva nodded and nudged Olwyn in the foot. He sat up slowly with Norah's help. "Here's your sword back," she said. "And I'm afraid that your suspect didn't survive."

Olwyn slowly nodded his head. "Good." He held out his hand and Reva set the pommel in it. She then turned and headed up the stairs.

Chapter 50

Reva stepped out of the hold and looked around. The two large holes in the deck still smoldered at the edges, and Reva thought that the ship was listing slightly away from the dock. She spotted Aavril standing on the raised deck at the back of the ship. She walked to the front.

Standing at the rail, Reva could see that a large crowd had gathered and was trying to get past the constables in order to see what had happened. *I guess having two pillars of fire come down out of the sky would draw a crowd.*

Reva heard the creak of the deck, but only turned around when Aavril called her name. He was bloodied on the arms and neck, and soot streaked his face. He stepped toward Reva, arms wide to give her a hug. She was too tired and hurt to stop him as he hugged her. It was a fierce hug, full of remorse, relief, and passion. She thought about staying there, to remain in his arms, but the longer he held her, the more she recalled the lies he had told her. The things he had kept hidden. She broke the hug and wrapped her arms around her shoulders.

Aavril pointed to the ship, taking in all the damage. "Does this mean that I'm no longer under arrest?"

Reva shrugged. "You'll need to ask Pflamtael about that. I'm not supposed to be here. Officially."

"You came to save me?"

Reva uncrossed her arms and pointed toward the holes

in the ship. She could feel her brow furrow slightly. "I came to stop a deranged elf who was killing innocent people and turning them into undead. You just happened to be here, too."

Aavril stiffened. "So, I don't mean anything to you anymore?"

"I didn't say that," Reva shot back.

"You didn't have to. It's always about the job with you."

Reva felt her ears heating. "Yes. My job is important."

"And mine isn't?"

"Stop putting words in my mouth. Maybe if you wouldn't lie to me about everything—"

"Lie?" Aavril cut her off.

"Yes, lie!" Reva poked a finger at his chest. "You lied about wanting to settle down and give up this," she waved a hand vaguely to take in the ship. "And you lied about getting a promotion that would keep you here. You broke your promise to me."

"I never made you any promises, and you never gave me a chance to explain about my promotion. You were too busy saving the city to even care that I was back home."

Reva sucked in her lower lip and glared at Aavril. "I was doing my duty."

He gave a derisive snort. "You care more about everybody else in this damn city than you do about me."

"If you kept your promises, I might."

"Damn it, Reva. Stop talking around the tree trunk. What promises? I said I would *consider* leaving the *Tern* if you'd *consider* raising a family. But you're too *dwarven* to do that." Reva felt her face flush at the insult. "So yes, I took the promotion because you haven't shown any interest in finding out what I wanted."

"I haven't..." Reva spluttered. "Every time you returned to Tenyl you'd tell me how you wanted to settle down. You didn't like being away from me. I thought you wanted to spend time with me. Here, in Tenyl. Not sailing to every port between here and Nephrin."

"I never said I wanted to give up sailing, though," Aavril shot back. "You never bothered to find out what I really wanted. If you'd have taken one damn night off so that we could have a real conversation, you might have known what I wanted."

"All those hours spent lying in bed and talking about our future apparently didn't count, then," Reva said. She could tell that Aavril was getting upset, and she wanted to end this before he lost his temper. She knew that they had spent a lot of time talking about a future together, and realized that, if she conceded something, Aavril might calm down.

"Well, maybe you'll have time now to tell me what you want. Your promotion won't matter now." She gestured to the ruined deck of the ship.

"Time? I won't have any time, and my promotion is even more important now."

Reva couldn't help letting her mouth fall open. She gestured to the still smoldering deck with both arms. "You have no ship, and your crew were all killed by a madelf. What could possibly be holding you here?"

"For someone who is always talking about *duty* you just don't get it. Loren and his father trusted me to do a job. My crew and their families trusted me to keep them safe—both at sea and in port. I was responsible for them, and I failed them. And because of that, I now owe a debt to all of their families."

"And you have to go back to sea to repay it?" Reva shook her head; she didn't understand what he was talking about.

"Who said I was going back to sea? But if I have to do that to fulfill my duty, I will." Aavril stuck his chin out defiantly.

"Now who's the one giving up on us? You are just looking for an excuse to go back to sea. It's not about any duty or debt. You're just afraid."

"Sure, I'm the coward because I need to do my job. That's the pot calling the kettle black."

"This is who I am," Reva said, pointing a finger at her chest. "You knew that when we met. You knew that I won't give up who I am for anybody. That was the deal."

"But everything is different now. Can't you admit that my own responsibility is just as important as yours?"

"But what about your responsibility to me? To us?" Reva softened her tone. "Does that mean nothing to you? Do I mean nothing to you?"

Aavril threw up his hands. "This is going nowhere!"

Reva's mouth formed a hard, thin line. "Going nowhere isn't a problem for me, but it apparently is for you." She walked away.

Chapter 51

Ansee found Reva talking with Constable Gania on the dock. A makeshift bandage was wrapped around her head and dried blood still streaked her face.

"Everything alright?" he asked.

She turned to him, "Sure."

"Because I saw what happened with Aavril."

"It's fine," she repeated. Ansee caught the tone in her voice, so he knew that it wasn't fine.

"It you want to talk about—"

"I want you to leave it alone."

Ansee felt his ears flush. He was used to Reva being stubborn, but she was just being mean now. "No, I will not leave it." His voice was firm, commanding, and before Reva could respond, he continued. "Do you know how far out on the branch you are right now? I could give a kobold's ass what is going on between you and Aavril, but it's distracting you. The LCI is going to have your ass—and possibly your job—for disobeying her. You need a friend right now, and the way that you are behaving, nobody but me is willing to do the job."

Kai started to say something and Ansee threw him the same glare that Reva used. Kai needed to stay away from this before he found himself in trouble with the LCI too.

Reva folded her arms and just stared at him. It reminded him of his first day in Acer Division when she'd piled all the tasks on him because it had been her day off. He'd reacted in a similar manner then, calling her out in front of the entire Stable, and he wasn't going to change now. Reva needed somebody to remind her when she was doing something stupid.

Uncrossing her arms, she took a quick step toward Ansee. He flinched, closing his eyes and expecting a slap—or a punch. Instead, he found himself being hugged.

"Áeorias," she said. "For being a friend."

A commotion on the dock caused them both to turn their heads. Stalking through the crowd were several constables, First Constable Aescel, and the Lord Constable Inspector.

"I hope you'll still be my friend when I'm looking for work tomorrow."

"We can be adventurers together," Ansee said. Reva gave a noticeable shudder.

The constables stopped to help keep the crowd back, but Aescel and Betulla continued forward. Aescel gave a nod of greeting to Reva and Ansee, but it was the LCI who spoke.

"You were suspended," she said, jabbing a finger at Reva. "Now you're fired. I know you are behind this mess. I want you gone."

Reva crossed her arms and it looked like it was taking all of her strength to not respond to the LCI.

"That seems like a rash decision, ma'am," Aescel said. "Perhaps we should—"

Betulla turned a baleful gaze on the First Constable. "Do you want to join her?" She turned back to glare at Reva. "I can't have constables that disobey me on the force."

Ansee knew that the LCI just didn't want anybody around who could show her up. He heard footsteps coming from behind him and turned to see CI Pflamtael and Seeker Pfinzloab walking up the dock. Both of them were covered in soot, their faces streaked with dried blood. Norah gave

Ansee a conspiratorial smile and a wink.

"Lord Constable," Pflamtael greeted. "Lunaria was critical to the success of this case."

Betulla barked a laugh. "A burning ship in the port is a success?"

Pflamtael ignored the comment. "Without Reva, the port would be overrun by undead. Maybe even the city."

"I'm not in the mood for hyperbole, Inspector."

"It's not hyperbole, ma'am," Pflamtael said calmly. "And if you fire Reva, I will be sure that the Mayor and the King know the truth."

"Are you threatening me, Constable?"

Ansee was sure that she used the generic title as her own veiled threat. If it was, Pflamtael didn't seem to be bothered by it.

"No, ma'am. Just that if Reva remains on the force, then I will be sure to mention in my report for you and the Mayor how important your role was in stopping this deranged killer."

"My role?" Her voice was a mix of surprise and curiosity. Pflamtael knew how to get her attention.

"Of course, ma'am. You had suspended Reva so she could infiltrate this crazy elf's cult. It allowed her to get close to the elf."

Ansee saw the LCI's head nodding slowly. He wanted to throw up. *How vain is she?* Pflamtael was just stroking the LCI's ego, and Ansee wondered if that was the best thing to do. Better to be honest and risk having Reva fired than to puff up Betulla's ego in this way.

"It was your foresight that allowed Reva to learn about the elf's plans. Without that information, I would not have been able to discover how to stop these undead." Ansee saw Reva's eyes go wide a bit at that announcement. "Reva was working under my direction, based on your insight. I was able to use what she learned to put together the plan that stopped the cult leader."

Ansee couldn't keep from rolling his eyes and he hoped that the LCI hadn't seen him. It was typical Pflamtael, exaggerating his own importance in the whole case. He felt Reva's hand on his shoulder; a gentle reminder that he should keep his mouth shut.

Betulla looked at the wreck of the *Majestic Tern*. The ship listed slightly, and smoke still drifted into the night sky from a couple of places on the deck. "And you had to destroy a ship to do it?"

"It was the cult leader's actions that caused the ship to burn, ma'am, but it is a small price to pay to stop a cult that was determined to convert the city's population into undead," Pflamtael said.

The LCI turned back to look at the group, and Ansee could see the saplings growing behind her eyes. He rocked on his feet and he felt Reva's hand squeeze his shoulder again. He was sure she knew what he was thinking. *It's dangerous to feed the LCI's ego like this. Giving her credit for something she didn't do will just lead to trouble in the future.*

"Fine," Betulla said, not bothering to meet anybody's eyes. "But we should play out the deception through to the end. Reva will serve out the rest of her suspension."

Ansee started to speak. The LCI was just being petty, and even though her decision benefitted Reva, it was no different than taking goods out of a merchant's hands. They were setting themselves above the law. Reva dug her nails into his shoulder this time, hard enough that he felt it through his armor. He clamped his mouth shut.

Betulla turned and headed up the dock, a gaggle of constables in tow. FC Aescel shook his head, a gesture full of amazement and disbelief. "You are twitching a warhawk's feathers," he said, giving voice to Ansee's thoughts. "I better have your report—exactly as you told the LCI—on my desk in the morning." He also turned and walked away.

"I didn't need you to defend me," Reva final said, turning to glower at Pflamtael.

"I know. But I couldn't resist the opportunity"

"Opportunity?" Ansee asked.

"To hold a favor over me," Reva said.

"Several favors, I believe," Pflamtael added. "Though I am open to how you want to pay me back. I think you may have recently broken up with your boyfriend." He gave Reva a lecherous smile.

Reva shook her head and headed up the dock. "Have fun staying up all night to write your report. I'll see you all in four days."

Chapter 52

The morning light rose over the deck of the *Majestic Tern*, the list of the ship casting long, distorted shadows on the dock. It had been two days since Erroll had destroyed the ship, and the smell of wood smoke was still heavy in the air. Aavril stretched and watched as several ships were getting ready to sail on the morning tide. Had things gone according to plan, they'd have been getting ready to sail as well, but Erroll had destroyed that plan.

Aavril was weary; his very soul ached. He'd spent yesterday talking to the wives and parents of the *Tern's* crew, telling them about their deaths, and apologizing to them for what had happened. Each of them, from the Blueleaph brother's parents to Donnel's sister, and Kelsey's widow, had told him that they didn't blame him for what had happened. The hardest had been telling Liam's parents about the young elf's death. His father had been stoic; he knew that being a sailor held many dangers, but his mother had been beside herself with grief. She'd been the only one to blame Aavril for her son's death, and even though he knew that it was the grief speaking through her, the accusation had jabbed a dagger into his soul.

Aavril had intended to visit with Captain Sterna yesterday as well, to tell him what had happened. The Captain knew about Loren's death, but Aavril owed the Captain an explanation for everything else that had happened, and what had caused his beloved ship to be destroyed. But after meeting with Liam's parents, Aavril had headed to the nearest pub where he'd deadened the pain and grief with cheap Highlands whiskey. He'd become numb, but the grief had remained. He didn't think that it would ever leave him.

He had no idea what he would do now. Beyond telling Captain Sterna what had happened, he was unsure about his next course—something that was troubling for a ship's navigator. He had always had a plan, an idea of what he wanted and where he was going. Now he felt cast adrift, without a course, and that feeling, coupled with the loss of his friends, was causing him to doubt himself.

Had Reva been right? Had he kept his desires from her? As he watched the ships heading out of the harbor, he had to admit to himself that he'd only really played with the idea of giving up sailing. He'd done it to stay close to Reva, but he had never embraced the idea of becoming a merchant. Sailing was in his blood, and he couldn't imagine any other kind of life. Even if giving it up meant that he'd be with Reva, he would have been miserable. *Did I lie? Maybe to myself, but never to Reva. She's wrong, I always told her the truth. She just never bothered to listen to me.*

"*Alvoe!*"

Aavril turned from the rail at the greeting and walked across the listing deck to the starboard rail. He saw three elves standing on the docks, two men wearing fancy cloaks —one blue and the other red—and merchant's guild chains around their necks. The third person wore a plain brown cloak, the hood pulled up to hide their features. It took Aavril a moment to recognize the merchants as Loren's backers, Ghalen and Vanya. *Shit. They are probably here to get their money back.* Everybody in the city had heard about the attack on the ship—hells, half the city claims they had seen the pillars of fire reach down from the sky to set it ablaze. Loren's partners had to know that the ship had been destroyed and wouldn't be sailing, so they had come to collect their investment. *And I spent over a hundred crowns paying for the supplies and provisions for the ship. I don't have the coin to pay them back what has already been spent.*

Aavril forced a smile and waved to the three people.

The elf in the red cloak—Ghalen, if Aavril remembered correctly—called out, "May we come aboard, *Isean*? We have some business we need to discuss."

Business? That was an odd way to say that they were coming to get their money back. But Aavril knew that he had to let them on board. They had the right to recover their money and could easily bring in the constables if they wanted to.

"Just a moment," Aavril called. He picked up the gang-plank and carefully set it into place. The list made it sit at an odd angle, so he held out his hand to help the three people onto the ship. Ghalen and Vanya smiled politely, but they didn't introduce their companion, who remained hidden within the deep folds of the cloak.

"Excuse the mess," Aavril said, unable to think of anything else to say.

"We were surprised to hear about the attack," said Ghalen. "It is tragic what happened to your crew."

"Áeorias." Aavril was trying not to fidget. This small talk was a waste of time, and he wished that they would just get to the point of their visit.

Vanya was looking around the deck, taking in everything like a spectator at the arena. "I hear it is a good thing that the zealot was stopped." He turned and looked at Aavril. "Is it true that you killed him?"

How had that information gotten out? The last thing Aavril wanted was any notoriety for being known as the elf to have stopped a crazed zealot from unleashing a horde of undead on the city. He wanted to deny it, to try to squash the rumor, but the expectant look on Vanya's face caused him to humbly admit that he had killed Erroll.

The briefest of glances were exchanged between Ghalen and Vanya, and then Ghalen said, "Can we head to the cabin? We have something to discuss."

Aavril nodded and led the group across the deck to Captain Sterna's cabin. Ghalen and Vanya stood aside and let the third person take the seat on the bench. Aavril quickly pulled out two stools for the merchants. Before either of the merchants could say anything, he knelt, opened the secret panel, and pulled out the strongbox. He handed the box to Vanya. "Here is your money back. We had to spend some of it on supplies, but I will pay it back. Even if it takes me years to do it, I will make sure you get your money back."

Vanya set the heavy box onto the deck. "I told you he was honest."

"And he is quite resourceful," added Ghalen. Aavril was wondering what was going on before he realized that they were not talking to him but to the third person.

"It's not many people that can face down a deranged killer bare-handed," Ghalen continued.

"And he does have a silver tongue as well," said Vanya. "He was quite the orator when we delivered this investment." He patted the strongbox.

Aavril looked between the two merchants and the cloaked figure. "What's going on?" He tried to keep his annoyance out of the question. It wouldn't do to piss off the elves who could demand coin from him that he did not have.

"Aavril," Ghalen said, gesturing to the seated figure. "We'd like to introduce you to our partner."

The figure stood up and raised delicate hands with red-painted nails to pull back the hood of the cloak. The hair was a deep amber color, and as the hair flowed out of the hood flashes of purple and red light danced across the strands.

"This is Caelyn," Vanya said.

Caelyn held up one hand, which Aavril took gently. He bowed to give her hand a kiss. "And a gentleman too," Caelyn said, a seductive smile gracing her lips. Aavril watched her eyes flicker up and down as she gave him a quick appraisal.

Aavril stood up and looked to the three elves. "So, is this about the money? I told you I will repay whatever has already been spent."

"This is about the money, in a way," Caelyn said. "But it is about a lot more as well. My partners and I had an arrangement with Loren. Part of the reason we backed him was that he was eager to work with us. I want to extend the same offer to you."

"What?" Aavril knew his jaw had fallen open. He had not expected this.

Caelyn reached over one finger and traced it up Aavril's throat, closing his jaw and giving him another smile. She started walking around the small cabin. "How much do you know about Loren's plans?"

"Only a little. He didn't tell me a lot of the details before he was murdered. I know that he wanted to sail directly to the Spice Islands to trade there, to bypass the Torollan and Oroman merchants, and to get the goods directly from the source. He said that we could get better prices and make more money doing that."

"Did Loren say what sort of goods he wanted to trade for?"

Aavril shrugged. "Not really, but the Spice Islands have a lot of goods that sell well here, from exotic woods and plants to spices, animals, and everything else. Whatever we traded for would be profitable for us when we returned here."

Caelyn nodded, "All of that is true, but it was secondary to what we wanted Loren to do for us. The Spice Islands have several other products that are more profitable here in Tenyl. Certain plants and roots that have stimulating properties when properly prepared."

"You mean Wake." Aavril had used Wake a few times with Reva, to allow them to make the most of the short time he had in port.

"Wake, and a few other special botanicals. There are many interesting things that herbalists and apothecaries can do with these materials, and there are people willing to pay for these materials, but we need the raw ingredients." She stopped her pacing and turned to look at Aavril. "That's where you come in."

"We have contacts in the Spice Islands," Vanya said. "People with similar interests who can supply these raw materials. We want you to step into Loren's boots. We want you to travel to the Spice Islands to pick up cargo, anything you think will sell well here, and that will earn us a decent profit. But we also want you to pick up these special botanicals and keep them secret. They will not be recorded in the ship's ledger. Those will be delivered to one of Caelyn's people."

Aavril was speechless. They were offering him something he'd always dreamed about but had never considered attainable; to be captain of his own ship. But something rustled the leaves in the back of his mind. "You want me to deliver contraband. Illegal goods."

"Is that a problem?" asked Ghalen.

"Captain Sterna never carried contraband or smuggled anything. He said the risk was not worth the extra profit. He taught me to run a clean ship." But as he said the words, he wondered how many of those lessons Loren had learned. Caelyn had said that Loren had been eager to work with them. And Aavril had always thought that Loren's plans had been too ambitious. Yes, better profits would be had by going directly to the merchants in the Spice Islands, but Aavril had wondered how Loren expected to be able to buy a second ship so quickly.

Caelyn gave a gentle laugh, running a hand through her hair, brilliant colors cascading through the strands. She then reached over to caress Aavril's cheek. "If you are reluctant to help us, we understand. We can make other arrangements to have you work off the debt you owe us."

Aavril found himself swallowing, his mouth suddenly dry. There was an implied threat in the words, and he wondered who Caelyn was. The secrecy of her being here, and the cargo that they wanted him to smuggle, meant only one thing. "You work for one of the thieves' guilds," he said.

Caelyn gave him a smile and patted his cheek. "You're right Ghalen, he *is* a fast thinker. I don't work for one of the guilds. I *am* a guild. I built the Corpse Tenders up from nothing, making a guild that controls more in Tenyl than even King Aeonis."

Aavril swallowed again. You couldn't work in the docks or on a ship without some interaction with the guilds. They were everywhere and demanded their cut of all the money that passed through the port. The Corpse Tenders were not as overtly ruthless as the other guilds; they generally didn't go in for open violence, but from what Aavril had heard, they were more dangerous because they weren't overt. When a sailor or a captain went missing, or an accident happened on the docks, the rumor was usually that they had crossed the Corpse Tenders. Some said they ended up dead, others said that these people worked as slaves in underground mines and workshops. A few of the rumors said that the guild got its name because anybody who crossed them became living corpses, undead serving at the beck and call of the Corpse Tenders leader. An involuntary shudder vibrated through Aavril's body. He'd just avoided becoming an undead follower for Erroll. He didn't want to become one for Caelyn. His eyes seemed to turn, on their own, to the strongbox. *I am in debt to the leader of the Corpse Tenders. If*

I don't do what she wants, at the very least I will be made to work as a slave to pay it back. At the worst, I'll be killed, and maybe raised to serve her still.

"I'm not reluctant," Aavril finally said. "I just like to know who I am working for." He managed to stand a bit straighter. Caelyn gave him a slight nod as if she knew the thoughts that had just run through Aavril's head.

"Well, *Captain* Paroth," she said. "I think we should sit down and discuss the arrangements of your employment with me."

Chapter 53

Reva finished lacing up her bracers, and then belted on her sword belt. She'd enjoyed the past few days off. She'd paid her debt to Rhoanlan, and taken him to see *Talia*, the new play at Pfenestra's Playhouse. She'd agreed with Pfletcher's assessment that it was a good play and, surprisingly, Rhoanlan had been a great companion for the night. He'd kept his fingers to himself as they'd gone backstage before and after the performance, and he had been respectful all evening. Reva still didn't know what had prompted Pfenestra to ban Rhoanlan in the first place, but maybe she'd find out. She'd had a good enough time that she'd agreed to go see more plays with him.

Reva had also taken a lot of long walks, each time ending up along the north side of the river in Old Grove, staring across the water to the port. Each time, she stood in silence for several minutes, her thoughts turning to all the times that she had spent with Aavril. She'd tried to bury them away. She didn't want to remember him, but the memories came to her unbidden. She fought the nostalgia, pulling up other memories of times when she was sure that he'd lied to her. She had to remind herself that he had always been only interested in himself, that he didn't care about what she wanted, or that he even really understood her. She would end these sessions by heaving a stone out into the river before turning back for home.

Reva closed her bedroom door and gave Gabii a playful scratch under her beak. She'd thought that Gabii would have reminded her more of Aavril—the parrot had been a gift from him—but now that Gabii no longer spoke in Aavril's voice, she'd stopped being Aavril's present and had become just Gabii. Reva was glad because she didn't think she could have parted with the silly bird. Just then Gabii squawked, "Reva is sexy!" but said it in Mister Peulldove's voice.

"Eww, that's just wrong." Reva shoved a handful of nuts at Gabii. "That will keep you quiet."

Reva headed downstairs. Her mother was sweeping the shop floor, getting ready to start her day. "Do you need me to get anything today?" Reva asked.

Her mom shook her head. "Nothing today, dear, though I will miss having your help around the shop."

Reva raised one eyebrow. "I thought you were mad at me for getting suspended."

"Of course I was," Aeollas said. "But you are so much more helpful than Gabii."

Despite being upstairs, Gabii called out upon hearing her name, "Aeollas's pots are amazing!"

"Well, I can't trust the bird around the kiln," Aeollas said. They both shared a laugh.

Reva gave her mother a kiss on the cheek. "Have a good day. I will see you tonight."

Her mother gave a wave as she started sweeping again. Reva headed out the door and gave a start as a shape loomed out of the shadows. "*Reis hoestii*, Inspector," Ansee said.

"Hells, are you trying to scare me to death?" She gave him a smack on his shoulder. "Did something happen?"

Ansee rubbed his shoulder in an exaggerated manner. "Nothing's happened that I know about. I just thought you might want to see a friendly face on your first day back."

Reva shrugged. "I've been suspended before. It's no

moss off my bark." She set a leisurely pace up Embankment Road.

"Well, I'm glad you're back. I won't have to endure Norah's glares at me all the time."

"Has Seeker Pfinzloab been that bad?" Despite being suspended, Reva had managed to keep up on the New Port gossip.

"Not really, I think she's just mad that nothing has happened. She filed a complaint with FC Aescel, but he just tore it up. He said that he didn't care what I was, as long as I did my job. She tried to get some of the other Seekers to side with her, to complain as a group to get me kicked out, but most of them also didn't seem to care. She's sitting alone in a clearing and I think that has her more upset than me being a sorcerer."

"Well, working in the Constabulary can change an elf's outlook on many things." Reva was actually a bit surprised that nobody was backing Norah. The prejudice against sorcerers was still a strong one among the wizard community.

"Or they all know that if it wasn't for me and my dragon-blood—or demon-blood, depending on who you ask— then Seeker Pfinzloab might not be here to make her complaints. That, and Willem and several of the other Senior Constables threatened to shove her head into the water trough if she kept it up."

Reva couldn't help but smile. That was the New Port that she knew and loved.

They crossed King's Bridge, weaving around the people, carts, and animals. It felt like such a long time ago— certainly longer than just a few days—that she had faced Erroll under the bridge and been thrown into the river. She made a quick look around, trying to see if Inquisitor Amalaki was lurking around. He'd tried to talk to her once during the last few days, and she'd told him to leave her alone until she was back at work. She had no desire to deal with him when she didn't have to. He'd implied that he'd see her the first chance he got, so she was surprised that he hadn't been the one lurking outside her home.

Ansee paused in the middle of the bridge and looked toward the mouth of the river. Reva stopped as well. Ansee's thoughts had apparently mirrored her own, as he looked around to see if they were out of earshot before he spoke.

"So, what happened to the necklace?" He asked, in a lowered voice that was practically a whisper. "The last I knew was that Pfastbinder was making overtures that the church of Banok deserved to claim it as compensation for services rendered."

"Somehow, the church of Basvu got wind of it, and their 'grand high whatever' convinced Betulla that they should be its keeper," Reva stated, clearly unhappy with the decision.

She sighed. "They should have just destroyed the damned thing and been done with it. But no, it's a 'divine artifact' and it 'has to be studied.'"

Ansee replied, "Then I guess it's in good hands."

Reva shrugged. They both stood there silently and watched as two ships were making sail to take advantage of the morning tide.

Ansee broke the silence. "I heard from Inspector Pflamtael that some merchants claimed the salvage on the *Majestic Tern*. They have started tearing the ship apart for scrap."

Reva didn't say anything.

"Did you hear about Aavril?"

Reva stayed quiet.

"He was hired by the same merchants as a captain of a new ship. I wonder if he's on one of those."

Reva knew he wasn't. He'd taken command of the *Emerald Wasp*, a small, fast merchant ship. They weren't scheduled to leave port for a couple of more days. *Maybe*

I'll stop thinking about him when he's gone.

"I'm sorry you and he couldn't work things out. It's not good to let things fester."

"Are you done?" Reva snapped. Ansee managed to not flinch, but she could tell that he'd been hurt by the rebuke. *Good. I don't need him, or anybody else, to dwell in the past.* She turned her back on the river, the port, and the ships. She looked at the people crossing the bridge, the buildings crowding the river's edge, and the rest of the city spread out upriver. "Then let's get to work."

Author's Notes

As with any creative undertaking, Coy and Geoff could not have started this latest Reva adventure without help from many other people. First of all, a huge thank you to everybody who has read *Wrath of the Fury Blade* and liked it enough to leave a review or let us know at cons. Knowing that people enjoyed that book helped motivate us to get *Joy of the Widow's Tears* out.

Second, a huge thank you to the folks who assisted us with the project. Mike Wagner, who again did a fantastic job on the cover for this book. We've worked with Mike before, not only on the *Wrath* cover, but also on our *Ados: Land of Strife* D&D campaign books, and we are always blown away by Mike's skill. Thank you as well to our beta readers: Tina Rak, Jessica Smith, Jennifer Vinck, and Zachry Wheeler. You provided us great insight into the story, helped find major plot holes that needed to be filled, and kept us motivated with your encouraging words interspersed between pointing out all the places where we need to add a comma because of an independent clause.

We plan on continuing to tell Reva's stories as long as you continue to read them. If you enjoyed this tale, we would appreciate it if you would let others know about it as well. Leave us a review on your favorite place on the web where people review books (Amazon, Goodreads, Bookbub, etc.) Getting reviews really helps, and is a way that you can spread the word about our books.

We also encourage you to follow us on social media. We maintain an author page on Facebook (**https://www.facebook.com/HabigerKisseeAuthors/**) and Geoff is active on Twitter (**https://twitter.com/TangentGeoff**). You can also check out our author website where we occasionally post updates about our projects, write smashing great reviews of books that we love (usually from other indie authors), and put out ramblings on our blog about our writing process and other things that strike our fancy (**https://www.habigerkissee.com/**).

About the Authors

The writing duo of Geoff Habiger and Coy Kissee have been life-long friends since high school in Manhattan, Kansas. (Affectionately known as the Little Apple, which was a much better place to grow up than the Big Apple, in our humble opinion.) We love reading, baseball, cats, role-playing games, comics, and board games (not necessarily in that order and sometimes the cats can be very trying). We've spent many hours together over the years (and it's been many years) basically geeking out and talking about our favorite books, authors, and movies, often discussing what we would do differently to fix a story or make a better script. We eventually stopped discussing other people's work and started developing our own material, first with RPGs and card games, and now we do the same thing with novels.

Coy lives with his wife and one cat in Lenexa, Kansas. Geoff lives with his wife, son, and two cats in Tijeras, New Mexico.